FRANKLIN PARK PUBLIC LIBRARY

7/13

Y0-CDQ-183

# THE
# OFFICER
## and *the Secret*

## JEANETTE MURRAY

sourcebooks
casablanca

FRANKLIN PARK LIBRARY
WITHDE
FRANKLIN PARK, IL

Copyright © 2013 by Jeanette Murray
Cover and internal design © 2013 by Sourcebooks, Inc.
Cover design by Brittany Vibbert
Cover images: © Blend Images/John Dedele/GettyImages,
SeanPavonePhoto/Shutterstock, Galyna Andrushko/Shutterstock

Sourcebooks and the colophon are registered trademarks of
Sourcebooks, Inc.

All rights reserved. No part of this book may be reproduced in any form
or by any electronic or mechanical means including information storage
and retrieval systems—except in the case of brief quotations embodied
in critical articles or reviews—without permission in writing from its
publisher, Sourcebooks, Inc.

The characters and events portrayed in this book are fictitious or are
used fictitiously. Any similarity to real persons, living or dead, is
purely coincidental and not intended by the author.

Published by Sourcebooks Casablanca, an imprint of Sourcebooks, Inc.
P.O. Box 4410, Naperville, Illinois 60567-4410
(630) 961-3900
Fax: (630) 961-2168
www.sourcebooks.com

Printed and bound in the United States of America
VP 10 9 8 7 6 5 4 3 2 1

*For Sam*

FIC
419-2608

# Chapter 1

CAPTAIN DWAYNE ROBERTSON'S BOOTS HIT THE blacktop and he nearly fell to his knees in relief. Only the fact that there were other Marines behind him waiting to rush off the bus and jump into their loved ones' arms kept him moving forward. Not that he had a loved one to rush to. But being trampled to death the minute he landed safely on U.S. soil wasn't his idea of a great redeployment.

Marine after Marine rushed by him, dropping their rucksacks as they went to spring into a welcome home hug. One lucky SOB had his woman all but climbing up his torso like a tree. His night was a guaranteed grand slam.

Someone behind him shrieked, and Dwayne cringed, flinched a little. God in heaven above. He should be grateful he didn't have anyone to freak out and fuss over him. His mom could never take time off work, and his sister was too busy being a single mom to make the trip across the country just to give him a hug.

Yeah. He didn't need a big welcome home… thing. He'd just grab his ruck, his locker, hail a cab, and…

Head home to an empty apartment. Order a pizza. And sulk.

Across the sea of camouflage, someone familiar caught his eye, and he smiled before he could remind himself he didn't care.

"Jeremy freaking Phillips."

"What's up, man?" Jeremy stepped over and gave him a slug on the shoulder, as if they'd just hung out the night before rather than over eight months ago. They stared at each other a moment, then both grinned and stepped into a hug.

"Damn, dude, it's good to see someone I haven't been stuck with for eight months. Even if it is your ugly mug." As Dwayne stepped away, he leaned down and hefted his ruck back over his shoulder. "You here to take me home?"

"Yup. Let's go find your locker and get the hell out of here."

"With pleasure." Though he understood the emotions surrounding all the spouses and loved ones, he was more than willing to leave the lovefest behind and go settle down in his quiet apartment to decompress. The entire ride on the bus from the airport had been a white-knuckle ride.

Twenty minutes later, after hauling his things out from under the ever-growing pile of olive bags and personal items coming off the moving truck, he tossed his duffle into the bed of Jeremy's truck.

"God," Jeremy swore as he hefted the black locker— the trunk holding most of Dwayne's personal items—over the edge and into the truck bed. "What'd you bring back? Rocks?"

"Among other things." Dwayne smiled. "Remember the last time, when we did our shakeout and that camel spider crawled out of Johnson's bag?"

Jeremy chuckled and snapped the door in place. "He screamed like a girl."

Dwayne hopped into the passenger seat. "I'm man enough to admit it. A spider the size of a house cat comes after me? I'm going to be biting back a scream too."

"Just shoot it," was Jeremy's helpful response as he carefully pulled out of the parking lot and onto the main street.

"Talk about overreaction." Dwayne smiled a little, taking in the sights of the base he'd left eight months ago. "Dang. Built up the new Burger King on the corner. That thing was just in planning stages when I left."

"Lots of changes." Jeremy pulled to a stop as he came to a red light, then signaled a turn. "Blackwater's gone. Though you'd have known that from news over there."

Good riddance. "How's the new guy?"

"Decent. Still getting a feel for him, but seems like a good guy overall. Not the prick Blackwater was. As always, we'll know more as time goes on." He laughed and shook his head. "No, you'll know. I'm almost done."

"Still can't believe you're separating, man."

"I'll be around all the damn time. I'm a contractor now, remember?" Jeremy grinned. "Or I will be, once my terminal leave starts."

"Still can't believe you're leaving the Marines. But hey, gotta do what's good for you. Well, what's good for you and Madison." Dwayne couldn't quite keep the amusement out of his voice when he asked, "Tim kicked your ass for sleeping with his sister lately?"

"No, I think we got that out of our system a while back."

Dwayne jerked as Jeremy sped through the turn a little too fast. His fist clenched around the handlebar, and he gulped down a moan. *Concentrate on breathing. In through the nose, out through the mouth.* Then he bit back a yelp when Jeremy tapped the breaks. Talk about screaming like a girl… "Jesus, dude, drive often?"

"Dick in front of me's the one who can't drive. You haven't met Veronica yet." Jeremy turned the air up a notch. "She's coming along. Couldn't get a read on her at first, but now she's starting to open up more."

"We've met."

"You have?" Jeremy shot him a quick glance. It was all Dwayne could do not to yell at him to keep his eyes on the road. Jesus. "When was this?"

"Skype. We kept crossing paths when she was at Skye and Tim's house, then when she moved in with Madison." He smiled a little at the memories. Some of the best moments of the deployment were from teasing Veronica until she blushed and fidgeted in her seat. She'd turned into some sort of mental mascot for his time over there. A bright spot to cling to when things turned to shit.

Something white fluttered next to the road in his peripheral vision. Dwayne grabbed at the *oh shit* bar and beat down the urge to jerk the wheel out of Jeremy's hands and avoid hitting the trash. They were going to get themselves killed driving like this. His eyes squeezed shut in automatic defense.

*No. Look again.*

Dwayne forced his eyes open and watched in the side mirror as the white object dipped and fell, floating and landing again as cars whizzed past it without a second thought.

*Plastic bag. It's a fucking plastic bag. You're losing your shit over nothing.*

Though he tried to let go, Dwayne's grip on the bar

was cement strong. He gave up and did his best to relax his fingers one by one before he lost feeling.

To distract himself, he asked, "What's some of the other changes? The new CO can't be all."

"Nope, definitely not all. For one, Tim's up on the board for promotion to major."

"Dickhead didn't say anything." He wouldn't have, though. Tim wouldn't see it as anything but another day in the office. Not out of overconfidence or arrogance. Just that he did his job, did it right, and did it quietly.

"Well, tease him over dinner about it. You can also tease him about getting married."

Dwayne raised a brow at that. "He's already married. Did he turn to polygamy while I was gone?"

Jeremy shook his head and came to a fast stop when a light suddenly turned yellow. God. At this rate, Dwayne was going to lose the two-day-old sandwich he'd scarfed down on the bus.

"No. Since his parents missed the first wedding—"

"We *all* missed the first wedding. They got married in secret in Vegas," Dwayne reminded him. "Though we happened to be in Vegas too and didn't rank an invitation," he added with a grin. The one and only time Tim had ever been impulsive, and it landed him a wife. It made Dwayne want to laugh just thinking of it.

"Yes, well, his parents want to do some sort of commitment ceremony or something. A fake wedding of sorts. And do the big reception afterward."

"Everyone loves a party. Can't argue there."

As Jeremy took an exit too early, his brows rose. "I know I've been gone eight months, but did you forget the way to my place? I'm two exits up."

"I need to pop by Skye and Tim's while I'm out this way. You don't mind, do you?"

Dwayne glanced down at his cammies—three days too late for a wash—and shrugged. Nothing Tim hadn't seen before. And Skye was too laid back to care, if she was even there. "Sure. I just need to get to a few things today, like calling the bank and utility companies and crap. The usual, you know."

"Yup, yup." As Jeremy slowed to take the turn into Tim and Skye's townhouse complex, Dwayne let himself grin. This was good. Seeing both Jeremy and Tim for a welcome home was good. Easy. He could handle this. Then he could slip home, shower, order a pizza, and decompress. Nothing stressful. One day at a time, he could ease back into stateside life without any problems.

He wouldn't have problems. No.

They pulled in behind Tim's SUV, but Skye's little hybrid was nowhere to be seen. He jumped down from the passenger seat and shut the door. "Skye at work?"

"Oh, uh, not sure." Jeremy ran a hand over his hair, which was getting a little long if you asked Dwayne. But you'll have that with someone edging up on terminal leave.

Dwayne tapped the toes of his boots on the driveway as they walked up to the front door. "This is good. I'll knock out seeing both my friends, maybe Skye if she's home. Then I can spend the rest of the day decompressing at my place."

"Need the peace and quiet, old man?" Jeremy joked, waiting for him to walk around the front of the truck.

"You know how it is. Get home and just need some time to put yourself back in the game, mentally. I do that best alone," he lied.

"I thought that was me who liked to be alone. I mean, before Madison." Jeremy frowned. "Maybe we shouldn't stop by now. If you need some time to—"

"No, it's cool." Dwayne stepped up onto the porch, taking his cover off. "Just stopping by for a few minutes with Tim won't kill me. He won't care if I bug out after a couple minutes. He'll get it."

Jeremy's hand froze over the doorbell. "Are you sure? We can get in the car now and head to your place for a beer."

Dwayne's brow lifted. "I just said I was fine with it. And when did we start having to ring the bell at Tim's place? Shit hasn't changed that much while I was gone, has it?"

Jeremy took a step back. "Let's drop your stuff off at your apartment. We can hang out later."

Dwayne shook his head and gave a quick courtesy knock before opening the door.

And stepping into his own personal hell.

———

Veronica Gibson settled the last platter of food on the coffee table. "Skye, what else do you need from me?"

Skye bounced on the balls of her bare feet, a broad grin spread over her face. "Relax. I need you to relax and enjoy." She took a side step and dodged a pair of Marines in polo shirts and cargo shorts heading to the kitchen for drinks. "Hey, Steve, Bryson. Beers are in the cooler on the deck, soft drinks in the fridge." Skye walked toward the front door where there was a small pocket of space, her frothy tangerine skirt swirling and draping around her legs in the process. Veronica followed automatically, though she couldn't call any-thing she wore frothy. Or even fun, for that matter. "Jeremy sent us a text right before he picked Dwayne up so we know they're coming."

"And he has no idea you're hosting a party for him?" Veronica glanced around the townhouse, decorated by Skye and Madison in preparation for Dwayne's arrival.

Skye laughed and waved that away. "He's a total social guy; he'll love it. Dwayne loves being around people. Plus, it's only us and a few guys from the unit. Nothing big."

"Hmm." One of the Marines from before—Steve—brushed by and touched her arm lightly to let her know he was behind her. She held back the urge to pull away from the simple, friendly, benign touch. "If you think he'll be all right with it, you know him more than I do. I don't know him at all."

"Oh, I wouldn't say that. You've talked to him sev-eral times now," Skye said with a smile.

"A few conversations on Skype do not count."

Madison saved Veronica from having to elaborate. "Hey, everyone!" Being short, Madison took advantage of the second step on the stairs and waved her hands in the air to grab the attention of the fifteen guests. "Jeremy sent me a quick text from the red light. They're almost here!"

Veronica wiped damp palms on her khakis. Why was she so nervous? Just another person to meet. This should not be such a big deal.

But it was. She could admit that to herself as she took her place behind the crowd. The few Skype con-versations she had had with Dwayne sparked something inside her. Something she didn't know she was missing.

Interest. Feminine interest in a man. Someone completely unattainable, but it was there nonetheless.

Through the computer screen, the attraction seemed so safe. They were on different continents, and she could turn the computer off whenever she was ready. But now he was back in the states, back to his friends, and she was going to be face to face with Captain Dwayne Robertson... the star of more than one of her nighttime fantasies.

She was ready for this. She could do this.

No, no, she really couldn't. Just as Veronica turned to slip into the kitchen—under the guise of checking the soft drink supply—the front door opened and her eyes shot to the man she'd been thinking about nonstop.

Terror. White-knuckled, silent-screaming terror was the first thought in her mind. Not hers. His. Though nobody else seemed to notice, Dwayne froze the moment everyone jumped up and yelled, "Welcome home!" And as the swarm of friends enveloped him in a hug, she could see him fighting with every tense muscle not to bolt, or worse.

Her heart ached just a little. Skye swore he was social and would greet the party with open arms, and maybe he was, on a normal basis. But perhaps the party had been too much too soon. She'd seen that look before, with other missionaries coming back to home base from a bad month of travel.

Jeremy clamped a hand on Dwayne's shoulder, and Dwayne's entire body jerked in response. He played it off well, though. With a tight smile, Dwayne shrugged until the hand fell away and nodded at something Tim said.

Every instinct in Veronica screamed to slip back into the kitchen, fade into the background, melt away from sight.

But something about him drew her across the living room until she mixed into her group of new friends. She said nothing, only watching the way his lips tightened in something that looked like a smile-grimace hybrid.

Skye wrapped an arm around her shoulder and pulled her closer. "Dwayne, you might recognize Veronica." She laughed a little. "You two probably talked more than the rest of us, thanks to luck."

Dwayne turned her direction, and maybe she was seeing things, but his face seemed to relax, just a bit.

"Hey, yeah. My Skype buddy." His smile grew. "How are you, Miss Veronica?"

She started to speak, then squeaked when he bent down and pulled her into a hug. Her hands, instinctively coming up to put a barrier between them, were squished between his chest and her shoulders. But Dwayne didn't seem to notice, only squeezed a little tighter before letting go. And when he let go, she dropped to the floor, the impact jarring her teeth a bit. The man was much taller than expected. Well over six feet.

Veronica quickly stepped back, more out of habit than anything. "Welcome home."

*Welcome home? The man has been starring in your dreams for months and the best you can do is say welcome home?*

If Dwayne noticed the weak greeting, he didn't mention it. "Glad we're finally meeting, sweetheart. I think Skye's right. With us crossing paths so often on accident, I talked to you more than these two idiots." He nudged Tim with his elbow and got a none-too-gentle nudge in return.

She nodded, trying to unstick her tongue from the

roof of her mouth. But along with all the saliva in her mouth, it appeared as though all her brain cells had dried up as well, because all she could do was keep nodding like the bobblehead on Skye's dashboard.

Dwayne hefted up his olive green duffle bag and tilted his chin at the stairs. "All I have is PT gear, but it's better than nothing. Mind if I change? Can't exactly rock the welcome home party in cammies all day."

Tim thumped him on the back again. "Yeah, sure. Mad ran to your place the other day and grabbed a few changes of clothes. They're in the office."

"You guys thought of everything." Though he said the statement lightly, his eyes were dark and darted around the room as if on watch for something. "I'll be back down in a few."

He disappeared upstairs, his footsteps from those huge boots still echoing clearly as he made his way to what used to be Veronica's room and shut the door.

"Damn, it's good to have him home." Tim grinned and reached over to pull Skye to him. Nuzzling against her temple, he placed a soft kiss there. "Thanks for throwing the party."

Veronica fought back against the overwhelming sense of longing at watching her cousin and her husband interact. Their marriage—though unconventional from the start, according to stories she'd pieced together from Skye and Madison—was a rock now, and enviable from her point of view.

*This is why you made the Big Change. So you could find something similar. Now stop feeling sorry for yourself and go help.*

Madison glanced at the stairs. "Did we plan this all

wrong? He didn't seem quite as excited to see everyone here as I thought he would be."

"Nah." Jeremy mirrored Tim's gesture with his wife and pulled Madison tightly against his side. "Dwayne loves a party." But as Jeremy tipped a bottle of beer up to his lips, Veronica couldn't help but notice his eyes darted toward the stairs too, just for a moment, as if thinking quite the opposite.

Moments later, Dwayne thundered back down the stairs to cheers from the partygoers. He smiled and waved like a goofy king, bowing at the foot of the steps. "Thank you, thank you."

Some of the worry smoothed away from Jeremy's eyes as he called Dwayne back over and handed him a bottle of beer. "You have got to be the biggest ham I've ever known."

"Hardly. You've known Madison for almost as long." He smiled when Madison leaned over to punch him in the gut. But her hand merely made a sharp smack against the man's stomach, like it had come up against a wall.

Veronica wondered what a stomach like that would look like. Then immediately flushed when she realized that was an awful thing to think. And when her eyes met Dwayne's, he winked at her as if he knew what she was thinking.

Time for a fast escape. Her specialty. "Anyone want anything from the kitchen?" She took a step back, then another, bumping into a Marine as she put some distance between the potent man and his cocky swagger that seemed to drain all her common sense.

Dwayne held up his beer that he'd yet to open.

"Actually, I wouldn't mind a bottle of water, if you're heading that direction already. Want to make sure I hydrate after all the travel."

"Of course. No problem. We've got someone out back manning the grill as well. Did you want anything?"

He leaned forward again, like he was about to share a secret. "Steak. Rare as he'll go." His lip tilted up a little at the edges and he leaned over. The sheer mass of his shoulders made her feel crowded in, though she had an open room at her back. His voice dropped down a little as he added, "If it's still mooing when you bring it out, now that's just perfect."

She couldn't help the little shiver that raced down her spine. Men in general were a struggle for her to interact with, but she'd made such great headway in the last few months. Now with one hot look, she seemed back to square one. Her tongue seemed to swell, rendering her speechless, so she just nodded and walked away as fast as she could.

But as she wound her way through the cheerful party attendants, she heard Jeremy's voice drift behind her.

"Damn, D. Did you have to scare the hell out of her with your Southern badass routine?"

# Chapter 2

DAMN, SHE WAS SOMETHING TO SEE. THEY'D MET accidentally—and then not-so-accidentally—over Skype several times while he was deployed. First when she'd lived with Skye and Tim, and then after she'd moved into Madison's guest room. But it'd been a couple of months since he'd last spoken to her, on accident or not. Long enough for him to convince himself he'd all but created a mirage to get him through the rough months. A sort of mental cheerleader.

Definitely long enough to convince himself she wasn't nearly as hot as he'd remembered.

He was wrong. Dwayne took a small sip of the beer in his hand, not wanting the taste but more something to wet his mouth while he watched her butt wiggle through the guests. Try as she might to cover it up in an ugly, baggy, shapeless khaki-colored skirt that fell below her knees, Veronica Gibson had one fine ass. And Dwayne considered himself something of an expert on the subject.

But she wasn't an easy read. Veronica had the understated look that plenty of men wouldn't even notice. They'd pass her over for a more obvious female model. One with huge tits or painted-on clothes. Fussy hair. Stilts for heels. A walking advertisement for pleasure. But this little mouse was almost more attractive for the way she didn't even try. Her clothes weren't huge, but they were more baggy than fitted. She kept her head down more than up. And as she turned to head back toward the kitchen, he could see her blond hair was pulled into a braid that was nearly as thick as his wrist and went down her back. All the way down her back. Lord, she had some long hair, the tail of which ended just above her aforementioned superb ass.

"Damn, D, did you have to scare the hell out of her with your Southern badass routine?"

He gave Jeremy an offended look. "I didn't know I had a routine. I'm as genuine as they come."

Madison snorted, then coughed as her water went down the wrong way. He gave her a slap on the back, a little harder than necessary. She could take it.

"Stop. Please. You're gonna make me lose a lung," she said, laughing. "No routine, my ass. Please. You see a female and suddenly your accent gets all extra-syrupy sweet and you break out the southern-fried Mississippi charm to whack them over the head with. You know it works. I've watched it."

"Ease off, squirt. If women fall for it, then that's their problem." Tim took a sip of beer.

Skye bit her lip. "Um, maybe you could just… not do the routine with Veronica?"

Four heads turned her way.

"You don't think she's in the market for a Marine?" Jeremy asked.

"I don't think she's in the market, period," Skye corrected.

Huh. Now that was a new one. Curious. "Are you warning me off from your cousin, sweetheart?"

Skye's eyes grew huge and she shook her head.

"That's not what I meant. Just that I don't think she's, well, prepared for your level of… awesomeness?"

"Nice save," Tim stage-whispered.

Dwayne shook his head. "I'm not exactly out for tail myself at the moment. Rest easy. Your cousin's virtue is safe with me."

"You mean *from* you." Jeremy laughed into his beer.

"Same thing."

"Hey there, Skye. I just saw you and wanted to say thanks for inviting the restaurant crowd too. We're… oh. I'm sorry." A woman he didn't recognize, this one of the "walking advertisement" variety of female, stopped short and acted like she was shocked. "I didn't mean to interrupt." She spoke to Skye but batted her eyelashes— those fake things that looked like spider legs—directly his way.

Madison snorted in disbelief, covering it by turning her face into Jeremy's shoulder. Dwayne shared her sentiment.

"I should go." But the woman didn't leave. Just stood there, with one hand over her chest. A large one, stuffed into a shirt a size too small so the buttons gapped in the front. She likely earned every penny of those boobs back in tips, if she worked at Fletchers as a waitress or bartender.

"No, that's okay." Skye's tone was formal, a little detached, and completely unlike her natural warmth. Which signaled to Dwayne she definitely wasn't this coworker's biggest fan. "Stephanie, this is my husband Tim, his sister Madison. And these are two of our friends, Jeremy and Dwayne."

She held out a limp hand to Jeremy, who shook it and

let go with lightning-quick reflexes. She then held it out for Dwayne.

"Nice to meet you." He shook her hand, careful not to squeeze or show encouragement of any type. Unfortunately, just the fact that he was breathing seemed encouragement enough for her. In earlier years, that might have been enough for him too. Now he knew better.

"It's wonderful to meet you too." She leaned in, leading with her breasts. "So you're the soldier who's just back from the front? Is that right?"

"Marine," Skye interjected quickly. "They're Marines."

Dwayne smiled at Skye's quick correction. How things had changed since he left. To Stephanie the Obvious, he said, "Yes, ma'am." Damn Southern upbringing. There were times when attracting flies with the natural honey had its drawbacks. "Grateful to be home."

She sighed a little, with all the finesse of a seventh grade drama production, and he wanted to stuff a napkin in her mouth and send her on her way. "I think it's just so brave what you boys do out there."

"Not to mention us ladies, right?" Madison asked dryly, then grunted and rubbed her ribs. Jeremy likely elbowed her.

"Madison here is actually in the Navy herself. A nurse."

"That's nice." Her tone said *I don't give a shit*. Stephanie's eyes never left his. "I'm sure you're very happy to be home. Must have been so lonely out there by yourself."

Yup. Lonely. Nothing like sleeping in a tent with forty other dudes every night, or stuffed in an airless

MRAP with six other guys like it was a clown car to create that lonesome effect. He said nothing.

"If you ever want to—"

"Stephanie." Skye's voice was sharp, uncharacteristically forced. "Weren't you scheduled for the night shift this evening? I'd hate for our party to make you late."

At that, Stephanie could say nothing. Skye was a manager at the restaurant. Off duty, of course. But still her boss. "Oh. Right. Well, it was nice to meet you. Welcome home." Her eyes held his a little longer than comfortable, then she turned and shuffled by them to the front door.

"Thanks," Dwayne said to her back. He breathed a sigh of relief. Despite the undeniable hotness, he could already tell Stephanie would have been way more trouble than a one-nighter would be worth.

Madison laughed. "Come on, Dwayne." She batted her eyes in a mock flirt and made her voice low and husky. "She was practically in your lap."

Skye shook her head in disgust. "I know we're off duty and all that, but... that was definitely not how I want my staff behaving. I'll have to talk to her about it."

Veronica appeared, as silent as any stealth recon team, with a bottle of water and a tray, likely borrowed from the restaurant, laden with plates of food.

"You didn't have to do that. I didn't realize it was already done; I'd have gone to get it." Dwayne reached for the tray—which looked way too heavy for someone with such skinny arms—but she stepped out of reach with the grace of a dancer.

"No problem; the food all happened to be ready while

I was out there. It's my job." When he raised a brow, she blushed. "I mean, I'm not at work or anything, just that I can handle it. It's fine, really," she insisted when he tried once more to grab the tray. Instead, she settled it down on the edge of an end table and began the fascinating process of serving them their food.

"Vegetarian plate for Skye," she muttered, almost to herself as she passed a thick paper plate to her cousin.

"Tofu burger for Tim," she said again in the low voice, passing off another plate before handing over Madison's pulled pork.

"Tofu?" Tim's voice sounded strangled. Veronica looked over at him, eyes wide.

"You wanted the tofu burger, right?" But she couldn't keep up the deadpan look and cracked a smile. Skye laughed and Madison snickered.

Tim eyed the burger warily and poked it with his potato salad fork. "It used to be alive, right?"

Veronica nodded and went on to hand Jeremy his plate.

Dwayne didn't want to, but he couldn't help noticing that her shirt was buttoned to her throat. Not a hint of cleavage. She was locked up tighter than a nun in her outfit.

Stupidly enough, it was more intriguing than anything Stephanie the Obvious wore. Or didn't wear. Two blondes, but only one made him look twice.

As Veronica bent an arm around his shoulder to grab his beer bottle and trade him for the plate with his steak on it, he tilted his head. At the angle she was twisted, their faces were inches apart. She froze, a lock of blond hair dipping over her eyes. Gorgeous, intelligent gray eyes, fringed with light lashes and carrying no makeup. Eyes that looked about as frightened as a deer caught in his crosshairs.

He tried to think of something witty to say, something charming to put her at ease. But he couldn't do anything but stare at her, feel their breath mingling between them. If he leaned in just a little, his lips would be able to—

"Moo."

Veronica jerked up straight at the sound. Dwayne looked to his left to see an amused Madison. She shrugged innocently.

"You said you wanted your steak to talk. Looks pretty rare to me. Compliments to the chef."

Dwayne gave her the stink eye, but she merely smiled and scooped up a bite of pork. He looked back up, but Veronica was already gathering the serving platter to take back.

"Is everything okay?" she asked the table at large, deliberately not looking at him.

"Everything looks great. Thanks. And make sure you sit down and eat. You're not on the clock." Skye gave her an encouraging smile and Veronica left without another word.

Everyone else dug into their lunch, something that told him they'd been waiting for him to get there before eating. His stomach was still a little raw from the travel, but he wasn't about to let a damn good steak go to waste. Settling down on the couch, using the coffee table as leverage, he went to town. And though the food was good, his mind kept drifting to another tasty morsel. One with a long blond braid and skittish nerves.

That was odd. Okay, no, he wasn't on the lookout for

a woman. Right now, his best chance for keeping his sanity would be to focus on reintegrating to a non–war zone. To normal life. To not jerking the wheel every time there was a piece of an old tire on the road or a sharp sound that might resemble the crack of a rifle.

But damn if he couldn't stop himself from getting one more good look at Veronica's backside as she disappeared around the wall that separated the dining room from the kitchen. His mind floated back to their Skype conversations, when she'd made him laugh when he needed it most. When she'd unintentionally given him a piece of home he craved desperately. When she'd lulled him to sleep by just being a voice at the other end of the Internet connection. Taking time out of her day to talk to a complete stranger halfway around the world.

"Ow!" A sharp kick to his shin got his attention quickly.

Tim was staring at him, his best *don't fuck around* face plastered on. "What are you doing?"

He shrugged. "Nothing." Truth there. Looking was, in all technicality, not doing. And besides, he wasn't obligated to explain his every thought to his buddy.

Tim shook his head but didn't say anything.

He was right, though. As sweet as Miss Veronica Gibson seemed, she wasn't for him. Nobody was right now. He wasn't in the right mindset for anything other than getting life back on track and doing his job.

---

Veronica tossed her keys in the little bowl on the entry table and kicked the door shut behind her. A door. A real door in a real apartment that she paid rent on without her parents breathing down her neck. Not a hut, or a tent, or some makeshift hovel. The comforts of Middle America were truly a blessing.

"Hey, you're home." Madison walked into the living room holding a bowl and a bag of chips. "Salsa time?"

"Yes, please. But let me change first." She scurried off to her room and peeled her wet clothes off before slipping into flannel pajamas and hustling back to the living room.

They plopped on the couch and propped their feet up. She reached in and grabbed a few chips. Junk food. Another luxury she would never take for granted.

"Work sucked, huh?"

Sucked… The word sounded absolutely dirty, but she knew it wasn't. "Right. Yes. Work sucked." Especially after Stephanie took out her frustration on a ditched table by spilling a tray of drinks on Veronica. The only bright side had been it happened at the end of her shift. Somehow, everyone thought she was the perfect scapegoat.

Likely because she never said a word about it.

"You know, eventually you'll have to tell me what your first language is." Madison picked up a magazine from the side table and started flipping through it mindlessly, still eating.

"What?" Nobody had mentioned her speech before. Was it really all that different?

Madison glanced up. "The way you talk is so formal. Either you were raised by nuns—"

Veronica nearly choked on a chip. Too close for comfort.

"—or your first language isn't English."

Veronica bit her lip, not sure of how much to explain. Only Skye knew the full background. Everyone else had, until now, accepted the simple explanation of being Skye's cousin from Texas and not having a story worth mentioning.

Slowly, with care, she answered as best she could. "My first language is English. I think it's just that I don't talk as much." She made sure to use a contraction that time.

Madison shook her head. "I wouldn't say that. You're just shy; nothing wrong with that. We can't all be social butterflies like Skye. Or amazing conversationalists like me."

Veronica smiled at that. Her cousin was so easy to talk with, such a good listener. It was hard not to confide in her. And Madison was, well…

Madison. God bless her.

"I just had a very isolating childhood. Some social slang is still new to me." There. That was the truth. Just not the whole of it. But even sharing that tiny scrap of information had her nerves buzzing, waiting for the judgment.

Madison shrugged and went back to her reading. Well. Okay then. Veronica made a note to borrow the magazine later. Anything to continue helping ease her into modern America. TV was wonderful, but she liked magazines. It moved slower for her. She could take her time to absorb.

"You don't mind if I invite someone over tonight, do you?"

The question startled Veronica out of staring at the woman with some bubbles taped to her dress. Why in the world would anyone choose a stage name like Gaga? And why did she want to look like a bubble factory? "No. Not at all. It's your place."

Madison sighed and tossed the magazine back on the coffee table. "It's our place. You pay rent here too."

"You were here first, though." She was blessed Madison had offered the spare bedroom in the first place. She'd been staying with Skye and Tim. But as newlyweds, they deserved their privacy. There were only so many rooms of the townhouse she could escape to when the couple started looking romantically at each other.

"I don't care who got the apartment first; it doesn't matter. You're my roommate, and my friend, so it's our place. But it's just Dwayne I'm talking about."

Dwayne. The handsome Marine. Her, what had he called her? Skype buddy. The one with blue eyes that stared at her like he was seeing into her, through her. She felt a little buzz in her head but didn't want to think about it. "That would be fine. I'll stay out of your way." She paused a moment, then went out on a limb. "Won't Jeremy be upset with you spending time with another man?"

Madison's eyes grew huge, and she flopped back on the couch and laughed, holding her stomach as if she had a bellyache. "Upset? About Dwayne? Dwa... oh my God... no!" That sent her into another fit of laughter.

Were relationships in America really so funny? Sadly, she couldn't say, as the concept was foreign to her.

Finally Madison calmed down and wiped her eyes. "No. Dwayne is like another brother to me. He's one of those guys that I love dearly... but not love like I love

Jeremy." Madison's normally analytical and shrewd eyes went a little hazy at the mention of the man she loved. "Nobody's gonna be like Jeremy, and the cocky bastard knows it. So no worries on that front."

"Ah. I see." No, she truly didn't. Dating and men in general were still a scary subject. When she was just getting used to how fast and quick conversation flowed with slang on a daily basis, the thought of jumping in to meet men for the purpose of a relationship was daunting, to say the least. But it was something she knew she had to tackle. And soon.

"We just both like action movies, and since he's missed all the new releases, I saved the one that came through last week from Netflix. I know how it is, coming back from deployment. Some people want to go out every night to bars and just be right back where they left things. But other people like to sort of slide back into the groove. D's in the second half. So just chilling out around the house will be good for him."

Chilling out. Relaxing. Right. "Makes sense." Her life had never been easy, wasn't designed that way. Relaxation was a sin, in her parents' eyes. The Gibsons firmly believed discomfort was somehow a quicker road to God's good side. But being at war was something even she couldn't imagine. "Of course he can come over."

"You sure you don't mind?"

"No. Not at all." Only a little. He was just so… large. And intimidating. The way he'd stared at her at the party the other night unnerved her, though she would not admit that to Madison. Or anyone else. The little mouse she used to be had no place in her new life. It wasn't allowed. She needed to learn to stand up for herself and not be such a wimp.

"Great. You can join us if you want to. It's an action movie. I know those aren't your favorite. But still, if you're bored you can hang with us."

"I might. But I'm really tired. And I have some work to catch up on for school." Another bone of contention that she hated to admit. Madison thought she was working on an associates degree through an online program. Veronica felt bad deceiving her, but when her roommate made the assumption, she didn't correct her.

In reality, she was working toward her GED. Living in the world's remote jungles did not make schoolwork an easy feat, and her parents just gave up after a while. She could read the Bible, so what more did she need?

Only Skye knew and was helping her catch up so she could take the test as soon as she felt ready.

Another secret. Another millstone hung around her neck, keeping her from experiencing real life to the fullest. She couldn't wait to be through the process.

No, that wasn't fair. Veronica breathed and did her best to push the bitterness from her mind. Many people would love to travel the world and traipse through thick, lush jungles and vast deserts.

Just not her. And not for what she had to sacrifice to do so. Too bad she had not had the choice.

"So when will he be here?"

"Probably around seven. We'll order a pizza, if you want some."

Pizza. Her favorite. "I would love some. Thanks for the offer."

Madison stretched out on the couch so that her feet draped over Veronica's lap. "No problem."

This sort of friendship, with casual ease and no barriers, was something she'd always dreamed of. No language barrier to fight through. No cultural divides to conquer. Just simple girl-speak. No, girl-*talk*.

"So what did you think of Dwayne?"

"Hmm?"

"Dwayne. Was he what you were expecting, after all your Skype chats? I'm sure you had expectations."

"Oh. He was nice." *Imposing.* "He's also very tall." *Huge.* "His accent is nice." She could listen to him talk for hours. He could probably read her GED prep book out loud and make it sound like a love sonnet.

Madison smiled. "That's Dwayne. He's a big teddy bear. All heart."

Teddy bear? The man looked like he could rip a car apart with his bare hands.

"He seemed a little more tense than normal, though. I hope he's okay. Sometimes guys have a little bit of trouble adjusting when they come home."

The worry in her friend's eyes made her sad. "Maybe he was just tired. The trip was a long one, I'm sure."

Mad's face cleared. "You're right. Dwayne's a tough one. I'm sure he's fine. You'll really like him. We all hang out a lot, the five of us. Well, six now that you're here."

Veronica was glad to hear it. Being one of the group was so exciting for her. Forced isolation for over twenty years will do that to a person.

Now if only she could get over the feeling of intimidation when Dwayne was around.

# Chapter 3

DWAYNE KNOCKED ON THE DOOR OF MADISON'S apartment. Nothing. No way would Madison forget their movie date. Plus, her car was in the parking lot. He knocked again, harder.

"Coming." The voice inside was definitely not Madison's. But he would recognize it anywhere. That voice echoed in his dreams… at least the ones that weren't nightmares.

Veronica. Right. She lived with Madison now. He remembered from their online run-ins.

She opened the door, her cheeks a little flushed, as if she'd run to get there. "Hey."

Her clothes were baggy again. A sweatshirt zipped up to her chin, simple jeans that weren't too tight, but not hanging off of her either. They hid her shape well enough. But her long hair was braided again, the thick tail swung over her shoulder. He had the strangest urge to wrap a hand around the woven locks, see if the stuff really felt as heavy in his hands as it looked.

"Madison came home late from work. She said to tell you she is changing and will be out in a minute." Her voice was whisper thin, like she was unsure. She opened the door wide and let him through.

"Thanks." He walked through and stood by the kitchen table, not sure exactly what to say. She closed

the door behind her and walked to the living room as if
he wasn't even there.

Well, okay then. Apparently he didn't register on her
radar. It bothered him, though it really shouldn't. She
shouldn't be registering on his radar either. Hell, his
radar should be turned off.

The doorbell rang and Madison yelled, "That's the
pizza!" from deeper in the apartment.

"I'll get it," he said, thankful for something to do
other than stand stupidly in the dining area by himself.
He paid the pizza guy and dropped the boxes on the
table. Madison ordered three. Bless her, she remembered he'd be starving and wanting good food again.
Thoughtful friends were irreplaceable. He opened the
top box and let the aroma of the loaded toppings, the
spicy pepperoni, the melting cheese, and sweet sauce
hit his nose. Pizza. Real pizza, not that horseshit they
served at the mess hall and dared to call pizza. With a
sigh of thanksgiving, he grabbed the first slice and bit in.

"Oh."

He whirled around, which only made the melting
cheese and a little sauce fly across his cheek. Gross. Not
to mention unattractive.

Veronica stood there, holding a stack of plates and
some napkins, wearing a slightly alarmed expression.

Right. Because in civilized society, people used
plates. Not just digging in rudely. Fuck, she must think
he was an animal. He chewed quickly and swallowed
while using the back of his wrist to wipe at his cheek,
wincing at the burn of the too-hot cheese. "Sorry. The
allure of good pizza got ahead of me. Haven't had much
decent food for a while."

Her expression softened. "Oh, of course. That's fine. Here." She handed him a plate and went back to the kitchen. "Would you like something to drink?"

*She's playing perfect hostess and I'm dripping sauce on the carpet. Great.* He plopped the slice on the plate and shut the box so heat didn't escape. "Uh, I can get it."

"I'm already in here. Would you like a beer? Madison has a few in here. I'm sure she wouldn't mind sharing."

He wanted a cold bottle more than she knew. But he wasn't an idiot. Right now, alcohol was the last thing he needed. "Just water." He sat at the table, not sure if that's what Veronica was expecting. He and Madison always just took the food into the living room and ate on the couch straight out of the box. Maybe the new girl was super uptight?

She brought out a glass with ice.

"You didn't have to pour the bottle out." He accepted the glass and took a gulp, hoping to wash down the awkwardness with it.

"No bottle. Skye has given everyone a filtered pitcher in favor of being more eco-friendly. Plastic bottles are the devil, she says." Veronica grinned a little.

Yup. Sounded just like Skye. Dwayne grinned at that. "But Skye's not here, and Madison hates those things."

"She does." Veronica smiled slyly. "But whenever I can, I hide the bottles she buys so she's forced to use the pitcher."

He laughed, and the sound felt rusty coming out. Rusty, but good. Needed. Amazing. "Sneaky little witch. I knew I liked you. All prim and buttoned up, but you've got a sadistic streak hidden in there."

Her eyes widened a little, and he wondered if he'd

gone too far with the joke. But then they crinkled in the corners, as if registering the humor, and her lips twitched.

And then there was nothing. Literally nothing. Veronica didn't grab a slice of pizza, and Dwayne wasn't sure if eating in front of her would piss her off. It was an Italian standoff. Why did he feel so damn uncomfortable? Was it the warning Skye had given? Or Veronica herself?

The fact that he didn't think she'd appreciate his brand of innocent Southern flirtation meant he was left with little to say. Wasn't that a pisser… While twirling his glass between his palms, he took a quick peek at her from the corner of his eye.

She sat there, prim as can be, hands folded in her lap, studying the box of pizza. Either she was memorizing the pizza chain's slogan printed on the cardboard, or she was completely avoiding looking at him. Maybe he made her just as nervous. At least they had that in common.

Finally, she reached for something. But it wasn't a slice of pizza. Her fingers grasped a napkin, then reached out toward him. He jerked back reflexively before realizing her intention. Her eyes widened, then she dropped the paper next to his plate.

"You still have a little…" She tapped a finger on her cheek.

The sauce. Right. He'd been sitting there the whole time with a smear of sauce on his cheek like a two-year-old. As far as first—or was it second?—impressions went… he was probably batting a zero in her eyes. And it shouldn't matter anyway.

"Hey, guys."

"Madison." Thank you, God. Dwayne popped up

and gave her a hug and a kiss on the cheek. "Hiding from me?"

"Not even close. Just got held up at the hospital. Training a new girl on the computers and she's clearly a little slow on the uptake." Madison glanced at the plates, brows raising in surprise. "Where'd those come from?"

Dwayne jerked his head toward Veronica.

"I brought them out. Should I not have?" She bit her lip like she was waiting punishment or something.

Madison waved the question off. "No worries. We just bring the boxes in with us to the living room. We're casual like that." She slugged his arm hard and pointed at the pizzas. "Grab those, pack mule."

"You just keep me around for the heavy lifting," he joked.

"Damn straight. You gonna watch the movie with us, Veronica?"

*Say yes.* He wanted to watch her all night. Just being in her presence reminded him of the calm she'd brought to his life during the deployment.

*Say no.* He'd embarrassed himself enough around her for one day.

Great. He couldn't even make up his own mind.

"Sure."

Well, damn. Or maybe not. Hell if he even knew what he wanted—or needed—anymore. He grabbed the boxes and headed toward the couch.

The good thing was that during a movie nobody was expected to say a damn word. Silence was currently his best friend.

---

Veronica covered her eyes and shuddered as a gang of rebel soldiers invaded a warehouse and walked right into a trap. A violent, deadly, graphic trap… one she couldn't watch without risk to her stomach.

Normally she took every opportunity to watch movies, picking up on slang and other social nuances. She treated it much like a game. Sheltered didn't begin to describe her upbringing, she was coming to realize. Veronica knew she would be behind the curve on a lot, but she hadn't realized just how far her parents had gone to keep her ignorant about all things average.

Of course, their reasoning wasn't to shelter her so much as they just assumed their calling to spread God's word was too important to ignore. For them or their daughter, who had no say in the matter. But the effect was still the same. Veronica was playing catch-up at twenty-six.

"I'm gonna go take a shower."

Veronica looked toward Madison. "What? It's the middle of the movie." At least she thought it was. Hard to tell one part from another with all the blood. She winced as another man fell with a shriek of pain and rolled offscreen.

"I know, but I didn't have a chance to take one earlier, and I feel gross. Not showering after the hospital isn't an option. Plus, D's asleep anyway. He won't even know I'm gone. I'll feel better after I shower." Without waiting for her answer, Madison headed for her bedroom with the connected bath.

Veronica glanced at Dwayne. He was, indeed, dead asleep. After seven slices of pizza—seven!—he'd moved from the couch where all three sat to the love seat. He'd said he wanted to lie down for the movie. Two minutes later, the not-so-faint rumble of snoring had started.

How he could sleep through people being slashed and shot to death, she had no clue. It was nightmare-inducing. Then again, maybe he was on to something. If his eyes were closed, he wasn't forced to watch the screen.

Why didn't she think of that?

She focused on the movie, but after another minute, she turned her attention back to the giant lounging to her right.

His body took up the entire sofa. One arm was flung over his head, the other rested on his abdomen. His shirt was pulled up just a little, showing a thin strip of bronzed skin and a little line of hair, just a little darker than on his head, leading into his...

Oh, no. Veronica's face flushed at the thought. She turned her eyes away.

You can take the preacher's kid out of the missionary work... but apparently you couldn't take the guilty mind out of the PK.

And just when she was starting to feel normal. She'd bet Madison wouldn't blink at seeing a man's stomach, or the reminder of where the little trail of hair led. Time to ditch the old mindset. She left her parents behind because she wanted to experience a new life. New life meant considering men for something other than platonic friendship. So she forced herself to take further stock of the specimen on the couch.

His hands were ringless, and a simple sports watch wrapped around his thick wrist. Forearms dusted with hair led up to the pushed up sleeves of his shirt. His wide shoulders stretched out a tight Henley shirt that had seen better days. She could see the frayed edges from here.

Long legs… Lord, were they long, encased in jeans that were more than a little worn at the seams. At least it was consistent, she thought with a small smile. She followed the line of denim, refusing to ignore his groin area. If she was going to start dating and being with men, she had to get used to it.

Okay. Maybe she should start with a less daunting subject. Her eyes drifted down until they landed on his boots. One foot was on the floor, but the other was on the coffee table. Right next to the pizza boxes.

For some unknown reason, it bothered her. A great deal. She tapped the boot with her own bare foot, but nothing happened. What was she expecting? The man didn't wake up when bombs went off on the TV speakers. A little tap wasn't going to move him. She debated the wisdom of her plan, then ditched wisdom and went for it anyway.

One hand grasped the toe of his boot, the other hooked under the cuff of his jeans. She waited, holding her breath, but he didn't move an inch. Not a flutter of lashes, not a twitch of the finger. Lifting slowly, she adjusted until she could place the boot with care down on the floor.

The snarl was her first clue she should take off running. But before her mind could even process the odd noise, she flew through the air. Landing on her back on the sofa, she tried to breathe, but couldn't. Her lungs wouldn't expand, like the time she fell from a tree limb and had the wind knocked out of her. She opened her eyes and saw what might be in her top five most terrifying sights of her life.

Dwayne pinned her down, one arm draped over her chest—explaining why her lungs couldn't expand—and his knee was holding her legs immobile. His face was red, eyes bloodshot, nostrils flaring. He was a raging bull, and his anger was one hundred percent focused on her.

She tried to gasp, to say something, to scream for help, but only a squeak came out. Her eyes watered, lungs burned like they were on fire. She clawed at his arm, struggled to be let up. Desperate for air.

And then the heavy weight was gone. Her eyes closed automatically in relief. She gasped in a cool, relieving breath of fresh air and nearly choked on it. Slowing down, she forced herself to breathe in through her nose, out through her mouth. To focus on slowing down the rapid pace of her beating heart. Shock and near-hysteria, she knew, could steal your oxygen almost as fast as anything. Her eyes stayed shut, but she could hear Dwayne moving on the other side of the room, but she wouldn't look. Couldn't. All that mattered was soothing her abused lungs, calming her racing heart. Not throwing up.

"What the… Veronica? Are you okay?" Madison was by her in an instant, kneeling down in front of the couch. She rubbed her arm soothingly. "What happened?"

Veronica pried her eyes open, not at all sure how to answer that. Because she had no clue herself. She shook her head, though she wasn't sure if it was a request for more time, or something else.

"Dwayne?"

Veronica finally made herself search out the man. He stood in the corner of the room, as far away from the couch as he could get without climbing out the window. He stared at his hands, which were shaking, balling them into fists, then unclenching them again. Stared at them as if they weren't his own.

"Dwayne, what happened?" Madison's voice sounded so upset.

"It's okay." Too scratchy. Veronica cleared her throat and tried again. "It's fine. I think I startled him."

What an understatement. He'd scared the daylights out of her, but all of a sudden, with the large man pressed against the wall, looking so disgusted and shattered, she couldn't feel anger or resentment. Something else was wrong, and it had nothing to do with her waking him up.

"Veronica, I..." He shook his head and screwed his eyes tight. When he opened them again, they were filled with regret. "I'm sorry."

Madison reached out an arm. "Dwayne, sit down and we can—"

"No."

And he left. Without giving either of the women a chance to say a word, he bolted for the door, brushing past Madison so fast she swayed with the speed. Before they knew it, an engine fired up outside and they sat silently, listening to it fade in the distance.

"Are you sure you're okay?" Madison rubbed a hand over her back. The caring nurse was in her element.

"Yes. I'm fine. But I don't think he is."

Madison sat on the couch next to her. "I don't think so either." She sighed and ran her fingers through her wet hair. "I need to make a few calls. You're sure you'll be fine?"

She nodded. Madison would call her brother, maybe Jeremy as well. And they would go to Dwayne, look out for him. Because that's the kind of people they were.

People who cared enough about each other to inconvenience themselves. To be there no matter what.

This was why she'd started her life over again. To be a part of that. As painful as the moment of fear had been, the aftermath was a good reminder.

———

Dwayne walked through the back door to Tim and Skye's townhouse patio. Both were already out there, along with Jeremy. He'd come to the impromptu cook-out early specifically to catch both his buddies before everyone was there and enjoying themselves.

Jeremy was slouched in a patio chair, glass of water in his hand. Tim stood by the grill, waving a spatula to get rid of some smoke. And Skye was stretched out on a wooden bench, flat on her back. She wore ripped jean shorts that showed off a mile of leg, some tank top thing that flowed down to the ground, and her feet were bare. Huge shades covered her eyes, and one arm was draped over her forehead like she was asleep. She couldn't have been any sexier if she'd been posed that way by some photographer looking for the perfect pinup shot.

His friend was a lucky bastard.

"Welcome." Jeremy toasted him with his water and took a drink.

"Hey, sweetie." Skye stood and came to give him a kiss on the cheek. When she nudged her shades to the top of her head, no pity shone in her eyes. If Tim told her about his freak-out the night before, she wasn't showing it. He appreciated that.

"Hey, beautiful. You ready to get rid of that loser and come be mine yet?" he drawled, making her laugh and swat his arm. "Hey, it's just my bad luck he spotted you first in Vegas, or I'd have walked away with a new wife instead of that unappreciative jerk."

"Trust me, he's plenty appreciative. Now," she added, her voice warming with obvious undertones that Dwayne pretended to not notice, "Tim, I'm gonna go in the kitchen and start slicing up some veggies."

"Sounds good. Thanks." He didn't move from his post at the grill.

She patted Dwayne's arm again once before shutting the sliding glass door behind her. Okay. She knew. This was her way of giving Tim and Jeremy time to talk to him in private.

The only reason he'd managed to put off the confrontation from last night until today was because he swore he'd come over early to the barbeque and talk then. They'd both called him, most likely after Madison informed them of his *unfortunate episode* with Veronica.

Unfortunate episode. Right. What a nice, polite way of thinking about it. Like he'd spilled his drink on her or something. No, he'd only damn near terrified the life right out of her. He still could see the fear in her eyes, hear the little desperate gasps for breath, feel her chest struggling to rise under his forearm.

After swearing he wasn't going to drink, do drugs, or engage in any reckless behavior, his friends both agreed he wasn't a danger to himself and left him alone. But only with the promise of coming to Tim's place the next day so they could talk.

He fell into the nearest patio chair and grabbed Jeremy's water from the table. Jeremy shrugged and reached into the cooler for a beer.

"There's nothing to talk about."

Neither man said anything. They all could play the patience game for hours. But they didn't have hours.

Dwayne sighed. "She woke me up, I heard gunshots from the movie, I reacted. It's really not the end of the world. I'll apologize to her when I see her next."

Tim glazed some marinade over a kabob. "You think it was a natural reaction?"

"For a guy who'd been stateside for not even forty-eight hours, yeah."

Jeremy shook his head. "You're smarter than that. You know the signs. You're just ignoring them."

Because nobody wanted to admit they were cracked in the head. That's what it was. No matter how widely known it was, no matter how many *20/20* specials Barbara Walters covered about returning vets, or how hard the military worked to erase the stigma... the fact remained.

To the public at large, people with PTSD were crazy.

He couldn't be one of them. Oh, a part of his mind knew it was a certain level of denial to think he could will away the effects. But he was tough. And a good person. He could do it.

"D. You need to take care of this." Tim closed the grill lid and gave him undivided attention. "I'm not kidding. It's not something to dick around with."

He was saved from having to make promises—sincere or otherwise—when the sliding door opened behind him. He glanced over his shoulder to see Skye's head peeking out.

"Honey, Madison and Veronica are here."

Veronica? Now? Damn. He scrubbed a hand over

his face. Couldn't he have at least had a full twenty-four hours before he had to think of what to say to the poor girl?

"Guess my bill's come due. Time to go pay the price." He gave the others a wink so they didn't worry, stood up, and headed inside to wait.

# Chapter 4

VERONICA WASN'T SURE SHE WANTED TO BELIEVE Madison's claims that she'd be welcome at the barbeque. After what happened the day before, it seemed kinder to give Dwayne some space, some room to breathe. The entire episode had scared her half to death, but only until she'd seen the effect his unintentional behavior had had on him. If she was scared, he'd been terrified of his own reaction. Maybe seeing her so soon would only make things worse.

"I don't mind taking your car and heading back to the apartment," she said once more as they turned into Tim and Skye's neighborhood. "Really. I could use the time to study."

"No. You're going in there and that's final." Madison parked her car behind Dwayne's huge pickup truck.

They grabbed the two bowls of fruit salad Veronica had sliced up before they left and headed to the door. Before their feet hit the front porch, the door swung open. Skye stood there, a wide smile for them. But the grin didn't reach her eyes.

"Hey, guys. Come on in." Her tone was warm but reserved. Not at all like Skye.

She shouldn't be there. Once again, she was the outsider in a group. And they were going to close ranks around their own—Dwayne. Not that she could blame them. He deserved their loyalty.

Didn't mean it didn't hurt. It hurt when she was ten, staying with her grandparents and trying to fit in with the other kids, only to be called a freak who didn't belong, chased back to her parents' side by hurtful words.

It hurt the worst at fifteen, when the words were more cruel and the emotions more raw.

It would hurt now, too. But she was old enough to soothe the pain and not give up on her dream of normalcy.

Skye didn't give her a chance to make an excuse and leave on her own terms. She took Veronica's arm and tugged gently until they were all in the foyer of the townhouse that she and Tim owned. "I'm glad you guys could make it. Thanks for bringing the salad."

They wound their way through the living room and dining room where she placed her bowl on the kitchen table. The sliding glass door opened, and Dwayne walked through, blocking out all the afternoon light with his massive frame. With the sun at his back, and the house dark, she couldn't see his expression to read his mood.

Nobody spoke, and she could hear her own heart beating in her ears.

Finally he said, "Hey."

Quite the start. She forced a smile. "Hi."

"So, Madison," Skye said. "Could you help me carry the fruit and this tray of veggies out to the patio?"

"I don't know if I—oof! Yeah, I'd love to." Madison headed into the kitchen, rubbing her side.

"Excuse us, sweetie." Skye waited until Dwayne stepped into the room before sliding around him and through the door. Madison followed and shut the door behind her.

And then there were two.

She really should apologize for causing him the grief. After all, she'd been the one to startle him awake for no good reason. And she was just about to find her voice when Dwayne cleared his throat.

"Can I, uh, talk to you? In the living room?"

She nodded. Apologies could be made on the couch just as easily as standing awkwardly in the kitchen. She followed and waited while Dwayne sat on the middle cushion of the couch. What did he expect her to do? Sit next to him? Or would he think that was weird? The chair would be safer. But she didn't want him to think she was scared of him... though she was. Just a little. But every day was a new challenge for her to step away from the scared introvert she used to be. So she boldly sat right next to him on the couch. One little shift and their thighs would touch. She just wouldn't shift, that was all. Screwing up her courage, she took a breath and started.

"I'm so—"

"I need to apologize."

"—rry... what?" Veronica blinked. Did he just...

He rubbed a hand over his face, through his short, buzzed hair, as if he wanted to be anywhere else but there. Because of the topic? Or because of her? When he spoke, he stared at the fireplace.

"What happened yesterday wasn't your fault. I'm still... wound tight. From the deployment. And you got caught in the wrong place at a really bad time. That had nothing to do with you. And I hate that I scared you. It might make me sound old-fashioned, but my mother taught me better. Doing that to a guy would have sucked.

But knowing I behaved like that with a woman…" His voice trailed off, shame ringing clear in his words.

His sense of honor, his own personal code of ethics, was tormenting him more than she ever could have. Not that she wanted to. Pity, and more so respect, rose up for this poor man. He'd likely seen so much. Without thinking, she reached out and put a hand around his wrist. It was too thick for her to wrap her fingers around. His pulse thundered beneath her fingertips.

"There's no need to apologize. I wanted to extend an apology myself, for startling you. I wasn't thinking and I caused your… reaction."

He glanced at her then. Wounded. He looked so wounded, and her heart melted just a little. A true gentle giant. "Thanks."

Suddenly, she realized she was still touching his wrist, and she started to pull back. But he laid his hand over hers and held her there. Not with force, but she was immobile just the same.

The little thrill of feeling his calloused fingers on the back of her hand shocked her. Warmth spread from her hand up her arm, through her body. That was definitely a new phenomenon.

"You're a sweet one, aren't you?" His drawl was thicker now, a little more syrup than melted butter. It mixed with the warmth spreading to her belly and she wanted to crawl into his lap.

No, she wanted to run away. She'd never felt like this before. Ever. She found men attractive, from a safe distance. But they didn't make her body react this way. It was horrifying. Terrifying. Confusing.

*It's nice*, she scolded herself. Her parents weren't

going to round the corner and scream at her for impure thoughts and sins of the flesh. She could be attracted to a man. She was twenty-six years old.

This was, however, a little more man than she ever bargained for.

She tugged a little and he released her with ease. "Maybe we should head outside. They're probably wondering where we are."

He watched her a little longer, and she started to feel uncomfortable. Finally, he nodded and put his hands on his knees.

"Confused too, huh?" When she didn't answer, he continued. "It's like we know each other, because of all the talks on Skype. But we don't, not really. And yet…"

*And yet…* She couldn't help wondering what he wanted to say. But he didn't go on. Just shook his head.

"I need to grab something out of my truck. You go on ahead outside. Grab something off the grill before Tim burns it all to hell."

Veronica stood and walked toward the back door through the kitchen. But she couldn't—despite her internal lecture—resist peeking back around the corner.

He sat, silent and still as a statue, on the couch staring at his hands. Much like the day before, but without the horror or dismay. It seemed to just be thoughtfulness now.

What a confusing, interesting man.

---

Feeling lighter, Dwayne settled at the patio table with his plate of food. Next to him, Madison stretched out on a lounger, her plate lying over her stomach.

"You could eat at the table like a civilized human

being." Jeremy tossed a baby carrot so that it bounced off her knee.

"It's a barbeque, not a night at the O Club," Skye chided, like they were all children.

Madison, in response to Jeremy's question, merely gave him a one-finger salute. He laughed in response.

"Can't you wait until later for that?"

Tim mimed covering his ears and sang, "La, la, la!" loudly.

Madison took the opportunity to set her plate aside and launch herself into Jeremy's lap, who caught her with ease. And making sure her brother was looking, she planted a smacking kiss on Jeremy's mouth.

"Is there no deccncy in the world anymore?" Tim moaned.

Dwayne smiled and shook his head, shoulders shaking with laughter. God, he'd missed this. Missed it all. The utter normalcy of things. Well, okay, Madison and Jeremy being an item was brand new for him. And Tim being married was still pretty new. But the bullshitting, the joking, the teasing and mocking. He missed it all.

"Your veggie kabob, babe." Tim slid the last plate across the table toward his wife and settled himself in front of his burger. "You wanna tell them?"

Skye picked a piece of green pepper off her skewer and popped it in her mouth. "Nope, you go ahead."

"Right. Everyone knows my parents want to do a big commitment ceremony thing, since nobody made our first wedding."

"That's what happens when you get shitfaced and marry a stranger in Vegas," Dwayne pointed out. He knew Skye wouldn't be insulted, given that it actually worked out.

The odds, huh.

As predicted, Skye just rolled her eyes and pulled off a piece of squash to nibble on. "So thanks to my mother-in-law's flair for planning, it's turning into something a little bigger than we originally planned. And as our best friends, we were hoping you guys would stand up with us."

"Wait. Who?" Madison sat up suddenly, plate tipping to the side. She caught it before her burger could splat on the wooden deck.

"All of you. I need two bridesmaids, so I was hoping you and Veronica would say yes." Skye gave them hopeful looks.

Madison, in all her usual subtlety, jumped up on the lounge chair and gave a whoop.

Skye laughed. "I'll take that as a yes. How about you, sweetie?"

Dwayne looked at Veronica for the first time since he sat back down outside. Her eyes were wide, face pale. Her fingers were tearing a napkin into little pieces that the wind whipped off the table and across the lawn.

"Stand up. Like, in front? By you?"

"That's usually where the girls in matching dresses go," Jeremy pointed out. All tact, that guy.

"Are you sure there's nobody from Vegas you would rather have?"

Skye smiled a little. "I'd love to have a dozen bridesmaids, but that would make Tim look a little lonely with only two groomsmen. Besides, you're family. If you don't want to, I won't be offended." She reached across the table to cover her cousin's hand. And Dwayne could feel the camaraderie there. Skye's soft heart understood Veronica was afraid of the attention, that she was already scared of the idea.

Just how he thought he understood Veronica's thoughts as well, he didn't even begin to know.

"No. No, I'll do it. I'd like to." The words were quiet, but the resolve was firm. And her eyes, those smoky eyes, said she'd push through hell and back to do it. Dwayne's admiration of the quiet one grew another size.

"Which leaves me with you two jackwagons for groomsmen."

"Hello, bachelor party." When Madison snorted in disgust, Jeremy playfully pinched her in the waist, causing her to twist and laugh. "What? Like you girls don't do the bachelorette thing."

"They're not bachelor and bachelorette. They're already married." Madison picked up a cherry tomato and bounced it off Jeremy's cheek before it fell to the wood deck with a soft splat.

"Doesn't the bride's family usually do the planning? Will your mom want to get involved?" Dwayne asked Skye.

She smiled. "My own parents aren't even married. To them, it's just a piece of paper with no significant meaning. I think it's a mild disappointment that I'm not cohabitating  instead of 'buying into marital oppression.' They'll come, to support me. But it's not really their thing."

"Which suits my mother to the ground. Give that woman the chance and she'd run her own small country." Tim saluted the group with his beer. "To our wedding party. Best group of friends a guy—"

"Or girl!" Skye chirped.

"—could ask for."

"Hear, hear!"

Veronica waited until her shift was over and she cashed out with the swing shift manager before heading over to the office. She found her cousin sitting at the desk, the room empty otherwise, and breathed a sigh of relief.

"I think I'm ready to start dating."

Skye looked up from the catalog she was flipping through. Commercial kitchen supplies for restaurants. She waved at the office door and Veronica shut it behind her, then took a seat at Skye's desk.

"You want to start dating." She said the words with care as she folded the magazine back up and placed it at the edge of her cluttered desk.

*No. No, I'm not ready.* "Yes. I do." She'd never be ready if she didn't have someone to push her along. Time to grow up and get out in the world. She wanted a family someday. That would need to include a man at some point. She was just old-fashioned enough to want it that way.

"And is there a particular reason why you think you're ready?" When Veronica stared at her, Skye smiled. "I'm not trying to play therapist or anything; that's not what I intend. But it seems sudden. You just mentioned the other day that you were getting used to regular conversations."

"I still have trouble sometimes with slang. But for the most part, I think I've adapted to modern society nicely." Compared to where she was six months ago, that was very true. Coming from living in jungles or barely populated areas of third-world countries didn't lend itself to modern American social practice. Nobody from the African Zulu tribe was going to ask her to the prom.

And the few months she spent in the states at age ten, and again at fifteen, weren't enough to help with the social awkwardness. More like cause for her to be gun-shy at the thought of trying again.

"So why now?"

"I just feel ready." If the spark that had zinged through her when she sat on the couch with Dwayne was any indication, very ready. Ready to make up for lost time, and then some.

"Hmm." Skye twirled a container of paper clips on her desk, the rattling sound like soothing rain on a window. "Do you have any prospects?"

*Yes.* "Not that I can think of. I'm just going to look." Like window-shopping. Only instead of a sweater, she was on the hunt for a man.

Manhunt. That sounded so… not like her. The thought thrilled her.

Skye opened her mouth, but before she could speak, her cell phone rang. She turned the screen forward, then pushed a button and set the phone flat on her desk. "Hey, Madison. Veronica's here too. You're on speaker."

"Hey, guys." Madison's voice, firm and loud as always, filled the small office. "Wanted to see if anyone was up for a girls' night sometime soon."

"Yeah. First things first, though. Veronica says she's ready to start dating."

"Skye!" She wanted to slide off the chair into a puddle of embarrassment.

Madison only laughed. "It's about time. I wondered when her cute butt was going to start getting out there. So is there a target in mind?"

"She says no. But I'm not sure if that's true yet."

"She should start with a gentle model. Someone easy."

"*She* is right here," Veronica grumbled, but couldn't hold back the smile. It felt right, like what all girlfriends would do. Calling about boys, teasing each other. Only the more grown-up, mature version.

"No bad boys," Skye agreed and tapped a pen on the desk. "We'll think about it. Pick someone for a test run."

Test run. Gentle model. Were they picking out a car?

Skye hung up the phone and smiled. "Madison is a good ally in this."

"She's not going to think I'm some… freak? For not having dated until now?"

Her cousin waved that away. "Not at all. Madison's not a judgmental person. Plus, I didn't say you'd never dated. Just that you were ready to start dating. How she takes that is up to her. Either way, you heard her. She was excited to help."

Skye tossed the pen on the desk and crossed her. "So tell me really. Who or what spawned your sudden desire to hop into the dating pool?"

Veronica looked toward the big window. She could never lie worth anything.

"Okay. We'll ignore that for now. How about Madison, you, and I powwow about it this weekend?"

She jumped on the chance to deflect for now. "Sounds good."

"I have to ask. And you know you aren't obligated to answer. But I'm curious. Why do you want to keep your past a secret?"

The million-dollar question. "Your parents didn't mention me. Ever. Did they?"

Skye shrugged. "No, but they aren't big into sharing their pasts. For all I knew, they were only children. It's how I was raised, and I accepted it."

In that, they were the same. "I didn't even know your mom—my mom's sister—existed for so long. With my parents dragging me from one 'God-forsaken,'" she used air quotes, something she'd picked up from Madison, "country to the next, spreading the gospel, I got sick of it. I knew this wasn't the way normal people lived. Age ten, I begged for us to move back to the U.S."

"Can't blame you," Skye murmured, rocking back in her chair.

"They sent me to live with my father's parents. I lasted about three months. The kids were merciless. I didn't know how to make friends, because I hadn't had anyone my age to talk to." She smiled a little. "Anyone who spoke English, I mean. I talked funny, I didn't understand the slang, and I was too hesitant in reaching out."

"Kids can be cruel."

"Very," Veronica agreed. Her fingers automatically picked at, then smoothed over, a fray in the arm of the chair she sat in. "I was sensitive. It hurt. And I thought I would rather be with my parents, so I went back. I tried again at fifteen. Surely, I thought, teenagers wouldn't be as horrible and mean."

Skye said nothing.

Veronica smiled a little. "I know what you're thinking. They're not as mean as ten-year-olds. They can be worse. I very quickly learned that telling people my parents were missionaries would lead to one of two results.

They either thought I was some religious zealot who would try to shove God down their throat at every turn and would avoid me. Or they would treat me like I was some odd science experiment, always asking questions, trying to prove something."

"At an age when you must have wanted to start dating…" Skye added softly. Intuitive as always, knowing without a doubt what wasn't being said.

"My parents did not care at all about my comfort or my wishes. I never had friends, because we moved so frequently. I didn't ever speak the language of wherever we were. And the one time there was someone else who spoke English close to my age to hang out with, it happened to be another teenager, a boy. And we were caught kissing. Just kissing." She shivered at the memory. "It didn't go well when my father found us."

She still had the scar from her father's belt across the backs of her thighs. Could still hear the harsh, biting tone of his voice as he quoted Scripture like a weapon while whipping her. Could see her mother weeping, crying out why they had been cursed with such a shameful, wicked daughter who couldn't—wouldn't—accept her own mission in life… to see to the reform of others.

She still held the shame he beat into her about her desire. Though she'd matured, grown, and done some self-searching and realized her desires were not only normal, but healthy, it was a constant battle. But it was a battle she would win.

"It's a little hard to vocalize to someone that your parents cared more for their mission than their daughter. And to make sure people don't think you're some zealot that will start smacking them with a pocket Bible the moment they transgress. My hope is that I can get to know people for a while and eventually bring it up. Once they know I'm not like that." *Eventually. One of these days. When I get the nerve up to talk about it again.*

Skye laid a hand on her knee in silent comfort, then squeezed. "Well, no time like the present to make up for your lack of dating. Think about whether there's someone you might be interested in."

Dwayne's easy smile came to mind. She pushed it aside with effort. Her cousin meant someone who had the chance to be interested back. Dwayne Robertson was not only intimidating, he was out of her league. "Sure. No problem."

# Chapter 5

Dwayne jackknifed up in bed, reaching under his pillow for his Ka-Bar. His hand grasped air. There was a deep, rasping sound that he couldn't place, and he strained his ears to figure it out.

Damn. His own breathing, rattling his chest. And he didn't recognize it. He wiped a wrist across his brow and it came away damp with sweat. The sheets were wrapped around his legs like a vine and he kicked them away. Nothing confining. Nothing on top of him. He couldn't handle it.

What woke him up at—he checked the clock—four in the morning, he had no clue. But there was sure as hell no way he was going to get back to sleep now. And he knew, knew with a bone-deep, gut-wrenching sort of dread, that this was the nail in the coffin he couldn't ignore.

Despite the time, he reached for his cell and punched in the first contact.

"Sup?" Though he'd probably been deep asleep, Tim's voice was clear, without a hint of grogginess.

"I need help, man."

"If you need to be bailed out of jail, call Jeremy."

Dwayne didn't laugh at the joke. He ran one hand over his head, noting absently he needed a haircut again. When he said nothing, Tim spoke again.

"Start with the chaplain. Email him, set something up. Go from there. He's a good guy."

"I hate that I need help."

"I know."

Tim would. Asking for help was a Marine's worst nightmare. Probably any man's worst nightmare. "I have to do this, don't I?"

Tim sighed, then he must have covered the mouth of the phone because his voice was muted as he spoke to— Dwayne could guess—Skye. Then he was back. "Yeah. You do. I'm just shooting straight here. If it's affecting you this much that you're calling me like this, then you need to talk it out. You never know, it might not be all that bad."

Dwayne didn't scoff, but he wanted to. Telling some stranger his problems and admitting there were issues, exposing that soft underbelly, the weakness... it didn't bring good things to mind. But if it had to be done, then it had to be done.

"Okay. I'm on it."

He set the phone down a moment later, then stared at it. Something had him picking the phone back up, wondering what Veronica was doing. Craving to hear her voice. When he'd been injured in Afghanistan, it was her voice, her calm presence that got him through.

Just as quickly, he let the phone drop back down to the bed in front of him. First off, he didn't have her number. And second, he wasn't calling some chick he'd met three times—not including their computer dates—to help him get back to sleep. She'd think he was crazy. Crazier, he corrected with a smile.

Well, at least his sense of humor was still intact. That was something.

He texted his sister instead, asking about his niece

and telling her to call him when she got the message. He knew Natalie wouldn't see it until the morning anyway, so no worry in waking her. She always put the phone on silent after the baby was in bed.

Not a baby anymore. He smiled at the framed photo on the dresser across the room. His niece was growing up too fast. He'd only met her once, thanks to them still being back in Mississippi. But he'd have to see her again soon, or he'd miss too much.

That finished, Dwayne stretched and laid back, hands beneath his head, and stared at the ceiling until exhaustion took him under.

—⁓—

"Let's get shopping!" Skye shut the car door behind her and bounced in the backseat with excitement.

"Do you have a sadistic bent or something?" Madison pulled out of the townhouse driveway and out of the complex. "I thought when you asked us to be bridesmaids you were going to go all nontraditional and let us just pick our own dresses. Or hell, wear tuxes. I'm down for a bow tie."

Skye laughed. "Sorry. I have just enough 'traditional' in my blood to want you guys to be all prettied up standing next to me. Matching. Like a pair of bookends."

"Bookends. Hell. What are we—Bobbsey twins now?"

"Maybe your brother and all his conservativeness is rubbing off on me."

"Other way around, I'd say. You're rubbing off on Tim. And it's a good thing. Someone had to yank the stick out."

Veronica sat in the front seat, watching the landscape

and letting the teasing surround her. Their teasing didn't bother her anymore. Before, she might have taken things too literally. She could almost laugh at herself as she remembered she used to think they were serious when they went at each other like this. She'd come quite a long way. "I think it's nice to want bridesmaids. I don't mind."

"Thank you, sweetie." Skye's voice was smug.

"Veronica, where's my backup? Roomies stick together."

Veronica shrugged, a smile tugging at her lips. Madison looked so disgruntled in the driver's seat, her mouth set in a pout like a belligerent child in time-out. "Sorry. I like it."

"You suck," was all Madison could say as they pulled into the empty parking lot of the formalwear shop. "At least it's not birthday ball season, so the place won't be full of spouses and girlfriends looking for gowns."

Skye and Madison started to walk in, but Veronica stopped.

"I forgot my purse. You guys go in." She ran back to Madison's car, used the keyless entry code Madison had given to her before, and grabbed her purse. As she shut the door, she stepped back and right into a wall.

Or a chest, she realized, as arms steadied her at the elbows.

"Easy now. In a rush?"

She'd know that accent anywhere. The heat from his body almost soaked through her shirt, warming her skin. His thumbs caressed the inside of her elbows. Unconsciously? Or on purpose? And why wasn't she jerking away? Men made her uncomfortable. Especially this one, she reminded herself as she took a step forward and turned.

"What are you doing here?" That sounded nice and calm, she congratulated herself.

Dwayne rocked on his heels and stuck his hands in his pockets. "Tim didn't want uniforms, so we're getting fitted for tuxes. Lucky for us."

"Lucky?" When he tipped his head, she fell in step with him walking to the door. "I would think you were used to the uniform."

"Cammies, sure. Those aren't so bad. Not the one we'd wear for a wedding. They're hot as a bitch in heat and twice as annoying…" He trailed off and she looked up. His neck was bright red and he looked sheepish. "Sorry. Uh, I just mean they're uncomfortable. A monkey suit should feel like pajamas in comparison."

Hmm. Though she'd become accustomed to cursing, not hearing it much before moving to the States, rarely did anyone apologize for it. It was almost sweet that he would be concerned for her and check himself. When he reached around her back to open the door, she tried hard not to feel the little thrill at the contact, at the security of his huge arm sheltering her body.

This was definitely not her assignment. She was supposed to be thinking of available men who would be interested in *her*. Not emotionally unavailable, never-going-to-want-her, too-much-to-handle men.

"Good luck with your fittings." Before he could answer, she scurried through the racks of dresses toward the left side of the store, where her friends were flipping through a binder with pictures. Her purse caught once on a rack and she had to stop and detangle herself. *Please don't be watching me. Please don't be watching me fight with a rack of clothes like an idiot.* She wouldn't look. She wouldn't look. She… okay, she looked back and watched Dwayne melt into the sea of display tuxedos on the right side of the store. One tiny peek at his back couldn't hurt. It wouldn't be that bad of an idea if she let her eyes just drift down the line of his back to his butt either. Not a problem at all. No problem—

Something sharp jabbed her on the temple with enough force to have her eyes water and stop her in her tracks.

"Ow!" With some quick footwork and unique hand placement, she managed to barely catch another rack of dresses before they toppled to the floor. This place was a death trap.

Rubbing the spot on her forehead, she kept her eyes straight ahead and sat down next to Madison. Madison was peering over Skye's shoulder, who was flipping through a binder full of dresses and color swatches.

Skye pointed to a pretty floor-length gown in teal. "I really think you should try this style on. The A-line is flattering for anyone and—"

"And my shoulders will look like a linebacker in that cut." Madison's tone said she'd rather take a bullet than wear the dress on page seven.

Skye blew out a breath, shifting the hair that frizzed around her face. "Okay then. Let's try this one on page nineteen. I think—"

"That green color will make me look sickly? Yes, I agree."

"Madison," Veronica murmured.

"Sorry." Deflated, Madison sank back into her chair. "I'm being a bitch, aren't I?"

"No," Veronica tried to soothe, though she sort of agreed.

"Yes," Skye said at the same time, then patted her knee. "But I still love you. And this dress comes in several colors."

"Oh." Madison was appeased.

"How about this one?" the bride asked, pointing to another page.

Skye finally chose two different dresses that she wanted to see. A quick consultation with the store clerk found she had one of each dress for Madison and Veronica to try on.

"I only have the dress from page nineteen in a size four."

"That'd be my size." Madison stood.

"And it's only in the green. But you can order it in any of the other colors, of course," the clerk reminded them quickly when Madison's face clouded over. "The important part is seeing how it fits."

"Just head to the dressing room, oh sickly green one." Skye gave her back a gentle shove and off she went, holding the dress with the interesting color palette.

The sales clerk held out the second dress, which happened to be Veronica's favorite. "It's a size too big for you, but when you come out we can use clips to hold it back so you get a good idea of what it will look like when it's properly sized."

It was a dusty rose color, with a strapless sweetheart neckline. The hem, at least on the model, hit right above the knee. Shorter than she was used to, but not too bad. Her favorite part, though, was the little belt that had rhinestones on the buckle. It added a fun little eye-catching pop. Something she wasn't used to, but couldn't resist. Veronica took the dress and made her way to the middle of the store, where the fitting rooms were.

"Madison, I'm going to need your help here in a second with the zipper."

She quickly shucked her clothing and pulled on the cute dress, but when it came time to zip the dress up, the zipper caught. She twisted her arm, tried to shift the material of the dress one way and the other, but nothing worked.

"Madison?"

No answer.

"Skye?"

Neither woman seemed to be around. They'd likely walked onto the mirrored staging area to check out their dresses.

She tried for the zipper again. No way was she leaving the dressing stall with the thing halfway undone. She might have graduated from wearing, as Skye called them, schoolmarm clothing to shopping for more contemporary styles that actually showed her arms and legs, but there was no way she could just flounce out onto the showroom floor and let her dress droop down around her back. If it fell, she'd be mortified.

Just as she started to wedge herself into a corner for leverage, thinking this time she finally had the right angle, the curtain shifted behind her.

"Oh, thank you." She breathed a sigh of relief and let her forehead drop to the wall. Her prayers had been answered. Madison heard her calling. "I apparently lack the third arm necessary to get into this dress myself."

The material tugged together in the back, drawing it tight across her breasts for a moment. The fingers that fumbled with the hook on the back felt thick, almost clumsy. After a moment, she couldn't breathe. No, it wasn't the fit of the dress. It was the realization that it wasn't Madison behind her, seeing her exposed more than she ever would have wanted.

She tried to turn, but couldn't. Though hooked at the top, the dress would still fall. All she needed for the humiliation to be complete would be to actually flash the intruder.

"Please go away." Her voice was so quiet, distant even to her own ears. The flush that crept up her neck and into her face burned almost painfully.

"Easy. I'm just trying to do you a favor. No ulterior motives here."

Dwayne. She should have known. For some reason she couldn't explain, the panic subsided marginally. But it was only replaced with a new form of tension when the back of his fingers brushed against the skin of her lower back, working to line the zipper up. Goose bumps spread up her back, over her arms, causing her to shiver.

"Cold?" He leaned forward and she could feel his warm breath on the back of her neck, where her braid was flipped forward.

She should pull away. Cover her front, jerk away, and scream. Men didn't just… come into women's dressing rooms like this. Did they? But her body was paralyzed from doing anything but shaking her head.

As the zipper found its track and he pulled it up, the rasp of metal on metal was one of the most intimate sounds she'd ever heard in her life. How bizarre, to be, what was the phrase? Turned on. To be turned on by getting dressed, and not the other way around.

"There." His voice was low in her ear, husky almost. "All trussed up."

She turned then. It was time for a blistering lecture on being rude, on assuming, on the arrogance of walking in on a woman undressed.

"Thank you."

Wait, that wasn't it. But she honestly couldn't form any heated words. She wasn't feeling them. They weren't coming from her heart.

Hallelujah. She was finally shedding her former mentality.

"That's quite a sight."

"Hmm?" She focused her eyes back on him. "What?"

He twirled a finger, and catching his meaning, she faced the mirror.

She still held one hand over her chest, since the dress was a size too big. But despite the awkward stance, she liked what she saw. There was a flush to her cheeks, just enough to add some color to her normally pale complexion, which complemented the dress's color. Her eyes were wide, amusement shining. And her mouth was split into a huge grin.

Joyful. She looked truly joyful. And not at all scared.

"Pretty damn beautiful." Dwayne placed his hands on her shoulders, his calluses feeling decadent on her skin. He leaned over and whispered, "The dress looks good too."

She could only nod.

"You should smile like that more often."

*I intend to.*

Dwayne shifted back into his own dressing room and shut the curtain tight. The throbbing in his head made him nauseous, and he pressed his thumbs to his eyes to relieve the pressure.

He shouldn't have gone in there. No ulterior motives his ass. He'd been drawn to the little breathless sounds, the struggles, and he knew damn well it was Veronica, and that she'd be in some form of undress. And despite his better judgment, he'd peeked.

Though startled, he didn't think Veronica had been scared. No, the way her breath had caught, her face had flushed, she looked almost like she was ready for him to toss her up against the wall, scrunch up her dress, and give her something to really smile about.

And his body was still tight with a desire to do just that. Except he couldn't, for more reasons than he wanted to think about at the moment. But the most important being... it wouldn't be fair to Veronica, on many levels.

"Dickweed, you ready yet?" The curtain flew back and Jeremy stood, annoyance on his face. "We've been waiting."

"Yeah." He shrugged into the suit coat and buttoned it while following Jeremy to the other side of the store, away from the women.

Tim stood, in a matching suit but lighter colored vest, waiting. "Took you long enough. You forget how to dress yourself?"

"Bite me." Dwayne stepped onto the riser next to Tim, Jeremy taking his place on the other side. Together they spun to face the wall-length mirror.

"Not bad." Tim adjusted his tie.

"So this is what we look like all cleaned up." Jeremy brushed imaginary lint off his sleeve and grinned.

"What made you go with suits? Thought we were doing the tux thing?" Not that Dwayne was going to complain. Hell no.

Tim shrugged. "Seems a little more low-key than black tie. Tuxes seemed overkill. Too Bond."

A saleswoman popped her head in, then another behind her. Their eyes were wide, and Dwayne wasn't too keen on the jackal-like smiles that stretched their dual bright red lips. "Can we help you gentlemen with anything?"

Given the way their eyes were devouring him and Jeremy, Dwayne wasn't sure how to avoid that land mine.

"Yeah, you know, is this tie right?" Jeremy, who was busy concentrating on the mirror and not on the predatory looks the women were sending their way, didn't see the hazard looming. "I'm just not sure; suits and ties aren't really part of our daily wardrobe."

"Oh my God," Dwayne muttered under his breath. "You gotta be shittin' me."

"Madison's gonna kill you," Tim sang softly.

"What?" Jeremy gave him a confused look.

The girls practically kicked each other trying to get to Jeremy first, but the taller blonde won. She cooed over how cute he looked in his suit, hands busy with his tie, brushing against his chest. Fawning. Straight up fawning. No other word for it.

"Need some help?" The smaller blonde's hands brushed against the side of Dwayne's neck in the pretense of fixing his tie.

He took a half-step back, hoping she'd take the subtle hint. "No, I think I'm good."

"Oh my God, your arms are huge!" the taller one squealed at Jeremy.

"Christ," Tim muttered. "This has death written all over it."

"Well, isn't this just cozy."

All five turned to see Madison standing at the entrance of the men's side of the store. Arms crossed over her chest, she tapped one high heel in rapid time. Her face was pinched. And if eyes were laser beams, Jeremy would be smoking. The woman next to him would have been ash.

Death just came knockin'.

"Hey, shouldn't you be over on the girly side with Skye?" Tim hopped off the riser and came to give her a once-over. "You look pretty good though."

Madison smacked his chest. "She sent me over here on a little recon mission. Making sure you guys look good in your suits so we don't have to change up the order. Everything fitting?"

"We're just double-checking," Tall Blonde told her. The tone, however, said, *Get lost; you're not invited to the party.*

"Hey, Mad." Jeremy took a step away from the saleswoman and shot her a smile. "You look cute."

"I look sick," she corrected, brushing a hand down the skirt. "This is so not my color. But you seem to be having… fun."

Five minutes too late, Jeremy must have registered the picture he was presenting. But rather than a look of guilt, he shot her a grin. "Hey, just getting a little help."

Madison just rolled her eyes, but she smiled a little. These two might kid, but Dwayne knew there was no real heat in their argument. "Dwayne, how about you? Everything fit okay? Need any help?"

"Fits just fine, sweetness." He took the opportunity to disengage fully from Shorter Blonde and walked over to give her a kiss of gratitude. Not that she knew she'd just saved him. "How are things on the shiny side?"

"Shiny side? Oh, right." She fingered the wide sash of the mint green dress. "Skye's dress is perfect. And Veronica is adorable."

More than adorable. But he wasn't exactly supposed to know that. So he kept his mouth shut. "Sounds like you ladies are all set."

"So we can get out of here?" Jeremy materialized by his side, looking anxious to get the hell out of the room suddenly. Whether he wanted to escape the overeager saleswoman or Madison's narrowed gaze, Dwayne wasn't sure.

# Chapter 6

THE GUYS HEADED BACK TO THE DRESSING AREA. As he shrugged out of his jacket, he heard Veronica call out.

"Tim, are you in here?"

"Yeah," he answered from the next stall over.

"Skye's coming back in, so you can't come out until she's secure."

"What is this—a military operation? Christ, why did I allow my mother to suggest all this?"

Veronica huffed. "Is that a yes?"

Tim sighed. "Yeah. I'll stay in here 'til someone gives the okay."

Dwayne poked his head through the curtain. Veronica scowled at him and shooed at him with her hand.

"Go away. You're not supposed to look."

"Hey, I'm not the groom. Maybe I just want a little sneak peek of my own." The peek he wanted was of Veronica.

She was too cute. Her braid was more out than in, her cheeks were flushed with happiness, and despite her stern look, her lips curved into a telltale smile that said she was in too good a mood to bother bickering with him any. The dress, which had gaped earlier, was now tight across her chest and torso, flaring out gently at the hips. But when she turned, he could see the white clips holding it back. Ah, so that's how they made it work. Just one more female secret.

"You look nice."

She looked down and smoothed the skirt in an unconscious gesture of pure feminine pleasure. "Thank you."

"Need any help with the zipper?"

Well, that burst the happiness bubble. She stalked to him, heels thumping on the carpet, and pointed her finger at his nose. "You… you…"

"Me?" He grabbed her finger—so tiny compared to his own hand—turned her wrist gently, and placed a kiss on her palm.

Her annoyance melted away, leaving only confusion. Her lips parted slightly, and he was dying to yank her into his dressing room and see if she tasted as good as she looked. But the moment he started to tug… he was stopped by Skye's voice.

"Veronica? Is everything okay?"

Wide eyes still staring at him, unblinking, she whispered, "Yeah."

A moment passed, then another, and Dwayne debated how fast he could toss Veronica over his shoulder and bolt out the front door, when once again Skye's voice intruded.

"Veronica? Is Tim hiding? Can I come in?"

That broke the spell. She blinked, shook her hand until he loosened his grip, and she scooted to the entrance. "Yes, it's safe."

Safe. What a lie. Dwayne slipped back into his room to finish undressing. What the hell was the matter with him? He'd been seconds away from dragging Skye's cousin to his car for… what? And to what purpose? She was a beautiful woman, sweet, and completely not for him. And that wasn't because of any deficit on her part. She was a little *too* sweet for him. She'd never be able to hang with his particular brand of clumsy country boy.

Not to mention the fact that he shouldn't be dating—or seeing—anyone right now. Not while he was still getting his life back in order after a deployment. And his mental health was still up for debate as well. They always warned against huge life changes directly after a deployment. Taking sweetie Veronica into his life wouldn't benefit either of them.

They were sound, logical reasons. He agreed with every one of them. If he brought it up, Tim and Jeremy would say the same.

So then why was he having to fight so hard to keep his hands off her?

—⁓—

Dwayne settled on the couch for a much-needed catchup of the shows he'd missed while deployed. First up, *The Walking Dead*.

But just as he hit play on the DVD, his phone rang. Of course. He sighed and reached for the phone, perfectly content to hit the ignore button and go back to his show. But when the display showed Natalie's name, he answered without hesitation.

"Hey, sis, what's up?"

"Deeeeeee!"

Dwayne held the phone away from his ear to save his eardrum from the high-pitched squeal. "Not sis. Hey, button, did you dial Uncle Dwayne all by yourself?"

His fifteen-month-old niece, Suzanna, squealed with delight again.

"Can you go find your mama?"

A muffled thump, an exasperated groan, and then Natalie was on the phone. "I'm sorry, Dwayne. I swear, this kid grew wheels when she started walking. I turn around and she's dumped out my purse and dialing you."

Dwayne stretched out on the couch and settled in. He loved his family more than anything, and missed them like crazy since the day he left for TBS. "Suzanna just wanted to talk to her favorite uncle. There's no harm in that."

"You're her only uncle," Natalie said dryly.

He wouldn't have been, if Natalie's deadbeat ex were in the picture. Guy had more brothers and sisters than Dwayne could remember. But he'd left her high and dry, repeatedly, in the past. The guy couldn't be counted on for anything. Though Natalie didn't see it that way, Dwayne saw it as a blessing he was completely out of the picture now.

But it killed him that his sister had taken the same path their mother had. Deadbeat loser boyfriend, who turns into a deadbeat loser dad, which leads to single motherhood and a rough life for everyone.

Something clattered in the background and he winced. "What'd she get into now?"

"Nothing. That was me. I'm putting groceries away." Her breath huffed out a little. "So how's the readjustment going?"

Immediately, his back stiffened. "What do you mean?"

"You know, catching up with friends, seeing what you've missed, all that. Can't be easy, being gone for so long and coming home to a brand-new world."

"Oh. Right." He scratched his jaw and sat up. "It's fine. Meeting people who came into town after I was gone."

"Veronica?"

How the… "How did you—"

"You mentioned her before, in emails."

"No I didn't."

"So I just made up her name?" Natalie laughed. Then a giggle sounded loudly. She must have picked up Suzanna. "You mentioned her at least four times in emails while you were deployed. I saved most of them to read over again later. You made her sound like a good influence."

He was so not doing this right now. "Suzanna stick anything interesting in her mouth lately?"

Natalie sighed, but moved on with the wisdom that came with twenty-five years of siblinghood. "Nothing new to report."

He paused, then decided to go for it. "Need help?"

They both knew what he meant. Did she need a check to make up for the lack of any support from Suzanna's deadbeat dad?

But Natalie wasn't having any of it. As usual. "Look at the time. Gotta go put missy here down for her nap. Call me later. And don't scrimp on the details about Veronica." With that, his sister hung up.

Well, damn. He'd pissed her off and made her curious all in one phone conversation. That was, as Madison would say, an epic fail.

Dwayne tossed his phone on the coffee table. Maybe the delightful image from a zombie apocalypse would cure his need to go find a punching bag and start wailing on it.

Veronica was glad she'd asked for the whole day off from the restaurant, rather than just the afternoon as she'd planned. Now she had all the time in the world to hang out with Madison and Skye for a girls night in, or GNI, as Skye liked to call it.

"Let's talk boys."

"Oh my God. Really? Five minutes into girls' night and you're already bringing a penis into this?" Madison threw a cracker at Skye, who batted it away.

"Yes. We promised we'd take tonight to go over Veronica's options for men." Skye glanced at her upside down since she was draped over the armchair with her legs dangling over the back. "You're still wanting to go through that? Ready to jump into the dating pool?"

Veronica thought back to her reaction to Dwayne's touch. The way her body had sparked and sang and almost… recognized his touch. That she'd craved more even long after he'd left the formalwear shop. "Yes. I'm ready."

"Well, then," Madison said, popping a grape in her mouth. "By all means, let Skye begin."

"No dating coworkers."

"Hmm?" She looked at her cousin and saw Skye holding a pad of paper and pen. "What are you doing?"

"Making a list," she said, like it was the most obvious thing in the world. "Dating rules, ideas, preferences. That sort of thing. Something to reference as you toss yourself into the great unknown."

"You make it sound like I'm about to go backpacking through Alaska."

"Close enough. Dating is an uphill mountain climb. You must proceed with caution, be ready for a long hike, and bring provisions."

"Hear, hear!" Madison toasted her with a bottle of beer. "Provisions for everyone."

Skye tapped her pen on the pad of paper and ignored her sister-in-law. "Nobody needy."

"Nobody who is emotionally unavailable," Madison added around another cheese cube.

"Is this your list or mine?" Veronica asked.

She gave Veronica a smug smile. "I don't need a list anymore."

Touché. "Nobody too young," Veronica added.

Skye and Madison both looked up at that.

"If it's my own list, I should contribute, shouldn't I?"

"No young 'uns," Skye said while scratching on the pad. "That's a good point. And no oldies either."

"What are we defining as oldies, and young 'uns for that matter?" Madison asked, leaning over to read the list.

"I don't think I'd like anyone younger than me. As for older…" She shrugged, not sure.

"Mid-thirties, I'd say." As if agreeing with herself, Skye nodded. "Yep, mid-thirties it is. Any older and I think you'll start feeling intimidated."

Veronica felt the stirring of annoyance. But she tamped it down. Skye was helping, and it was kind of her to do so. Even so, she couldn't help but wonder if she'd said she wanted a guy in his forties if these two would have talked her out of it.

Not that she did. Principle of the thing.

"Veronica?"

"Yes?" Glancing over, she realized both Madison and

Skye were staring at her. "I'm sorry. I think my mind drifted again. What did you say?"

Skye smiled gently. "I was just asking if you had any ideas of specific men. Someone you found attractive, that met your ideals, so on. A starting point."

"Well," she began, fidgeting with the hem of her shirt. "I was thinking about David."

"David who?" Madison asked.

"Oh, he's perfect!" Skye cried at the same time. To Madison, she said, "David was a server at Fletchers, but his class schedule and work weren't compatible so he had to give notice. He's a grad student now. Cute, nice, polite, not a coworker anymore. And a sweetheart. In other words, a great choice."

"Sounds like a paragon of virtue," Madison joked as she took a sip of her beer.

"I think he's nice, so leave him alone," Veronica shot back, then covered her mouth. Oh, no. She'd snapped. That was rude.

Madison laughed. "That was awesome! You really need to get pissy more often. It's fun."

Skye just grinned and shook her head.

What a reminder. That she could have a negative thought, say a cutting remark, and wouldn't be struck down for it. That she could be sarcastic, or even rude, and the world wouldn't come to an end. A smile tugged at her lips, and she couldn't hold back the giggle that escaped.

After she and Madison calmed down, Skye asked, "So what's your plan with David?"

Veronica paused for a moment, grabbing a cube of cheese from the tray and chewing slowly. She already knew, of course. But the reaction from her cousin and friend was what worried her. "I think… I think that I will just ask him out."

Skye and Madison stared at her, unblinking.

"Is that wrong? Did I mess something up?"

"Nope. I'm just surprised. It's good. Gutsy." Madison grabbed a handful of grapes and tossed one in the air, catching it in her mouth. "Way better than playing coy and doing something weird like stalking him and showing up wherever he is." Madison smirked. "Not that I'd ever do anything like that…"

"Moving on," Skye interjected.

"Then it's settled. I'll email David and ask him out for coffee." It sounded so bizarre to hear herself say it, but the thrill of anticipation excited her.

"Here's to your training wheels," Mad toasted her with a mock salute. "May you have a lot of fun, get in a little trouble, and live a little. Time to break free from the shy-girl routine, sweetie."

Routine? Did they think this was an act? She nibbled on a cracker while pondering that.

Maybe Madison was right. She didn't often feel shy, just unsure. After years of having every action, every word scrutinized by parents who thought she could do nothing right, she'd lost any semblance of who she really could have been.

Well, she could be that woman now. There was nothing stopping her from doing—or saying—whatever she wanted any longer. And it was time to get living.

~~~

Dwayne shifted on the cushion, trying to find a comfortable spot while maintaining posture. The room was quiet, so much that he could hear the clock ticking out every second. Every awkward, silent second of every torturous, agonizing minute. Maybe this was a bad idea. Horrible, actually. He should excuse himself and just—

"Captain, why don't we get started?" The chaplain sat back, relaxed, in his office recliner. He was a few years older than Dwayne, likely just on the other side of forty. Old, by military standards. Gray colored his temples, lines etched around his eyes and mouth. But despite the rank and extra years, Dwayne still felt like he was looking at a contemporary instead of a superior.

He'd never been in the chaplain's office before, but it wasn't what he expected. An overstuffed couch with wild floral print sat facing a La-Z-Boy recliner. The sitting area was completely separate from the more businesslike side with the man's desk and bookshelves. Homier, more relaxed.

"I was referred, sir." Not with an ultimatum, but close enough. "A friend suggested I come speak with you." Because talking to the chaplain was a better idea than seeing a shrink. At least for now.

Major Dunham waited patiently, not saying a word. To fill the silence, Dwayne went on. "I'm having… a few problems. Minor ones."

"Reintegrating to daily life."

It wasn't a question. Dwayne could only imagine how many times he'd heard the same thing, with Marines beating around the bush. "Yes, sir."

"Let's, for now, drop the sir. And I'm begging you, sit back. Kick up your feet if you want. You're making me stressed just looking at you. The couch was meant to be lounged on." Major Dunham gave him a smile. "You seem uncomfortable enough with the visit; why bother making it worse with a stiff neck?"

Dwayne sank back at that, grateful for the chance to loosen a little.

"Let's talk about what made you seek help. Anything specific?"

"Typical stuff, I guess. Driving still freaks me out a little."

The major nodded. "Of course. You spent seven months not going over ten miles an hour, having to suspect every bit of debris that crossed your path as an IED. Driving seventy on the highway and ignoring typical roadside litter is bound to be tough."

Just hearing that it was understandable, his tension started to melt. "I also scared the life out of someone. She woke me up, startled me. We'd been watching a movie and I fell asleep. I felt a tug on my leg, heard the sounds of gunfire from the speakers, and…"

"I assume she's okay?"

"Yeah."

"Your wife?"

Dwayne snorted. "No. Acquaintance." Or could he just think of her as a friend by now? He'd like to.

"How did she react?"

"Fear first. Then, it almost felt like pity."

"And that made it worse?"

He got it. The chaplain was all but reading his mind. Talking around the lump in his throat, he choked out, "Yeah."

"Captain." Major Dunham leaned forward, resting his forearms on his knees. "This isn't uncommon. You are aware of that. You lead the briefings on looking for the signs of PTSD, of reintegration problems for your men. You know this is normal, almost expected. After living in a state of heightened awareness for seven months, where your very job has life or death consequences attached, coming home to daily life and all its trivial, silly moments that civilians can ignore with ease is not as simple as flipping a switch. Nobody expects it to be."

Dwayne shook his head.

"And it doesn't make you crazy, no matter what you want to think. You served the country, and you deserve the time to pull yourself back to rights. Give yourself a break. You've come seeking help; you're not a danger to anyone. I don't see you snapping anytime soon. All in all, I think you have a healthy grasp on the situation. And you'll work out that *left seat, right seat* mentality soon enough. Give it some time."

"Can I do anything to speed it up?"

"Keep hanging out with your friends, the ones who will notice changes in you. Talk about it if you need to. If there's someone you trust to air your worries with, all the better. You're not married, as you said. How about a serious girlfriend?"

"Nope."

"Dating anyone?"

"Not yet." Hold on, what did that mean? "I mean, not currently, no." He shouldn't be thinking of dating anyone. He couldn't dump his problems on anyone.

"Then stick close to your buddies. They'll know if you're struggling, and they can do what is necessary to help you out. If you trust them—"

"With my life."

"Then don't disconnect. Keep those relationships open, and communicate. And come back." He chuckled at the wide-eyed stare Dwayne gave him. "It's not an order, merely a suggestion. My door is always open. And despite the fact that you might hate handing your problems to someone else for analysis and help, it can sometimes be the best thing. A person once-removed from your inner circle can provide perspective. So, if you need to talk, my door's open."

He nodded, stood, and shook the major's hand before showing himself out.

As he opened the outer door of the chaplain's area, it opened in, hitting him on the shoulder.

"Oh, sorry, ah. Robertson." Captain Bryson Beckett looked up from the stack of papers he was carrying. "Welcome back."

Dwayne took the offered hand. "Thanks. Good to be back." He squinted. "You shave today, Beckett?"

The younger man smiled and rubbed at his jaw. "That bad already, huh? I blame my Italian mother. Dark hair and the background means I get the five o'clock shadow around lunchtime."

Dwayne smiled in sympathy. Shaving daily wasn't fun, but having to do it twice would just suck. "You're just lucky you got here after the old CO took off. He'd have you shaving every hour, on the hour."

"So I hear. Managed to transfer in at the right time, right command." Bryson had transferred in after receiving his promotion to captain. They shared a rank, but Dwayne had a couple years on the new guy, both in age and time in service. "Is the chaplain in?"

"Yeah, he's in. I'll let you get back to your errand.

See ya." Dwayne held the door open and let Bryson pass by to—he assumed—deliver the papers to the chaplain. He walked back into his office ten minutes later and shut the door behind him. He'd meant to head straight there from the chaplain's office, but his first sergeant intercepted him with forms to sign. When he was able to sit down in the quiet, peaceful silence of his own office, the enormity of what he'd confided to the chaplain finally hit him. Added to that, the realization of the work he had ahead of him made him want to lay his forehead down on the desk and take a nap.

His mind, without permission, drifted back to the small woman with the long golden braid. The shy sweetheart that looked at him so watchfully with those clear gray eyes. On the quiet side, but always absorbing, taking it in. His hands remembered the smooth skin of her back as he'd zipped her up into that dress, and he clenched them, shook them out to relieve the feeling.

The chaplain wanted him to keep his friends close. That wasn't a problem. Tim and Jeremy had his back, always. There was never any doubt about it. And they would pull him away from the edge if he even started looking at approaching it. But staying close to them meant staying close to the group as a whole. And he was afraid that one tiny, blond woman might end up getting in his way more than anything.

A knock on the door sounded, and he ignored it. Let them figure out problems for ten or fifteen minutes. The Corps wouldn't fall apart in the meantime without his help. But all the same, his conscience made him sit up a little straighter and open his email to clear out the spam. Starting something with Veronica could end in disaster. For her. He couldn't let that happen. Wouldn't let that happen. She deserved more than a guy with a screw loose. Even if he could get it back together eventually, right now was the worst possible time to start forming something—anything—with a woman. And with her sweet, sensitive nature that he instinctively sensed… she could get hurt, big time.

She deserved more.

# Chapter 7

VERONICA STROLLED IN BEHIND MADISON, CLOSING the garage door to Tim and Skye's townhouse behind her, using her foot. Her hands were freezing from the fruit platter she carried in from her own fridge.

"Can someone tell me exactly how a coed bachelor and bachelorette party works?" Jeremy asked, dropping the box of decorations on the coffee table.

"Pretty self-explanatory, isn't it?" Madison picked up a rolled-up crepe streamer and tossed it at him. "It's the same theory as a regular bachelor or bachelorette party. Only difference is, both sexes will be at the party together. Duh."

"I fail to see the difference. There are usually women at a bachelor party." Jeremy threw the streamer back at her.

"Strippers don't count." She bent her head to pick through the box.

"Now that's just hurtful. Strippers are people too." Jeremy grabbed the box from her with a grin.

Madison rolled her eyes and ducked out of the way when he tried to steal a kiss. "This isn't even really a bachelor or bachelorette party, given they're already married. It's just a relaxed celebration before the more stressful hype of the real ceremony gets here."

"So, you're telling me I should call and cancel all those sweet girls working their way through college on the pole? Well, all right, but it seems a little cruel now." Jeremy took his cell out of his pocket and pretended to dial.

Madison rolled her eyes. "You're such a gentleman." She ignored when Jeremy wiggled his eyebrows comically at her and turned very deliberately, giving Jeremy her back and facing Veronica. "Poll time. What do you think? Lots of decorations? Or use sparingly?"

Veronica chuckled under her breath and shook her head. It was like watching children with a toy. But she knew they had just as much fun snipping at each other as they did being sweet with each other. It was purely how they operated.

She glanced around the townhouse that Skye and Tim had abandoned earlier that day. The couple were out doing a cake testing and something about invitations. They wouldn't be back for a few hours, which provided plenty of time for the four friends to sneak in and decorate to their hearts' delight for the surprise party.

Bringing herself back to Madison's question, she set the fruit bowl down on the coffee table and surveyed the room and the box at Madison's feet.

"Sparingly. Too much of anything and it will start to look like we let a child handle things. Or a pair of children." She gave Madison a pointed look. Her mature friend stuck her tongue out and went back to sorting through the box.

Dwayne strolled in through the garage door they'd left unlocked. "Hey, boys and girls. I just texted Tim, and apparently he's already close to falling asleep, and they just got started. Something about rosettes and fondant and I don't know what any of that meant. I started tuning out and it was just a text message. I can't blame him for being bored out of his gourd."

Surprisingly, Dwayne came and sat on the couch next to her. Maybe not so surprising, though, since Madison and Jeremy had already moved into the dining area to bicker about another subject entirely. The heavy weight of him directly to her side was the biggest shock of all, in that it was more comforting than anything. When had she become so at ease with men she barely knew?

They both watched in silence as Madison threw up her hands and let out some agitated animal sound and Jeremy crossed his arms over his chest.

"Have they been doing this all afternoon?" he muttered to her, leaning close so she could hear.

"Only since the minute we walked in," she confided, giving him a smile.

His gorgeous blue eyes crinkled back at her when he grinned. He leaned closer and she breathed in. He smelled wonderful. Nothing thick or sickly sweet. Almost smelled like what she imagined an open country road would smell like. Fresh, inviting, daring her to sit in the back of a pickup truck, toss her arms up to the sky, and feel as if she were flying.

And oddly, the panic, the thick weight that normally felt like it rested on her chest when she spoke to strangers, was no longer there.

He chuckled and nodded toward the other two. "They get like this sometimes. Really, we should just lock them in a room together and see who comes out alive. God knows how these two ended up together, since they constantly argue."

"It's sweet. It's their thing. It might be exhausting

to someone else, but it works for them." At Dwayne's expression, she realized maybe she was absolutely off base. Maybe she hadn't picked up as much about how people interacted after all. "I mean, I just thought that…" She raised her hands helplessly.

Dwayne shook his head slowly. "No, you know what? The more I think about it, you might be right." He turned to watch as Madison smacked Jeremy on the shoulder with a stack of paper cups, only to have Jeremy rip them out of her hands and poke her in the stomach with them. But before an all-out fight could break out, Jeremy swooped in and planted a kiss on Madison's lips that silenced any protest she might have put up. When Madison wound her arms around Jeremy's neck, Veronica flushed and looked away. Their voices were too low to hear, but it was clear whatever words they were saying to each other were not of the *sweet nothings* variety.

"No wonder he's always sucked with women. His style hasn't improved since the fourth grade."

She couldn't hold back a snicker. Partly from the image the words brought up. And partly from relieved self-gratification at having read the situation correctly. It was then she realized Dwayne had walked in empty-handed. "Did you leave the party cake in your truck? You really should get it; the heat will make the icing run."

"What cake?" He didn't look at her, his eyes fixed on how expressively Madison and Jeremy argued, and then quickly made up, in the dining room.

"The cake for the party." He didn't respond, just kept staring into the other room. "Dwayne. Hello?" With no response, she got feisty—as Madison would say—and grabbed his chin in her hands. Forcing his head to turn her way, she repeated slowly, "The cake? For the party?"

When he just looked at her, then one side of his mouth quirked up, she realized her fingers were still tight around his jaw. She snatched her hand back quickly. But she wouldn't apologize. Nope. People touched like that all the time. It meant nothing. And he wasn't offended.

She hoped.

"Darlin', I have no clue what cake you're talking about. So why don't you run it by me again?"

Oh, that voice. It lulled her into a happy place, and her body wanted to melt back into the couch and just relax. But Veronica's brows lowered in thought. "I could have sworn Madison said she called you and asked you to stop by the shop to pick it up on the way over here."

"She might've. But I didn't get it." He shifted one hip off the couch to reach into his pocket. From her shoulders down to her thighs, he pressed into her with unconscious intimacy. She repressed a shiver of awareness. This man was not her training wheels man. He flipped the phone open with one hand, propping the other arm over the back of the couch. Its heavy weight pressed slightly against her shoulders, and she resisted the urge to snuggle farther back so that they draped over her as well.

"Yup. Look at that. She did leave a message. Just didn't notice it while I was busy figuring out what Tim and Skye were up to. Well, guess I better go back out and get it."

They both turned to the dining room, now empty. Something clattered in the kitchen, and Veronica didn't even want to know what that could mean. But she was not moving off the couch to find out.

"Uh, are you going to be okay here? Or do you want to come—"

"Yes!" She jumped up, ready to bail out on the intense duo. Every woman for herself.

"…with me," he finished on a chuckle. "That answers that. Okay, let's roll."

Before she shut the door leading out to the garage, she called out, "We're going to get the cake!" toward the direction of the kitchen. Sure, it might be cowardly to not go back and tell them to their faces. But self-preservation demanded she scoot out the door as fast as possible.

Madison and Jeremy never called back, so she shrugged. "Guess they don't care." Or couldn't hear her. She wasn't about to stay longer in order to figure out which it was.

"Come on." Dwayne grabbed her hand with easy familiarity and laced fingers with her, tugging gently to lead her to his truck. "They won't even miss us."

She liked the feel of his hand. It enveloped hers completely. Strong, capable, a little rough but with a gentle touch. She locked the memory away.

After unlocking the truck door, he gripped her hips without warning and popped her up on the tall seat. Her stomach dropped just a little, partly from the weightless feeling, partly from his touch. But he didn't even seem to notice, just pushing her feet in and shutting the door like it didn't matter.

Noted.

---

Mistake. It was a mistake to bring her with him. Not that he could take it back now.

He shook his hands while walking around the front of the truck. He'd almost been able to fit them around her entire waist, she was so tiny. But the look she'd given him when he boosted her up... Whether she realized it or not, it was one that said she was interested. Curious. Wondering about the really untimely spark that seemed to happen between them. And it scared the shit out of him.

Dwayne hopped up into the cab and, before she could speak, he turned on the radio to a level high enough to discourage talking but not so loud it'd blast her eardrums out. He needed to think. Not chew the fat.

Untimely was only the first of a billion words he could use for the thing he felt around Veronica. It wasn't outright lust. No, that was easy to define, and he could identify that in a second. And what's more, lust could be substituted easily with a simple one-night stand. Or hell, his hand.

This was more comfortable than a hot punch of lust. Like they'd been friends for years. Like they could just lie on the front porch, shoulder to shoulder, watching the sun go down and say absolutely nothing. And enjoy it.

Which was crazy, given he'd known her for less than a month.

She couldn't be right for him anyway, even if he was looking. She was shy, quiet. And he'd guess she'd cower if he said boo.

Except, when he'd momentarily freaked out, she

hadn't cowered. Oh, he'd startled her, so who wouldn't have been a little frightened? But she hadn't freaked out or called him a monster, which was how he'd felt at the time. Still felt sometimes, if he was being honest with himself.

And now that he thought about it, she'd been changing a little bit more each time he saw her. Becoming more assertive. A little more free with the jokes and laughter and teasing. Maybe she was just a late bloomer, coming out of her shell.

He noticed her shiver and flipped down the AC automatically.

"Which cake shop is it?" she said, fighting to be heard above some classic Garth.

He turned it down with reluctance. "According to Madison's voice mail, it's a little bakery downtown. Not the one Skye and Tim are using for the wedding, luckily. Not much of a surprise if we ran into them while they were doing a tasting."

She nodded and said nothing more. He liked that. Didn't have to fill the void with chatter that meant nothing. Another point in her column.

Wait, why was he keeping score?

They pulled off the exit and made a beeline for the bakery. When he parked, she opened her door and jumped down before he could help her. She looked up at him with a smile. "A girl could break an ankle getting down from there."

"Most females wait for help." He led the way into the shop, a little silver bell chiming as he opened the door for her and followed her in.

Veronica stopped so fast he almost bumped into

her and breathed deeply. "Mmm. Oh man, that smells like heaven."

The look on her face said she'd just gotten her first taste of ambrosia and couldn't wait to get back in line for more. Dammit, now he was going to be fighting a boner through the rest of this little errand. *Thanks a lot, smell of donuts*. Though, really, when he stopped to take a breath, she was right. Oh man, that was good. Like warm sugar and vanilla and a little hint of chocolate.

A short, grandmotherly woman with graying brown hair and flour on her cheek stepped out from the back of the shop, wiping her hands on an apron. "Can I help you?"

"We're here to pick up a cake," Dwayne said, nodding between himself and Veronica. "Should be under the last name O'Shay." Okay. He should just focus on the baker lady and think of grandmothers. That should help keep the boner at bay.

The woman smiled sweetly. "Oh, and you two are just the cutest couple we've had in here in ages."

He took an automatic step back, as if her words were actually a swinging punch coming for his nose. "Oh, no, we—"

"Thank you." Veronica cut him off and wrapped a hand around his wrist… or around what of his wrist she could reach with her tiny hand. "I happen to think he's a keeper."

The bakery worker tittered and walked back toward the other room, calling, "I'll be right out," behind her as the double doors swung shut.

"What was that?" He glanced down and saw her biting the inside of her lips. He couldn't stop his own from twitching a little.

"Oh, come on. She was cute and really excited for us. No harm done." She patted him on the arm, but then started to look nervous and let go. "Sorry it's such a trial to pretend to be my fiancé."

"That's not what I—oh, hell. Never mind." This was what most men would call a no-win situation. "It's not a trial. I just didn't understand where you were going with that."

Veronica shrugged, her back to him as she inspected the baked goods on display. "She thinks we're a couple, she said we were cute together. It might have embarrassed her to be corrected, and she was nice. It's not like we'll see her again, so why not?"

Why not, indeed? He really didn't need to react so fast to the whole thing. She was right—no harm done. He might have tried the same thing if it were Madison with him. Someone who he had no plans or hopes of ever dating. Why did it seem so much more denial-worthy with Veronica?

"Here we are." The woman backed through the doors and swung around with the cake in hand. "I have to say, I think it's just so interesting how couples are doing their bachelor and bachelorette parties together now. Whose idea was that?"

"Hers."

"His," Veronica said at the same time. They both turned and locked eyes on each other, then started laughing. The worker just looked confused as she handed over the cake.

"Have fun then, you two. And many blessings on your marriage."

"Thanks," Veronica said brightly, holding the cake out as they left the shop.

Once he helped her settle the dessert in the backseat of the extended cab, he lifted her up once more. But she didn't stare down at him, just looked straight ahead.

"Are you angry with me?"

Her head turned, confusion written all over her face. "No. Should I be?"

"You just looked… never mind." He was about to sound like an insecure chick any second. Time to stop the insanity. He got the truck back on the road and started the drive, turning the music down enough so he didn't feel like a douche for discouraging her from talking to him if she wanted to.

She only hummed along to the tune. Badly, and not in harmony at all. But she was trying. It made him smile.

*Fuck!*

Dwayne swerved to miss the debris littering the road, overcorrected, and did his best to get the Humvee back on track. Sweat trickled between his shoulder blades, and his cammies felt like a furnace, trapping all his body heat. The white-hot sun penetrated through his shades. He was blinded for a moment, unable to watch for another IED. Unable to watch for the far-off glint of an insurgent sniper in waiting.

Who the hell was yelling in his ear like a girl? Christ Jesus, they were Marines, for the love of God. Could they not pull their shit together and keep it shut for five minutes? Didn't they see him trying to keep them alive?

"Dwayne, Dwayne, pull over. Take the exit."

Fucking almost hit a goddamn possible IED and some jackass in his Humvee can't even shut the…

The black haze started to drift, the horns started to

penetrate his mind, and Veronica's shaky voice was making sense now.

"Right here. To the right. You have a clear lane, just merge over now. There we go."

He followed her directions almost by rote, not trusting himself to make the right decisions anymore. He was sweating. Why was it so hot? He was only wearing a polo. But his arms were shaking. And he could smell burned rubber. Worst smell in the world… it stayed with you forever.

"To the right there's a parking lot. Turn in. Let's park over here in the shade. There we go. Now turn off the car."

He sat, fists clenched around the wheel, breathing deeply. He didn't trust his voice, with his throat dry as dust. But he felt her. Knew she was rubbing his back lightly, talking some nonsense that was soft and low, like she was soothing an upset infant. It should have pissed him off. But it felt good, and he didn't want her to stop.

"Let go of the wheel now. Come on, it's okay," she whispered. One small, cool hand wrapped over his and started to gently pry his fingers off the wheel one by one. They ached as he flexed; he'd held on so tightly. She took one hand between her two and kneaded and rubbed, saying nothing more. Giving him time.

*Thank you, God, for small favors.*

Finally, the shaking stopped, the sweat that coated his body started to cool, and he felt confident enough to reach for the bottle of water in his cup holder and take a sip without spilling it all over himself.

It washed the taste of panic and shame from the back of his throat, made him want to gasp with relief.

Except there was no relief from the embarrassment of not only freaking out in front of Veronica for a second time, but that he could have gotten her killed. His hand tightened around the water bottle, releasing it when the crinkling plastic threatened to break. She must be terrified of him. He really was some sort of monster.

"Are you okay?" He stared at the wheel, unable to look at her.

She breathed in, and he could hear the shaky quality. "Yeah. I'm fine. What about you?"

He made some noncommittal noise. He wasn't hurt. But fine? Far from, it seemed.

Another minute passed, with her rubbing his back and the long-past sounds of war fading from his ears. Finally he sat up and let his head drop back against the headrest.

"I'm sorry." The words sounded inconsequential, even to him. But it was all he had to give.

She didn't reply. Not a "Stuff it" or a "Bite me" or even an "I accept." Just sat, facing him. He still couldn't face her.

Then, in her low, soothing voice, she said, "Tell me about it."

And to his amazement, he did.

# Chapter 8

"I THOUGHT IT WAS GETTING BETTER. I WAS DOING SO well. Huh." He grunted and looked out the driver window. "Doing well," he repeated, voice mocking.

She could guess. Though she and her parents had stayed close to whatever village or town they'd set up camp in, other missionaries were intent on reaching the truly needy. The ones on battlefields, in the middle of genocides, dying in third-rate hospitals. The horrors they saw, she knew, stayed with them a long time. Sometimes haunted them for years. Though she didn't go through the trauma with them, she watched as they fought their way through it, as others helped them cope.

"If you'd rather not—"

"I have no excuse for this. That's the worst part. I wasn't badly hurt. None of my men died, or were even severely injured. Bumps, one broken bone—already healed—and a concussion. Nothing major."

Clearly their definition of "nothing major" differed greatly. But she wouldn't point that out.

"I think that adds to the problem. It's bad enough, coming back from that place and having… problems." His lips twitched up into something resembling a mocking smile. "But knowing there's no good reason for it makes you feel weaker still."

How could he think that? It broke her heart. She bit

her lip to stop the burning behind her eyes and just held his hand. Though she doubted he even realized it.

"It was such a simple thing. I stayed inside the wire ninety percent of the time. Safe, secure." He laughed, a chilling, unamused sound. "I used to actually complain about that. That I was stuck playing desk jockey while other guys got to get out, have all the fun. Fucked up, right?"

She said nothing. She'd never heard him curse like that before, and she doubted he'd be happy to know he slipped up later. But now, it was his story and he didn't need to censor himself.

"It's not like I wanted to get into a firefight or anything. But with my job, I just wasn't expecting such inactivity. You stay inside the wire and you start to forget that there's so much else going on. Tunnel vision. Mentally and physically, I was on alert. But emotionally, I wasn't ready or prepared for anything to happen. Like I blocked the possibility out. Though really, how else can you function?"

She rubbed his arm and silently agreed, even as the thought of Dwayne having to emotionally numb himself made her want to cry. Her tears weren't going to do anything for him.

"The one time we had to move operations…" His breath shuddered in and out. "The one time we were going to step out of the wire, and we run over a goddamn IED. Driver tried to swerve it, but it still got us. Humvees are protected, but they're not impenetrable. They can only take so much before they break. And the bottom on those things aren't meant to withstand blasts like an MRAP."

His voice turned hollow, as if he forgot that he was

even talking to someone. "We all walked away. Except for one guy, who had the broken leg. But I mean, compared to the possibility…" He trailed off, then shrugged as if it were no big deal he'd been hit with a bomb and lived to tell about it.

Veronica listened in horror. Despite living in some of the world's poorest countries, during some serious conflict, her parents had managed to shelter her enough to keep her from such sights firsthand. She knew they existed, but she'd never left the protection of the missionary camps or their host homes. And yet Dwayne had lived it, lived through it, survived it.

"I went through the briefs, the required meeting with higher-ups, everything. Over there, I was fine. Pissed, upset, but functioning at the same level. Maybe higher, since I guess my subconscious went on high alert or something. But over here, where there's no war, nothing to be on alert for, where everyone's relaxed and it's business as usual…"

He looked so lost, as if he couldn't even figure out how to end the sentence, let alone how to get through the next minute. He had survived a deployment yet was struggling to drive home.

"Do you… have you talked to someone? Professionally?"

Dwayne rubbed the back of his neck and closed his eyes like he was too weary to go on. "The chaplain, yeah. He said I needed to talk with friends, keep things open."

"Did you? Talk with Tim and Jeremy, I mean. Or other Marine friends. I'm sure they know something's up, but in detail?"

He shook his head, then nodded, then shook again.

Maybe it was perverse, or wrong, or selfish, but she felt a little pride, a small sense of honor that he'd trusted her enough to let himself spill out.

She reined herself in before she became too prideful. Maybe he just didn't feel like he had a choice. It was twice now he'd had an unfortunate episode with her as a witness. Maybe he just felt like he owed it to her. Or maybe he hadn't even meant to spill the story out, but in his state, he just went with it.

"Sometimes it's just hard, and my brain flips back and forth. I'll be fine for days. I was fine for over a week. And then that blown tire on the side of the road startled me, and it was like a switch flipped and I was right back in that moment, in the Humvee. Only this time I know how it ends before we hit the IED, and I'm just anticipating, doing what I can to change history."

He sighed and finally looked at her for the first time since before they pulled over. His eyes looked exhausted, but almost with a hint of relief in them. She could easily imagine why. Carrying the burden of such pain alone would be so hard.

She rubbed his hand briskly. "Time to get out."

"Out?" He surveyed the parking lot. "It's a Walmart. Not exactly our destination."

"Of course not. But now I'm driving."

His eyes widened, and he looked as if she'd just told him she was about to bomb the Capitol Building. "Wait. You? Drive my truck? You can't be serious."

Veronica hopped down and cut his protests off by shutting her door. She didn't know why, but she had a hunch about what he needed. No pity, no petting. Coddling not allowed. Just no-nonsense tough love.

Love—okay, maybe not the best choice of words. But it was a saying. Not the real thing.

So when she said it in her mind, why did her heart dip down to her stomach?

Veronica walked around the truck and opened his door, tugging on his arm. "Step out or scoot over. We've got a cake to deliver."

"Shit. The cake." He looked sheepish. "It's probably ruined."

"I'm sure it's not. Now out."

He stared at her. "Do you have your license? Are you insured?"

"Sure I do. And of course I am." As of a few months ago. But he didn't need to know that. Trying to reassure him, she added, "I'm a very safe driver."

He didn't look convinced, though whether that was about her driving skills specifically or just the thought of turning his truck over to anyone other than himself, she wasn't sure.

Men. They were such babies over their vehicles. It was just a truck, not a prized heirloom.

Taking another tact, she shoved at him until he scooted over enough for her to climb in. "Shoo. Go. I'm driving this big thing." Big monster was more like it. The truck was huge. But she wouldn't let him see her apprehension. That was a surefire way to get him to say no.

He shifted to the passenger seat. "This is my baby. I beg of you to not screw her up."

Giving him the *yeah, duh* look, she hopped up into the driver's seat with only one false start. Buckling in, she took a minute to look at the dashboard and figure things out.

Then she threw the truck into reverse and stopped short. As they both jerked forward and back, she gave him a sheepish look. "Whoops. Just getting used to the pedals."

Dwayne mumbled something as he buckled his seat belt. She had a feeling whatever he said was dirty, so she didn't ask him to repeat it. She cranked up Garth Brooks, who she'd heard once or twice but was really starting to enjoy, and drummed her hands on the wheel while waiting to get back on the highway.

"You have really awful rhythm," Dwayne said, a smile in his voice.

"Shh. I'm doing you a favor. You don't mock the favor-giver."

"Maybe I'm doing *you* the favor, letting you drive my truck."

She snorted, and he laughed. It was nice. For the first time, she felt completely, one hundred percent at ease with a man, minus a few butterflies here and there. It was almost as if she was just another normal woman.

Imagine that.

---

Tim waved his arms and tried to make a *settle down* gesture. Not that anyone was paying attention. "Okay, okay, everyone, listen up."

The noise inside the townhouse was too much to be heard over. Nobody noticed Tim's attempt to grab attention, as if everyone was having too much fun to listen to the guest of honor himself. Dwayne smiled, waited a moment, then stuck two fingers in his mouth and whistled. Everything but the music halted, and then someone turned that down too. He grinned at

Tim and swept out an arm, as if taking a bow. "You were saying?"

Tim flipped him off. "I could have done that."

"But you didn't. Now, go on."

"Right." He stepped up on a chair—something he never would have done a year ago—and waved his arms. "Everyone, over here. My wife and I—"

"That's sexist. Why don't I have a name?" Skye asked from behind him.

Everyone laughed. Tim rolled his eyes, but a smile tugged at the corner of his mouth.

"Skye and I," he corrected, then paused, waiting for an objection. Hearing none, he continued. "We would like to thank you guys for coming to our not-so-bachelor and bachelorette party. And a special thanks to our friends who set the whole thing up. You guys seriously scared the hell out of us when we walked in the door. It means a lot to us that you guys are here, partying with us. And that you'll be there in two weeks when we tie the knot." He gave a sheepish shrug. "Again."

Another round of laughter followed, along with cheers.

A few people took their leave of the party, and things started winding down. Dwayne watched as Veronica helped Madison start picking up abandoned plates and carrying them to the kitchen. He followed, wanting a moment alone with her.

"Hey, Madison. Kick-ass idea. And great work with the decorations." He leaned around her at the sink to give her a kiss on the cheek. She patted his face with a soapy hand and he wiped it off.

"No problem. We all contributed. I'm just glad we

somehow managed to keep it a secret for as long as we did."

"Yeah, luckily someone's big mouth didn't spoil the secret. That sure as hell surprised me." Jeremy dumped his plate in the trash and stood at the edge of the kitchen.

"Bite me." Madison didn't look up as she sang the words.

"Save that talk for later." Jeremy reached around her waist and pulled her back up against his chest. He might have said something else, but his words were lost as he bent down to nuzzle against Madison's neck. And though she rolled her eyes, she tipped her neck to the side to give him access.

If those two were going another round, he was getting way out of range. He touched Veronica's wrist and motioned with his head. "Can I talk to you for a second?"

She gave him a curious look but nodded. "Just give me a minute to wash my hands." She wiggled them and he saw they were covered with frosting from scraping plates into the trash. His mouth watered at the sight of her skin coated in all the sugar. He could think of a few things to do with those fingers…

No. No, he could not. That wasn't the right track at all for his mind to be racing down. Excusing himself, he stepped outside the patio door and down the wooden stairs to the small yard below, out of eye range from anyone inside. If he needed even a remotely good reason why he shouldn't be thinking anything remotely sexual about Veronica's fingers—or any other part of her body—all he had to do was think back to his stellar display on the highway a few hours prior. Nothing sets the romantic mood quite like war flashbacks.

The door opened and shut, and he straightened. Watching her walk toward him was like an erotic dream. Or nightmare. White shirt and matching skirt, little ballerina-type shoes, her long blond hair braided and swinging around her shoulders. She was pure innocence. And he was… not.

"Hey." She stopped on the bottom stair of the patio and laced her fingers together in front of her. The height of the step still put her a good few inches below him. But not as much as normal, with her tiny stature. "So, you wanted to talk?"

He took a deep breath, then just let it go. "I wanted to apologize one more time for earlier. You must be scared to death of me by now, and I can't blame you. But I need you to—"

"No."

No? "No what?"

"I'm not scared of you. Far from it." She gave him a sweet smile that seeped into him and spread through his chest with warm waves. "I actually think it takes a gentle soul to be so affected by what you'd seen. If you hadn't been the least bit affected, it might be concerning. But despite your job, I feel like you're more of a lover, not a fighter. I can sense that in you. If it were up to you, you wouldn't hurt a fly, would you?"

Wow. Insight from someone he barely knew. And she was dead right, which was the really amusing thing. He shook his head, then nodded, then tried to remember what her question was.

She just laughed. "Don't worry, Dwayne. I'm not frightened or mad. And I know you didn't ask it of me, but I won't be saying anything to anyone about what we talked about either. That's your story to tell, if you choose to or not. So no worries." She patted his chest lightly, and he caught her hand there.

He was about to do something completely stupid and unnecessary. Maybe a little dangerous. And he couldn't wait.

---

Dwayne trapped her hand flat against his chest. An impressive, rock-solid chest. Wow, they really built men like this? But she looked up to his beautiful blue eyes and they weren't amused, or laughing. Or even upset. They were intent, like she was on his radar and he was ready to go. Before she could even begin to guess what he was thinking, he leaned down and pressed his lips to hers.

Oh.

*Oh.*

She wanted to melt. Her first real kiss, if that one sloppy kissing session with Robbie at sixteen could be discarded. Because this was nothing like that fumbling, embarrassing, discovering time. This was, as Madison would say, a whole new ball game.

His lips, warm and firm over hers, were gentle but insistent at the same time. Acting on instinct, she slowly wrapped her arms around his neck. He responded with an arm around her waist, locking her against him. His body was warm, like a rock that had absorbed the sun's rays for the day and was a nice place to lounge. Tilting his head slightly, she did the same, and his tongue outlined the seam of her mouth.

He wanted her to open. Would it be like she imagined?

No time but the present to find out. And she wanted to find out. She wanted to know everything that this moment had to offer, because it felt so good. So right. And if it wasn't going to last forever, because it couldn't, she would take what she could.

His tongue dipped in, quietly probing, silently asking for a response. When she did, tentative at first, he moaned and crushed her against him. The slightest response from her managed to push him further, as if he only wanted more and more of her willing participation.

One huge hand nudged the hem of her shirt up, lightly caressing the skin of her lower back between the shirt and her skirt. And shocked her system into overdrive. Whatever came next, she had absolutely no clue. But it didn't worry her. Nothing but the curiosity of that moment, the absolute fire that was burning alongside her veins, could possibly matter.

"We should stop," he said, lips moving across her cheek, resting on her temple. It was so sweet her heart ached a little.

"Stop. Right." The words were breathless, and she didn't mean them one bit. But it seemed a token show of resistance was warranted.

"I didn't mean to do this. I'm no good for you." His words were stronger this time, and his hand slipped out from under her shirt. The lack of warmth was instant and regrettable. He moved away, and she almost stumbled off the step. Using the rail, she caught her balance.

"Don't…" She licked her now-dry lips, still tasting him, and tried again. "Don't I get a say in what is or isn't good for me?"

He shook his head. Not a hint of regret shone in his

eyes now. They were simply cold, indifferent, as if he'd just finished a good meal instead of a great kiss. "Not in this. In this, it takes two yeses. But only one no. And that's my answer. It's gotta be."

Embarrassment filled her from head to toe. Did he feel like she was throwing herself at him? That she couldn't resist?

*Only bad girls like to kiss that way.*

No. That wasn't true. There was nothing wrong with wanting someone, being attracted. But the realization that she was swimming in a pool too deep for her was lowering. A man like Dwayne wasn't right for her, and obviously he didn't want her anyway. David. A guy like David was more her speed.

Using what little pride hadn't been crushed, she tilted her head and gave him a cool stare. "Fine. If that's how you feel, I won't bother you about it." She turned and walked into the house without looking back, pleased with how she had reacted.

And maybe just a little bit disillusioned.

# Chapter 9

KICKING A PUPPY WOULD HAVE BEEN JUST ABOUT THE same level of low Dwayne felt as he got in his truck and pulled away. He hadn't even bothered to go back inside the house, just walked around the side yard and took off. Things were wrapping up, and only minimal cleanup would be necessary at that point. He'd send a text later to Jeremy apologizing and giving the best excuse he could invent between now and then.

Going inside, facing her right then, was not an option. Not with a hard-on that could hammer nails and a weak-ass grip on what was left of his control and good common sense. The combination of lingering vulnerability and shame from his freak-out earlier mixed with the disgust of using Veronica so easily and giving in to his own impulses without even the slightest resistance wasn't making him the best of company. Good idea to just avoid people all around.

He knew she was different. Special. She had that quiet, serene personality that was something completely different than what he was used to. And maybe a little naïve. But sweet, compassionate. And as far as he could judge, trustworthy. Not to mention trusting in others.

Too trusting.

Dwayne ran a hand over his hair and managed to merge onto the highway without any complications. It hadn't hit him until his lungs started to burn that he was holding his breath. He let it out on a slow, controlled puff until the burning eased.

He'd barely known her. Why was he so sure of his assessment? Was he really the best judge of character anyway? He thought Blair was a decent person. He thought he might even be edging up to love her. And she turned out to be a manipulative bitch. There was no other way to describe a woman who faked a pregnancy to get a guy to marry her. Lowest of the low, as far as he was concerned.

Veronica just didn't strike him as anything close to that. Not manipulative, not bitchy. Almost too quiet. Oh, she had pride in her, though. He smiled at the memory. Tilting her chin, looking at him like he was suddenly dirt on her shoe instead of a guy she'd been tangling tongues with seconds earlier, using her haughty, superior voice to set him down and walk away. Yeah, she was something. Feisty when she wanted to be. She should let that side out to play more often.

No. He didn't need to be thinking of any woman's sides. He didn't really know her, and shouldn't want to know her better. He was in the middle of fixing his own life, and that was a one-man job. Dragging another person into his own version of hell wasn't fair, wasn't right, and wasn't going to happen. Not a sweetheart like Veronica, not someone more worldly. Nobody, period.

He pulled into his apartment complex and hopped down from the truck. Another engine roared behind him, someone on a motorcycle pulling into the complex. Not unusual, since many of his neighbors—also Marines— owned bikes. But this one's engine he knew well.

Jeremy. The bastard had followed him home.

Momentary paranoia set in, wondering why. Did Veronica tell him about his problem on the highway earlier? Was he sent to babysit?

*No. Calm your ass down.* She said she wouldn't tell, and she wouldn't. He didn't know where the complete and utter confidence in her word had come from, someone he'd only known a little over a month, but he accepted it at face value and didn't question it.

Jeremy pulled his helmet off, ran a gloved hand over his flattop, and grinned. "Thanks."

Dwayne leaned back against the side of his truck and crossed his arms. "For?"

His friend hopped off the bike and tucked his helmet under his arm. "For leaving. When we realized you were taking off, I volunteered to go make sure you were okay."

"You could have just called. Or sent a text," Dwayne pointed out.

"Yeah, but if I did that, I'd still be back at Tim's place cleaning, wouldn't I?"

Dwayne couldn't help but laugh and shake his head as he walked to his apartment. "Coming up for a beer?"

"I wouldn't say no." Jeremy followed him in, setting his helmet down and unzipping his jacket to drape over a kitchen chair. "You know, I don't think I realized until now how bare this place is."

"Yours is just the same." Dwayne popped one bottle cap, handed a beer to Jeremy, and sat in one of his chairs with a bottle of water. "That's the bachelor way, my friend. Functional."

"Yeah." Jeremy took a long pull as he turned a three-sixty in the living room. "But I'm just now realizing it.

Tim's got all sorts of stuff everywhere. I mean, a lot of the weird shit's Skye's. The fertility statues and burning stick stuff, it's obvious what's hers and what's not. But even before she moved in with him, he had little things here and there. Pictures. Art. Stuff."

Dwayne had pictures of him and his family in his bedroom. Not for public display. He wasn't hiding them, but they were simply more personal. Jeremy had never been in there, for obvious reasons. Guys just didn't go into other guys' bedrooms for anything. It was weird. But he took another look around the room and started to see what Jeremy did.

Two recliners, one couch. Mismatched end tables. A kitchen table he'd taken for free when another single Marine was getting married and refurnishing the new love nest. The flat screen, of course, and entertainment console. Nobody could accuse him of scrimping on those. Hell no. A man had priorities, after all. But the walls were white, bare. No plants, no pictures, nothing that gave any hint to who lived there. Coming from Tim's welcoming place, full of signs of the lives of those who lived there, it was a little... hollow.

"Huh. Never really thought about it. But it's not like I'm here a lot anyway. I'm either deployed or I'm at work so much I don't really care about anything in here except for a place to watch the games and to sleep. I couldn't keep a plant alive with my work schedule."

"Good point. Clearly I'm of the same mind, since my place is no better. Though if Madison keeps bringing crap over, who knows what it'll look like?" Jeremy sank into the other recliner, well broken in from years of guys' nights. He swiveled a few times. "So what do you think of Veronica?"

Dwayne choked on his water. Coughing a few times, he leaned forward to set the bottle down. "What?"

Jeremy raised a brow. "Water goes down the other tube."

"Thanks." Catching his breath finally, he gave Jeremy a look. "What were you saying?"

"You heard me; don't make me repeat it."

Yeah. He'd heard. Didn't mean he wanted to answer. "She's nice."

"She's quiet. And weird."

"Don't be an ass." Dwayne shook his head. "She's not weird."

"She talks funny," Jeremy argued. "Like English isn't her first language. But apparently she's not fluent in anything else."

"I talk funny," Dwayne shot back, using an exaggerated drawl for emphasis.

"You talk stupid. Matches your face. There's just something about her. I don't know. Secrets or something." Jeremy shrugged and took another drink. "Not saying she's not nice. She is. In that silent, invisible, *I'll just sit over here so nobody remembers I exist* sort of way."

Dwayne thought back to how she'd smiled in the bakery, laughing and joking and playing up the role of a bride in love for the benefit of the worker. Not exactly invisible.

"Having any more problems?"

The question was quiet, more serious. As much as they gave each other shit, Jeremy was one of his best friends. And he cared.

"Saw the chaplain the other day. Talked about it a little." When Jeremy said nothing, he went on. "Said it's normal, not surprising, not to worry about it. Talk it out. Ask for help. That sort of thing. Expected stuff."

"Did it help any, to talk to someone?"

"A little." He couldn't not say anything. Despite Veronica's promise to keep it to herself, he knew he needed to work through the incident with someone else. "I freaked out on the road today. When Veronica and I went to get the cake. Saw a tire on the road, and when I tried to get around it…" He swallowed some water to wash the taste of shame out. Didn't work. "She had to help me pull off the highway and wait for me to snap out of it."

A long silence pulsed. "She freak out?"

"Ha." Dwayne put his water down, then picked it back up again. Always easier to have something to do with your hands. "Not even close. She was probably terrified at the time. But cool, calm, collected was all I saw. It was like she was inside my mind, knew exactly what I needed at that moment, and went with it. I was probably better off with her than if I'd been alone."

"That's surprising. I would have figured she'd be scarred for life from something like that. But during the party I started to wonder—"

Dwayne waited, but Jeremy didn't finish. "Started to wonder what?"

His friend set his empty bottle down and kicked back. "I noticed she was looking at you. Trying to be covert about it, which was cute since she sucked so badly at it. But my first thought was amusement more than anything."

"What's so funny about a girl wanting me?"

Indignation in his voice covered the excitement that vibrated through him. She'd been watching him?

"And my next thought," Jeremy went on, ignoring the question, "was that this could be a huge problem."

Problem. Hadn't Dwayne just been telling himself that any sort of attempt at a relationship—with Veronica or anyone else—would be a mistake? But hearing an outsider say it only pissed him off, irrationally. "Problem my ass."

"Look, she's cute, I guess." Jeremy's face said he didn't really think so.

Dwayne wanted to kick him.

"But she definitely doesn't have the type of personality to hang with a guy like you, or any Marine in general. She seems a little on the needy, high-maintenance side. Not always the best combination."

Blair had been high maintenance. At first he thought it was a cute, weird quirk. Later, though… "She handled both freak-outs of mine with serious balls. I wouldn't think someone seriously high maintenance would do so well."

Jeremy shrugged again. "Like I said, I just think it would end in disaster. We have a nice little group going, the waters are calm. Why go and fuck it up with something that wouldn't last anyway?"

"Like when you and Madison went through your little *thing*? You didn't really appreciate all my advice back then, did you?" The words were out before he could stop them, and he immediately wanted to erase the entire conversation from both their memories.

Jeremy's eyes turned stormy and his fists clenched on the arm of the chair. "Leave Madison out of this. That was my fault, and we're past it now."

"Look, I shouldn't have said it. It wasn't a dig, I just meant—"

"Shouldn't have said it. Perfectly put." Jeremy stood. "Let me know when you're in the mood for company. Clearly today isn't the day." He snatched his helmet and jacket up and stormed out, shutting it tightly behind him.

Always a little on the dramatic side, that one.

But Jeremy had a point. What else did he have to do besides sit and think about what would happen if he really went after Veronica? It wasn't as if he was going to go after someone else.

He stood and picked up the empties to place in the recycling bin Skye bought him for a welcome home gift.

That made two people now who warned him off from starting up something with Veronica. Neither had used his reintegration issue as the reason why, though. Her own gentle heart and secret past seemed more the problem. As if he would be clumsy with her. What, did they think he'd leave her broken and damaged as he trotted off to his next victim?

That was bullshit. He was a good guy, minus his current unfortunate issues. But he'd work those out. If willpower had anything to do with it, he'd be better soon. And then why not Veronica? There was attraction there, definite chemistry. She'd already seen him at his worst and hadn't run the other direction screaming.

A part of him wondered why, out of all the women in the area, the one with the most secrets was the one he was drawn to. Why Veronica?

Then another, stronger part argued… why not?

—◁◈▷—

Veronica checked the hem of her skirt once more in the long mirror. It covered to her knees, but that was all. And while it was okay—she knew it was okay— the small voice that sounded too much like her mother whispered she was in the wrong. Still, nerves had her second-guessing everything.

"You're sure this skirt is okay? Not too short?" She looked at Madison in the mirror.

Her friend flopped back on the bed in obvious exasperation. "Again, yes. That skirt is long compared to what most people wear on a date. It's fine. I swear, you must have been a nun in another life."

Veronica smiled, wanting to tell her how close to the truth it really felt. But not now. Still not yet. She wasn't confident enough in being open about it, somehow wanting to lock in the friendships securely before admitting her beyond-unique upbringing.

"Should I do something different with my hair?" It was braided, as always, down her back. It was so much longer than most other women's, unfashionably so. Braiding was the only way to style it without worrying about massive tangles later. Maybe soon she'd get the courage to finally cut it off. Not all. But some.

*Your crowning glory, Veronica. To cut it off is to spit in God's eye.*

"No, it's fine. This is supposed to be casual, remember? Just a quick meet-up. You shouldn't think so hard about it." Madison toyed with the edge of the bedspread. "I'll admit, though, I'm impressed that you asked him out. Shows guts."

The reminder made her blush. She'd asked another coworker for David's email address—asking Skye

would have been wrong, since she was the manager—
and sent him a message asking to go for coffee. Madison
had agreed with the idea of a coffee date. Coffee, as
she said, was a good way to start. Not too long, in case
things weren't working, and it was easy to duck out of.
But if things went well, they could always segue into
something longer, like dinner or a walk.

There was a knock at the door and Madison popped
up. "I'll get it. You stay here. It's the whole effect thing."

Veronica raised a brow but didn't bother comment-
ing. No point with Madison; she was already out the
bedroom and bounding to answer the door. She turned
back to the mirror one final time and turned around to
see front and back.

She looked good. Normal. Like she'd done this a
hundred times.

Except she never had. She shook her hands to relieve
the pins and needles feeling, to dry the sweat. It was just
a first date. No pressure. David was a nice guy, a real
sweetheart. It's why she'd chosen him to begin with. He
wouldn't push, or make her feel uncomfortable, or like
she wanted too much.

Unlike someone else she could mention. It still burned
to recall the way Dwayne had acted after their kiss.

"Veronica, David's here!"

Shock. Veronica bit back a giggle at the sarcastic
thought. She smiled and stepped out to see David standing at the door, looking almost as nervous as her. In
pressed khakis and a light blue button-down shirt, he
looked good.

She waited for the tug of excitement, the little jump
to her system at the sight of him. But it didn't come.

Maybe some things were simply meant to go slower. She smiled and walked up.

"You look nice."

"So do you." He opened the door and smiled. "Are you ready to head out?"

Veronica grabbed her cardigan and purse and stepped out. As they headed to David's car, he directed her with a hand on the elbow. But nothing. No shiver of reaction, no heat.

Okay, she had to stop analyzing the entire thing, or this whole afternoon would turn into a disaster. And David didn't deserve that.

Putting on a very cheerful, if a little false, smile, she said, "I'm really glad you agreed to meet with me. We didn't work together for very long before you left. I was afraid you wouldn't remember me."

He closed her door and walked around to get in the car himself. "Of course I did. I was glad you emailed me." His smile was warm, his eyes matched. But there was no heat there.

This might be a very long afternoon if she couldn't stop comparing him to Dwayne.

—∿∿—

"Yeah, I'm getting the order now." Dwayne waited for the line to crawl forward and gripped the phone tighter. "Well, it wouldn't take so long if you would just take coffee from the freaking McDonald's drive-thru like everyone else. But no, you need your special coffee from the one place that doesn't have a drive-thru. And everyone and their grandma thought today was a good day for coffee."

"Chill," Jeremy said on the other end of the line. "I suggested coffee. You didn't have to stop and get some if you didn't want to. Leave if the line's too long."

"I'm staying now, just on principle," he grumbled. Twenty freaking minutes already. It was enough to make a guy want to drink. But that was the entire point. He and Jeremy weren't drinking, at least for the weekend, in Jeremy's case. It was his way of supporting Dwayne. Just as he'd suspected, ten minutes after their disagreement both had moved on from it. Guys, unlike girls, managed to not drag crap out for another fifteen years. So when Jeremy called Dwayne to hang, he saw it for the peace offering it was and didn't hesitate to accept.

Another inch put him on the other side of the massive display of international coffee. Still several people back from the line, Dwayne really regretted offering to swing by for drinks before heading over to Jeremy's for poker night. The coffee better be the best damn thing he'd tasted since…

A long, golden braid caught his eye and he turned automatically, as if drawn to her by some magnetic pull.

Veronica sat at a small table in the corner, elbows on the table, chin in her hands as she listened to her tablemate say something. A guy. A guy Dwayne didn't recognize.

His fists curled naturally into loose fists before he shook them out. He had no reason to care. She had friends he didn't know? Big deal.

The guy reached out and touched her arm. Just a quick touch, but it was full of obvious intent. She laughed and didn't pull back.

"Hey, buddy, the line's moving."

Dwayne startled and looked forward. He was a good

four feet away from the next person in line. "Sorry," he mumbled and shifted forward.

He took one last glimpse of Veronica and the guy she was with—still with his damn hand on her arm—and shifted forward. His cell buzzed and he opened it to check the incoming text.

> *Did you forget how to order? Use sign language. This is taking forever.*

Jeremy, busting his ass about it. Again. Like his pissiness was going to make the line move any faster. He shot a text back, something along the lines of getting his panties out of the wad they were bunched in, and shoved the phone back in his pocket. He shouldn't, he really shouldn't…

Okay, he looked.

Veronica's back was still to him, but she'd turned her head slightly, just enough for him to see her profile. She looked happy. Like she was having a good time. And cute. From this angle, he could see she wore a skirt that didn't hit her ankles. Legs. Despite how short she was, she had a seriously drool-worthy pair of legs. And the smallest feet he'd ever seen. She definitely didn't look nunnish, like Jeremy would stupidly say. She looked completely normal. Like any woman on a date.

Date. Was that what was going on? Was this a coffee date? But a coffee date wasn't as big a deal as a dinner-and-movie date; everyone knew that. So it couldn't be all that serious. Maybe this was their first time out. But how did she know that guy?

Oh, for the love of Christ, he was starting to sound like Needy Chick, the one nobody wanted to date.

Veronica wasn't his girlfriend. She was allowed to see whoever she wanted.

"Dude. Move."

But if she was dating someone else, why had she kissed him back?

He didn't have time to think that one through before something hit him square between the shoulder blades. He stumbled hard enough to knock into a display of travel mugs. Instinct had him crouching low and sweeping the area for the insurgent. He took two blind steps forward before his vision cleared enough to remind him he was in a coffee shop in California, not an abandoned building in Afghanistan. No insurgents. Just a pushy bastard who had more impatience than sense.

"What the fuck is your problem?" he growled, crowding the man who shoved him. Suddenly, Impatient Asshole didn't seem so confident in his decision to push like a second-grader.

"I just, you weren't moving and I'm tired of standing here and—"

"Dwayne?"

Aw, shit. Just what this whole thing needed. He stepped back quickly, out of the asshole's personal space, and forced two calming breaths. Only problem with that plan was forcing calm never really worked. He turned, hoping his face looked surprised instead of guilty. "Veronica. Hey, didn't know you were here."

The guy behind him snorted, but one angry look from Dwayne silenced him.

"Yeah, we've been having coffee."

Veronica stood on the other side of the displays, and

he stepped around it to talk. "We?" Did that sound casual? Or forced?

She turned and waved at the guy from their table. "This is David. We used to work together at Fletchers before he started grad school."

Dwayne held out a hand, resisting the urge to squeeze a little harder than necessary during their shake. "Nice to meet you. So, uh, I'll just let you two get on with your, uh… " And crap. Now he'd left it hanging out there, boxing himself into calling it a date.

"We were just about ready to head out," she finished for him smoothly.

"Yup." David nodded once to Dwayne. "It was nice to meet you."

"Yeah, you too." Was his nose growing? "Have a good one, guys."

Veronica stared at him a moment, but when David placed a hand on her lower back, she turned toward the door. Just before they left, David looked back and said, "I think you lost your place in line." The front door closed quietly behind them.

Smug bastard. Wait, what did he say? Dwayne turned to see Impatient Asshole already receiving his order. Yup. Line definitely moved on without him.

Dwayne counted to ten, giving Veronica and D-bag time to get out of the parking lot, then stormed out of the shop himself. Jeremy was getting coffee from McDonald's. And he was going to like it.

# Chapter 10

"This was fun," Veronica said, shivering in the car. Why did men always have to keep the interior of their vehicles at such chilly temperatures? There was no way to slip her cardigan on now with her seat belt on. So she would just suffer silently.

"Yeah, it was. We'll have to do it again soon."

"Yup. I had fun." She'd already said that. The urge to beat her forehead against the dashboard until all the awkward fell out was almost too hard to ignore. Why was it such a chore with David? He was so sweet and funny and nonthreatening. So how was it that the entire evening had been a struggle from the beginning?

*It wasn't like this at all with Dwayne.*

*Stop that. It's not fair. Dwayne's not even an option, and it's unkind to compare David to anyone else.*

The silence was thick and heavy, and she fought hard to figure out some way to fill it. But nothing that came to mind sounded even remotely good, so she kept quiet until he pulled up to her home. But he didn't open her door for her, not that he had to. Twenty-first century and all that. No big deal. He did touch her though, in small ways, as he walked her to the front door. On the elbow, small of her back. Brushing their hips together. Little things, whether on purpose or by accident, that reminded her that he was near.

Didn't matter. It wasn't giving her any feelings one

way or the other. He could have been a Labrador retriever for all the spark she was getting.

As she fished through her bag for her keys, he waited patiently. When she finally found them, she looked up. But surprisingly, he wasn't giving her a patient smile any longer. He was already leaning in for a kiss.

She waited for the moment of angels singing, for the feeling of *yes, there it is.* For the spark she'd been missing all night.

Nothing. Just warm skin touching, simple contact. Impersonal—on her side anyway. Poor David, he seemed to be trying so hard. But it just… wasn't there.

She patted him on the chest and he stepped back with her signal. Not one to push, he didn't advance again. "Can I call you?"

*No.*

Not fair…

"Sure," she said weakly. Another chance wouldn't kill anyone. So what if he didn't make her shiver with excitement? He was a good guy, and she enjoyed his company. He deserved more than one shot. And she didn't exactly have men beating down her door either.

That seemed to make him happy, and when she opened the door, he gave her a big smile. "Have a good night."

"You too," she said softly as she closed the door behind her. Exhausted at smiling so hard, jaw still aching, and more confused than she'd ever been before, she sank down to the floor, back still pressed against the door.

"Didn't go well?"

Madison popped her head out of the kitchen.

Veronica nodded, then shook her head, then shrugged. How to explain?

"Uh oh, that didn't seem like a home run. Want to binge on a carton of cherry fudge dream and talk about it?"

Veronica started to say no, because it was private. But this was what girlfriends did. She picked herself up, tossed her purse and cardigan on the nearest table, and walked to sit on the couch. Then realizing she wasn't going to be comfortable, she ran down to her room to change into a sweatshirt and sweatpants. Something that would horrify her mother. Naturally, she wore them with glee.

Madison was already in position on the couch, carton of ice cream next to her, two spoons in hand. She held one out as Veronica sat and started digging in.

"Won't Jeremy wonder where you are?"

Madison snorted around a spoonful of Cherry Garcia. "He's with Dwayne tonight."

The mention of the man who made her body shiver after such a lukewarm evening made her bite her lip with guilt.

"So, start talking. And go slow. My dating life is pretty much nil at this point so I'm living vicariously."

Veronica laughed and scooped up some ice cream. After the shock of cold passed, she said, "Your dating life is nil because you have a man. It doesn't count. But… it was nice."

Madison groaned.

"What?"

"Kiss of death. Nice. I worried about this." She peered off into the distance, spoon held straight up, locked in thought. "He's too much like you. Too easy."

"You and Skye said I needed to start easy," she huffed. Could these two not agree on anything?

Madison shrugged. "So maybe we were wrong. It's happened before. Not often, of course," she added with a wink. "But everyone has an off day. But I digress. Continue with the niceness."

"We went to the coffee shop. It's a cute place. I like the local businesses; more personal. Got a table in the corner, drank our coffee, and talked."

"About?" Madison prompted.

Veronica sighed and spooned out another bite. "Fletchers, other coworkers and what they're up to now. School." Which had made her insanely nervous. What if he asked where she went to high school? Or college? How did she answer, "Nowhere. Ever," and not look like a weirdo? Or an idiot?

"So lots of talking. Any touching?"

"Madison." She blushed and turned away. The only touching that came to mind was Dwayne's hands on her waist, on her back, on her skin. The pressure of his mouth on hers…

"I see from that little smile you've got going that the touching might have been a little more than nice," Madison teased.

She wiped her face clean of any emotion. "He kissed me at the door. It was… nice."

Madison rolled her eyes. "Doesn't sound like the guy knows how to kiss properly, if you ask me."

"It was just fine. There was just something… missing? I don't know how to explain it."

"You don't have to. I know what you mean. The chemistry. It's gotta be there or it's pointless."

Her friend spoke with such sadness all of a sudden that Veronica looked up in surprise. Madison stared off in the distance, and Veronica couldn't help but wonder who she was thinking of. Was it Jeremy? Was there no chemistry between them, or too much?

It wasn't her business, so she would not pry. To bring things full circle she said, "All in all, the date was simply fine. Nothing outstanding, but nothing wrong either. He asked if we could see each other again and I said—"

"No."

"—yes." She stared at Madison. "No? Why no?"

"You just said yourself there was no chemistry. Why bother?" Madison tossed her spoon on the coffee table and leaned back as if she were too full to move off the seat just yet.

Veronica mimicked her pose. "Guys are not exactly waiting in a queue for the chance to date me, if you haven't noticed. So what is the harm in going out one more time with him? Maybe I'm judging him too quickly."

Madison tossed her hands up. "Whatever. Your life. If you want to waste time on a dud, go right ahead."

"David's not a dud," she said, indignant. He might not be the one for her, but he wasn't that bad either.

Madison was quiet for a while.

Finally, Veronica said, "I saw Dwayne at the coffee shop."

"Oh yeah? Was anyone with him?"

In other words, was Jeremy with him? Veronica was getting good at this whole *reading people* thing. "He was alone. I think he almost got in a fight with someone standing behind him."

"What?" Madison sat up quickly, jostling the couch. "Why?"

"I only caught the tail end of it, but I believe the other

man started it first by pushing Dwayne. Who knew a coffeehouse could be so exciting?"

"Huh. Dwayne's normally so mellow, definitely the most laid back of the three guys. I hope he's okay."

Veronica bit her lip. It wasn't her secret to tell. Even though she knew Madison would only ever have his best intentions at heart, if Dwayne wanted anyone to know he was having problems, he'd have to tell them himself.

"Moving on then. A date for Tim and Skye's not-wedding. Any ideas? Will you invite David or go stag?"

"Oh, right. That is coming up soon, isn't it?" She hadn't really thought through a date yet. But then again, David would likely be willing to attend with her. The main problem there was if she wanted him to or not. That was something she would have to consider. Asking him to a wedding seemed like such a large step. Or maybe not. What did she know of normal dating practices?

"Few weeks. I'll be honest and say I'm so thankful I no longer have to do the 'where do I get a date' dance like I had before. So I sympathize with your plight."

"You had trouble finding dates before?" Veronica had a hard time seeing that.

"You'd think being in a male-dominated career, it'd be easy to find a man." She laughed. "Maybe I was the exception to the rule. Anyway, how about we make a deal. If you don't get a date that you're happy with, then we just go together."

"What about Jeremy?"

Madison thought about that for a second. "Jeremy will be busy all day with the guys, and we'll be with Skye for most of it. So really, it's not that big a deal. You can be my sexy mama date. And who knows," she added, that typical Madison mischief coming back into her eyes, "there might be a sexy guy we haven't met before just waiting for you to show up so he can sweep you off your feet."

Veronica wanted to say she'd already met a sexy guy, and he'd already done some unintentional sweeping. But she couldn't, because nothing was ever going to happen between them.

Even though she was starting to think he was much more the type of guy she should be aiming for.

—⁂—

Dwayne stared at his boots, at the dog tag twined under the laces. "Should I just start talking?"

The chaplain sat back in his chair. "You asked for the meeting, Captain Robertson. What would you like to talk about?"

Nothing. Everything. "I had another freak-out. I was driving this time."

"I assume you weren't injured."

"No. There was someone with me; they managed to talk me through getting off the road and parked."

"Lucky." He paused. "How did they react?"

He breathed deeply. "Better than I expected. She just sat there, waiting for me to calm down, then drove us home." But first he'd spilled his guts. About his deployment, the IED.

"Sounds like a good friend. Are you worried about—"

"What about dating?"

The chaplain stopped mid-sentence and looked at him, surprised. "What about dating? In general, or for you specifically?"

He felt like five kinds of fool for blurting that out so suddenly. It wasn't what he came here for. Or was it? He still wasn't sure what made him want another appointment. But maybe he should just roll with it.

"I guess for guys in general with my specific problem."

"Ah." A knowing look crossed his face. "Are you worried then about how a relationship might affect you and your efforts to move past the issues you're dealing with?"

*No, not worried. Terrified.* He nodded.

"Well. On that I can only say… I don't know."

Dwayne stared at him, waiting for more. Nothing came. What the hell kind of rip-off was this? He came for guidance, and all he got was "I don't know"?

The corner of the chaplain's mouth twitched. "Obviously my answer isn't satisfactory. And I don't blame you. I'd like someone else to give me all the answers to life too. A cheat sheet would be splendid. But that's just not how it works. All I can say is, there's no way to know. A relationship could only highlight the struggles you're going through, distracting you from your progress. Or it could give you an anchor, something to hold onto when things get tough. A built-in support group. How it actually works out is just something nobody can know until it's over. Or not over."

Dwayne flopped back in the chair and stared at the ceiling. Waiting, maybe, for a sign.

No divine answers came from above.

"You don't have to answer, but I'm curious. Is it the girl from the freak-out? The one who waited for you, helped you calm down, drove you home."

"How did you—" Great. His chaplain could read his mind, but not the future. Helpful.

He smiled. "Comes with the job. Over the years, I've become a bit of a people-reader. All I can say is what I said before, that nobody knows ahead of time. But the fact that she didn't freak out herself, that she handled the situation so efficiently, tells me that maybe this won't be as hard for her to deal with as one might think. Something to ponder."

Something to ponder.

He stepped out the door and nearly ran into Captain Beckett.

"I think this is becoming a thing with us," he joked, steadying himself on the wall.

Beckett grinned. "If you were a chick, I'd think you were stalking me. I'd have to start dating you just to get rid of you."

"I'll pass, thanks. You heading in here?" Dwayne motioned at the door and started to grab the handle.

"Yeah, thanks."

"You're running a lot of errands in this end of the building lately. I know you just got promoted, but you know you can use one of your office minions for stuff like this, right?" Some guys got nervous after gaining a rank, not wanting to rock boats with those who hadn't advanced yet. They took on more grunt work than necessary.

He smiled and shrugged. "I like handling my own stuff."

Dwayne mirrored the shrug. "Your choice. Have a good one." Dwayne went back to his office and shut the door. Only a matter of time before someone came knocking. But he needed a minute.

Would there be guilt in tangling someone up in his life when he was still so confused about how to deal with his problems? Was it fair? Was it right?

She knew, though. It's not like he would be hiding anything from her. She'd seen the worst of his problems, and she hadn't treated him like he was diseased. She still kissed him, still wanted more after. So maybe it wasn't his decision to make. Maybe Veronica would say no anyway. Turn him down.

The thought went through his spine like ice. Not having her by his own choice was one thing. But to put himself out there and have her walk away, reject him…

He'd think about it some more. Ponder, as the chaplain said. He just hoped he thought fast, 'cause keeping his hands to himself was more than a little of a challenge.

---

Disaster. That was the only word that really fit the entire situation. Veronica sighed to herself, then did her best to turn the sigh into a sort of cough.

David drove on, heading home after their movie. The movie—which was awful, thanks to way too much violence and too little plot—that followed a stilted and yawn-inducing dinner. They'd barely spoken, each picking at their food and every so often making a random comment about how delicious it really was.

It tasted like sawdust. But that was more likely because of how uncomfortable she'd been. She never should have agreed to go out for a second time. Madison was right. It was a waste of everyone's time, including poor David's.

But she felt so wrong just saying no after only one

afternoon coffee. He was so sweet. So she'd said yes when he called for a real date.

And now they were alone, in the car, with no dinner to talk about and no movie to focus on. Why was this just so different from her time with Dwayne?

*This isn't Dwayne. So get over that. Move on. He surely has, since he doesn't want you.*

After another few moments, she realized they'd passed the exit for her home. "David, you missed it. We were two exits back."

"I know. I have one more thing to show you before we head home."

Oh, boy. Was there any polite way to say she'd rather eat her GED studies book than spend another minute of forced silence or uncomfortable conversation with David? Probably not. Best to just play nice.

Another minute, he pulled off and swung into the parking lot of what looked like a playground.

"I played here as a kid," he said as he got out of the car. Like that just explained everything. She waited for him to open her door, and she got out to survey the area.

It was nice, well-kept. The equipment looked new, the grass around was mowed. And she still didn't understand why she was here at night.

"David, it's getting late and—"

"I wanted something else for us to do while we talked. I figure conversation over dinner is tricky and nonexistent during a movie. But swinging," he said, grinning as he walked toward the swing set. "Swinging and talking are pretty good ideas. I've had some of the best conversations of my life on a swing."

"Really?" Okay, it was a little cute. She walked over

and sat on the seat he held steady for her. With a push, she floated forward gently.

"Oh yeah." David plopped onto the swing next to her and pushed off at a much faster pace. She pumped her legs a little to go faster.

"What kind?"

"Let's see. When I was in kindergarten, I learned girls had cooties while swinging with my best friend."

She laughed.

"In the fifth grade, I learned that maybe girls didn't have cooties after all. Now in seventh grade, I took a girl for a walk to the neighborhood play area, and I stole my first kiss while she was asking for a push. What else…? Oh, I think one of my favorite moments of being an uncle is playing with my nephew on the swing set."

"That's sweet." Adorable, really.

"How about you? Any favorite swing set memories? Or were you more of a monkey bars kinda girl?"

Playgrounds weren't a part of her own childhood, but she knew the general concept. Her parents hadn't really wanted her playing on one, given she always wore skirts and that was just unseemly. But the urge to fly, to feel the wind in her face, to reach for the stars overtook her and she pumped harder to go faster, ignoring his question.

He went faster as well, and she understood exactly what he meant. With the free feeling of being air bound, conversation really wasn't so hard.

"Tell me about school. How are classes?"

He grunted. "Hard. But I'm pushing through. I should have gone for my masters right after I graduated, but I just wanted the break, you know?"

No, she didn't.

"How about you? I seem to remember you at the restaurant mentioning a need to study or something."

She smiled, remembering the excuse she'd given to avoid going to a party thrown by a fellow server. Though it was true—studying was important—she had been too intimidated to join in the social aspect, so she'd chickened out and given the first excuse she could come up with.

"What are you majoring in?"

"Right now I am mostly doing general studies." The misleading comment slipped from her lips before she could catch herself. The response to avoid the truth was so automatic in this area, it didn't even occur to her to try the truth.

David nodded and kept swinging. "Keeping it general. Yeah, I've had lots of friends do that while they're figuring out the right major."

It was a good conclusion, and one most people came to on their own. But the truth that she wasn't even in college, that she was studying for her GED rather than any college courses, was one she wasn't ready to share with anyone. The embarrassment of being a twenty-six-year-old without even a high school diploma to her name was overwhelming. Just one more thing that separated her from the average. One more thing that made her too different.

She pumped her legs harder, wanting more freedom, however fleeting it was. Wanting to simply escape the past. But you could never run fast enough for that. She'd always be the weird one who grew up in jungles. The one people thought was either a weird native or a religious freak.

"You might wanna slow down," David called at her. She ignored it.

What would it feel like to just let go? Go flying, not care about holding on so tight to the chains? Why not try? She took one more swing back, then launched herself from the seat.

The feel of weightlessness, the moment of no fear, of going where the wind literally blew was incredible. The wind blew against her face and she closed her eyes for a second, reveling in the flight.

Until she landed on her feet and her ankle rolled into the dent in the sand. She crumpled and bit back a moan.

# Chapter 11

OKAY. THAT HURT.

"Veronica! Hey, what happened?" David was by her side in a moment. Of course, he dismounted the right way, and still had the use of both legs.

"I think I landed in a little hole on one side. I'm all right, really. No big deal." But she gratefully accepted his arm for support and stood, brushing sand off as she straightened. Trying to put weight on the leg made her gasp in pain. "Maybe it's a little deal. Just a tiny one."

"Let's just take it easy then." He helped her hobble to the car and worked to ease her down onto the seat carefully. He bent down between her and the open car door and lifted her leg on his knee. "Can I check?"

She nodded.

He rolled up her pant leg and took a look, hissing through his teeth a little. "It's starting to swell. Probably just sprained, but it's not going to feel great. Do you want me to take you to the doctor?"

"No. I feel dumb enough already."

"Not dumb. Just… impulsive." He looked up at her, smiling. The street lamp caught his hair, the little crooked smile he gave her, and she wanted her heart to melt.

Instead, nothing. Nothing at all. No reaction. No silent feminine sigh of happiness. No clenching of the heart. But he raised up and pressed a kiss to her lips, and she responded. Because it was a nice kiss, and he was a nice guy.

Just not the guy for her.

It was finally time to accept that. She gave this a shot, and it didn't work out.

Before she could pull away, he broke contact. "This isn't working, is it?"

Startled, she stared at him. When he gave her a small smile, she responded, "No, it's not. I'm sorry."

He sighed and sat back on his haunches. "Nothing to be sorry for. If the spark isn't there, then that's just a fact. No sense in pushing, right?" He waited for her to shift in her seat, swinging her legs in, and then closed the door and walked around to the other side to climb in.

She wanted to scream. Or maybe cry. Not from anger, but frustration. David was exactly what she thought she needed. And instead of feeling safe, confident, ready… she just felt more trapped. He was perfect on paper.

Maybe perfection was the problem.

As he started the engine, she said softly, "For what it's worth, I wish it was there."

"Yup. Me too."

—◦◦◦—

Wedding rehearsals sucked, plain and simple. This was the seventh wedding Dwayne had been in in the past four years. Most of the time, he was just a generic sword bearer, doing his stoic duty when the couple came out of the chapel. Of course, he never could deny the fun it was when he was on the end and got to swat the bride in the ass with the broad side of his sword.

Just a little *Welcome to the Corps* gift. Hey, it was tradition. You don't mess with tradition.

But there'd be no ass-swatting for this ceremony, since the groomsmen weren't even in uniform. And nobody was asked to wear theirs as a guest or attendant. Dwayne was all for it, since their dress blues choked him to no end. Someone his size with a neck as thick as his wasn't meant to wear a collar that tight.

Of course, the choice to go sans uniform had, apparently, horrified Tim's parents. But they were cool enough, they'd get over it... eventually. They were just a little more traditional. Skye would break them in.

The minister, a short, completely bald man who had to be at least ninety-five, started talking about the service. Tim's parents had brought him from their hometown. Apparently he was the guy who married them forty years ago. It was actually kind of cool, the more Dwayne thought about it. That familial connection that would span generations. His mom never even got married, thanks to the jackass of a sperm donor that was his biological father leaving as soon as the stick turned blue. His sister's sperm donor was a repeat performance. So he envied that generational connection Tim's family shared.

Except the minister seemed a little confused. He rambled on about something involving unity and what the sanctity of marriage meant, and how they were *about to* enter into the most holy of all contracts. His voice was creaky with age, pausing in interesting places.

"They did tell the guy they were already married, right?" he muttered to Jeremy from the side of his mouth.

"Beats me. I would think so." Jeremy shrugged

and kept staring straight ahead, not willing to break character.

"And so," the minister went on, "I am so pleased to be here to witness this, Timmy, your wedding day, when you first join in holy matrimony with the woman you love."

Skye fidgeted, and Dwayne bit his lip to hold back the smile. Skye wasn't one to hold back.

"Have you already obtained the license?" he asked. "Don't want to be forgetting to make this legal now."

Skye leaned in and stage whispered, "Sir, we're already married. This is just a commitment ceremony."

The minister stared at her blankly, like she'd spoken another language.

Tim groaned.

Skye's parents laughed in the front row.

Tim's dad looked suspiciously like he was fighting to hold back a smile, while Tim's mother, Suzie, hopped up to talk to the minister.

"Remember, Reverend Todd, how we talked about the ceremony?" she asked loudly, probably because the guy was deaf. "They're already married; they just want to recommit themselves to each other." She was all but shouting now.

The minister's bushy eyebrows—quite a shock since he was a cue ball—drew together. "They're not getting married?"

"No," Suzie said, shaking her head for emphasis.

"Because they're already married," he clarified.

"Yes," she, Skye, and Tim all said at once, nodding like a bunch of bobblehead dolls.

The minister looked down at his ceremony script, then back up at the couple. "Then why the hell am I here?"

There was a moment of stunned silence, then Skye broke into peals of laughter. Bent over, she grabbed Tim's arm for support as she dropped to the top step of the platform they were using as a makeshift altar. The long skirt of her pale blue dress draped around, tangling in her legs, and she sprawled in a rather unladylike pose. Her parents started in, laughing as hard as their daughter, and even Tim cracked a smile before the whole thing was over.

Dwayne chuckled quietly, watching the show. Then he glanced over Suzie's head and caught sight of Veronica, and for the second time, his heart stuttered.

She was beautiful, no other word for it. The pale lavender cocktail dress showed more skin than he'd ever seen before. Strapless, to the knee, figure-hugging, it fit like something from his dreams. Even her hair was different, down around her shoulders in waves rather than the usual thick braid, looking soft and sweet.

And she was laughing so hard tears were coming out her eyes. He couldn't not smile at the picture she made. Having fun, not stiff or unapproachable.

Tim finally managed to pull himself together enough to quiet everyone down, and they continued on with the rehearsal. But by the time rehearsals were over, she was back to her quiet self. A small smile for Madison, a little bigger one for Jeremy as he walked her back down the aisle. But past that, nothing.

"You can put your eyes back in your head, Romeo."

He looked down to see Madison's head tilted up at him, amusement written all over her face. "I don't know what you're talking about."

Madison snorted. "You've got to be kidding me if

you think I'll take that at face value. You've been staring at Veronica most of the night. You know that, right?"

"You wouldn't know."

"Hell yeah, I would. I've been standing across from you the whole time, you idiot. And you practically stopped breathing when she walked in the door carrying her fake bouquet of ribbons." She waved her own ribbon cluster in his face for emphasis. "Trust me, you're not all that hard to read." An impish expression took over. "She does look pretty hot, right?"

"Not answering that." He tapped her nose with one finger. "Good try, though. This country boy's not that stupid." If he gave an inch, Madison would be all over him in a second. How she would react to his crush on her roomie, he had no clue. But her interference on the matter wasn't required, regardless.

She shrugged, holding her pretend bouquet out for inspection. "Suit yourself. I mean, she's always got David."

"David." David from the coffee shop? She couldn't be serious.

"I don't think he could make it to the wedding. I didn't get all the details. But he's pretty cute, if I do say so myself. They'll make a nice couple."

The involuntary urge to punch his fist into the wall was abated only by the fact that it was brick, and he'd break something for sure. "That's great. Good for them."

Madison laughed. "You're going to break a tooth if you don't relax your jaw there, sweetie. Look, I don't think he's the guy for her. But at the same time, maybe you're not either. For all I know, you're looking for a quick fuck."

Shock drew his eyes to her. Had Madison ever actually used the f-word before?

She rolled her eyes. "Please. I'm a sailor. It's a job requirement to have a potty mouth. Just because I'm a girl doesn't mean I don't have an impressive dirty vocab. I'm a big girl. I can cuss if I want to."

He glanced over her shoulder. "Hey, Mrs. O'Shay."

Madison paled for a moment and she whipped around, staring at air. Her brows drew together as she tried to kick him in the shin. He laughed and scooted out of the way of her lethal high heels. "Not funny, D."

"I thought so." He laughed again, then calmed down. "I'm not out for a quick fu—screw. You know me better than that."

"I do. But at the same time, I also know you just got back. I don't have a clue if you're ready for anything serious, and you probably don't either. She's a great person, but she's a softie. So I can't really endorse a relationship between you two if I have no idea what your intentions are to begin with."

"None of your business, that's what they are." Why did everyone seem to think this was the worst possible idea? Even he'd first thought it. But now he wasn't so sure. The more he saw of her, the more he liked being with her. And despite his current issues, maybe her calming presence in his life would be a help, not a distraction. Even the chaplain had suggested it wouldn't be an automatic disaster.

Which was all well and good, except for the part where he basically told her he didn't want her. Oh, and the part about her having a guy already.

Great timing. Couldn't be better.

The rest of the crowd gathered in the lobby, chatter echoing off the high ceilings, waiting for everyone before carpooling over for dinner. Normally he'd be in the middle of the chatter. He wasn't feeling too social at the moment.

Madison nudged him with her elbow. "Okay, I'm a bitch. I'm sorry. You didn't deserve that."

"Thank you." He kept his eye on Veronica, across the lobby of the hall where they were having the ceremony and reception the next day. She was talking with Skye and Tim's parents. And he wanted to walk up behind her, pull her back against him, and nuzzle into the soft pillow of hair at her shoulders. Except at this point, she'd likely step on his foot with her heel rather than let him touch her. Worse, he'd deserve it. And that sucked.

Okay. He could do this. They weren't engaged or anything. He wasn't breaking up a marriage. He still had a shot.

"Just be there. You don't need anything elaborate, you know."

Madison's soft words jarred him from his thoughts. "Be there…"

"Just simple as that. I have my suspicions that this thing with David won't work. And when it runs its course, then just be there. I think that would be the best option of all."

Except that meant waiting around, sitting on his hands, and generally feeling helpless. Not his favorite situation. So maybe he might just move things along. Nothing so drastic as stealing her out her bedroom window at night or anything. But if she was mentally comparing David to, oh, say, someone who made her pulse race, and realized it wasn't happening, then that wasn't so bad, was it?

He'd just keep telling himself that.

———

Dwayne took his chance at the end of the rehearsal. Everyone broke up, and he quickly claimed Veronica as his passenger. Though she didn't appear thrilled, she kept mum. Probably thinking that now wasn't the time for a scene or a fight. Thank you, timing and manners.

"I promise I'm doing better. No dodge and weave on the highway," he told her as she climbed up into the cab's passenger seat. He'd offer a hand, but she'd likely bite it.

"I don't have any concerns about your driving," she said, words short and clipped. Before he could tell her that was good, she yanked the door closed on her own.

The moment he started up the engine, she turned the Dixie Chicks CD full blast and stared out her window. Not-so-subtle message received. There was no way she wanted to speak with him. He smiled at the little attitude she was putting out. With him, she didn't play the quiet mouse. Oh, her tactics might involve the silent treatment. But she wasn't afraid to let her displeasure be known. And he liked it.

After a few minutes of driving, he took the risk of turning the music down. She glared at him, then whipped her head back to stare once more into the night.

"I have to apologize. Again."

She said nothing.

"For what I said before, about our kiss. That was wrong of me."

"Yes, it was." The dressing down was short and sweet, but potent.

"Agreed. So I'm hoping you'll forgive me. Because the truth is, I'd like to do it again."

"What, apologize?"

Damn, she was cute when she got feisty. "No. Kiss you. I liked it."

Nothing.

"A lot," he prodded.

Nope. Still nothing.

He sighed. "You can't be upset at me forever. I'm just a simple country boy who doesn't quite well understand matters of the heart."

She snorted in laughter, then clamped a hand over her mouth.

Bingo.

"Fact is," he continued, his Deputy Dawg accent in full force, "I just don't right know what to do with womenfolk that I happen to take a shine to."

She giggled, and he knew he had her then.

"But when one sure is purdy, I just seem to lose myself and I say the darndest things."

"Okay, okay." She waved a hand at him in surrender. "Stop. I get it."

He grabbed the hand before she could pull it back and pressed a lingering kiss to the inside of her wrist, over her pulse. "Do you? Get it, I mean."

Her breath was shaky when she took her hand back. "I thought so. Now I'm not sure."

Sneakiness be damned. He had to go with his gut on this one. "I like you, Veronica. A lot. I'm sorry I made a mess of it earlier, but I was just nervous and being stupid. I thought things weren't the right timing, and I let that do the thinking for me."

She was quiet. So quiet he wondered after a minute if she'd gone back to the silent treatment. When she finally spoke, her soft voice had him breathing a sigh of relief.

"I accept your apology."

Such a formal little phrase. He smiled and held out a hand. When she placed hers in his, his heart did a little dance.

---

"So Dwayne's picking you up, huh?" Madison gave her a sly wink as she grabbed her purse and heels. Like Veronica, she was wearing flats until they reached the ceremony site, where they would change into their official bridesmaids heels.

"Yes, as I said four other times. He's giving me a ride." She fiddled with the hem of her matching shawl, not wanting to look her friend in the eye. She'd guess far too quickly that Madison wasn't as cool about the simple ride as she tried to seem.

"I, for one, am glad I'm driving myself. I hate depending on rides with someone else. But remember I've got my car, okay? If you wanna leave for whatever reason, come find me."

"Thanks." She sat back on the couch and forced herself not to check the clock for the ninth time in two minutes. He wasn't late. He wasn't even remotely late. She was disgustingly early. Eagerness, much?

As Madison picked up her keys, she stopped and looked back. "Uh, I thought I should mention that I sort of hinted to Dwayne that you and David were still an item."

"Madison!" She sat up and stared. "Why would you do that? And what do you mean, *still*? We were never an item to begin with!" She'd told Madison about her decision to break things off with David the same night of their disastrous last date. She knew better.

"Come on. It totally forced him to make the move. You can't be mad at me for that. Males are notoriously slow at everything they're in charge of, including letting girls know whether they're interested or not. It's some deficiency with the Y chromosome. You learn about it in nursing school. Anyway, the fact is, it worked, right?"

She sat back and crossed her arms. "I'm not exactly thrilled that it took a threat to get him to ask to be my date." Was that the only reason? Some ingrained, natural male instinct that wanted what they couldn't have? She didn't want that. Nothing about that said *here's a spark!* or *this could be love.* It was more akin to a wild dog who didn't want a bone until another dog came along and sniffed at it.

Madison didn't seem at all concerned at her deception. "Meh. I don't think that's why. He stared at you through most of rehearsals last night anyway. I think he was holding back 'cause he thought you were happy with David. A little hint, a friendly nudge, and here you two are. Cutie-pie dates for the wedding. Are you really upset about that?"

Veronica, soothed by the thought he'd stared at her, could only laugh. "No. Fine. Shoo, go away. I can handle myself just fine, thank you very much."

Madison paused, hand on the doorknob. "You know, I thought David would be a good choice for you."

"So did Skye. So did I," Veronica reminded her wryly. How wrong they'd all been.

"Yeah. See, the thing is, I think that David probably is a good guy overall. But the reasons for wanting him were wrong. I think what you want in a guy wasn't exactly what we were looking for." She headed out the door, shutting it quietly behind her.

Veronica thought back to what the three had discussed when brainstorming men. How many of those ideas had actually been hers, anyway? Had she really let Skye and Madison— however well-intended—steamroll her into who she should be dating?

Oh boy. She had.

A knock on the door jolted her. She stood, straightened her dress, grabbed her purse and shoes. And realized this was definitely a big moment.

From the time she was born until the moment she stepped into the United States as a grown woman, her parents dictated every single decision for her, sheltering her, keeping her from learning about life, from living. And she let it happen again with well-meaning friends.

No more. She was going to go with the moment, let her heart and her instincts dictate what she should do next. And stop shying away from taking chances.

They couldn't all be bad, right?

# Chapter 12

AT SOME POINT, DWAYNE WAS SURE THERE WAS A wedding. Or, rather, a recommitment. But he was too busy watching Veronica watch the ceremony. Every expression crossed her face, from joy to soft envy and back to pure contentment. He could read her like a book, no hiding it.

Imagine that. A woman who didn't try to hide things. Novel. Now if only he knew what was hiding under that bridesmaid's dress…

"Move," Jeremy hissed behind him.

What? Oh, shit. Madison stared at him, arm out, ready for him to escort her back down the aisle. He missed the entire thing while mentally undressing Veronica. Luckily they weren't in a church, or he'd be toast from a lightning bolt.

He walked with Madison, glowing with happiness, down the aisle and led her to the little area where the bridal party would congregate, ready to enter the reception room next door. The girls all huddled together in a little hidden alcove, gushing and doing their little happy dances over Skye in her dress. That it was white was a surprise in itself. Dwayne was sure she'd buck tradition and wear something more multicolored than Joseph's dreamcoat. But the little dress, while a little more daring in cut, was definitely appropriate enough to have Tim's parents beaming with joy while still not looking like a cookie-cutter bride.

Veronica caught his eye and gave him a shy smile. And he went with instinct to walk over toward her, ignoring the guys behind him attempting to herd guests to their assigned tables in the hall. That was likely where he should be too, but he couldn't resist the pull of her eyes, her body language. Neither of the other women seemed to notice when he reached out a hand and pulled Veronica away, down the hall of the conference center and into a small, unused room. A boardroom table with a dozen chairs dominated the center of the room, a whiteboard took up all of one wall, and that was all.

She still hadn't said a word. But she watched him with careful eyes, meandering through the room, tracing the tops of each chair with her fingertips as she put the table between them.

What would those fingers feel like running down his body? Would they make him shiver, or heat him up?

"Do we need to have a meeting?"

He watched her, knew automatically she was forcing the confidence. This thing, this spark between them, got to her almost as much as it did him. She was on the same level of confusion as he was. Thank God.

"Meetings come in all shapes and sizes." Judging her reaction, he started to walk around the table. She didn't move, let him draw closer. No fear, no panic. Just a sense of curiosity, as if she was watching a lesson in progress. Only the underlying heat, the small tremble of her hand as her fingers outlined the top of one chair, told him she was interested.

"And what are you hoping to accomplish with this meeting?"

"Test the waters." When he came up to her, she turned,

bottom pressed against the table, between two chairs. He watched as she unconsciously placed one hand on the table, then bent back a little to look up at him.

Perfect.

He dipped his head and gave her a soft kiss that she returned easily. Then he increased the pressure of his lips, partly for pleasure, partly as a warning.

*This is going to get hotter. Now's your chance to say no.*

But she only kissed back, angling her head, and taking it a step farther by tracing the seam of his lips with the tip of her tongue in a sweet request.

Without breaking the connection, he lifted her up. She stiffened a moment at the surprise, but relaxed instantly when he placed her butt on the table. And when he finally let loose, cupping her face with his hands and putting his everything into the kiss, she moaned like a starving woman eating her first meal in weeks.

God, she was good for a man's ego. Every little movement, every action was given an instant response, verbal or silent, and he never questioned whether she was enjoying herself. And when he gently, tentatively slid his hands down her neck, over her shoulders, and grazed the sides of her breasts, she didn't even budge. He tried his luck and slid his hands down to her hips to squeeze. She only squirmed, but in the good way. Not the "Hands off, cretin" sort of way. So he took one more chance and lifted her enough to scoot her dress out from under her ass.

Veronica gasped, the sound wet and unbelievably sexy into his mouth. Well, the table was probably cold on her skin. He'd warm her up fast enough. Hands creeping over the tops of her thighs, he was about to inch them apart when—

*Thump.*

Veronica seemed completely unaware of the muffled sound, if her little mewling sounds of desperation were any hint. And hell, if she didn't give a rip, then why should he? He wasn't about to give up a perfectly good—

*Knock knock.*

Fuck. He stepped back, hands quickly shifting to her shoulders so she didn't lose balance and face-plant off the table. Now there would be a delightful way to woo a woman. In a voice that sounded too gruff to be his own, he barked, "Occupied."

Some giggling, a male grunt of annoyance, and then nothing.

He looked back down at Veronica, whose hand was now covering her mouth, eyes wide with shock. "Hey, are you—"

"Oh my…" She tilted her face to look at him, eyes glassy. Was it really that upsetting to almost be walked in on?

"It's fine. The door's locked." He helped her off the table, knowing the moment was officially over, whether he liked it or not. Almost in a daze, she straightened her dress and brushed invisible wrinkles from the front of her skirt.

"We almost… I mean, I almost let you…"

Okay, not everyone was in for the thrill of a semi-public tryst. But she really seemed to be startled that they'd gone so far. "I'm sorry. I wasn't thinking."

That seemed to snap her out of whatever funk she'd

dug herself into. "No, please. Don't apologize. That was wonderful. Just a little shocking, actually." Her lips twitched, then she seemed to give up the fight completely and a full-on grin broke out. "Thrilling is a better word, I think."

Thrilling. Not the adjective he'd use to describe it, but it sounded positive enough so he'd take it. When she looked down again once more to assure herself she was decent, he took the opportunity to face away and straighten his pants and shake a leg. A much-needed feel of relief washed through him, and he could breathe again. Jesus. He wasn't into being watched any more than the next guy. The knock should have sunk his battleship faster than a torpedo. Not with Veronica. If she asked for it, he could have his battleship docking her harbor in moments.

Glancing up, he laughed to himself when he saw her standing by the door, hands primly laced in front of her. Looking like a damn schoolteacher waiting for her pupils to show up for the day.

Yup. She wasn't going to ask him for a boardroom quickie any more than he was going to give her one. Miss Veronica Gibson required more than that. And so did he, he realized as he walked to the door and opened it for her. He needed more than one quick table-shaking hour to see where things were headed. If she was as special as he thought she might be, as important as she might be, then it just wasn't the right way to start things out.

She paused before they hit the ballroom entrance and bit her lip, eyes shifting between him and the door. "Do you think they missed us?"

Was that code for *Does anyone know what we were*

*up to?* Probably. "I doubt it. But we can just slip in through the side. Little more inconspicuous."

Ten pounds of worry slid off her shoulders and her smile was back. "Good. That's good. I don't want to mess anything up for Skye's beautiful day."

Her consideration and care for her friends was just another feather in her cap, as far as he was concerned. Walking them around to the side, where servers had been slipping in and out discretely with plates of food, they quickly melted into the crowd surrounding the dance floor with ease. But it soon became apparent, while their entrance was discrete, their absence had not been.

———

Madison fought back tears, watching her brother twirl his wife around the floor for their first dance. They'd been married almost a year now, but since she'd missed the wedding, this felt like the first time. And her happiness for her brother was trumped only by the smugness that she was right from the start. He needed a wife just like Skye to shake up his world and keep him on his toes. Thank God he found her.

"They look good together."

Jeremy's deep voice rumbled behind her. The heat from his body seeped in through the thin material of her dress, to her bare shoulders. "I thought you didn't like Skye."

He chuckled softly. "You have to admit, they didn't start off like normal couples."

"No, that's true, they didn't."

"I was reserving judgment on her until later. But she

makes him happy, and she's a good person. Doesn't get much better than that."

"No," she said softly, "it doesn't."

The DJ's mic boomed. "And now, the bride and groom would like to welcome their wedding party out onto the dance floor."

"Come on." Jeremy tugged at her hand, surprising Madison.

"You're an eager beaver." As he swept her easily into a slow step, she smiled. "Never would have taken you for much of a dancer."

"Dad had me take lessons. Something about how all officers should know how to do basic dance steps should they be required to." He snorted. "Like all company grade officers need to know how to bust out a tango at the drop of a hat."

Madison raised a brow. "Could you?"

"Wouldn't you like to know?" He leaned down for a quick kiss, one that had her biting back a groan of frustration. How long did they have to stay before they could slip away?

Slip away… Madison glanced around. "Shouldn't you be dancing with Veronica? You escorted her down the aisle, and I walked with Dwayne."

Jeremy shrugged. "I didn't figure it mattered, long as we were all out here."

"Yeah, but…" She pushed until he spun her in a three-sixty spin. "They're not out here."

Jeremy did the owl-pivot on his shoulders. "Huh, you're right. Wonder where they went."

Madison started to smile, laughing a little as her grin spread. "Gotcha." As she spotted both Veronica and Dwayne slip slyly into the back of the crowd from the server entry, she crooked a finger at them. "Get out here."

Veronica hesitated, but Dwayne grinned his idiotic grin and tugged her behind him. Veronica was too sweet to say a word otherwise, though the mutinous look she shot D proved how much she disliked being dragged without a word.

"Hmm. Wonder where those two have been," she thought out loud.

"I know where I wish I was. A dark room alone, with me *not* in this tuxedo and you still in that dress. I want to watch you peel out of it, one inch at a time. Exactly how fast do you think I can get you out of it?" Jeremy's hand smoothed up and down her back, as if searching for the hidden zipper.

She punched him on the shoulder once, then remembered they were the center of attention when a table nearby laughed.

"She's a cold one."

"Really?" Madison glanced up in surprise. "You think so? I thought she was extremely warm. Just struggles with how to show it sometimes. But she's getting there."

Veronica laughed then, dipped back by Dwayne, suspended while he held her nearly upside down. Dwayne's smile wasn't full of humor anymore, but pleasure and something more. Something that had Madison's throat closing with the happiness of it.

That bitch Blair had stolen something from him. He used his sweet Southern personality as a shield, though it was a true part of him as much as anything else. It was cute and quirky and drew the women in like bees to a fragrant flower. But then the flower would close, keeping the bees at a distance.

"And now, we open the dance floor to all those wanting to celebrate Timothy and Skye's love," the DJ announced smoothly, and they shifted slightly to make room for new couples joining them on the dance floor.

But Madison kept Dwayne and Veronica in her eyesight. D was opening up again, and Veronica was the reason why. Or maybe it was just time that healed the wound, and Veronica was in the right place at the right time. Either way, they were good together, and she was happy to see her friend—both her friends now— enjoying each other and making each other happy.

"Wow."

"I know. I've got smooth moves." Jeremy led her into a quick twirl ending in a dip of their own, which he capped with a quick kiss on the nose. "Try not to swoon."

"Oh yeah, Casanova. You've got me." She rolled her eyes, but smiled anyway. "I meant watching Dwayne and Veronica."

Jeremy glanced around, but by now the sea of people had swallowed them up. "Gonna elaborate on what 'wow' meant?"

"Just that I'm happy, watching them move together, toward each other, and enjoying each other. It's like this sweet, slow slide from friends into something more. And I wondered if this was how other people felt watching us."

"Probably not, since we didn't do the slow slide so much as the quick bang." He wiggled his eyebrows to indicate he knew damn well the double entendre he'd just used.

"Sicko."

"Yes, but I'm your sicko."

Madison sighed and rested her cheek on his lapel. "Exactly."

---

Veronica waited to hear the door close and the light by the hallway to illuminate the room before sitting up on the couch. "Want some—"

"Ahh!" Madison screamed, jumped back, and held a hand over her chest. "Christ on a crutch, Veronica."

Veronica mentally winced at the phrase, almost as a reflex. Then reminded herself no bolt of lightning was going to fly down and strike them. "Sorry." She held up the carton in a peace offering. "Ice cream?"

Madison glanced down the hallway toward her bedroom once, longingly, before dropping her bag on the floor and shuffling to the couch. "Why the hell not?" She snatched the carton and spoon from Veronica's hand and dug in.

Veronica debated reaching for the spoon to get another bite in, but the look on Madison's face stopped her cold. She didn't want to lose a finger, so she just gave the treat up for lost. "How was your night?"

If looks could kill, Veronica would have an appointment with St. Peter.

"I'm getting tired of this whole back-and-forth junk between our place and Jeremy's apartment."

"Why didn't you stay over there tonight?" Veronica eyed the ice cream longingly, wishing she hadn't given it up for lost so quickly.

"Because our place is closer to work. Plus, his place is gross. I spend as little time over there as possible."

She dug back into the ice cream, heedless of the drips on her bridesmaid dress. She stuck the bite in her mouth then pointed the spoon at Veronica when she dared reach for the spoon. You know, her own spoon, the one she'd gotten out of the drawer herself. "You had your time with the ice cream. Now Ben, Jerry, and I are having our quality time."

"Why does Jeremy not just come here, then?"

Madison shoveled another bite or two into her mouth without looking up. Veronica waited patiently, then when Madison kept on eating, she prodded her with an elbow. "Madison. What is it?"

"Okay, okay." Madison set the ice cream down— with great reluctance, Veronica noted—and straightened. "We thought it might make you uncomfortable."

She sat for a moment, silent and stunned. "We, as in you and Jeremy?"

"Yeah." Madison reached for the ice cream again, then changed her mind and sat back. "I just, well…"

Veronica bit back a smile. For a woman who was so confident in herself and so open, Madison looked very uncomfortable. "You thought I would be offended that you two would share a bed?"

"We just decided to keep that… elsewhere." Madison shrugged. "Plus, I have to admit having a boyfriend come over when you've got a roommate just feels very college-like. Know what I mean?"

No, she didn't. But she nodded wisely, as if in complete understanding. "I hope you won't let my prudishness stop you from having someone over." With a small smile, she added, "Whether he be staying the night or not."

"You're not a prude. You're just… more conserva-tive." Madison tipped her head down and raised a brow. "You know, I liked you better when you were meek and unresponsive. Those were good days, back when you wouldn't give me lip and just nodded and smiled a lot."

Veronica grinned. "The meek, unresponsive girl is no more."

"I was kidding. Oh, happy topic. And bonus, a topic not about me." She scooted until she could cross her legs under her. A very unladylike position for one wear-ing a cocktail dress. But who was Veronica to judge? "You disappeared after the ceremony for a bit. And come to think of it… so did Dwayne." When Veronica felt her eyes widen, Madison nudged her with a foot. "Don't think I didn't notice you two sneaking back into the ballroom."

She tried, really she did, but she couldn't hold back the small smile that curved her lips. "We might have disappeared together."

"Good going. You know, the more I think about this, the more I think I was entirely wrong when I gave you all those suggestions earlier about who you should start dating."

Veronica waved that away. "No worries. I already had decided to ignore you and Skye." She clasped a hand over her mouth. "Oh, I mean… I meant that with… I didn't mean to—"

Madison burst into laughter. "It's fine. We needed to hear it. A backbone won't kill anyone. Thinking back, we really were a little pushy, weren't we?"

Veronica tried this time for diplomacy and simply shrugged.

"We meant well, I hope you know. But we just didn't know what the hell we were talking about, clearly. You found Dwayne. And I think…" Suddenly the laughter died from her eyes. "Not to lose the moment but… you are aware of his issues, right? The whole reintegration thing?"

"Yes. It was sort of hard to miss, what with me flat on my back on the couch." Veronica chewed her lip. "I don't think there's anything I can do to help him. But I'm hoping that my presence won't harm him, either. I just want to be there, if he needs me, for whatever I can do."

"Well." Madison clapped her hands and rubbed them together. "That's a healthy attitude to take. I'm sure he will appreciate the extra support. He might need it. Or might not. These sort of issues can clear up as suddenly as they start. But until then, I think we're forgetting something extremely important."

Veronica looked at her.

Madison wiggled her eyebrows, a gesture that made Veronica laugh until she snorted. "While you and Dwayne 'disappeared' together… what were you doing?"

"I don't disappear and tell," she answered, channeling her mother's prim voice for effect. The whole thing was ruined when Madison hit her with a pillow and she snorted again.

"I'll drag it out of you then. I have to live vicariously through someone, and I can't do it through Skye, given she's got my brother in her bed and that's just gross. Give! Give the details!"

"Never." She threw the pillow back at Madison and sprinted for her bedroom, laughing when Madison made threats behind her.

Just another normal moment of life that she'd been craving. And she had it in the palm of her hand.

# Chapter 13

DWAYNE STOPPED BY JEREMY'S APARTMENT, BUT THE lights were all out. A quick check told him Madison's car wasn't there, but both Jeremy's bike and truck were in the lot, so he had to assume Jeremy was just as alone as he was. While Dwayne would love to find someone to hang out with—misery loves company, wasn't that how the saying went?—he wasn't about to wake the dude up.

The only problem was, he had too much nervous energy to just head home. After dropping Veronica off—and settling for a simple chaste kiss at the door—he was still wired for action of some kind. A fight, a hard workout, a sweaty, moaning roll between the sheets…

Okay. That wasn't happening. Not tonight, anyway. But at least now that he had a candidate in mind, the prospect looked much better. He walked down the apartment steps to his truck, resigning himself to a quick workout before bed to beat out some tension, when his phone vibrated.

Veronica. He fumbled with the pocket of his suit, then almost dropped the phone in his haste to open it. She wanted him to come back. Wanted him to take her back to his place. To finish what they were starting in the boardroom. Wanted—

No, not Veronica. Blair. Fuck. His stomach twisted painfully. Not only was it not Veronica, but it had to be *her*. The one person God put on this earth to make him suffer more than an insurgent cell. He debated deleting it, then some sick version of curiosity took over his fingers and clicked the "read message" button.

*A little birdie told me you were back. I'm glad you're safe.*

A little birdie, his ass. His Facebook profile was public, and he intended to keep it that way in case anyone from previous bases or deployments wanted to find him. But that meant Blair could see him too. Sure, he could block her, but that would give her way more power than he ever intended to. Two seconds on his Facebook wall would tell her he was back. He rolled his eyes and hit delete, but his phone vibrated again before he could pocket it.

*I miss you. I think about you. All the time.*

He tightened his grip around the phone until it was close to snapping. The lying, conniving, deceitful bitch. The one positive he could come up with about deployment was he didn't have to deal with her constant attempts to smooth the waters. Half the time she played the victim, and half the time she acted like nothing happened. Both ploys were bullshit. But that's the only thing Blair had to offer... bullshit and ploys.

He almost shoved the phone back in his pocket when it vibrated again. The growl stuck in his throat though when he saw it was Tim, not Blair.

*Where did you all head to? Thought we would do a post-celebration get-together at the house.*

Dwayne texted back as fast as his thick fingers would let him. They really didn't design phone buttons for guys with big hands.

*We wanted to give you some space. Now go have a kick-ass wedding night.*

*Thanks bud. Don't mind if I do. :)*

"Lucky-ass bastard," he muttered as he tossed the phone into a cup holder and started his truck back up. Yeah. Tim was lucky, not that he didn't deserve Skye. She was perfection, but only for Tim. Dwayne couldn't begrudge him the happiness he found. Just because his own near-miss with the preacher was a disaster of untold proportions didn't mean everyone else should suffer like he did. So he could appreciate the way Skye made Tim smile, the way he could make her laugh. And if the jealousy pinched his heart just a little, there wasn't a problem in that.

Though come to think of it, that small pinch was almost unfelt entirely now. Huh. Maybe the amount of time was the reason. They'd been together almost a year now; it wasn't brand new.

Or, he thought with a grin as he threw his truck in reverse, he didn't feel the pinch because he had something of his own now. Something that might turn out to be just as special as whatever Tim and Skye had. And jealousy was no longer an issue.

The freeway was almost deserted as he headed back to his own apartment. But the occasional spear of lights from traffic illuminated his cab, glinting off his phone. He threw it another disgusted glance.

Veronica was nothing like Blair. Not even close. If she had a deceitful bone in her body, he'd be shocked. And she wasn't pushing for the relationship. The opposite, really. She had reservations about the whole thing, though he didn't think it was just about him. Some ass must have burned her in the past, maybe. Something. But they'd work through it together.

There was something good there. He knew it. And

for the first time since he returned from the sandbox, his heart felt light.

―⁀⁀⁀―

Veronica leaned back in her chair, rubbing at her tired eyes. After a lunch shift at Fletchers, she really was not in the right frame of mind to work on these math problems. But she had to finish her preparations for the GED test, and soon. The constant reminder that she was twenty-six years old and had nothing, not even a high school degree, to her name was one of the most worthless, shameful feelings in the world.

*But I'm correcting it. It wasn't my choice to stop my schooling. And I'm doing the best I can.*

The little mini pep talk helped to boost her confidence, just a little. Rolling her shoulders, she bent over, prepared to keep plugging away until she mastered this stupid quadratic equation. Because really, who would ever need this in daily life? Wasn't that the beauty of a calculator?

No. Buckle down. Block out the negativity. Focus. No outside distractions. No thinking about anything but math. Especially not clear blue eyes, deep twangs that made her shiver, kisses that had her forgetting they were in the middle of a wedding reception…

No. Bad. Veronica physically shook herself, as if to knock the heated memories back a few steps. Math was number one. She could wonder why Dwayne hadn't called in the two days since the wedding once this was done.

The phone rang, and she nearly knocked over her glass of water scrambling to reach the lifeline saving her from problem 2b.

"Hello?"

"Hey." Dwayne's warm Southern twang melted through the phone and into her body, relaxing her muscles the way a good massage might.

"Hi," she replied, annoyed with the breathless quality her voice took on.

"What are you up to?"

"Homework," she said, then instantly squeezed her eyes shut on a wince. Such a juvenile term, and it would only lead to questions.

"Really? What subject?"

Questions like that. "Uh, math." She shut the textbook quickly, as if he could see she was struggling with high school trig instead of college-level calculus. "But I can always use the break."

"I don't think we've ever talked about school before. What are you studying?"

She knew exactly what he thought. School, for someone in their twenties, equaled university. College. Or at the very least, community college. Nobody assumed someone her age was stuck so far behind, which was exactly what she counted on any time she sidestepped the topic with acquaintances. Even Madison didn't know. "Oh, a little of everything right now." There. Truth. As much as she could give at this point.

"Well, math was my best subject, so if you need help, I'll be your study buddy." The suggestive purr in his voice made her shiver, both with delight and apprehension. These feelings, still so new, almost scared her in their intensity. And she immediately retreated from the fear into her old personal.

"Thank you for the offer." The cool distance in her

voice made her want to cry. This reaction had to stop. She would end up chasing him away at this rate, just like her parents did to anything that might bring her pleasure when she was with them.

Maybe he wouldn't notice.

Of course he noticed.

Dwayne cleared his throat a little, clearly uncomfortable. "Right. Well. I was calling to see if you work tonight."

She forced more warmth into her tone. "I worked this afternoon. Why?"

The pleasure was clear through the phone. She could almost picture him standing there, smiling broadly. "Then, Miss Veronica Gibson, I would love the pleasure of taking you out on a date."

The words, in all their Southern gentleman glory, made her giggle. It wasn't the first time she'd been asked out. But it was the first time she wanted to leap up and shout, "Yes! Yes, yes, yes!" So she overcompensated by meekly squeaking, "Yes, please."

Yes, please? She let her forehead drop to the desk, not even minding when it banged harshly.

He only chuckled. "Good. Tonight at eight? That work okay for you?"

"Yes." Progress. She didn't squeak this time.

"See you then, Miss Veronica," he crooned as he disconnected the phone.

Veronica tossed the phone onto her bed and sat back. What was it about Dwayne that made her so nervous? Was it his size? No, that wasn't right. He was large, definitely. One of the biggest men she'd ever met. But never once had that intimidated her. Maybe because along with his size came such a gentle personality, a kind understanding of other people's feelings.

Maybe his job then. But that wasn't really true either. She'd known Tim for months now, and he was a Marine as well. No nerves with Skye's husband.

So it had to be the way she felt about him. Her hands shook just a little as she stood to look through her meager clothing. He'd already seen her in everything remotely normal. That only left the last dredges of her old wardrobe—ankle-length skirts and blouses that covered her to the wrist and up her neck. Nothing wrong with those clothes, if that's what a person liked. But it's not what she wanted. Not in the slightest. They'd been what her parents forced upon her, and she hadn't been willing to rock the boat.

Well, she'd just have to create something out of one of the outfits he'd already seen. Her budget from the restaurant left almost nothing extra from month to month. Maybe she could borrow a top from Madison or something. That's what girlfriends did.

And here she was, standing in front of the closet, dying to know what he would think of how she was dressed. For twenty-six years, clothes were nothing more than something she put on daily to protect her modesty.

Modesty—and its preservation—took on a whole new meaning when she thought about Dwayne looking at her. Sitting on the bed, she closed her eyes and remembered the feel of his mouth on hers, his hands skimming down her sides, the way she wanted him to keep going, that she had no intention of stopping him at all.

Scary. And thrilling. Which one she'd feel more if she let him continue, she wasn't sure. But, she realized, she wanted to find out. That was something she was positive about. Looking down, she saw her hands had ceased their shaking.

Decision made, she stood again to pick out an outfit with more confidence. She was twenty-six years old. And she'd been saving herself because someone else insisted it was the right thing to do. But she was on her own now, and it was her choice, her body. And if she wanted Dwayne Robertson to make love to her, she would.

And she wanted. She wanted very much. But first, she needed to test how far she had come.

———

*I'm ready for a change.*

Veronica stared in the mirror and forced herself not to wince as the pair of scissors came closer.

Skye stood behind the stylist, a frown on her face. "Sweetie, you look a little green. Are you sure you want to cut that much off? Maybe a compromise, somewhere in the middle."

*Your hair is your crowning glory.*

"No," she said, a little more forcefully than necessary. She smiled in apology at the stylist and tried again with a softer tone. "No, I'm sure. I need to change things up."

The stylist nodded and fluffed her hair between her fingers. "Honey, I can't argue with that. This is the longest hair I've seen since beauty school. We won't go too short. But taking a good deal of length off will make you feel so much different." She gave the back of Veronica's head a more thoughtful glance and ran her fingers through the hair, measuring the texture and weight of it. "I think it's actually long enough to donate. Are you at all interested in donating?"

She hadn't even thought about it, but the stylist told her enough to know that it was worth doing. If she was going to leave the hair behind, at least let someone else benefit from it.

"Good. That sounds good. Let's do that." She settled deeper into the chair, staring straight ahead. "Skye, I'm fine. You can sit in the reception area. You'll get bored standing there."

With one last worried look, Skye left and the woman pulled her hair into a loose ponytail in the back.

She watched once more as the stylist picked up the shiny shears on the table in front.

"It's okay if you close your eyes," the woman whispered, giving her a small smile in the mirror.

"Thank you." She breathed and did just that. The first snip, taking all the weight from her hair, was like a bomb exploding in her mind. And she instantly wanted to scream, "Stop!" and run like the wind. But the damage was done, she realized when the woman placed the ponytail on the table in front of her, eye level. She could always grow it back if she wanted.

*This is what I need. It's just hair.* But the change had to start somewhere. She needed to know what it felt like to make her own choices… starting with a small one.

As the woman swapped out scissors for a smaller pair, she shook her head. The lightness was unbelievable. No heavy mass weighing her neck down.

Symbolic, that.

The woman took up her post in back and tilted

Veronica's head down gently so she stared at her shoes. "So why the big change?"

"Hmm?" Veronica closed her eyes and kept them closed.

The woman talked easily as she snipped here and there. Thank God Veronica didn't have to look. It would have driven her nuts to see even more hair fall bit by bit. "The way I see it, this is a drastic change for you. Nothing wrong with that, but it usually comes because of—or in spite of—something else in that person's life. Is it a new job?"

"No." The panic in her chest started to ease a little. She took a few more deep breaths and realized that truly, this wasn't as hard as she thought it would be.

"You won the lottery."

She laughed. "If only." Yes, the fear and panic had definitely receded. Maybe they weren't even real. Maybe it was just her body—her mind—playing a trick on her. Reminding her of what the consequences would have been had she done this while still with her parents. Instinct at play, rather than her own thoughts and feelings.

That angered her more than anything. That her own mind didn't know what it wanted, its own instinct was to fall back to what she had lived for the past twenty-six years, rather than to move forward to the life she wanted.

It would change.

"Has to be a man, then."

No. Not really. True, her date with Dwayne had set the idea to do this today in action. But the pure rebellion of the act… that was all her. And for nobody else. She wanted a change, and she was starting here. Something so small, so inconsequential to some women. A haircut.

A new look. But for her… it was like a talisman signaling her true freedom from her old life. The last little bit of the old that needed to be shed… or sheared, as it turned out.

The hair dryer ran a little, and she kept her eyes closed until the chair spun enough to make her a little dizzy.

"Here we go, sweetie."

She didn't want to look. What if her first true act of independence was a disaster? What if she looked like a rabid chipmunk?

*Then you'll buy a hat. Open your eyes.*

She peeked with one eye, then opened both wide with shock. Where was she? She wasn't facing the right mirror—

Oh. Oh, she was…

Veronica's eyes watered a little, and the stylist gave her shoulders a pat. "I'll go get your friend."

She could only nod in response. As she walked away, Veronica shook her head a little, watched as the strands of hair danced, then fell back into place.

It wasn't short. Not even close by normal standards. Her hair brushed past her shoulders, still long enough to pull into a ponytail or braid. But short enough that she wouldn't sit on it, or struggle to brush it every morning, or dry it.

More than the practical aspect… she just liked how it looked. She was younger almost. Not too young. But it was as if, along with that long rope of hair that the stylist took off, the exhaustion and fear she had been living with was also cut away. As if she was truly cutting away the last of her old life and ready to step out into the life she had always wanted.

As far as haircuts went, this was nothing short of a life-changer.

How much did someone tip for a life-changing event?

"Oh my… Veronica."

She looked up to see her cousin's face in the mirror above hers. Skye's eyes were wide, a hand covered her mouth. And she had no clue if this was a good sign or a bad one.

"Do you like it?"

Skye just stared a little.

Her cousin, the one who could never stop talking, never hold anything in, was speechless.

Finally, she lowered her hand and rearranged her face until it was impassive, completely neutral. "I think the question is… do you like it?"

She looked once more at the new her. The one without the world's problems on her shoulders. The one who was ready to make her own choices and do so without any fear. Who was twenty-six years old, damn it, and ready to make love with a man she liked and respected.

"Yes. I like it very much."

# Chapter 14

DWAYNE STOOD ON THE FRONT PORCH, RELIVING HIS late teens. Only this time, he was driving his own—newly cleaned out—truck instead of his mom's twenty-year-old Buick, and he didn't worry that a well-meaning father would open the door and interrogate him for an hour before they left.

But when Veronica stepped out onto the dimly lit porch, he found himself wanting to know where his date really went, and who the woman standing in front of him was. Because this was not the Veronica he saw last.

Her hair, usually so long and pulled back into a tight braid, was free and drifting down to just below her shoulders. That in itself was unbelievable. But her outfit was another shocker, and in a good way. A cute little tank top with only the thinnest straps over her pale shoulders covered all the right stuff, and would have been almost modest by another woman's standards. But on her, it was unbelievably sexy. Maybe it was the contrast from such buttoned up shirts with long sleeves to this. Her jeans weren't skin tight, but they didn't hide her figure either. And the heels.

He'd be thinking about those heels later tonight. In his dreams. Or maybe nightmares. The difference likely depended on how the date went.

And that was a jackass thing to think. He held out the small bouquet of flowers he'd picked up on impulse on the way over. Truthfully, he would have arrived at her place almost half an hour early if he hadn't stopped for the buds, looking like a creep who was too anxious for their date. So they served a dual purpose. And he couldn't even be remotely sorry he'd bought them when her eyes went so soft, almost liquid with pleasure.

"Oh, Dwayne. Thank you." She did the girly thing and sniffed a little, petting the individual blooms with one delicate finger. He shifted. This was definitely too early to be having the thoughts that raced through his mind as he watched one fingertip trace the soft skin of one closed rose.

"Well, I figured we'd been dancing around this long enough that you deserved the works."

She smiled at him absently, still looking at the flowers as if they were completely foreign to her. Had nobody ever brought her a handful of blooms before? The simple, almost mindless gesture on his part suddenly seemed much more important.

"I'll just slip back in and put these in—"

The door slid open and a hand darted out to carefully snatch the blooms. "Got 'em. Have fun!" And the door snapped shut again.

Dwayne stared at the peephole. "Was that Madison?"

"Yes, it was." More loudly, Veronica said, "And she can stop spying on me anytime now. Go do something else."

"Love you too!" was the cheerful reply through the door, just before the dead bolt slid home with an obvious snick.

Veronica stared up at him a moment, almost horrified. Then she jerked, as if she'd hiccupped. After another, then a third, he realized she was trying to hold back laughter, and he couldn't stop the chuckle himself.

"Oh, what the hell. Let's go grab some food."

As he walked her to the truck, she stopped. "Dwayne. Did you have any serious plans for tonight?"

He shook his head as he opened the door. "No. Nothing that can't be changed. Why? Got an idea yourself?"

"I think I'd just like to go back to your place."

He thanked God he'd already set her on the seat, because if he'd still been holding her waist, he would have dropped her in the parking lot. He cleared his throat. "Uh, my place. Are you sure that's what you—"

"I mean, we can just relax, right? Order a pizza or something? Watch a movie?"

Right. Pizza. Movie. Not an invitation for a delicious and completely mind-blowing sex-a-thon. Of course. "If that's what you want. But are you sure you don't—"

"Oh, yes. I do. That's exactly what I'd like."

Having her home, shoes off, kicked back on the couch with nobody else there to answer to but himself, was going to be a huge test of his willpower. But with her staring at him, those big beautiful eyes working him over, how could he say no?

"Yeah. I'll take you home."

---

Dwayne led her up the stairs to his apartment. Twice, he knew she stumbled in her heels, but he didn't say anything. She caught herself, and he knew that's what she wanted. Turning around to steady her would have only been embarrassing. So he fought the urge to offer his hand and left her to her pride. But the adorable thought of her wearing heels on their date despite not being used to them was definitely not something he was going to deny himself. A caveman moment, sure. But if a man had caveman thoughts, and nobody knew... did they really exist?

He opened the door and thanked whatever deity was listening that he had been bored enough to do a half-assed cleaning job the other day. He wasn't a slob like Jeremy, but he was no clean freak like Tim either. The living room, though, was presentable. Maybe some dust, but not too bad. He at least liked to give the impression that he knew how to keep things neat. But he made no guarantees about what his bedroom looked like. Luckily, they wouldn't be heading in there to find out.

He watched, waited with an unease he didn't really care for, as Veronica took a slow trip around his living and dining room, stopping to peek into the kitchen for a minute. Then she smiled.

"You always hear the silly horror stories about men left to their own devices. But nothing too scary."

The sigh of relief was, luckily, inaudible. "Don't look in the fridge then." He shrugged out of his jacket, glad he'd worn a polo instead of a more uncomfortable shirt. Lounging required comfort. "I'm going to order the pizza. What do you want on it?"

"Anything is fine with me," she said, not looking at him. Crouched in front of his DVD rack, she seemed engaged in checking out his movie collection.

"Are you sure? I like a lot of spicy toppings."

She tilted her head, glanced at him from the corner of her eye. And with a serious tone, said, "I'm willing to try some spice."

Their eyes locked for only a moment, then she broke the connection to continue perusing his DVDs.

Okay. Was that comment meant to be suggestive, or was his imagination playing tricks on him? She said it so simply, without a hint or a wink or anything to give him a clue as to her motive. Either way, he turned his back so he wasn't staring at her ass in those jeans while he called in the order. No rushing. You didn't rush a woman when it was serious.

And especially not one like Veronica.

Not to mention, he still wasn't sure exactly how his little… problem was going to handle taking the next step. Would getting wild in the bedroom trigger some sort of crazy response? God, he hoped not.

The fact that he had to question himself only pissed him off. He waited until the moment passed before looking behind him.

And there she was, standing right there. Only, a little shorter than before. She'd kicked off her heels, leaving them in a pile by the TV.

"Sorry. I thought since we were relaxing, it'd be okay."

"Fine with me." The sight of her toes peeking out from under the hem of her jeans was almost more erotic than anything he'd seen before. And how pathetic was that? "Did you find a movie?"

She smiled a little then produced the cover from behind her back. "*Legally Blonde*?"

He reached for the cover but she danced back, out of arm's reach. His masculinity just dropped five points. "It was a gag gift. Madison got it for me one year for Christmas."

"Hmm. But… it's open." Her lips tilted with an impish smile. "Seems to me someone's been enjoying a… what's the term? Chick flick."

"Reese Witherspoon is hot," he grumbled. There went another five masculinity points. This time, when he lunged, she turned her back to run. Winding one arm around her middle, he brought her back flush up against his chest. She struggled, wiggled, laughed, and twisted around. But he didn't let go. It felt too good. Not sexual—okay, well, a little—but the fun, easy feeling of playing. Just goofing with a woman, with no other motives in sight.

After a long drought of fun, he soaked up the moment like a dry sponge. And when he realized another minute of this would make him appear less fun and more creepy, he let her go. With reluctance.

She swatted his arm and smiled. "Just for that, I am definitely picking this as our movie for the night." She gave the DVD player her full attention.

"Haven't you seen it before? Don't you want to pick something you haven't seen?" He walked into the kitchen, found a few dishes on the counter, and tossed them in the sink. Then, realizing they were no better hidden in there, he picked them out and put them in the cabinet under the sink. He got down two glasses—they didn't match, but she didn't seem like one to care—and filled them with ice water. When he came back out, she was already sitting on the couch, staring at a blank screen, remote in her hand.

"Here. Remotes are still completely worthless to me. I'll break it if I try."

"Figures." He traded her the remote for her glass of

water and sat next to her. Not touching, but close. "Last chance to change your mind about the movie selection."

"I've never seen it. And now my curiosity is piqued."

"What woman hasn't seen this movie?"

Her brow scrunched for a moment. "I guess that would be me."

"Okay then. I offered. Just remember, nobody gets blown up in this one."

"Already scoring high points." She settled deeper into the welcoming cushions of his couch. A piece of furniture bought for comfort, not style. But she hadn't complained about the ugliness yet. Nor had she commented on his lack of decor or pictures. So maybe she didn't care much about decorations. Fine with him.

He started to fast-forward through the trailers, but she put a small hand on his wrist. "No, I like them. Do you mind?"

Who liked trailers? But he said nothing, only put the remote down and let them play through.

He didn't pull any of the crappy seventh grade tricks, like stretching and leaving his arm around the back of the couch. Or coughing so that he shifted closer to her. But then again, he didn't have to. After the third trailer, she was already settling in next to him, her side nestled in against his. Her head right in the crook of his arm. Hand placed oh-so-innocently on the top of his thigh. Almost as if she was nesting.

And it felt good.

〜

Veronica was following every instinct she had—which wasn't saying much—to get him to make a move. And despite her new haircut, Veronica wasn't really ready to take the next step herself. Or, at least, entirely by herself. She needed a little guidance. And he was ignoring her every subtle attempt.

What was she doing wrong?

Though really, she had to admit, simply sitting here next to him, his body heat mingling with hers, breathing in the clean masculine scent of him, snuggling... she wasn't all that upset by the turn of events. And if she angled her head just a little, to breathe in a little deeper, take in more of him to create a memory of the moment, at least it was a good second to what she really hoped was going to happen.

As she watched the blonde in the movie work hard to get into Harvard, she had a pinch of regret about leading him to think that she was in the process of earning a degree. But at the rate she was going, perhaps she could finish her GED soon and get ready for college. And nobody would be any the wiser. The dishonesty ate at her gut, but she didn't see a way to correct everyone's assumptions without appearing to be a liar.

She turned and soaked in just a little more of whatever made Dwayne Dwayne when he chuckled.

"Darling, are you doing what I think you're doing?"

*Painfully trying to seduce you and doing a horrible job at it?* "What do you think I'm doing?"

"I think you might be smelling my shirt."

Horrified, she looked up, only to see an amused smile on his lips. Well, he didn't seem weirded out by her. "You smell nice," she mumbled and started to shift away.

"Oh, no." One thick arm wrapped around her, keeping

her pressed tight against him. "You can't escape that easily. So, I smell good, huh?"

The flush that crept up her neck and spread to her cheeks was almost painful, it burned so much. "Maybe."

"That's good news to me, then." His hand rubbed down her back, up her arm. Now they were getting somewhere. Goose bumps of anticipation and excitement covered her arm. But he rubbed more briskly. "You're cold. I'm always running warm so I keep the air up. Let me get you something."

"No, I'm not—" Her words were lost as she face-planted into the couch cushion. Dwayne standing up so abruptly left her no time to shift her balance. And without his body there, holding her, she flattened. *Very graceful*, she thought and pushed hair out of her eyes. Not that he noticed. The silly man was already in his bedroom—she assumed—and rummaging through drawers from the sound of it. Veronica pushed herself up and waited, blowing a few stray strands out of her face.

"Here we go. My alma mater." He held out a sweatshirt that would have fit her, Skye, and Madison all at once. When she didn't reach for it, he took matters into his own hands and plopped the shirt down over her head, rendering her blind as hair swooped back into her eyes.

"Dwayne, I'm really not—"

"I should have thought about you. I like the air cold, helps me sleep better. After so many months in suffocating heat, it just feels better. But your shoulders and arms…" He trailed off as he helped nudge her arms through the correct holes and rolled the sweatshirt down to her knees. He laughed a little, then stepped back.

She blew again, using her fingers to scrape the hair

from her face. So much for her newly styled do. And for the shirt she borrowed from Madison. The entire effect from the knees up was covered by soft gray fabric. But Dwayne didn't seem to mind her odd appearance. Actually, he was looking at her a little strangely. Like they'd just met, and he knew he'd seen her face before but could not place it.

Finally, he stepped to her again, cupping her face in his large, warm hands. "I forget how small you are sometimes. How delicate you are. I'm clumsy, and big. And I don't think I've been delicate a day in my life." He stared at his thumb while it rubbed over one of her cheeks. "I feel like sometimes you might startle easily. I hope that's not out of fear from me. My size, or my... issues."

"Oh." Oh, this sweet man. So big, tough, and so soft inside. She wanted to cry a little at the gentleness. Mirroring his position, placing her hands on his face, she shook her head. "No. Not afraid. Men can make me nervous. But not you." It was the total truth.

Something changed in his eyes. They almost darkened in color, if that were actually possible. And it was the last thing she saw when he bent down and kissed her.

Nothing gentle this time. No, more of a claiming. A declaration to the world—even though there were only two there—that this was what he wanted, and nobody could stop him. She desperately fought to make mental notes. To remember every taste, every move. And when his tongue probed inside, she didn't even gasp. No. She wanted it. Here was exactly what she had been looking for. The passion previously denied her. This was what she craved, deeply, darkly. And the satisfaction of grabbing it for herself, of sharing it with Dwayne, was almost too much.

His hands slid down her arms, over the back of his sweatshirt until he gripped her bottom. She inched forward at the touch, and he took the invitation for what it was. Gripping just under each cheek, he hefted her up. As if the entire thing was natural, as if they did this every day, she knew what he wanted her to do. She wound her legs around his hips, as if clinging to a tree.

She squealed a little when he started to walk. Where, she had no clue. But she wasn't going to break their kiss to look and see. When her back nudged against a wall, she let out a puff of breath. And he took the chance to work his way down to the pulse of her neck, beating so hard she thought it might just jump out through her skin and run laps around the room.

"Oh. Okay, yes." The words were a whisper; she didn't even mean to say them. But Dwayne heard, and it only seemed to encourage him. He squeezed her bottom, then one hand was on her stomach, under the sweatshirt and tank top. The skin-to-skin contact startled her, but she wasn't about to stop him.

"We still okay?" he asked, lips now just below her earlobe.

"Mmm." How could he form full sentences? His hands brushed, massaged her stomach, and her whole body clenched to wonder where he was headed. Up… or down?

She knew he was wondering the same thing, and the tension in his shoulders told her he'd made his choice when—

*Knock knock.*

His body jerked, as if he'd been shot. Then he let his forehead thump against the wall next to hers. His breath was hot on her neck, still damp from his kisses.

"I'm sorry." He groaned the words out, as if he couldn't believe himself. "I'm so sorry."

How did you say *I don't accept your apology, now get over it and do it again*?

The knock came again, pounding so hard the door rattled in the frame. "Pizza delivery!"

This time, he let go of her legs slowly so she slid down his body in a kind of evil torment. Her skin felt alive, like it was ready to be brushed all over. But he didn't give her a second glance as he walked to the front door.

# Chapter 15

DWAYNE WAITED UNTIL VERONICA'S SHIFT WAS ALMOST over before walking into Fletchers. She didn't know he was coming, had warned him she wouldn't be available today for a date because she'd be too exhausted to think straight after working a double. But when he'd mentioned offhand that she worked too hard and could use the break, she'd simply said she needed the money.

He could relate, as much as he hated to think that she might be scrimping. Paying for college was hard, he'd been there, though he'd lucked into a football scholarship to pay the way, and ROTC to help with the rest. She didn't have those options. And much as he'd like to help, he knew she wouldn't accept any assistance. But really, letting him buy one textbook or something wouldn't hurt, would it?

Come to think of it, he didn't actually know where she was going to school. He'd assumed the local community college, but maybe she was taking courses online through a distance program. What the hell was she even studying?

Well, that's what dating was for. He'd ask her. Tonight. His plan of having a late dinner in her apartment's oven—thanks to Madison—would be just the thing to help her relax. And with Madison and Jeremy eating with them, no temptation to push her well past the boundaries he'd set for himself.

Pushing too far too fast wasn't going to do either of them any good. This was something serious—for him anyway, and he hoped for her too.

"Hey," the hostess, a short redhead with a nice smile beamed at him. "I remember you. Skye's friend Dwayne. Right?"

"You got it. But I'm here waiting on Veronica now."

The woman checked her book. "She actually got hit with a last-minute table, poor thing. So she'll be hanging back a little longer than usual. But I'll let her know you're here."

"Don't worry about it," he tried, too little too late. The hostess scrambled back toward the kitchen to tell her he was there. Not that he didn't mind the anticipation. But he also knew she had a job to finish, so he hoped she didn't feel pressured to hustle. He'd just tell her he would come back in a few.

"Hi there." Another server, tall with obviously bleached hair, walked over. "I hear you're looking for a waitress."

If there was a picture for the term *blatantly sexual*, this female would have it all. From the bedroom eyes to the practiced pout to the way she stood just a little too close, it made him want to run the opposite direction.

A little funny, actually, since before his deployment, the type of woman out for a simple night of fun would have been much more appealing. He took a nice big step back and stuck his hands in his pockets. "Waiting for one server in particular. Veronica."

Her eyes widened in surprise and the bedroom kitten routine was quickly replaced with an attitude of *You're shitting me, right?* "The little mouse? I mean, don't get me wrong, she's a sweetheart. But I'm just a little shocked."

The kitten calling his woman a mouse. Now there was something he didn't care to hear. "Right. Well, if you see her, let her know I'm—"

"Hi." Veronica popped up from behind the other woman, completely oblivious to the predatory glances fired her direction. She stopped short, not reaching for him. But he wasn't disappointed. Not in her nature to do the whole PDA thing, especially at work. He kinda liked that about her. That her affections were special enough to keep them quiet. "I heard you were up here. I'm sorry, did I get dates mixed up?" She glanced up at him, then back to the dining area, as if only half her attention were being given.

"No, I thought you'd be done by now, but it's fine. I just thought I'd surprise you if I could with some dinner. Madison's getting things started, and I thought we could hang out at your place afterward, just relax." Now that he said it, it was starting to sound more stupid by the minute. She looked completely worn out and run-down, as if she'd been running around for hours. Probably had. She'd be too tired to even sit and watch TV with him. This was dumb.

"Oh," she breathed. He felt her full attention on him now, like a blast of warmth, and when she smiled the warmth curled through his body and landed in his gut. "That's really sweet. I'd like that. But I just got set with a table and—"

"And you'll be later than normal. Yeah, she told me. That's fine. Do your thing, no rush. There's a bike shop two blocks down. I'm gonna walk down there and look for a birthday gift for Jeremy."

"Okay." Then more strongly, "Okay, great." She grinned. "I think I have enough energy to push through now." She placed one hand on his arm and squeezed. "Thanks."

Even after she left, he still felt the tingle on his skin from that one moment of contact. It was more than she'd normally given him in front of others, and he didn't want to read into it, but he couldn't help but feel a little encouraged. Turning on his heel, ignoring the bleach-blond server still standing in the area like a mannequin, he headed back out and walked to the bike store, intent on finding something for Jeremy... even though his birthday was four months away.

～∽～

"Spill the magic beans, blondie."

Veronica didn't say a word, just continued to punch in her last table's order, double-checking it before hitting the button to send it back to the kitchen. When she was finally done, she looked up at Steph. "Hmm?"

Steph rolled her eyes. "Nice act. I'm talking about the guy. The one with the muscles up there at the hostess stand? Tall, brawny, sexy as sin? He was here for you. So how the hell did that happen?"

"Oh. Dwayne." She stepped carefully around the other woman and made her way to the silverware tray, trying to look busy so maybe she'd be left alone. No luck. Steph just followed her like a child's pull toy, as if she had nothing better to do. Which was a total lie; there was always something to do in the back of the restaurant. "He's friends with Skye."

"But he was here to see you. Told me so himself."

He had? That made her smile as a reflex, which Steph caught and almost sneered back. "So I know you're not burning the sheets up with him. What's the catch?"

"Burning the sheets." She said it slowly, not liking the way it sounded.

"The horizontal tango. Bumping uglies." When Veronica said nothing, Steph's lip curled with disgust. "Jesus, you don't know shit, do you?"

She placed another silverware roll in the tray with precision and lined it up perfectly with the others, avoiding making eye contact. Why encourage her? "You're referring to making love. I actually realized what you meant from the start. I just didn't feel like responding to the crude way you described it."

"Making love. Right. Whatever." All at once, Steph seemed to lose the hostile attitude and slumped back against the wall. "A man like that is the definition of the word virile. A woman's ovaries itch just looking at him."

None of that sounded very pleasant, but Veronica didn't want to encourage her so she kept her mouth shut.

Sliding her a sidelong glance, Steph smiled. But as usual, the gesture looked more like a threat than a sign of friendship. "A woman would have to double down on her protection to avoid getting knocked up by a strappin' country boy like that."

Veronica filed the information away in the back of her mind, but wasn't entirely sure what she was supposed to say to that. What she *was* sure of was that it didn't need to be a conversation they had at work. "I think we all have chores to finish for closing."

Not at all dissuaded, Steph gave her a slow look up

THE OFFICER AND THE SECRET 195

and down. "You're cute. I mean, cuter now since you whacked off all that freaking hair."

"Thank you." *I think?*

"But really, I don't get what in God's name he'd have to do with a girl like you."

Veronica counted to ten while she rolled the last set of silverware and placed the bundle in the bin. "If you'll excuse me, I need to finish up my work so I'm ready to go." Steph didn't say a word, though Veronica half-expected Steph to trip her as she walked past.

Then it occurred to her—she didn't have to walk away like a sweet little lady. She had claws too, though they might not be as sharp. Might as well start sharpening them. She turned to see Steph still leaning against the table. No shock there, since she had the work ethic of a snail.

"Maybe Dwayne sees something in me that he doesn't in you. Like manners and good company. Maybe he wants to be happy instead of dealing with drama." With that, she turned on her rubber-soled heel and headed out to clear plates from her last table. In the world of set-downs, it wasn't exactly an Olympic effort. But it felt good. Darn good.

It occurred to her ten minutes later, as she was dumping the last of the ice, that Steph was likely jealous. Of her. Because of Dwayne. Part of her wanted to feel sorry for Stephanie. She didn't have many female friends, it seemed. Though if this was the way she treated others, it was no wonder. But the other half of her—the half her mother would be horrified to know she had, and therefore she reveled in it that much more—wanted to do a little dance with glee. Dwayne was hers... at least for the moment. He seemed interested in her, surprising as that may be to many others, and she was not about to look a gift horse in the mouth.

---

After a delicious dinner, Veronica and Dwayne claimed KP duty, since Madison and Jeremy had set up the late meal for them. The couple slipped back into Madison's bedroom and shut the door behind them. Veronica did her best not to stiffen at the reminder. This was part of having roommates, and she needed to grow up and get over it.

After the last dish was in the dishwasher and the counter wiped off, Dwayne walked to the door, hands in his pockets.

"I better head out."

"Oh, but…" Veronica wrung the towel in her hands, then realized the cliché picture she presented and tossed it back on the counter to follow him. "We could watch a movie here. Madison has a nice selection. I won't even complain if you pick something with bombs and blood."

He smiled a little at that, then shook his head. "I need to get back. Thanks though." He opened the door and she stepped onto their small doorstep leading to the building's staircase. "No, don't walk me down. I'm good."

"Of course I'll walk you down. You're—" She couldn't finish the thought, as Dwayne's mouth slanted over hers and pressed the sweetest of kisses to her lips. Before he could pull back, she instinctively wrapped her arms around his neck and tugged, bringing him more fully against her. He groaned, nudged her against the wall next to the front door, and kissed her back. Hard.

Deliciously hard. They didn't stop until both were gasping for breath and Veronica felt a little dizzy from lack of oxygen.

"Stay."

Dwayne dropped his forehead to hers and squeezed one of her hands. "I can't. I would if I could but… I just can't. I'll see you tomorrow night."

She nodded and waited until his truck drove away before slipping back into the apartment. She turned out the kitchen and living room lights, then headed down the hallway to the bedrooms. But before she turned into her own, she paused, grabbed Madison's laptop, and scurried in and shut the door.

Hey, she wasn't going to use it tonight. She was busy with her boyfriend in the other bedroom.

Lucky.

But Veronica had other things she needed to worry about besides mild jealousy issues. Hesitating only a moment, she opened up Google and got to work.

Twenty minutes later, she sat back, wide-eyed and regretting every moment of that Google-fest.

Okay. So, she knew where babies came from. But her sex education had been… nonexistent living with her parents. She barely saw doctors as it was for illnesses or injuries, and none of the missionaries her parents worked with were going to give her the straight truth about anything involving sex, safe or otherwise. It would have been seen as a sort of dirty sin.

As if the real sin wasn't keeping their daughter as ill-prepared for the real world as physically possible for their own selfish reasons.

It was upsetting, honestly, to know that she was so far

behind anyone else in her exact same age group. That people born the decade behind her likely knew more about sex and just things in general than she did, were prepared for more. But logically she had to remember... she hadn't been given a choice. The Internet was still new to her, along with so many things she was just discovering. And up to now, she hadn't exactly had a reason to research the subject.

But now that she'd followed the Internet spider-web from one place to another dealing with all things reproductive—several of which she wished she could now scrub from her brain—she knew it was time to face facts. And it would be embarrassing. But she had to.

She closed the computer and headed back into the hall to plug it in at the desk. Then she knocked softly on Madison's door. She heard the bed creak—and only winced a little—then Madison's face appeared in the crack of the door.

"What's up?"

"I'm sorry." Right. Now was not the best time for this. "I'll catch you later."

Madison paused a moment, then looked over her shoulder. "I'll be back."

"Huh?" Jeremy's voice called out from the dark.

"Girl talk. Make yourself useful and fold something in the laundry basket in the corner." She slipped out of the door and shut it, muting Jeremy's grumbling protests. "Into your room."

Veronica let herself be pushed at the bed until she sat down. Madison, wearing boxers that she could only assume were Jeremy's, and a large T-shirt, sat beside her, cross-legged. "What's up? Is Dwayne gone?"

"Yeah, he is." Thinking back to Madison's not-so-subtle exit, she smiled. "I'm glad you and Jeremy aren't avoiding the apartment for my sake anymore. But you didn't have to slip away so fast after dinner."

Madison gave her a wink. "Oh yes we did. We had some fun of our own planned. Plus, I wanted to give you two some time. You don't need a chaperone."

Veronica cleared her throat. "About that kind of fun…" When Madison cocked her head to one side, she almost lost her nerve. So instead she blurted it out as fast as she could. "HowdoIgetmyselfsomebirthcontrol?"

Madison's eyes bugged. "Come again?"

Veronica screwed hers tight. "Don't make me say it again, please?"

"Okay, fine. Well, I guess you'd just head to your regular doctor and ask them. If you don't have one, there are always basic clinics that you can go to. They usually have pharmacies attached where you can fill the prescription right there in fifteen or twenty minutes."

She nodded. Though she didn't have a regular doctor, she knew of a few clinics in the area. She'd driven a fellow server to one after he'd cut his hand and required stitches. "Thanks."

"Do you want to… uh, talk about… it?"

Madison looked as miserably helpless as Veronica felt. But while she appreciated the effort, she wasn't a teenager needing parental advice. This was something she'd figure out on her own. She shook her head, thanked her friend, and watched as Madison headed back to her room and her lover.

One more step on the way to becoming an independent adult who had boyfriends and experienced life. The real thing, not a watered down version that was picked out for her. But she had to be smart about it.

———

The only sound signaling the attack was the soft whistle of air. Dwayne came to life, swinging his arm to block the incoming blow. He rolled up, naked, and crouched on the corner of his bed and willed his eyes to adjust. But the first thing he realized wasn't from sight. It was the soft feel of the bed's mattress beneath his feet.

Bed. Not his rack.

The present came to him in a rush of sensations. His teeth were chattering so hard they actually hurt. His skin was covered in sweat, even though the room was cool. And his head pounded out a drumbeat the cast of *Stomp* would be proud of.

He ran a hand down his face, wiping sweat away and flicking it off. What the hell time was it, anyway? The place where his alarm clock normally sat was empty. A quick search showed the alarm clock—turned to static and on—behind the nightstand, with a good-sized dent in the wall behind it. The sudden sharp pain when he flexed his hand told the rest of the story. As his alarm went off, he'd mistaken the radio static for… something else.

God, this was ridiculous. Why was he acting like this? He hadn't even been in the thick of combat. Guys who saw way more shit than he ever had came home without a problem. Hell, his first two deployments were way more action-packed and he'd walked away without a hitch.

So why now? And why, period?

He flexed his hand again and walked to the kitchen

for an ibuprofen. Hopefully it would work double-time to clear the headache up and dull the pain in his hand. After chasing the pills with a glass of water, he did a quick calculation and realized his sister was probably feeding Suzanna her breakfast. He needed a little innocence, combined with the unconditional love and support of family, to clear the rest of the nightmarish fog out. Taking a chance, he gave her a call.

"Hello?"

She sounded tired, and it broke his heart a little. "Hey, Nat. How are things?"

"Dwayne, hey." The pleasure in her voice spread, edging out the exhaustion. "What's up?"

"Just was thinking of you guys, wanted to see how things are going."

"They're good." A loud squeal penetrated through the phone and had Dwayne wincing. "Okay, baby, okay. Cheerios, coming right up."

He heard the scatter of food hitting the plastic high chair tray and Suzanna's delighted laugh and clap.

God, that sounded good. Normal sounds, familial sounds, comforting sounds. If things had gone differently, he knew Natalie would be exhausted because she was pregnant, and her husband would be off to work already, making enough to support the family and provide.

But instead, she was dogged out from two jobs and a toddler she handled alone.

"Natalie…" He paused. "I miss you guys."

"We miss you too. Tell Uncle D how much we miss him."

Babbling, which might or might not have been English, filled his ear. He grinned and made the appropriate sounds back at her. Damn, his niece was going to be a pistol when she could actually form real sentences.

"She's so chatty in the mornings." Natalie again. "I swear, the minute she picks up words I'm in trouble. Okay, honey, here are your eggs. Let mama help you."

"I won't keep you; I know you're always rushed in the mornings."

"Aw. So soon? I can give you my full attention; she's preoccupied now with her milk cup. So what else is going on? How's that girl you were thinking about?"

"Veronica." He smiled a little at her name. "She's good. Things are… progressing," he decided was the best term. "You'd like her."

"I'll like her even more if she's up for babysitting. Bring her with you next time you fly over. I'd love to meet her."

"Yeah." The idea held real appeal. "I'll do that."

"Bring any help you want. Hell, bring me a man with you."

"A man?" He blinked. "You want a man?"

His sister laughed. "I'm not dead, I'm just a mom. You were the one who kept telling me to give up on Suzanna's dad."

"And you should." But dating? His little sister? He got a chill just thinking about it.

Dwayne listened for a few more minutes while Natalie talked about Job Number One, which she hoped would earn her a promotion soon that would cancel out the need for Job Number Two. He shared her hope, then sent his love to both and hung up the phone.

The thought of his baby sis dating had done one thing… he wasn't in a cold sweat from his dream any longer.

# Chapter 16

Dwayne grabbed a PowerBar out of the cabinet and a Gatorade to top it off. Breakfast of champions. What he wouldn't give for Natalie's breakfast right now. Scrambled eggs, some slobbery Cheerios, and a sweet, gummy face smiling at him from across the table.

Wow, where'd that come from? Time to back up. He tore open the wrapper and tossed the foil in the trash while he chewed the bar.

He was enjoying time with Veronica. She was sweet as can be, smart, funny when she let herself be, and now that she was more comfortable with him, things were starting to get red-hot. Though now that he thought about it, maybe he should slow down in that area. She struck him as a female who hadn't had much experience in the bedroom. Maybe a few failed attempts as a teen—as most teenage attempts at lovemaking were dismal failures—and it'd scared her off. Maybe some college Joe Schmo Dickhead bungled her first time, treating her badly. She just needed some more time to ease into it.

But he needed time too. Time to get to know her better. He knew almost nothing of her background, nothing of her life outside their group and work. She didn't like talking about it, or shied away from talking about herself. She was shy, yeah. But eventually they needed to dip into that area.

But there was time for that. Hell, he had another date with her tonight. Dinner, conversation, they'd get it sorted out. He had a feeling things could just hit the right mark with Miss Veronica.

―――――

"Do you want to come in?" Veronica held the door to her apartment open in invitation.

He wanted. He wanted very much. But when his day began by accidentally smashing his alarm clock against the wall, he wasn't at all sure about whether coming in was the best option. He'd kept his date, like the chaplain suggested. Let his time with Veronica soothe away the most ragged edges of his fear and worry. But going in just didn't seem right.

"No, I think—"

"Madison's not home tonight. She's working late, then heading to Jeremy's."

That was so not what he wanted to hear. But a man had only so much strength, and they'd been dating for way longer than he even imagined being able to hold out. So in the end, he had to believe if she thought the time was right, it was.

"Yeah." Decision made, he nodded firmly. "Yeah, I'll come in."

"Good." She shut the door behind him and left her bag on the table by the door. "Do you want something to drink? I know we have water, and Madison sometimes has beer in the fridge. I'm sure she wouldn't mind if you had some."

Dwayne watched as she twined her fingers together, untwined them, played with the zipper of her jacket. She was nervous. Was it from him? Worries about if he was getting better? Or something else?

He stepped up and covered her fingers with one of his hands. "Veronica." He paused until she looked up at him. "We can just sit on the couch and watch a movie if you want. We don't have to do anything."

As the truth of that sank in, he watched the nerves flow out of her eyes, saw them heat with something new. Something entirely more welcome. Anticipation.

"No, I don't think I want to watch a movie. I think I want… "

"What?"

"You." She breathed it, as if afraid someone could overhear her. But her hesitation was short-lived when she reached up on her toes and kissed him. Not one of their sweet, or even sensual, kisses on her front porch or by his truck. One that told him exactly what she wanted, and that she wasn't going to wait any longer.

And if she wasn't going to wait, who was he to try and make her?

She jolted as he gripped her ass with both hands, then melted against him. And when he hefted her up, she didn't waste time in wrapping her legs around him. The position was perfect, his erection lying right against her sex, feeling the heat between both their jeans. God, he was already on fire and they were still fully dressed. If he survived this night, it'd be a miracle. Carrying her back, he paused at the end of the hall until she ripped her mouth away long enough to say, "Left." Then she giggled and said, "No, other left. My left," when he turned the wrong way.

"Right. Right. Got it." Using her back to nudge the

door open, he shut it again with his foot. Sure, they were alone. But who knew if Madison would be coming back early from wherever she was. That thought should have given him pause, should have made him put the brakes on the whole thing until he could take her back to his place, sans roommate. But he couldn't stop now. Not with her little throaty sounds and total abandonment to pleasure in his arms. Not with her squeezing her legs around him, only bringing their pelvises more fully together, increasing that amazing friction.

Oh yeah. He was as likely to walk out the door now as he was to dance naked in Times Square on New Year's Eve.

He toed off his shoes, all while still holding on to her, then let her control drop to the bed. He gave her no time to move, only came down on top and resumed right where they left off.

Kissing had always seemed so seventh grade to him. So unnecessary, now that he knew what else there was to the whole sex thing. But with Veronica, it was like discovering that fun all over again. Maybe because of her enthusiasm, maybe because of her, period. But something was new and bright and exciting with Veronica, every step of the way. And it soothed him even as it excited him.

She ground up into him, panting as she clawed his back to pull his polo from where he tucked it in. "Off. Please."

"Slow down." But he let her pull the shirt up and over his head anyway. The pants, though, those were staying on. He couldn't take any chances and so he was going to keep as many barriers between them for as long as possible. Though her own top seemed a little unnecessary now that his was off. With her hands roaming the skin of his back, sending goose bumps up and down his spine, he lifted her shirt until he found the white, simple cotton bra that held two perfectly proportional breasts. The simplicity of her underwear was more exciting than something designed to rev his blood. And not waiting, he lifted the bottom of the elastic and took one nipple in his mouth.

"Oh my…" She gasped, as if she'd been dunked into a vat of ice-cold water, and arched into him. Not wanting to lose the friction, he ground down with his hips as he circled the tip of her breast with his tongue, flicked the nub, sucked it in deep. And changed his direction with his hips as he moved to her other breast.

"D… something's… oh my…" Her body tensed, she scratched up his back and gripped his shoulders in a surprisingly strong vice, and then he felt her whole body tighten and release with the most shocking orgasm he'd ever witnessed.

Shocking for both of them, it seemed.

He raised his head and looked at her, mouth open. When was the last time a little dry humping had been enough? When he'd brought a woman so close that she'd jumped over the edge of orgasm?

Back in seventh grade, probably.

"Holy shit."

Her eyes fluttered open, almost wild with confusion. But she didn't say a word. Just reached out for him and brought him back to her lips.

"You okay, darlin'?"

"Mmm. More."

Her hands reached for his belt, pushing in on his

lower abdomen, and he had to roll off to get his shit together before he was the second one to lose it with their jeans still on. Christ, she undid him. He needed a breather. But looking back at her, sprawled over her bed with her shirt and bra under her chin, arms and legs limp like a rag doll, he knew the breather wasn't even an option. He reached over to help her remove the shirt and bra, then worked his fingers on the button of her jeans. Kissing her neck, below her ear, her shoulder, he gave her ample opportunity to slow him down, to stop, to say she changed her mind.

She said nothing.

She was a matcher, he discovered. One of those women who matched their panties and their bra together. Normally, he found this was a hint that they would be one of those complicated females. But with her, the entire matching thing seemed to make more sense, like she just did it because it was the thing to do rather than because it mattered a whole lot.

With her pants completely off, he dipped one finger under the band of her panties to find her completely ready for him, no assembly required. She squirmed, twisting her body until her face was smushed into the nearest pillow, though whether that was coincidence or out of bashful instinct, he didn't know. But he wouldn't push. Instead he pulled the underwear down and shucked his own jeans off. Holding back at this point would just lead to more pain than necessary. There was delayed gratification, and then there was masochism.

"Dwayne?" She looked up, and he had a hard time placing the look in her eyes. It wasn't fear, but it wasn't exactly confidence either. He paused in reaching for his wallet in the back pocket of the jeans he'd just dropped.

"Yeah, darlin'?" *Please don't say stop. Please don't say stop.*

She bit her lip, then shook her head, fire overtaking the uncertainty in her eyes. "Nothing."

He froze, waiting for her to take it back, but she didn't. Careful with the rubber, he rolled it on and positioned himself over her. Her face said she was caught in the moment, but her body remained stiff as a board.

What kind of experience had she been through before to freak her out? What jackass had treated her badly before…? He clenched his teeth against the anger and forced it from his mind. For now anyway, his main concern was Veronica.

With soft kisses, he soothed the best he could. Supporting his body on one forearm, he used his other hand to smooth up and down her body, massaging a little. As her muscles relaxed under his touch, he nudged a little into her center. She tightened, and he started the process over again.

Her uptight posture made it all the more tight as he inched in. He gritted his teeth against the amazing pressure, and nudged one of her legs wider with his knee.

"Need just a little more room here, sweetheart." He kissed her, continued kissing her, because he realized she wasn't one to open her eyes during sex. Pity. But she loosened up a little and spread out wider for him, making the rest of his entry easier.

"Oh my…" Her eyes popped open, and it was like looking into a beautiful mist. She wiggled around a little, experimenting with how much range of motion she had. "That's wonderful."

Between the extra slap on the back to his ego and all her wiggling, he wasn't going to last. Not at all. He kissed her again, hoping to distract her from her below-the-belt exploration, and pumped into her. With one hand he slid around her hip and found her clitoris, speeding her along as best he could.

The sound she made deep in her throat would have driven a saint to sin.

"God, forgive me." He wasn't going to be able to wait. Dammit. Praying she wouldn't think he was a total jackass, he followed the rhythm his pounding blood sent him on and pushed into her over and over, still working her with his thumb and forefinger.

But just as he reached the point of no return, she clenched around him. Her mouth opened in a silent "O" and her eyes fluttered closed. She even came quietly, with dignity. No screams or thrashing around wildly for his woman. Just a contented smile that spread over her face and the constant pressure around his cock that told him he was out of the doghouse and could grab his own release without guilt.

And grab he did, until he couldn't keep himself up any longer and collapsed next to her on the bed.

"That was fun." She said it with such wonder.

"It usually is, when you do it right." He immediately cursed himself for being an idiot. Way to make her think she'd been doing something wrong up to now...

But then again, he sort of thought he'd been doing it wrong, too. Nothing he'd ever experienced in the past had come close to what they'd just shared. So maybe it wasn't so much about something wrong, but *someone* wrong. And then finding someone right.

He let that thought wind its way through his mind as Veronica curled up next to him and sighed into his neck like a sweet kitten ready for a nap.

———

Veronica woke to the sound of running water. She opened her eyes and saw nothing but darkness. Though the bed was still warm, Dwayne was gone. She sat up and glanced at her bedroom clock. 3:18 a.m. She breathed a sigh of relief. Still plenty of time left in the night… if he wanted to stay.

Pushing through the bedroom door, he appeared, silhouetted in the hallway light. He flipped it off and crawled back in bed, pulling her to him. She sighed and snuggled closer. This was something she had been missing out on. The idea that she could be intimate with a man, even without sex. The touch, the feel of another body close by. The actual act of making love was truly splendid—even the pain she'd read about had only been more of an uncomfortable pinch, then gone—but this. This was what she had truly craved.

He jostled her just a little as he settled further in the bed. "You know," he said, voice rumbling in the dark, "we really need to do this at my place instead. This twin-sized bed? Not cutting it for my frame."

She softly laughed and realized he was all but hanging off the mattress on all sides. No wonder, with as tall and broad as he was. "Sorry. I didn't think that one through, did I?"

He squeezed her tighter. "No worries." With one

hand, he drew light circles down her arm, going up under her nightshirt—which he'd asked her not to wear but she'd insisted—and down to her wrist. With the other, he twirled a lock of her hair. Almost as an afterthought, he asked, "What made you decide you were ready?"

Did he know? Had it been so obvious she'd been a virgin? She fought to keep her breath even.

A twenty-six-year-old virgin wouldn't exactly be what Dwayne was expecting. Much as she cared for him, she just wanted to have a bit more normal before she could explain her history. So she hedged. "Ready?"

"For us. You know." He squeezed her hip a little. "I knew you weren't the type to hop in the sack at the word go. Not that there's anything wrong," he added quickly when she sucked in a breath. "To be honest, I appreciated that more than you can probably understand. You know, with my issues. Time was a good thing."

She relaxed, let her body melt around his like chocolate to a strawberry. "I think we just both were ready." *Me more than anyone.* "And it felt right. I couldn't ignore that any longer."

He shifted until she was under him, his face hard to make out in the dim light. But the intensity of his look wasn't hard to miss. "I'm really glad to hear that." Burying his face in the crook of her neck, he held her gently, and her heart absorbed the sweetness of the moment. "You have no idea how glad I am."

Because he seemed to need it, she rubbed her fingertips over his back, stopping just before she hit his butt. Unlike her, he had zero issues sleeping in the nude. It seemed almost deliciously wrong, in a good way. But baby steps. Sleeping with a man at all was a massive jump for her. Maybe she'd get used to it.

She prayed she'd have the chance to.

—⁓—

As dawn crept in through the blinds of her room, Dwayne shifted over her. He crooned, his honey-tipped voice smoothing over her still-sleepy senses, waking her up with gentle ease. His hands roamed over her body and she resisted the urge to open her eyes, just letting her skin do the work. She wanted to feel him, smell him, hear him. Imprint the memory of what it was like to have a man like him in her bed—so intimately in her life—so that she wouldn't forget.

And when he nudged one knee aside and high, probing between her legs with his erection, she sighed and cracked one eye to find him grinning over her.

"Morning, sunshine. You're a hard one to wake up." He punctuated the greeting with a kiss on the nose and a short pulse against her wet center.

"Mmm. Someone cut into my sleep time last night. And I'm not an early bird." She glanced at the clock. "It's not even six yet. Give a girl a break."

He pushed in, and though her body resisted a little, it was nothing compared to last night. And she was able to mentally relax enough to let him slide in without pain. Discomfort, a little. But the pain was gone, she was relieved to find out.

"This is definitely a nice way to wake up," he murmured below her ear, nipping his way down her neck to her collarbone. One hand pulled her nightshirt up until he could see her breasts. She managed to resist covering herself, but the automatic flush that took over her skin wasn't something she could control. Luckily it was still dark enough, he probably didn't see.

With one hand massaging one breast, he took the other nipple in his mouth. She moaned, then wanted to bite her tongue. What if Madison was home?

"We're still alone, darlin'. I checked when I hit the head a few minutes ago." He spoke against her skin, lips brushing an intimate caress over her cleavage before settling around her other nipple.

He'd checked to make sure they were alone before starting another round of sex. Though modesty wasn't his thing—clearly—he still cared enough that he knew she would mind. Her heart did somersaults in her chest beneath his touch, as she realized that not every man would care.

But that's why she was comfortable with Dwayne. Because instinctively, she knew he would. He would be the kind of man to make sure her natural modesty was preserved as much as possible.

The slow, leisurely climb to climax was sweeter, more relaxing than before. Not the sweaty race to the finish from the night prior, but more a floating, serene existence that ended as sensually and calmly as the entire thing began. One minute she was feeling the lovely tug at her breast, the next her stomach contracted and spasmed, and she couldn't hold back the pressure that built below until it overflowed, taking Dwayne with her.

She sighed and loved how his weight settled over her a little more fully, yet still not pushing against her too hard. A man his size could suffocate her, but he seemed to know it and was conscious of how he relaxed. And when he pulled away, she regretted the loss of warmth, the delightfulness of the moment, the quiet—

"*Fuck.*"

# Chapter 17

WELL, THAT WASN'T AT ALL SWEET OR QUIET. THAT he cursed so violently in front of her, when she knew he took care to watch his language in front of women, was more disturbing than the word itself. She sat up and concentrated on his shape in the dark room. "What?"

He was silent for a moment, back turned. Then he stood up and walked to the bathroom without a word.

Had she done something wrong? New as she was to the love-making process, she didn't think so. Maybe he'd stepped on something. Their clothes still littered the floor. Or perhaps he'd forgotten a meeting—she glanced at the clock again—at six thirty in the morning…

No, not likely.

Speculation didn't last long as he walked back to the bedroom, one hand on the back of his neck, completely unaware or unbothered by his own nudity. "Sorry for the language." When she said nothing, he sighed and grabbed his jeans from the floor, pulling them on without bothering to look for his boxers. After the jeans were snapped, he sat on the bed and held on to her foot, still under the covers. Massaging her instep, he said, "The condom broke."

The words filtered through her mind. Condom. Broke. She wouldn't pretend to know everything there was to know about sex. But that couldn't be a good thing. It was never good when something broke. Mentally she started flipping through the different facts she remembered from her short online search.

He finally looked at her, and his face was etched with anxiety. Her chest pinched a little in confusion, not sure what the problem was or what he wanted her to say. But he spoke first, saving her the effort. "I hate to ask this, and I feel like an as—a jerk. But are you…" His big hands gestured in some random circle.

Oh. That was helpful.

She stared at him. He looked so uncomfortable, so completely out of his element that she had no idea how to respond. Mostly, though, because she had no idea what he was asking.

He finally sighed, shook his head, and started over. "Are you on birth control?" he managed to ask, the words sounding like he squeezed them out of his throat.

"Oh." Now that was an easy one. She gave him a reassuring smile and crawled over to him, curling into his side. When his arm slid around her and tugged her closer, her heart did another little flip-flop. Being away from him, even for that short amount of time, wasn't any fun. "I am. It's okay."

His breath whooshed out in a relieved gust. "Thank God." He laid back down for a few minutes with her, mumbling something about how he wanted just a few more minutes before he had to leave to get ready for work.

She listened to his heart for a few minutes, thinking back just moments ago. His entire moment of panic made her curious. Was it having a baby outside of marriage that made him so worried? Or just having children with her, or having them at all? Did he even want kids eventually?

And why was she thinking these things so soon? There was no way she should ask something so personal so quickly. Could she? Should she?

He transferred his weight and she rolled back so he could stand. She covered back up with the bedsheet and watched as he dressed, his moves smooth and uninhibited in the dark of the room. Almost as if he had night vision.

"I've got to get to work. But can we meet later tonight?" Dwayne stood over the bed, smiling down at her, his face relaxed once again. All signs of distress or apprehension were completely gone, and he was simply happy Dwayne.

And he wanted to see her again. She resisted the urge to do a little happy dance and nodded. "That'd be nice."

With a kiss on her forehead, he tucked her a little deeper into the bed that still held his warmth from the night. "Good. I'll call you later." And then he was gone. She waited until she heard his truck start up in the quiet morning and the sounds of his engine faded away. Then, knowing she was alone, she got up and did her happy dance, barely containing a little shriek of joy.

She was still a dignified woman, after all.

But a true woman. With a social life, and friends who spoke the same language as her, a job she liked, and a boyfriend.

You could call someone you slept with and were dating a boyfriend, couldn't you?

Well, she was going to. Because it was a massive step in the right direction. She was in a relationship with a guy who she was falling for more each day, who she had a small idea might really care for her back.

At that very moment in time... life was good.

—w—

Dwayne whistled as he walked into the break room to nuke a breakfast burrito. Normally he would have snagged at least a bowl of cereal or another PowerBar at his apartment before coming to work, but he hadn't had the time. He'd wanted to spend every minute that he could in bed with Veronica before leaving.

His mouth curved at the memory of her draped over him. She was so small—though he was rather large in comparison to anyone—but so trusting. Quite a difference from the shy, almost skittish woman he'd met only a few months earlier. In general, she'd changed a lot. Though maybe she was just being more comfortable around him.

And, better still, he hadn't had a single nightmare while sleeping next to her. Maybe his brain was too tired from the exercise to be bothered. But then again, on a more fanciful—and more welcome—level… maybe the chaplain was right. Maybe Veronica was just that good for him. He wanted to be good for her, too. Though he was going to have to be more careful, he thought with a frown. The condom breaking was bad luck. Nobody's fault. And thank God she was on birth control herself. But that wasn't an experience he wanted to repeat. He'd gone through the whole "What's gonna happen?" thing before with undesirable results. He wasn't going to do it again.

The microwave beeped and he grabbed the hot burrito, passing it back and forth between his hands as he walked through the open offices toward his own door. Tossing the nuked breakfast on a paper towel on his desk, he sat down and started his morning routine of checking email.

"What in the good grace are you so fucking happy about?"

"Morning, Jeremy." He clicked another email open, not bothering to look up from his computer screen.

His friend flopped down in the chair across from his desk with dramatic flair. Though he didn't look, Dwayne could easily imagine the sullen look on his face. Jeremy carried the "tortured artist" look off with ease. He sighed, deleted the email, and opened another.

"You were whistling."

"Was I?" *Delete. Open next.* "How rude of me, quietly making a cheerful sound in the relative privacy of my own office."

"Agreed. So really, what's got you in such a good mood?"

He wasn't about to tell him he finally made it with Veronica. No stranger to swapping vague conquests in the past, this time it seemed beyond wrong. Not only because Jeremy would know who he was talking about, but because… it was Veronica. Just different.

Everything seemed different with her.

"You got some ass. Didn't you?"

The comment was meant to raise his hackles, and it did, no question. But Dwayne just punched the mouse with a little more force than necessary to open a reply window and started typing.

"I knew it."

Dwayne gave him the middle finger between sentences. Finally, Jeremy gave up being an ass for attention and leaned forward. "Seriously, man. You're hung up, aren't you?"

Dwayne sighed again, finished the email, and hit send before leaning back in his char to face Jeremy. He looked well rested, though Dwayne wasn't stupid enough to think he'd gotten a full night's sleep if he was spending it with Madison. But now that he was in relationship bliss, suddenly he had to be all Nosy Nelly into everyone else's business.

"Hung up is a little juvenile of a term for it. But yeah. I like her. I care about her. And I want to see how things keep going."

Jeremy leaned back at that and looked thoughtful. For all his annoying tendencies, the guy was a thinker and definitely didn't jump to conclusions easily.

Except with Madison.

"She's not your usual. Not flashy or loud or your female counterpart."

"Female counterpart?"

The corner of his mouth tipped up. "You know… country to the bone."

He couldn't deny that.

Tilting his head, Jeremy studied him with an intensity that made Dwayne itch. "She seems like she fits though."

Dwayne raised a brow at that. "You know, you were so against Skye when she and Tim first got together. I'm a little surprised you aren't in here giving me shit too."

"That was different. Different situation, different people. And you know I love Skye like a sister now. So it's all water under the bridge."

Dwayne chuckled at the ease with which he dismissed

his concerns from a year ago. True, showing up on Tim's doorstep and announcing she was Tim's forgotten wife was not the best introduction to Skye McDermott. But she'd quickly won them over. All of them, including her runaway husband.

"You're just different with her. Like your soul relaxes."

Dwayne squinted at that. "*My soul relaxes*? What the hell kind of mumbo jumbo is that?" Other than the truth, of course. But guys didn't say shit like that out loud. "You writing a book with all these witty remarks there, Dr. Phil? You should stick to the mystery and suspense genres."

Jeremy rolled his shoulders and peered out the tiny office window. "Never mind. Just trying to say that I like her and you together. That's all."

"Well, good. 'Cause it's gonna stay *her and me together* for the foreseeable future." Which sounded like more of a commitment than he'd mentally admitted before. But it was just the plain truth, so why bother sugarcoating it? He wanted her. Now, tomorrow, and he didn't see that changing anytime soon.

And there was nothing wrong with that at all.

---

Veronica propped herself up on her elbows. Her feet were by Dwayne's chest, next to the headboard, where he rubbed her calves and ankles. Exhausted after a long shift at work, he'd come to pick her up and bring her back to his place, promising a foot rub in the bargain.

She would have said yes anyway. But a foot rub, well, that just sealed the deal.

With a sigh, she let her head plop back to the mattress.

"This is probably what heaven is like." Hot man, a foot rub, hopefully making love a little later, and a warm bed to snuggle in after.

Her parents, of course, were currently praying for her immortal soul somewhere in Africa, and didn't even know why. She giggled a little, just thinking about their faces if they knew how their only daughter was spending her time in America.

"Glad you're enjoying yourself. And glad you agreed to come over."

"I was so tired, I never could have made the drive myself." Plus, with Madison and Jeremy holing up in their apartment, she didn't mind the added privacy of Dwayne's apartment with no roommates. But the sweet way he'd offered to come pick her up echoed in her mind. He knew how to take care of a woman he wanted.

A woman he wanted. That was her. What a comforting thought.

What a completely abstract, daunting thought. That she would be worthy of a man like Dwayne's affections. That a man like him would want a woman like her...

No. That was not positive thinking. That was her mother's voice creeping in again, uninvited. She shook away the pessimism and doubt and focused on him.

"So how is school going?"

The question jarred her from the little happy bubble she was rebuilding in her mind. "School?"

"Yeah, you've mentioned you were in school. I meant to ask, what are you studying?"

"Oh, you know. This and that." Her first instinct—to lie—made her stomach ache. She smoothed the bedspread to hide the shake of her hand. So soon, so fragile the thread of their relationship. She didn't want to take a chance of snapping it. Not just yet.

"Well, have you picked a major?"

"Teaching." It was out of her mouth before she could call it back. Eventually, yes, she would love to go to college for her teaching license. Out of all the tasks she was assigned in the missionary camps, working with the children and teaching them English—as best could be managed, thanks to the language barrier—was her favorite.

"Nice. Good, solid career choice. Lots of the guys' wives at the battalion are teachers. Seems like a pretty mobile career."

"Hmm." Her discomfort shifted a little at hearing him mention wives. A mobile career. Mobile, because Marines moved around often. And so would their families. But why was he mentioning it?

*Because you are flying off the deep end, as Madison would say. Stop reading into things.*

"I assume you're still in your core classes then, huh?" When she didn't answer—because she had no clue what core classes were—he added, "If you ever need help, let me know. I can't proof an English paper, as my professors would have told you. I tend to want to add a few y'alls in there every so often, just for spice." She giggled at that. "But I can rock calculus and I'm pretty good with sciences."

"Thanks." She wanted to cry. This was so not how she hoped the night would go. And now she'd accidentally misled him into thinking she was already in the process of earning a teaching license. Time to deflect. "Thank you for coming to get me."

He shrugged one shoulder, as if it was no big deal. "I

wanted to see you, and you were too whipped to make it. I wasn't. Problem solved." He gave her a head-to-toe inspection, then quickly yanked on her leg so that she flew at him, laughing the whole way. Settling her more comfortably over his chest, he pushed her hair back. "I can think of another subject I could always tutor you in."

"Oh?"

His grin was wicked, and sent chills of anticipation running down her spine.

"I always wanted to have a study buddy for sex ed."

---

"It's too easy."

Dwayne paced the floor of the chaplain's office, hands fisting by his side, then crossed over his chest, then back down by his side again.

The chaplain, by comparison, lounged back in his chair with ease, as if the world wasn't tipping on its axis, as if things weren't starting to go ass-backwards.

"You'll need to elaborate, Robertson." With a wry grin, he pointed to the couch with one finger. "And sit down before you wear a hole in my carpet."

He sat, letting his boots thud gracelessly out in front of him on the floor. Stared intently on the dog tag laced in next to the tongue of one boot. If he focused on one spot, then he didn't feel so off balance. Like those tea-cup things at the Disney park. Keep your eyes focused and maintain a semblance of balance.

"Start over. What's too easy?"

"Life. Things." He tossed his hands up in the air. "Her."

"Ah." Like a wise man who just discovered the secret

to life, he gave a secret smile and walked around from behind his desk to the armchair across from the couch. "So it's the woman."

"Yes. Maybe. I don't know." Dwayne squeezed the back of his neck to relieve the tension. "I keep expecting more episodes. I'm on guard for them. But nothing's happening. The nightmares are slowing down, only mild when they even happen. I haven't spazzed recently or scared the shit out of anyone."

"And this is a bad thing?"

"Yes!" He jumped up only to sit back down again when he got the stink eye. "It's exhausting, always being on guard. Always waiting. Staying vigilant."

The chaplain nodded, but stayed silent.

"Okay yeah, and it's her too. Veronica." Just saying her name brought a sense of calm to his heart rate. It slowed, coming closer to a more normal beat. "It's just... smooth sailing. Nothing wrong. She's easy-going, she's sweet. She just sort of slipped into my life at the right time, giving me exactly what I need. Helping me..."

No, that was stupid.

"Helping you what?"

Well, confidentiality and all that. "Helping me heal," he mumbled.

"Sounds pretty well like a good deal to me. What's the problem?"

Dwayne stared at the man. Had he been talking to air the last ten minutes? "It's too good."

The chaplain tossed the pen he'd been holding onto his desk and stretched his back. "The whole 'too good to be true' theory at work, am I right?"

"There's truth to the theory."

"So who burned you before?"

Dwayne's mood, so light from just thinking of Veronica, darkened. "Doesn't matter."

"Sure it does. Clearly. Otherwise, the baggage wouldn't be sniffing around for a fault in the relationship like a bloodhound on the trail. Something has told you in the past that good is never right. Who."

It wasn't a question. Dwayne could kiss lunch goodbye. He wouldn't be going anywhere. Settling down in the couch cushions, he got comfortable. "Blair. Her name was Blair."

Silence.

"She and I dated while I was stationed in North Carolina. She hung out at the same sports bar I did."

Glancing up to see if he was about to get off the hook, he wasn't surprised when the chaplain sat with stoic patience, waiting for him to continue. With a sigh, he did.

"We dated, we got serious. I was getting closer to a PCS, and I didn't know how the relationship would hold up over long distance. I didn't know where I was headed yet, but I knew I'd be moving out of the area, likely to California." He spread his hands in a *and here I am* gesture. "But I wasn't anywhere near ready to ask her to move with me across the country. Not when her entire family lived on the east coast. And so I started to resign myself to losing a good relationship, mostly due to timing."

"But?"

Damn the perceptive man. Wait, was that some extra sin, damning a man of God? He'd look it up later. "Then she found out she was pregnant."

# Chapter 18

HE SCOFFED. "A BABY HAS A WAY OF TIGHTENING THINGS up pretty damn fast. Went out and got a ring the next day."

"It didn't occur to you to wait? People have children out of wedlock often these days."

Dwayne looked up, surprised to hear the chaplain's thoughts. He smiled and spread his hands. "It might not be God's favorite thing, but it doesn't make it less than the truth. I might be a man of the Word... doesn't make me blind to the way things work."

Nice. A chaplain with an understanding. Nevertheless, Dwayne shook his head. "Not for me. My mom raised me alone, no dad in sight. I couldn't tell you his last name. Never even listed on the birth certificate."

"You don't have to be married to claim responsibility."

"I was going to. We were serious, and at the time the only thing stopping us from continuing on was the distance. Once I would be transferred to a new base—"

"Inevitable," the chaplain put in.

"It is. And then I could be across the country from her. But with a baby on the way, marriage was the right thing to do. I wanted to be with that kid. Every night that I could." He stared hard at the chaplain. "We're gone enough as it is in this business. When my boots are on U.S. soil, I want to tuck my kids in at night."

"Commendable." He waved a hand as a sort of white flag. "Continue."

"We were both happy. Excited even. Her mom started planning a small wedding for the next month. And I knew I could easily spend the rest of my life with her, our baby, any other kids that came along. Setting up a good life. Then I surprised her one day, took the day off work to bring her to the doctor for one of those monthly checkups."

He shook his head and stared at the purple-gray carpet between his boots. "Take her to the doctor," he said more softly, scoffing. "She didn't have an appointment that day. Or any other day. She wasn't pregnant. Never had been. Oh, first she tried to play it off, layering lie after lie, trying to make me think she'd lost the baby and was scared to tell me and she didn't want to ruin the wedding with the news. When that didn't hold water, she tried that she'd only been confused, truly thought she was pregnant, but she was wrong. And how sad that made her, that she wanted to try again for a baby, soon as we were married."

"Did you believe her?"

"I wanted to. Christ, I wanted to." He gripped his temples with his thumb and forefinger, squeezed his eyes shut. "But slow country boy that I am, even I knew that nothing added up. She finally gave up, got tired keeping track of the lie, admitted it all."

Nothing but the quiet hum of the ceiling fan greeted him.

"She saw the writing on the wall. Knew I'd leave and we'd drift apart and that'd be the end. Coming from less than nothing, from a trailer park in the middle of nowhere with barely a high school diploma to her name, I was a catch. I was security. Wanted to shore up a nice guy with a steady paycheck and good health insurance. I'm guessing the fact that I'd regularly be out of the country for seven months of the year was pretty attractive too. I could have been any dumbass in cammies. Didn't matter who I was. I was just the lucky SOB that she ran into first."

"That's a little harsh on yourself, don't you think?"

"No, I don't. I should have seen it coming. It was right there in my face the whole time, and I was blind to it. The only good thing that happened was there was never a kid involved. She could have gone all the way and actually gotten pregnant, though I'm not sure how. I'm just glad it was a hoax rather than the real deal."

The chaplain said nothing, and Dwayne felt too empty to go on. There was nothing left. He'd spilled it all out, laid it at the other man's feet. The embarrassment, the shame, the absolute terror of not being sure he could trust his own judgment again.

"And so, because of this Blair, you think Veronica is the same?"

"Veronica is nothing like her." The words were too fierce, even he knew it from some impartial part of his own brain. More calmly, he added, "It's not her. It's me. I just need to figure out why my brain can't let go. Can't accept that things aren't always just waiting to fall apart. That the other boot isn't always hovering, waiting to drop."

"What would happen?"

He stared at the man, eyes gritty now from squeezing them too tight.

The chaplain stood and started back around his desk to sit. "What would happen if the other shoe does drop?

Maybe you relapse and have another panic episode. Or Veronica turns out to be not the right woman for you, for any number of reasons. Then what?"

Dwayne flopped back once more and stared at the ceiling. "Then, I dunno. I deal with it."

"Can you? Are you able to handle that load?"

"Yeah." He said it with confidence, even arrogance, before he could think. But it was true. He wasn't some pissant weakling who waited around for things to go ass up. If shit hit the fan, he'd weather it and push through as hard and as fast as he could. It's what he would do in his job, and it's what he would do in life.

The chaplain smiled at him, almost like a proud teacher to the star pupil. Proud as can be. "I thought so." And with that, he picked up his pen and started writing, as if Dwayne wasn't still sitting on his couch, having an internal crisis.

But there was no crisis. It was all a reaction to the situation that he needed to get a grip on. The chaplain was right. No matter what, it wouldn't be the end of the world.

As he shut the office door behind him on the way out, he wondered if he'd earned a gold star for the day.

---

Madison flopped down in the armchair in Skye and Tim's living room. "That was absolutely unnecessary, not to mention awful."

Having had a rare day off together, Veronica had come over to hang out and wait for Madison to end her shift in the ER.

"What was unnecessary?" Skye asked from the ground, her feet propped up on the arm of the sofa.

"That entire rotation in the ER. Thank God today was my last day. I have to say, emergency medicine was never my thing." She visibly shuddered and threw an arm over her eyes. "Too much drama."

"Too much drama in the trauma… unit?" Veronica said, deadpan. Then when both women stared at her, she laughed. "Okay, that was bad."

"Very," Skye agreed. "But yay for finishing a bad rotation! We should celebrate, if you're up to it."

"Anything celebrating the fact that I won't have to see the inside of the ER for a few months is worth losing sleep over. Plus I've got three days straight off, so I'm good to go."

They laid around for a minute, enjoying the simple pleasure of company and letting the air conditioning cool them on the hot afternoon.

"Dwayne?"

Veronica tilted her head to look at her cousin. "What about Dwayne?"

"How are things going with him?" Skye asked, her tone implying that it should have been obvious, so why did she have to spell it out.

"Ah." She let her head fall back to the cushion. How to answer that one…"Things are going… well."

"Since you barely sleep at home anymore, I think things are going better than well," Madison teased.

Veronica threw a pillow at her. "I'm sorry, I thought you enjoyed the privacy with Jeremy. If you want, we can go back to me sleeping at the apartment and you bunking at his place. What was it you referred to his apartment as again? The gateway to hell?"

Madison shuddered and stuffed the pillow under her

legs. "I apologize. Really, sincerely. Don't kick me out. I can't sleep over there."

"Back to the topic. So you two are…" Skye waved a hand in the air.

"What she means to say is, so you two are doing the humpty-hump?"

"Madison!" Veronica covered her mouth with her hand, trying to muffle the laughter. "What a lovely image."

"You're telling me," Madison agreed. "So?"

"We enjoy spending time together." There. That was as close as they were going to get.

"Riiight. I'm assuming a good chunk of that time is horizontal."

"Madison."

"Just saying. I love him like a brother, but I'm not oblivious to the charm and attractiveness of Dwayne Robertson."

Skye sat up and gave her a good long look. "Are you happy?"

"Oh, yes." That didn't require any thought at all. Her life was right where she'd always hoped it would be, and where she'd thought for so long she'd never get to.

"Hmm. Well, this is lovely and mushy and all, but back to me." Madison tossed the pillow back at her and she let it hit her chest before wrapping an arm around it. "How will we celebrate this lovely occasion of me being out of the ER?"

They were silent for a moment, the only sound a lawnmower a few houses down.

"Shopping?" Skye asked, almost hopefully.

More silence, then Madison said, "I could go for that."

Veronica bit her lip. Buying more things wasn't

really an option. But the thought of spending the day with her friends, that was more appealing. "There's an outlet mall about an hour north of here. Maybe since we all have the whole day off, we could—"

"Sold!" Skye jumped up and pumped her fist in the air. Pointing a finger at Madison, she said, "You go change out of those scrubs, meet us back here at oh-whatever-hundred."

Madison laughed. "A year with my brother and you still don't know military time?"

"I'm *incorrigible*," Skye said back, in an almost dead-on imitation of Tim.

"That's so my brother. Okay, I'll run home and change. And then we can head out. But first we have to stop and grab me something to eat. I'm starving."

"They have a huge food court," Veronica offered.

"Fantastic. Cheap shopping and some junk food on top. Perfect girls' day out." Madison headed for the front door. "Let's get this show on the road!"

―∿∿―

Dwayne flipped from ESPN to ESPN2 to catch the second half of the next game.

"You didn't TiVo it? Damn, man, we can't watch the first half now."

He tossed Jeremy a disgusted look. "I didn't realize I was going to have company tonight, so you'll have to forgive me for not taking your wishes into account."

"All is forgiven." After a long pull of his beer, he set the empty on the coffee table and resettled in the armchair. "I'm surprised you're not with your lady love tonight. You guys have been almost inseparable for the last two months."

"Lady love? Christ, Jeremy, who talks like that?" Dwayne rubbed the heel of his hand against his chest. "She's just hanging with Skye and Madison, as you well know. Don't give me that look. I know you check in with Madison when you're not together like an old married couple. You wanna pretend you're not whipped like Tim, but you got it just as bad."

"And you don't?" Jeremy shot back.

Dwayne shrugged. "Maybe I do. I don't seem to have the same problem with it as you do." Whipped? Nah. Not really. But he did like knowing what Veronica was up to. Was that a crime? Nope. Just considerate. Yeah, considerate. Not whipped. That was stupid.

As the whistle blew on a play, someone knocked at the door.

"You order food?" he asked Jeremy, who shook his head in response.

He frowned and went to the door, expecting to not answer when he checked the peephole. But his frown morphed into a wide grin when he saw Veronica standing on his doorstep.

"Hey. What are you doing here?" He pulled her into a hug before she could answer. Her arms wrapped around his torso like she was trying to keep her balance, burying her face in his chest.

Taking a few steps back, taking her along with him, he shut the door.

"You have company," she said, voice muffled in his shirt.

"It's just Jeremy."

"Love you too, bro. Hey, Veronica."

"Hi."

She was soft-spoken by nature, but even so, her voice sounded much less steady than it should have. He rubbed a hand down her back. "You okay?"

She tilted her head to look him in the eye, and he could see the paleness of her skin, the slight flush that had nothing to do with pleasure.

"Hey, you feeling all right?" Automatically, his hand went to her forehead. What he was feeling, he didn't know, but her skin felt cold to the touch, slightly damp with perspiration.

"I was fine, but a few minutes ago, just before I turned into the parking lot, my…" She drifted off, then peeked around his arm to see if Jeremy was still listening.

Without looking behind him, Dwayne said, "Jeremy, we'll be right back." He guided her to the kitchen and propped her up on one of his barstools. "Okay, talk."

She spread a hand over her stomach. "I just don't feel great, that's all. I'm sure it'll be fine." But the glassy look in her eyes, the odd tint to her skin said otherwise.

"You sure you don't want me to run you over to a doc-in-the-box? There's one a few blocks down."

She shook her head, then let it drop to the counter as if she regretted the movement immediately. "No. Please no. Just let me stay here until the room stops moving."

Okay. What the hell was wrong? It was starting to freak him out. Hundreds of illnesses, diseases, and ailments started running through his head, most of which likely weren't even connected to an upset stomach. Pulling back on his imagination, he tried for something more helpful. "I've got some antacids; think those would help?"

As if just the mention of putting something in her stomach hurt, she groaned. Then, without warning, she slid off the stool with all the grace and elegance of a wounded animal and ran toward his bathroom, bumping her shoulder into the wall along the way. The door shut behind her with a snap, and he winced as he heard the unmistakable sound of retching.

She could be coming down with a summer bug, he reasoned with himself as he got a washcloth from the hall closet and dampened it with cold water at the kitchen sink. Or maybe she could be…

Pregnant.

No. No, not a chance. He wrung the washcloth out with a little more force than necessary, caught himself, and started the process over again with steadier hands.

He wore protection, always. And he… shit.

The first night the condom split.

But no. She said she was on birth control. It would be fine. It had to be. She told him it was fine.

He wanted to believe her.

Clearing his thoughts, he knocked on the door and opened it just a crack. "You okay, darlin'?"

"Does it sound like I'm okay?" It was the closest she'd ever gotten to being peevish with him, and he found the whole thing making him smile for some stupid reason.

"Here's a washcloth." He held the cloth out with two fingers, not daring to open the door further to look at her. If he knew women—and he thought he did—she wouldn't take kindly to his walking right in on her in such a vulnerable state. When the cloth was jerked out of his hands, he smiled.

"Thank you," came the reluctant reply.

He wanted to ask. It was on the tip of his tongue to demand she tell him.

*Are you pregnant?*

A jingle sound came from the living room that didn't belong to the TV.

"That's my phone," she croaked. "Can you see if it's Madison? And tell her I don't feel well so I won't be back home for a while?"

*You won't be back home at all. Not tonight anyway, if I have anything to say about it.* He headed back to the kitchen where she'd dropped her bag, searched through it for a moment, checked caller ID, and flipped it open.

"Hey, Mad."

"Dwayne?" The voice on the other end sounded vaguely like Madison, but more like a version of Madison that had been drawn and quartered, then run over by a herd of cattle.

"Yeah, Veronica's... busy. She asked me to answer her phone."

There was a pause, then a sigh. "So she got to your place okay?"

"She's not feeling too hot," he admitted.

"Well, that confirms it." A clank, a bang, and a groan followed.

"Confirms what? Mad, are you okay?"

From the corner of his eye, Dwayne could see Jeremy sit up straighter in his recliner. Then lean forward, but toward the TV, as if that was his main focus.

Right.

"Food poisoning. I just got off the phone with Skye. She's sick too. If Veronica's miserable, that's three for three." She moaned, and he heard something flop, like maybe she fell into bed. "Stupid food court burritos."

"Food poisoning." Not pregnancy. Never had the idea of bad Mexican burritos ever had him so relieved.

When he heard a groan in his ear, he snapped back to the moment. "Madison, do you need something? Can we bring you anything? Jeremy's here; I can send him with—"

"No," she croaked. "Don't worry about me. I just wanted to make sure Veronica got there okay and wasn't keeled over somewhere on the road. Can you watch over her?"

"Of course." He wanted to ask. *But who will watch over you?* when he saw Jeremy tossing his empty can in the trash and grabbing his keys from the coffee table.

Well, that answered that one. Madison may not like it, but he felt a hell of a lot better about it if someone was with her for the next few hours. "Call me if you need anything. You know I'll come get you."

"I know. But thanks." She clicked off without saying good-bye, in true Madison fashion.

He shut Veronica's phone and set it on the kitchen counter, watching Jeremy and fighting a smile.

Jeremy shoved his hands in his pockets and looked uncomfortable.

Amused, Dwayne asked, "Going somewhere?"

He shrugged, took his hands out of his pockets, then replaced them immediately. "Yeah, well, you've got Veronica here so…"

"Yeah." He smiled then. "Drive safe."

After Jeremy left, he listened for the sound of his motorcycle starting, then fading out. Then he headed back to the bathroom where his girlfriend was draped over the small tile floor.

"Darlin', you doing better?"

She mumbled something into the ground, and he felt a moment of panic. When was the last time he cleaned his bathroom? Okay. The weekend. That wasn't too bad. Having a female over regularly had kept him on his toes with cleaning.

He sat down, back supported by the door frame, and scratched her back lightly with the tips of his fingers. She sighed and turned one cheek to the floor so she could squint at him.

"That feels good. Please never stop."

"You got it." The moment stretched, both quietly sitting on the bathroom floor, his fingers drawing patterns over her shirt, which was quickly cooling from the perspiration she'd been coated with. The fabric still stuck to her back like a second skin, though.

"You wanna change out of those clothes and into a pair of my sweats?"

Looking a little stronger, she propped her cheek on her forearms and looked at him. "You sure you want to risk your clothing?"

"To make you more comfortable? No risk at all."

She gave him a beatific—if a little weak—smile. "Then yes, I'd love… a change of clothes."

His heart tightened and did a slow roll as he stood. Why? She asked for sweatpants. That shouldn't freak him out so much. What made his body react so…

Love. For a second, he thought she was going to say she loved him, even if it was just for his sweats. He shut his fingers in his dresser drawer and bit back a curse. How did that feel? Was the way his heart pitched and tumbled in his chest a good sign, or a bad one?

Things were good. Great. But was he ready to step out and make that next leap of faith into love?

He stood in the hallway, watching as she pushed up off the floor and sat back against the bathtub. Her skin was sheet white, her eyes had dark circles, and her bottom lip looked almost bruised from biting it. Her hair stuck up in some crazy nest on one side, flat and damp on the other. She was, in total, a complete mess.

But she was his mess. And he wanted nothing more than to take care of her at that moment.

Maybe that was love. Maybe it took a bad burrito to kick him over the edge. But for right now, he'd just enjoy the feeling without a label. Labels could come later.

# Chapter 19

JEREMY RODE INTO MADISON'S APARTMENT COMPLEX, guns blazing. Or, rather, temper blazing.

She'd called Veronica, but not him. He understood why she'd called her roommate first. Driving down the road while you were sick was no joke, and he didn't begrudge that one. But her second call should have been to him. But there was no second call. And he'd immediately heard her shoot down Dwayne's suggestion to send him over to help.

Why? Why didn't she want him here? She was sick, and she needed help. That's what people did for each other when they were in love.

But she didn't want him there. Yet here he was, standing on her doorstep like an idiot. Other than being a complete fool, of course.

He gave himself to the count of five to either knock or leave. One or the other. By the time he hit ten, he knew he wasn't leaving. It took until fifteen before he actually raised his fist and rapped on the door.

Silence. He was positive she was there, since her car was in the parking lot. But he didn't hear a word. Not a sound, not a creeping by the door as if she'd checked the peephole and decided not to answer. Nada.

"Madison?"

Now she'd have to acknowledge him.

As the silence stretched out, he thought *or maybe not*.

Starting to worry—Veronica seemed like death warmed over, and Madison seemed to be the same—he felt zero remorse reaching for his spare key she'd given him. Though he didn't use it often, preferring to knock in case Veronica was in there and he startled her, he used it occasionally when she asked him to. But first, he tried the doorknob. And when it twisted easily, he sneered and walked into the apartment, closing the door behind him.

"Madison, it's me. Your front door was unlocked. And by the way, that's a great way to get yourself robbed and killed."

Nothing. Not a curse, not a flying vase, not even a weak insult.

Okay, now he was officially scared.

Creeping in slowly, he cleared the living room and kitchen first. No Madison, but he did see what looked like the beginnings of homemade soup scattered. A chunk of ham waited to be chopped by the butcher knife lying next to it on the carving board. A recipe book was tilted open. A large, empty pot sat on one of the back burners, luckily still turned to off.

"Mad. Where are you?"

He headed for the one place he prayed she wasn't in, but found her anyway.

Sprawled in the empty bathtub, she looked like a drunk still sleeping off a night of pure booze-soaked debauchery. Or a woman on the wrong end of a bachelorette party. Head lolled at an uncomfortable angle, one arm draped out of the tub in a position that she'd regret later, both legs curled into her chest, as if trying to make the pain go away, fresh tear tracks damp over her cheeks, still spiking her eyelashes that rested against the thin skin under her eyes...

The entire thing broke his heart.

He crouched down and placed her arm back in the tub, knowing otherwise she would wake up to the pins-and-needles feeling. Rubbing up and down her arm, bare thanks to her now-sweaty tank top, he waited to see her reaction.

She was so still, he stared at her chest to make sure she was still breathing. But the rise and fall, deep and steady, told him everything was fine. She just needed the sleep.

She would hate him for it later, but he couldn't just leave her in the bathtub. No matter how independent she wanted to be. Carefully, as smooth as possible, he got a grip under her and lifted her in his arms. She barely moved, just shifted almost imperceptibly in his arms until she curled towards his chest.

He carried her to her bedroom, picking his way through the minefield of scrub tops and bottoms, socks, and a pair of flip-flops littering the floor. God, she was worse than Skye. Her bed, still unmade, just provided an easy place for him to deposit his cargo.

She settled into the mattress with a murmur of nonsense. He covered her up, then debated it. She looked hot, but cold at the same time. Like she'd been sweating, and the sweat cooled over her skin so now she was clammy. Did that mean she should stay cool? Or warm? Shit, he wasn't the nurse, she was. But it was food poisoning, not the plague, so he took his chances and covered her up. A little wispy sigh of relief escaped her lips, and she turned on her side, facing him.

He brushed the hair that clung to her face back behind

her ear. Glancing around, he grabbed the wastebasket and placed it by the bed, just in case. But it looked like maybe she weathered the worst of it. Because he couldn't resist, he sat on the edge of the bed and rubbed her arm through the covers.

Madison cracked one eye open. "Hey."

"Hey, pukey."

She smiled, though it was a small one. "Didn't anyone tell you name-calling is a horrible way to get girls to like you?"

"I only need one girl to like me. And she's stuck with me already." He brushed her hair back from her neck. "Why didn't you call, baby?"

"I can take care of myself," the stubborn ass said. "I don't need you running to rescue me."

"I didn't run, I drove my bike." When she didn't laugh, he sighed. "I want to be here when you're sick. I want to know. I want to help."

"It's food poisoning. I'm fine."

"So then tell me that. I never would have known if Veronica hadn't shown up at Dwayne's place."

"You would have made your way here eventually."

"Maybe. Or maybe I would have given you your space for the night and missed out on all the fun."

"Lucky you," she moaned and turned her face into the pillow.

He rubbed circles over her back some more, waiting until her muscles relaxed and the wave of pain passed. "Maybe we should just move in together. Then I'd always know if you're sick."

He said it as a joke, but after it was out, he knew it was exactly what he wanted.

She said nothing, and he thought maybe she'd fallen asleep. Which was just as well, since he didn't want it hanging over his head that he'd asked her to move in together while she was—

"Did you say what I think you said?" Madison's voice was muffled by the pillow, but still clear.

"Uh… yeah."

"Nice timing, champ." She raised her face from the pillow, and he held back a smile at the pink crease down one cheek. "I'm near death's door and you're asking to move in here." She frowned. "What about Veronica?"

"So we move into my—"

"If you even think about suggesting we move into that apartment better known as the gateway to hell, I will hit you."

"Weak as you are, that couldn't be too bad."

"Don't tempt."

She looked ready to try it, so he shushed her and helped her rotate onto her side in a more comfortable position. Then he crawled in behind her and pulled her back against his chest. "Sleep now. We'll talk about it more later."

"Love you."

"Love you too, pukey."

---

Veronica sat up slowly, her head pounding. A bright light shone through her eyelids, but she didn't want to crack them open, too scared of what she'd end up seeing.

*Is this the light that I'm supposed to walk into? Have I died? Because my body sure feels like it took a big enough beating.*

She let her senses return one by one. Body aching, beaten, battered. Moving her arm an inch felt like it took forever. But she brushed up against something warm. She could smell Dwayne, his aftershave, the detergent he used on his bedsheets. The whirl of a ceiling fan and the quiet sound of crickets outside.

And taste, well, she wasn't going to there just yet.

Taking a chance, she cracked one eye to see that yes, she was indeed in Dwayne's bedroom. But how had she gotten there? Last thing she remembered was driving down the road, changing stations, and suddenly feeling like her head was a little fuzzy, like her body was being taken over. And now here she was.

"Hey. You're awake." The mattress dipped and Dwayne slipped into her line of vision, blocking out the light from the lamp. "How you feeling?"

She opened her mouth to answer, but she croaked like a frog instead. Attractive. When she started to try again, he shook his head and touched a finger to her lips. "I'll get a bottle of water. Just sit tight."

It even hurt when the bed jostled as he jumped up. No, she wasn't going anywhere. With slow, pained motions, she gripped the covers and drew them over her head.

No more. No more.

But all too soon, he returned and helped her shift to sitting up, despite her croaky protests.

"You need some water. Soothe that throat of yours, and rehydrate. They always say getting sick depletes the body of water."

After another few sips, she felt the cotton clear from her mouth and was ready to try talking. "How did I get in here?"

"You don't remember?" She shook her head. "You walked in the front door and barely said a word before you headed right to the bathroom to get sick."

Yup. It was all coming back to her. And she almost preferred the memory loss to the knowledge that she'd vomited in front of her boyfriend. How sweet.

"You were a little too tired to get up, so I brought you in here."

"That's nice." Feeling her head swim a little, she leaned back, then realized she shouldn't. "Help me up."

Dwayne eyed her skeptically. "You sure you should move?"

"Seriously. Now." She spoke through clenched teeth, feeling the telltale tightening in her jaw.

He gave her a hand and she maneuvered as cautiously as possible out of his big bed and shuffled to the bathroom. Dwayne hot on her heels, she managed to gently close the door in his face before he could follow her all the way in.

"Veronica, come on. Let me help."

"Go away." She hunched, knowing he was about to hear her get sick and there was nothing she could do about it. Humiliating didn't begin to describe it.

"But I—"

"I'm begging you. Go to the living room. Turn on the TV. Turn up the music. Something. Whatever."

She waited, and a few moments later heard what sounded like a football game on TV, before she couldn't hold back any longer and dropped her dignity to relieve her stomach.

Twenty minutes later, she all but crawled from the bathroom to the kitchen for another bottle of water.

She'd rinsed her mouth out, swished with mouthwash, but she still felt more than a little gross.

Dwayne appeared at her side, as if by magic. "Let me help. Go sit down."

"I just want a bottle of water." She grasped the fridge handle and tugged, but nothing happened.

"Let me."

"I can do it myself." Another tug, and the thing didn't budge. "What did you do—have this reinforced with steel since yesterday?"

"Yup, you're on to me. Now go sit on the couch."

Giving up the good fight, she walked to the couch and gingerly sat. A minute later Dwayne came in with a bottle of water and some antacids.

"I don't have anything for upset stomachs, but this might help. I could go run out and grab some of that liquid stuff, the pink junk. It's supposed to be good for this." He ran a hand over his hair, looking frustrated that he couldn't offer more, which was silly since he already gave her way more than she needed.

"These will be fine. Thanks." After she chewed the chalklike tablets and washed them down with blessedly cool water, he sat next to her and patted his thigh.

"Rest your head."

It was too tempting an offer to refuse, so she did. And sighed with lazy contentment when his fingers started playing with her hair. The sweet pressure on her scalp lulled her, and she dozed on and off in front of the TV, which he'd turned down low now that it wasn't masking anything. At one point, while she listened to him muttering whispered curses at the referees, she wondered how she'd even begun to be embarrassed about feeling ill around Dwayne. He was the ultimate protector. One sick woman wasn't going to throw him off his stride, as seen by how easily he comforted her.

When she knew the next wave of nausea passed, she wanted the bed again. But he didn't let her struggle, no. One word from her and he swept her up in his arms to carry her back to bed, where he tucked her in so carefully tears stung the backs of her eyes. Then, gracefully for a man of his size, he climbed in beside her and gave her a chance to settle in his nook, her head on his shoulder.

Just before she drifted off, she made sure to thank him again for looking out for her.

He pressed a kiss to her forehead. "I always want to take care of you."

That sweet confession eased her into sleep.

———✦———

Veronica waved a hand as Madison closed the front door. "I'm over here."

Rounding the couch, Madison stuck her hands on her hips and looked down at her sprawled across the couch. "This looks like a productive day."

Staring up with one eye, Veronica was half-tempted to imitate one of the rude gestures Madison used and flip her off. But she wasn't that far gone. So she just pushed up and half-lounged across the cushion. "I still feel awful. Why are you so chipper?"

Madison dropped her hands and sat on the floor by the coffee table. "It was your burrito. Skye and I just had a few bites. You're the one who insisted that taking on the challenge of a burrito as big as your head must be a good idea."

"Bad idea," Veronica moaned as she flopped back down and covered her face. "Bad, bad idea."

"And now you pay the price. Skye's not great, but she mostly has a headache. Likely dehydrated, and that'll fix itself over the next few days. But you, well…" With regret in her voice, Madison added, "You'll probably recoup soon. I'm sure."

"Uh-huh." No effort for sarcasm, she dropped her hands. "I had to call in sick. I've never called in sick before." And she couldn't afford to do it again.

"Good thing, since you serve food all day. Frankly, I wouldn't want someone who looks as sick as you do passing me a bowl of pasta." And when Veronica stuck her tongue out, she added more gently, "The smell of all that rich food wouldn't have made you feel much better either. So it's best you took the day off. Food poisoning isn't a huge deal. You'll be back to normal in no time."

Scooting closer, Madison did what Veronica mentally thought of as *the nurse thing* and scooped her hair back to feel her forehead with one hand, checking her pulse with the other. The move was so practiced, so efficient, if she hadn't been overly sensitive already, she might not have even noticed.

"Have you been drinking lots of water?"

She shook her head, then regretted it. "I try, but it doesn't always hit my stomach well. Dwayne's bringing me some sports drinks. Said the electrolytes will help my body recover faster. And something about how it might stay down better than water."

"Good old simple country boy's got the right idea."

"He's not a simple country boy," she snapped, the words sounding too sharp even to her own ears.

Madison didn't miss the tone, either. Her lips tilted in an amused look. "Defensive of our man Dwayne, aren't we?"

She shifted and twisted until her back was facing her friend and spoke into the couch cushions. "I just don't like people calling him that. He's so smart." *Way smarter than me.*

Madison rubbed a hand over Veronica's back, like a mother soothing a child. "Yes, he is. He's a good guy, one of the few men I'd say I loved. He's another brother to me. And I like the look of you two together."

With a last scratch on her back, she stood and shook out her scrub pants that had bunched. "If you're good here, I'm gonna take a hot shower and then crawl in bed. I didn't get hit nearly as hard as you did, but I'm still wiped out." She headed down the hall, calling, "Drink some more water!" before shutting the bathroom door behind her.

～w～

Veronica knocked on Skye's office door and poked her head in. "Hey, I'm here today."

Skye rolled back in her chair and crossed her hands over her middle. "Are you sure you're up for a full shift?"

She stepped fully into the office and shut the door behind her. "Yup. No problems. A little tired still, but Madison and Dwayne are pushing liquids at me every time I turn around so I think I avoided a dehydration headache."

Skye grimaced. "Lucky you. I felt awful the next day, even though my stomach had settled."

"Sorry about that. I mean, it was my burrito and all."

Her cousin grinned. "You can't order a burrito as big as your head and—"

"And expect to walk away unscathed. Yeah, yeah. Madison gave me the schpeal already." When Skye gave her a funny look, she held up her hands. "What?"

"Your attitude. It's so… sassy. I like it." With a grin she stood up and shooed her toward the door. "Now, off to work, sassy pants."

*Sassy pants.* Hmm. She kind of liked that. With a grin she headed to the server alley and clocked in with her time card. Sitting down to roll silverware, she avoided contact when Stephanie walked in. But there was no hope when she sat down and grabbed another stack of silverware to help her roll. Much as she'd love to ignore the woman, it wasn't in her DNA.

"Thanks for the help," she said as quickly as possible. There. Duty done. No need for any more conversation after—

"So how are things with your lover boy?"

So much for no conversation. She tried to conjure up some sass, but it wasn't coming. So she sighed and set her roll down, picking up the fixings for another. "Dwayne is just fine, thank you."

Steph bumped shoulders. "No, I mean between the two of you. It's been, what, couple of months now you've been dating? And you're still together? Definitely beat the odds."

"What odds?" she asked, a little louder than necessary. She flushed immediately when people around them stopped working and stared. "Sorry," she whispered and looked back to Steph. If she had it in her to claw the satisfied grin off her face, she would have.

Wow, she was developing a little bit of a mean streak. Sass was one thing. Time to tone down the attitude.

She polished the set of silverware in front of her, and asked again, with cool calm, "What odds?"

"Uh-huh. Let's just say that it's a miracle you two are still together."

*Walk away now. Walk away now.*

"Why is that?"

*That's not walking away.*

The smile turned just a little hard, a little smug as she placed another sloppily-done roll in the bin. "Men like that—the ones who are all walking sex and cool confidence—they don't go for little church mice like you. The ones who don't have anything to give them beyond a sweet peck on the doorstep. They need someone to keep their attention." She paused, an obvious, calculated move. "In the bedroom, I mean."

It was easier now to ignore her. The jealousy made it impossible to take her seriously. She would not fight fire with fire. Or, in this case, fight crude with crude.

"Right. Thank you for enlightening me. I suppose should things ever start to crumble, I'll know why." Adopting her best serene expression, she picked up the bin of rolled silverware—knowing she'd have to redo all the ones *she* had done—and walked away before she could add another unwelcome comment.

There. That wasn't so hard. So what if one jealous server thinks they're doomed? It doesn't mean a thing.

*Men who get the milk for free never buy the cow. A man who wants sex will want nothing else.*

*Oh, shut up, Mother.*

Slamming the container of silverware down, she covered her eyes with one hand. She was officially crazy. The food poisoning had seeped into her brain, and she was carrying on a mental conversation with herself. Even better, an argument. As if one side could win or lose.

But then it occurred to her. She might not have been able to give her mother a solid set-down in person, but at least, in her mind, it was one more thing she could check off her list.

# Chapter 20

"I THINK THAT ONE LOOKS FUN!" SKYE POINTED TO another roller coaster, Tim and Madison responding enthusiastically.

Dwayne looked to Veronica, but he knew it wouldn't matter. She was along for the nice, calm rides, and to hold the bags while everyone went on the big ones. She'd made it clear up front she wasn't about to step foot on any of the big monster rides. "You sure you don't wanna try just one? Looks like a shorter ride than the others."

She shook her head and smiled. "Really, I'm fine. I'm having fun just walking around. And I get to stand in line with you guys for company until you get on, so it's no loss for me."

He would have argued otherwise, given the entire reason *he* came was to get a few thrills. But she truly did seem content so he let it go. "How about a bottle of water?"

She looked up at him with gratitude. "That would be fantastic. I didn't realize I was so thirsty until you said that."

He frowned and resisted the urge to put a hand on her forehead to see if she was overheating. He wasn't her mom or a nurse. But still… "You're still recovering from that wicked poisoning. You need to stay hydrated."

Patting his arm in a gesture that said *you're sweet,*

*and you amuse me,* she nodded and said, "I'll do that. Soon as I hit up that drink stand and grab a water."

"I'll get it. Go on ahead."

He watched as she took a few steps forward, catching up with Skye, Tim, and Madison, then headed to the nearest drink cart. Jeremy followed on his heels.

"I think Madison and I are moving in together."

Dwayne nearly dropped the wallet he'd taken out of his pocket. "Come again?"

Jeremy shrugged. "Yeah, with me getting out of the Corps and starting the contractor job, it just feels like it's time to take the next step. And the next step is moving in together. The timing is right."

Dwayne nearly rolled his eyes. "And when Tim gets word that you and his sister are living in sin?"

"Like he's one to talk. He didn't really do things by the book with Skye."

"And how about the Colonel?" Dwayne asked, referencing Tim and Madison's retired father. He couldn't quite bite back the snicker as he watched the blood drain from Jeremy's face.

"Well, I guess he'll just have to get used to it."

Dwayne nodded at that. He respected Tim and Madison's father as much as anyone else. He was the father he wished he'd had growing up. But Madison was a grown woman now, and if she chose to live with the man she loved, so be it. Glad Jeremy was sticking to his guns, he slapped him on the shoulder. "Well, good luck with the transition."

"Thanks. I guess the only issue now is figuring out how to handle the move with Veronica."

"Hmm?" Dwayne inched forward. "How so?"

"Well, do we move into Madison's place? If so, that's weird for Veronica. It's one thing for me to do an overnight, another entirely to live there."

He agreed with that, and the thought of Veronica living with them both didn't settle well with him.

"But if Madison and I get our own place, since I know she won't move into my apartment, that leaves Veronica with the lease. And I don't think she can afford a two-bedroom by herself." Jeremy stepped up and paid for two bottles of water.

Either way they sliced it, Veronica was out in the cold. Well, not entirely, Dwayne corrected. Skye and Tim would take her back in an instant. Or maybe she could find a small one-bedroom.

Or maybe she could move in with him.

Or… not. No. Way too soon for that. Dwayne handed the cart vendor four freaking bucks for a bottle of water, and decided to give the matter some thought later. When he caught up to Veronica, he placed the bottle, wet with condensation, over the back of her neck.

She tilted her head back and sighed so lustily, he started fighting a hard-on there in the freaking line.

"Wanna get out of here?" he whispered in her ear.

She reached back and grabbed the bottle, opening it and guzzling half the contents at once. *There goes two bucks.*

"Where are we going?"

Grabbing her hand, he said, "Guys, we're gonna hit a tame ride; they have shorter lines. You'll probably still be here when we get back."

The group grumbled but agreed that yeah, they likely would, so they took off toward the boat ride.

"This one?" She glanced up at the outer shell of the ride. "It doesn't really look like your thing." As she spoke, a mother with two toddlers got in line. She raised a brow as if to say *really?* This *is the one you want?*

"I think you're missing the virtue of this." He led her to the back of the line, which the sign indicated would only be fifteen minutes, and pointed. "See? Already, it's a winner. Short wait time."

"Uh-huh. As if you were really suffering before, standing in line for all those rides you love." She crossed her arms behind her back, pulling her tank top tighter over her breasts. Was it his imagination or were they… nah. Probably just the shirt. It was the skimpiest thing he'd ever seen her wear—well, when she was wearing clothes—though to be honest it was still more conservative than half the women in the park.

"What are the other virtues?" She lifted her ponytail off her neck and waved a hand over her skin to cool her down.

He leaned in and blew on her damp skin. "It's in the shade, so we get a break from the sun."

She angled her neck so he could reach more surface area. "That's a good point."

They inched forward a little. Though the ride was low on wait time, it still wouldn't be a speed. Each boat only contained two seats. Which brought him to point number three…

Leaning in further, as if he were still blowing on her skin, he whispered, "And it's in the dark, so nobody will know when I slip my hand down your shorts."

She gasped loud enough to have the mother turning around to give her a dirty look. Covering her mouth with one hand, she turned shock-wide eyes to him. "You're not serious."

"Sure I am. You think I wanted to ride around in a boat just for the hell of it? With no explosions or water-falls or anything? Gotta get the thrill another way."

She poked him in the chest with one finger. "Told you. You need the thrill."

"But this is my favorite kind." He reached around and brought her back against his chest, resting his chin on the top of her head. "Anything with you seems to be my favorite."

He waited to see how she would react. But she didn't say anything, didn't tense, didn't relax. He almost won-dered if she'd even heard him, but he knew she had. Then, as if knowing he was waiting for it, she settled back just a little into his hold.

"I could fall asleep just like this, I think." Her voice was drowsy, like when they turned to each other in the middle of the night to make love.

But it was the middle of the day, and they'd barely done a third of the park. "You tired?"

"Exhausted."

Okay, she wasn't an athlete, but she wasn't a slug either. She spent entire days on her feet at the restaurant. So far this wouldn't compare. "Maybe you're not as re-covered as you think from your food poisoning. Do you want to call it quits early? Tim and Skye can bring both Madison and Jeremy home."

"Uh-huh. Just needed a little break. So your boat ride has four good points. Not three." She shifted enough to look up at him over her shoulder as they inched forward again. "Thanks."

Her little smiles, the ones that she gave only to him, he loved those most. So he squeezed her gently and vowed to keep an eye on her just in case.

———※———

She shook her hands out, trying to wish away the nerves. This wasn't easy, but she needed to ask someone and Skye was her cousin. The closest thing she had to a sister. So she knocked and waited

A minute later, Skye answered the door wearing a pair of huge sweats, likely Tim's, and a towel wrapped around her head. With a clean-scrubbed face, she beamed. "Hey, you. I didn't know you were coming to see me."

"Is that okay? I know you work the late shift but if you have things to do before then I can—"

Skye grabbed her arm and tugged her inside. "Don't go back to that. Don't go back to assuming you're intruding. You know I love seeing you. So come in."

Had she done that? She was nervous, a little confused. But had she really slipped back into old habits? Definitely not okay. "Thanks," she said, instilling some confidence in her voice and heading for the living room.

Skye started to fall into the armchair, then caught herself at the last moment. With a sheepish grin, she pushed a few magazines and catalogues off before sitting down for real. "I still can't manage to keep the place clean for the life of me. Luckily Tim puts up with it… mostly. So, what brings you by?"

Veronica was pretty sure Tim would put up with way more than just a few scattered magazines to keep Skye in his life, but she didn't say anything. She could waffle, deflect, pick a starter subject. But in the end, it was easier to just ask outright. "With birth control pills, should I have had my period by now?"

Skye blinked a few times and her eyes drifted off to the other side of the room, a thoughtful frown puckering her forehead. "I mean, I'm not a doctor. I'm sure Madison—"

"She's working. And I still don't have health insurance. So if I'm being silly and this is an obvious question, I'd rather not spend the money on an office visit to hear, 'You're worried over nothing.'"

Skye bit her lip and stared off into the distance for a moment. "For the record, I think Madison is a better person to ask. But I'll answer what I can, and suggest you defer to an expert for the rest. How long has it been?"

"I started the pills just over two months ago."

"And since then you haven't—"

"Nope."

Skye's eyes widened. "Why did you wait?"

Veronica shrugged. The truth was embarrassing. But also, "I just thought it was my body adjusting. Could that still be it?"

"Maybe," her cousin said slowly. "I think my cycle was tossed off guard a bit when I switched brands, so it's possible."

She sat in silence, waiting for more. But Skye was unusually quiet. Unnervingly so. For a woman who didn't like to leave anything unsaid, it was disturbing to see her still and quiet as a statue.

"Skye, tell me what you're thinking."

Skye screwed her eyes shut for a moment, then nodded and blinked them open again. "I think we need to go upstairs and pee on a stick."

"Why do you have sticks in the house?"

"Right. Yeah. That's definitely not one you're gonna know. Sorry. Pee on a stick, sort of lingo for taking a pregnancy test."

"A pre—oh. No. Okay, you're right. I should have gone to Madison." Veronica laughed, relieved for a moment. "I told you, I'm on birth control."

"Which is only about ninety-eight percent effective, when taken correctly. Have you missed any pills?"

"Nope."

"Taken any antibiotics?"

"No. I haven't been sick in…" Her mind flitted back to the memory of her body draped over Dwayne's bathroom tile, too weak to even crawl to the bedroom. "Okay, well, I did have that bout with food poisoning. But I didn't take anything for it. And it passed after a few days." Mostly. She was still tired, but that was just rehydration. If she were better about drinking water, it wouldn't be a big deal.

"Uh-huh. You know, you could have lost your medication while you spent that two days puking up everything that went down."

"But he still wears condoms," she said quietly.

Skye glanced around the living room. "Why are you whispering?"

"It's embarrassing, and I don't want anyone to hear."

Skye smiled. "The house isn't bugged, and Tim's gone. It's just us." She held up her hands. "I'm not an expert. But it might be possible. In the meantime, I have an extra test from when I bought a three-pack a few months ago."

"Why do you have pregnancy tests if you're on birth control?"

Skye shrugged. "False alarm, my period started late and I just ran out and grabbed one. I'm impatient."

"Were you upset it was negative?"

Her cousin laughed. "Not at all. I know I want kids sometime, but not yet. I want to be married first, newlyweds, before we toss in the addition of babies."

"Oh. That sounds nice. But I don't want to waste your other test. It'd still be a waste of money."

"Tell you what." Skye pushed up from the chair. "Just take it. I'll buy you lunch when it turns negative, and I'll feel better."

Skye looked so earnest that she couldn't say no. "Fine. But I'm picking a nice restaurant and ordering steak." Actually, no. Steak didn't sound good. Meat didn't sound good at all. Maybe a salad.

"Let's go upstairs and prove me wrong." She bounded up the stairs and Veronica followed her to the hall bathroom, where she would be proving her cousin wrong.

# Chapter 21

"Shit."

Skye stared at her from the ledge of the tub. "I'm sorry, did you just curse?"

Had she? It didn't even register. With a dull voice that felt rusty coming out her throat, she asked, "Does it matter?"

"Oh, honey." Skye slid onto the tile and gathered Veronica in her arms, rocking her just a little like she was a child. "It will be okay. I swear."

She wanted to believe. Wanted to think it would all just go away, be a bad dream, a nightmare. She could wake up tomorrow and there would be no plus sign haunting her.

And the worst part was… she couldn't help that small voice in the back of her mind from whispering harshly, *Your mother was right.*

"What have I done?" she whispered, mostly to herself.

"Nothing." Skye's voice was fierce as a warrior as she sat back up and cupped Veronica's face with her hands. "You have done nothing. It is what it is, and it will be okay. Dwayne is an amazing guy, and it will all be fine. He's half in love with you already, anyone can see that." She stood and held out a hand. "Let's go downstairs and get some lunch. I'll make us some sandwiches."

She took Skye's hand, not even feeling the pressure as she stood. Numb, that's all she could register. Like she was sleepwalking down the stairs, into the kitchen.

Skye started to make sandwiches and stayed silent. As if she knew Veronica couldn't handle anything more right that moment.

She would have been right.

So why was it, when she most needed a quiet minute to absorb the shock, did one particularly loud voice continue to rudely echo through her mind?

And did it have to be her mother, of all people?

She shut it down as best she could and laid her head on the table.

"Babe?"

Tim's voice filtered into the kitchen and she lifted her head.

"Tim? What are you doing here?" Skye walked over to poke her head out of the kitchen.

He walked in and gave her a quick peck on the lips. "Half-day, since we'll be in the field all weekend. You making lunch?"

"Just sandwiches for me and Veronica. If you wouldn't mind—"

"Oh, hey, didn't see you there. How are ya?"

Before Veronica could answer, he started walking back out of the kitchen. "Hold that thought. I'm gonna change and wash up. Dwayne is meeting me here for lunch. We can all eat together, if you guys don't mind waiting another few minutes."

Veronica sat there, feeling like she'd just been the victim of a drive-by greeting.

Skye rubbed her back. "I can get rid of him easy. Just tell him we planned a girls' day and—"

"Hey, Skye," Dwayne's voice called out from the front door. "I saw Veronica's car outside. Is she here?"

Veronica let her head thump to the table. If things weren't so very wrong, it would almost be comical.

Skye waited a moment before answering. But Veronica just shrugged. He knew she was there. They could talk later. As Skye called out they were in the kitchen, she worked on her smile. Now wasn't the time to go into it.

Dwayne's boots thudded, announcing his entrance before she could see him. With monumental effort, she put on a smile. It hurt. Actually, physically hurt to stretch her lips into the fake gesture. But now wasn't the time. She just couldn't have the conversation in Skye's home, with her cousin and husband listening in.

"Hey, darlin'. Didn't know you were over here. Nice surprise."

Surprise. Right. Word of the day.

No, the word of the day would be *panic*.

He leaned down and gave her a kiss, and she breathed in the calming scent of his soap and scent. It did something to her insides, calmed the fluttering nerves just a little.

"How about you two go and sit in the living room? I can bring out the sandwiches in a few minutes."

"Do you need help?" It was the polite thing to ask, but Veronica felt about as capable of helping as an infant, so when Skye shook her head she was relieved.

Dwayne unbuttoned his uniform blouse and draped it over the arm of the sofa before sitting down with a groan, stretching his long arms over the back. She watched as his olive undershirt stretched across his chest, and new fluttering happened low in her belly. The stirrings of want.

Inappropriate timing. But when he patted the cushion next to him, she sat.

"Okay. I've got the mother of all lazy lunches here." Skye walked in from the kitchen and set a big plate on the coffee table with one hand, and set a few bags of chips down with the other. "Some are simply PB and J, four are turkey—" she shuddered visibly, her vegetarian side clearly objecting "—and there are a few different kinds of chips. Dig in."

"Thanks, babe." He reached over and snagged a turkey sandwich in each hand.

"Skye?" Tim thundered down the stairs, landing in the living room, looking more flustered than Veronica had seen him, ever.

"Lunch is on." Skye started to sit down, but Tim grabbed her by the arms and spun her around.

"Is it true? Are you?"

"Am I lunch?" Skye looked as confused as Veronica felt.

"I saw the test. You're pregnant?"

Oh. No. No, no. Please no.

"Maybe we should go," she whispered in Dwayne's ear.

Dwayne apparently didn't hear her. "Holy shit. Tim's gonna be a daddy?"

"Uh…" Skye looked like a caged animal, which Tim didn't seem to register as he picked her up and spun her around while laughing with pure euphoria.

Veronica, meanwhile, had never felt lower in her life.

Tim was in for a massive letdown, and it was her fault. "Let's go," she said a little louder, tugging on Dwayne's arm. She knew Skye would let him down easier in private.

"I can't believe this. Did you just find out? Are you feeling okay?" His hands roamed lightly over Skye's arms, her face, her stomach, as if checking for himself that she was okay.

"No, I, um." She looked over at the couch.

"Oh. Right. Private moment." Dwayne finally picked up on the fact that their presence wouldn't be welcome at the fake announcement. He stood, pulling Veronica with him. "We'll just head out."

As she followed Dwayne, Veronica turned to mouth, "I'm so sorry," over her shoulder. Skye, watching over Tim's shoulder, mouthed, "It's okay," and gave her a smile.

It didn't help much.

As they stepped out on the front porch, Dwayne let out a whoop. "I can't believe it. My best friend's gonna be a dad." He all but skipped toward his truck, the thick soles of his boots thudding on the concrete.

"Let's not get too excited. It could be a false alarm," she said weakly, trying to think of the most neutral way to let him down. The enthusiasm he showed for his own friend's—fictional—impending fatherhood was beautiful to watch, but it only made her feel that much worse for the deception.

"Is that even possible? I think I—crap."

"What?" She glanced back to see Dwayne heading for the front door again.

"Forgot my cammie blouse; be back in a sec."

"Oh, okay. Wait, no."

She hustled after him and into the front door just

in time to hear Tim ask, "If the test wasn't yours, then whose was it?"

———— ∞ ————

Dwayne immediately realized his error as his hand froze over the blouse. Neither Tim nor Skye were looking at him, still engrossed in their convo by the fireplace. He could slip out now, leave as if he hadn't come back in.

Except the tension had changed from elation to anger in the last five seconds, and now he felt stuck.

"If the test wasn't yours, then whose was it?" Tim asked, shoulders bunched beneath his shirt, hands clenched at his sides.

Test? What?

"That's not my information to share," Skye said, voice thick with regret. "I'm sorry."

Well, hell. He'd accidentally walked onto the set of a freaking telanovella. With as much stealth as he could manage—let's face it, Delta Force he was not—he lifted the blouse from the back of the chair and took a few steps backward. He needed to turn around, walk forward, ignore them. But it was like watching two cars heading for each other dead-on. You couldn't look away, despite the imminent crash.

"No. I can't accept that. This is too important. I need the full story. Now."

He couldn't blame the guy. But he was so close to the front hall so he kept backing up slowly, carefully, each step planned with care.

"You can't just accept that the test wasn't mine?"

Tim shook his head. "If it wasn't yours, then who's pregnant? Wait."

So close. Just a few more steps and he was home free…

"Is it Veronica? Is that why she was here with you? Is Veronica pregnant?"

And stealth became a nonissue as he tripped and crashed into a side table, knocking over a bowl filled with keys to clatter on the floor.

Both turned to stare at him, Skye with her eyes wide in shock, Tim with his mouth hanging open. But neither said a word.

Veronica. Did he say *Veronica* and *pregnant* in the same sentence?

"I'm sorry."

Both turned their eyes to something over his shoulder, and numbly he forced his body to shift and look as well.

Veronica, white as a sheet, stood by the front door, looking ready to burst into tears at any minute.

"I'm so sorry. I just… I didn't… I wasn't ready to… and then he thought…" She blinked rapidly, then spun on her heel and took off through the door. In some rational part of his mind, he registered the start of her engine and her car pulling away.

"Dwayne."

Tim's voice. He shook his head.

"Dwayne, please, before you—"

He held up a hand, still staring at the front door where Veronica had bolted through, leaving it open. He didn't turn around as he asked, "Is she?"

"It's not for me to—"

"Skye."

She sighed, then he felt her small hand on his back,

slipping around his waist, her forehead resting on his shoulder. "Please just talk to her. That's all I can say."

Her nonanswer was as good as a billboard sign.

Oh, God. She was pregnant. Veronica was pregnant.

And it was Blair, all over again.

---

Veronica rocked on her bed, arms drawn around her knees. Though she wanted to block it out, the scene kept replaying in her mind.

The one-second-too-late realization that Dwayne was walking back in Skye and Tim's door. Hearing Tim ask Skye whose test it was. Watching Dwayne stumble when Tim spoke her name. The look on his face, a cross between horror and something so deeply painful it didn't have a name.

That was nothing compared to the feeling of her own heart as it cracked down the middle. The force of the shock of the positive pregnancy test layered with Dwayne's reaction was just too much.

And what was she going to do? Leaning back, she placed a tentative hand on her stomach. Nothing. It was almost impossible to believe there was something there.

She jerked when a pounding echoed through the apartment.

Skye wasn't going to knock like that, and Tim was too controlled to knock like that. Madison had a key, and Jeremy wouldn't be knocking if Madison wasn't here. Which just left…

Dwayne.

Childish though it was, she'd rather sit in bed alone and mope. So she didn't move.

The pounding continued. How long would he go on?

"Veronica, open up."

Even from the back of the apartment, she could hear him clearly. His voice boomed. He wasn't yelling, but he meant business.

"I will stand here all day if I have to. And eventually Madison will let me in."

Darn it, he was right. With a sigh, she crawled off the bed and walked to the front door. She opened and stood back as he barged in like a bull looking for a fight.

"Talk. Now." He stood with his arms crossed.

"What do you—"

"Are you? Are you pregnant?"

"I just took the test today. As far as I understand—"

"How could this happen?" He threw his hands in the air and headed down the hall, then spun around and came back. "I was always so careful."

She'd wondered too. But there was that one time… "When the condom broke?" she said weakly.

"When the condom…" His eyes narrowed. "But you said it was fine. You said you were on birth control."

"I was. I am! Was. I guess." Didn't seem like she would need it now.

"Then explain to me how this happened?"

"Do I look like a doctor to you? Back off!" She immediately slapped a hand over her mouth, appalled at the anger in her voice. Then she remembered. She sure as heck had a reason to be angry. She didn't have to censor herself any longer. "I didn't ask for this, you know."

"Didn't you?"

She stared at him, trying to figure out what in the world that cryptic comment meant. But he gave nothing away.

"Okay. Here's what we're going to do." He crossed

his arms again. "You and I are making an appointment with an OB."

She wanted to argue, but what was the point? She needed to see a doctor anyway.

"If they confirm you're pregnant—"

"Why wouldn't they? The test said I was."

He shook his head. "I am going to be in the room when the doctor says yes or no. That's not negotiable. And if you are, then we're getting married."

This, out of all, was the hardest blow. A proposal from the man she loved… out of obligation and duty. It was the worst thing ever. "That is not a good idea."

"Why not?"

*Because daily my heart is going to break being around you.* "It's clear to me we all need to just take a step back and reevaluate."

"If you're not pregnant, then that's a fantastic idea. But if you are, then this is just how it works. I'm not letting that kid grow up without a father. And I'm not just going to turn into some dad who sees his kid whenever he has breaks or can make a few hours. I want you and that child under my same roof. Every night."

Said more sweetly, it could have been a beautiful proposal. But he was so angry, so frustrated, and his words came from a place of resentment rather than affection. God, how that hurt.

It was a null and void issue anyway, until she found out if the test was a false positive… did those exist? If so, now was one doozy of a time to get one. "I'll ask Madison for a recommendation for a doctor."

"And you'll let me know when your appointment is." It wasn't a question.

When she didn't answer, he repeated, "You will let me know. Don't play with me on this one. I'm going with you and I'm going to hear it firsthand."

She watched his face, hoping for one glimpse of the lovable, playful Dwayne she'd known the past few months. The man that made her laugh, made her comfortable, made her feel like she was so special.

It was as if he'd closed himself up in a hard outer shell that even a tank couldn't penetrate. Something was driving his immediate, intense reaction to this news. Was it all because of her? Or something more?

Compassion. Though she did not always agree with her parents and their beliefs... this was one she could grasp ahold of. Maybe after a show of good faith, he could relax and show a little in return. With a softer voice, she said, "Fine. I'll let you know as soon as I can."

He visibly relaxed, though he didn't drop the hard exterior. "Good. Call for an appointment today." And he walked by her and shut the door quietly behind him.

Marriage. A baby. A very angry, very hurt Dwayne. This was not one of her best days.

And if there really was a baby? Would she be able to marry Dwayne, knowing he was harboring some ill will about the situation? But how could she walk away from the father of her child, a man she loved?

*I didn't ask for this, you know.*

*Didn't you?*

The words came back to slap at her. Did he mean she did this on purpose? Or that he thought she was lying in some way? How could she convince him that she was telling the truth? That she never wanted to deceive him, never wanted to bring this on them?

She balled her fingers into a fist and rested it against her stomach. "This was absolutely horrible timing. Just so you know."

Whatever was or was not in there didn't respond. Not that she expected it to.

---

Despite her reservations, she made an appointment with the same clinic she had gone into for her birth control pills. Control. Right. Failure on that one. But as it turned out, they would administer the test, but not provide pre-natal care. She would have to see an actual OB for that. And the OB they recommended could not get her in for another few weeks, because she was not high risk and there were no complications health-wise.

Her hands shook as she picked up the phone to call Dwayne.

"Yeah?"

Her eyes closed as she remembered the sweeter greetings. "I can go in any time for an official test. And from there I have to make an appointment with a different doctor."

"What's the official test?"

"I don't know. I guess I have to go in and find out. It's just a walk-in clinic, so I can go whenever I have time."

"I'll be there in ten minutes."

"Just meet me at the clinic in twenty," she decided. "I have work in a few hours and I can just drive over after this."

"I want to—"

She rattled off the address of the clinic and hung up, ignoring his call back. If he wanted to play the jerk, then she would respond appropriately. After a moment to grab her bag and a change of clothes for work, she hurried out the door. It wouldn't shock her to see Dwayne pulling up to the apartment in an attempt to strongarm her into riding along. So she would beat him to it and leave now. The thought of the little rebellion, however small, brought a smile to her face.

But an hour later, the smile was long gone. She sat in the passenger seat of Dwayne's truck, a handful of paperwork clutched in her fist. And every page of it was a reminder of one thing.

She was really pregnant.

Dwayne stared straight ahead, the truck still turned off, still parked in the lot of the clinic.

"Now what?" she asked quietly.

"Did Madison talk to you about the apartment?"

"What?" Not at all sure what that had to do with anything, she tried to catch up. "Our apartment?"

"About Jeremy moving in with her, or them getting their own place."

"Oh." The thought brought on another wave of panic. Where would she live? "No, she hadn't mentioned it."

He tilted his head from side to side, as if stretching his neck, but said nothing more and wouldn't turn to look at her.

"Okay then." Slowly, she opened the passenger door. "I'll just head to work now."

"Be safe."

It wasn't quite the endearing good-byes he'd left her with, but it was still a reminder that he cared. Or was it just the baby he cared about? She decided right now to stick with positive thoughts.

She pulled into work an hour early and went up to Skye's office. Nobody else was in there, luckily, and she pulled the door shut and stepped into the storage room to change. When she came back into the office, her cousin was sitting at her desk.

"Hey. How was the doctor?"

"If you mean, am I pregnant? The answer is yes."

Skye's face revealed nothing. "How do you feel about that?"

Veronica started to laugh. Because really, how could she begin to explain how she felt about it? But the laughter soon turned into hiccupping sobs and she buried her face in her hands, knees coming up under her chin.

Skye waited until she finished her emotional outpouring before slipping an arm around her shoulder. "It isn't the end of the world. I know it's not quite what you grew up knowing, but here in the States it's not uncommon. You're an adult, and a smart woman. You'll get it figured out."

"Smart. Right. I don't even have my GED yet." The reminder brought another hiccup from her.

"A GED is a good piece of paper to have, but it's not an indication of how smart you are. And I think you know that." Skye brushed a lock of hair back from her forehead. "Need the night off?"

"No." Veronica took the tissue her cousin handed her and blotted her face. "I still have an hour before my shift. I'll pull it together. Plus, I need the money now, if I have baby things to buy." And extra health care costs. Day care once the baby was here. More food, bottles, diapers… Oh, God.

"Dwayne will help, I know that. Don't stress about the money. He's going to step up, I know that."

"Right now I think I would rather take a bribe from Satan himself."

Skye smiled a little. "I know what you're saying, but cut him a little slack too. He just found out he's going to be a father. Maybe he's not handling it well, but he might have his reasons. With a little time to accept the idea, things could turn around. Have some faith."

It made sense. This wasn't just a surprise for her, but for Dwayne as well. She could give them both time to figure how things would work out. It wasn't too much to ask.

"You're right. I need to be patient. I'm not exactly handling this perfectly myself, so he's reacting on emotion like me."

"Good." Skye stood and rubbed Veronica's shoulder. "Stay up here as long as you need. Come down when you're ready."

"Thanks, boss."

Skye smiled and left her alone.

Somehow, she would figure this out. She wasn't sure how, but she would.

# Chapter 22

HE GAVE HIMSELF A DAY TO CALM DOWN A LITTLE, then called, ready to apologize. She hadn't answered. Then she'd sent him a text message saying she was able to get an earlier appointment for the doctor and could he meet her the next morning? After clearing it with his CO, he agreed to swing by and pick her up in the morning.

But when he not only showed up, but came into the exam room with her, she wasn't all that thrilled about it.

"Do you have to sit there? Can you not wait out in the hall?"

Dwayne shook his head. Like hell he was going to go through that again. He'd stayed out of Blair's way the whole time she was playing him, thinking OB visits were some sacred woman thing. But not this time. At least not the first appointment.

"Could you... I mean, if she needs to examine me, could you at least not watch?"

Her knees were bouncing, her hands clenched around her legs. And she wasn't looking at him. Hadn't looked at him since they'd walked through the doors of the OB office together.

He was still angry at the situation. But with her, he couldn't figure out yet where he stood. Skepticism was high up on the list. As was confusion. But as much as he wanted desperately to comfort her, keeping his distance right now was the only way he could think to safeguard his own heart.

"If there's an exam, I'll step outside."

She looked at him then, finally. And even shielding himself, the resigned, grateful look pinched his heart a little.

"Thanks."

Blair had made him feel that way once. Like he would do anything to take care of her. And she'd proven he was a fool. And he had to admit, he hadn't felt for her half of what he felt for Veronica. The fall would be that much longer, the landing that much harder.

There was likely no coincidence that he'd woken up in a cold sweat, hearing screams in his mind, echoing in the darkness of the pre-dawn morning. For the first time in a while, he'd woken up without Veronica curled up next to him, without her calming influence. Without the security of her affection locked tight in his heart.

A knock on the door pulled him from his thoughts in time to see a woman slip in and grant Veronica with a warm smile.

"Ms. Gibson?" Veronica nodded and the doctor's smile brightened. "Excellent. I'm Dr. Smithson; nice to meet you." They shook hands, then the doctor turned to him. "And who have you brought with you?"

"This is my…" Her voice trailed off, and he knew she was about to introduce him on autopilot. As her boyfriend. God, he hated that she'd stopped. Things were weird. They weren't great. But still.

"I'm Dwayne." He stood and shook her hand, ignoring the raised brow at his lack of title. He could easily read her mind. Friend? Lover? Husband? Why no clarification?

He'd love to answer that. But just now, not happening.

"Well, okay then." She turned to the table and opened the file. "Your HCG levels from the initial testing look great, so that's on track. I assume you are hoping for a dating ultrasound here."

"Sorry, HCG?" Veronica looked as overwhelmed as he felt. Glad she asked, 'cause he had no clue either.

"HCG. The hormone that indicates pregnancy."

Veronica's hand slipped over her stomach, trembling a little. He wanted so badly to reach over and grab that hand, squeeze it. But at this point, he wasn't even sure what was going on.

Clearly seeing neither of them were following, the doctor laced her fingers together and set them on her lap. "The HCG hormone is what a home pregnancy test measures. It says on your file that you had a positive home test, and then an official test at a local clinic. Is that correct?"

"Yes. I didn't know if it was false, or wrong or…" She trailed off, and everyone was silent for a moment.

The doctor glanced between them, clearly sensing the unease there. "There are options. If this pregnancy isn't planned, isn't wanted, then you—"

"No." The sharp fierceness of her voice had both him and the doctor blinking in surprise. But Veronica's face was set, unapologetic. "Not planned. But it's here. Right?" She looked to the doctor for confirmation, who nodded. "Then wanted."

At the doctor's direction, Veronica laid back on the table and pulled her shirt up. The doctor must have told her something, but he suddenly found he couldn't hear anything but a low buzz. Like he'd had target practice at the rifle range and didn't wear his earplugs. The doc dropped some gloop over her stomach, and he realized he promised to leave the room. Standing up, feeling numb, he started for the door.

"Stay."

Looking over his shoulder, he raised a brow. "I said I would—"

"Please."

She looked so small on the exam table, so scared that he couldn't say no. He walked back to stand close to the head of the table. There, but not invading her space.

"Okay, let's see what we've got here." The doctor pressed some wand thing to her stomach, making her gasp a little, and gave her a sympathetic smile. "Sorry, I know. Cold, and definitely not fun when your stomach is already upset. I'll hustle." She clicked around a few times, and the black screen went sort of gray, like a TV without signal. Wiggling the wand around a little, she found some weird black circle. And then some gray bean-looking thing.

"Is that a kidney?" He couldn't look away now if he tried. Morbidly curious, he leaned closer, watching the screen.

"That would be the fetus. And this," she added with a few more clicks, zooming in slightly, "is the heartbeat." With her finger, she pointed to a flicker that he'd first thought was just a blip on the screen.

He heard Veronica gasp, saw out of the corner of his eye when her hand covered her mouth that her eyes watered. But he couldn't stop staring at the screen.

Heartbeat. His baby had a heartbeat. And it looked like a kidney bean.

Holy shit. There was a baby in there.

"Looks like everything's on schedule, from what you told the nurse. I'm going to say right now that we're measuring around nine weeks."

Nine weeks? But that wasn't right. They'd had sex for the first time less than two months ago.

"The weeks are a little deceptive," the doc went on as she handed Veronica a few tissues to wipe her stomach off. "You likely conceived seven weeks ago. But how we count, you go back to when your last period was. So, nine."

Now it made more sense.

"Do you need to sit down?"

He looked at Veronica, expecting her to look faint. But she was already lying down.

"No, I meant you, big guy. You look like one poke away from pulling a timber like a felled tree."

"No, I'm…" A little lightheaded, now that she mentioned it. He sat down with a thump in the plastic chair. "Okay. Now I'm good." What a lie.

"Can you tell me how this happened?" Veronica asked. "I was on birth control from the start of…" She waved a hand around. "I took them every day at the same time, like they told me to."

The doctor glanced back through her charts. "If the information the clinic faxed over is right, you started birth control just about two months ago."

"Yes."

"And you conceived about seven weeks ago. That's not enough time for it to become effective. Odds are, they didn't mention that part at whatever clinic you got the pills from. Usually, hormonal birth control takes a

month or so to fully be active. It's suggested to use a
backup method for the first month of use." The good
doctor gave him a look that would have shriveled his
balls on any normal day. But he was too intent on
breathing properly to care.

"Oh, it's not his fault. The condom broke, but I
thought…" She trailed off again, looking pale. "This is
my fault, isn't it?"

"Takes two to tango, as we often say in this office.
I'm going to leave you two in here. Check out with the
nurse at the front desk, okay, sweetie? They'll have information on nutrition, prenatal vitamins, all that good
stuff. And they can schedule you for another appointment in about a month."

Veronica nodded, pulling her shirt back down.
"Thank you."

"No problem." She looked between the two of them,
then made the pointed gesture of turning her back to
Dwayne and facing Veronica alone. "And if you need
to talk about anything, please call me. I'm always willing to chat."

Even in his stupefied state, he knew what that was
reference to. Him. As in *The jackass you brought to the
appointment isn't disrespecting you, is he?*

Much as he wanted to be upset about that, he could
appreciate a doctor that cared.

Dwayne waited until she checked out from the
nurse's desk, carrying a folder full of papers and a little
white sack that he overheard contained a thirty-day supply of vitamins. And still, he couldn't talk. They walked
to his truck in silence, and she didn't fight him when he
gave her a boost up to the seat.

The drive back was painful, to say the least. He had to say something. Anything. "Um, when we're married, if you want to see a doc on base, we can probably fix that up."

"No, thank you. This doctor is fine." She was still as a picture, staring out the window, voice so taut it might crack the air.

"Well, I'm sure we can figure out how to keep you off base if you like this doctor."

She said nothing.

Annoyed? Pissed? Terrified? Probably a combination of all three, just like him. Now he knew it wasn't a joke. He was going to be a dad in approximately seven months. But holy hell, what was he supposed to think? The one time the condom breaks, her pills fail? Or, rather, they weren't working at all. Did she really not know? Was this her first go-round on birth control?

Exactly what *were* the odds of that? He didn't think to ask, or see if Veronica knew. He filed it away for something to think of later. The kid was here now. Or, well, sort of. It existed, no going back there. Time to man up, do the right thing, and make sure his child had the best life possible.

But he realized she hadn't actually agreed to marry him. At first he thought it was resistance based on the unknown. But it was official now, and they couldn't look back. But the fear that she might reject him was almost overwhelming.

*Time to man up, grow a pair, and do the right thing.*

"I need to know. Are you going to marry me?"

Veronica stared out the window of the truck, her body on autopilot. Despite the fact that she was sure the test was right, confirmation from the doctor meant she couldn't ignore it any longer. Couldn't pretend or bury her head in the sand. She was, officially, the very picture of what her mother always feared most out of her daughter.

And though she knew—knew to the bone—that her mother was wrong about many things… this wasn't what she'd wanted for herself either. And yet here she was.

"Um, when we're married, if you want to see a doc on base, we can probably fix that up."

"No, thank you. This doctor is fine." It was automatic, saying no. He could have asked if her name was Veronica Gibson and she likely would have said no.

"Well, I'm sure we can figure out how to keep you off base if you like this doctor."

Her fingers tightened, crunching the bag holding her vitamins. She forced them to relax and rolled her neck once to release as much tension as possible. Not that it helped much.

It hurt. It hurt so much that he might have ever doubted whether she planned it or not. And he still hadn't taken it back. She watched as another exit flew by, and felt like her grasp on her own life was following the same path. Falling back farther and farther behind her.

"I need to know. Are you going to marry me?"

Just another knife in the wound. She bit her lip to keep it from trembling and swallowed a few times. This was definitely not morning sickness that made her nauseous. It was knowing the man she loved just asked her if she was going to marry him… because of an obligation.

And knowing she wouldn't be able to say no.

"Can we talk about it later?" Her voice was hoarse, probably from not speaking much. She thought she would have to repeat herself when he surprised her and nodded.

"Yeah. Sure. Just think about it. Please." His hands gripped the steering wheel, knuckles turning white.

Was it stress of impending fatherhood, or the idea of marrying her that made him so tense? "Thank you."

The scenery rolled by and she did her best to block out anything resembling a conscious thought. More often than not, those thoughts were tinted with her own mother's voice. Not helpful. Not in the least.

When he pulled up to her complex, she waited for him to help her down. Though touching him wasn't on her short list of things she wanted to do at the moment, jumping down and spraining an ankle was the worse of the two evils. So she sat silently as he walked around the truck and opened her door. But when he normally would have grasped her waist to lift her down, he slung an arm over the door, used his other to prop himself up on the frame, and leaned in just a little.

For a man of Dwayne's size, *just a little* was more than enough to crowd.

"I lied."

She blinked and refocused on his face. Nope, not joking.

"I lied about waiting for later. I need to know now. If you'll marry me."

His drawl was thicker, she realized. And she doubted he would have liked to hear it. "I don't know why we need to—"

"Rush?" He rubbed a hand over his neck. "Yeah. See,

I think we were doing a pretty bang-up job of going slow in our relationship. But things changed. And there's a lot more at stake now. So if you'll step into my boots, you need to know where I'm coming from. The simple practicality of the situation is enough for me. Health insurance for you and the kidney bean, you moving in to make things easier on you, someone there to take care of you. Help. Easier for me to be there for the baby. And I want to be there. I need to be there."

Practicality. The word didn't quite invoke a passionate swoon. But she had to set aside her romantic ideals and embrace the reality. Everything he said was true. She couldn't afford a baby while she was waitressing and finishing up a GED. That alone was true. But what's more… wait.

"What's the nonpractical reason?"

His face twisted like he was trying to mentally translate Latin. "What?"

"You said that the simple practicality was enough. But is there more?" *Let it be love. Please let it be love.*

"Oh." He sighed and stared at his feet. "Can we just say that the thought of my kid growing up without me there every night makes me really uncomfortable? That kidney bean's mine too, and the idea that I would have to schedule days to see him… it doesn't taste right. I don't like the thought of leaving either of you behind."

She closed her eyes and refused to let him see her fight back tears. No, not love for her. For the baby. Which was more than many other women could say. With that mental slap she swallowed what tears were close to the surface and opened them. And she nodded.

He blew out a breath and gently wrapped his arms

around her in a sort of semihug while lowering her to the pavement. "Thank you," he whispered in her hair. There was no kiss, no sweet caress. Just a man, thankful for the opportunity. And a woman who already wondered if she'd made a mistake.

She couldn't have said no. Never intended to. But oh, it hurt to say yes.

# Chapter 23

DWAYNE ENTERED HIS APARTMENT AND LOOKED around. He wanted to go back with Veronica. Wanted to be there with her constantly. But she'd made it clear with her body language that, although she'd said she would marry him, she wasn't in the mood for spending time with him.

She agreed to start looking into packing and moving in with him as soon as possible. He just hoped she wouldn't actually start the packing itself. He would handle all that. As much as he wanted things to go fast, he refused to have her lifting heavy boxes.

Hm. Should she still be working at the restaurant? All those heavy platters of food, the long shifts on her feet… would it be out of line to call her doctor and ask for himself?

And why did he need to call a doctor when he had an expert within his own family calling plan? He pulled out his cell and hit speed dial three. She picked up on the second ring, and for once there were no toddlerlike sounds greeting him before his sister said, "Hello?"

"Congratulate me." Dwayne sank onto the couch. His head hit the back of the couch with a thud, and he winced a little.

"Congratulations," Natalie said on cue. "For what?"

"I'm going to be a daddy."

Dead silence met his declaration. Not even a squeal

from his niece. It dragged out so long he pulled the phone away from his ear to see if he'd been disconnected. "Nat?"

"I think I heard that wrong. Did you say…"

"Yeah. I did."

"Oh my God," she breathed. "Veronica?"

"Well, yeah," he said, annoyed. "Who else?"

"I don't know. You dropped a bomb on me. Sorry for being confused for a second. You've always been Mr. Careful, even before Blair. Wait." She breathed hard. "I hate asking this but—"

"Yes, she really is pregnant. I went to the doctor with her, saw the ultrasound as the doctor did it. No faking that."

"Oh. Well, she didn't sound like the type to fake it anyway. So things happen. At least it's with someone you love."

Love? He hadn't gotten around to figuring that part out when he got hit with the bomb. "It shouldn't have happened at all."

"I know, but sometimes these things do happen. Protection fails. Mistakes are made. And then you get to nine months later, and you forget you thought it was a mistake." He could hear the smile in her voice. "I can't ever look at my little girl and think she was a mistake."

"Of course she isn't. Speaking of, where's the little rugrat? It's too quiet over there."

"On my way to pick her up from day care."

"Should you be driving while on the phone?"

"Easy with the big brother routine. Even my crappy cell has speakerphone. As we speak, you're sitting in the cup holder."

"Comfortable. Should she be working?"

"By she, I assume you mean Veronica. And working where?"

"At all."

Natalie laughed. "Well, does she work on a construction site? Is she often exposed to hazardous chemicals?"

"Natalie."

"Oh, come on, Dwayne. Pregnant women aren't disabled. She sounds like a smart person. I doubt you would have fallen for a moron. If she needs a break, she'll ask for one. If she is struggling, she'll take time off. If she keeps up with her doctor and listens to her body, she will be fine. I worked up until the day Suzanna got here."

The pause stretched out ten seconds before his sister spoke again. "Dwayne? Are you happy?"

*Happy, scared shitless... same thing, right?* "I don't know what I am."

"If you love her, you're allowed to be happy. I know I haven't met her, but she sounds like a great person. And I know her chats with you helped so much while you were deployed. She brought the calm to you. Isn't it just possible this was all a big coincidence, and she's just as scared as you are? Not every woman thinks the way Blair does. Not everyone sees gain from someone else's misery."

She was right, and he knew it. He'd reacted like a jerk, without even giving her the chance to explain. Maybe there was an easy explanation.

"Give it a chance. If things had been different, I'd want two parents for Suzanna. I know you would have given anything for a dad. I would have. Don't push her away because of assumptions and hurt feelings from the past."

"When did you get to be so smart?"

"I've been growing up while you were out there saving the country. Parenting is its own crash course in life."

"Love you, Nat."

"Love you too, D."

—∿∿—

With the truck loaded with boxes, Dwayne drove Veronica home. Their quick dinner at the restaurant, set up by Skye so they could make the formal announcement, was a quiet affair. Everyone put on smiles, but behind the façade, there was the underlying knowledge that this wasn't the typical pregnancy announcement. And after a quick trip to Madison's place, they were on the way home.

Home. Their home now. She'd officially agreed to move in with him before the wedding. Though the date for that little detail hadn't been decided. When he'd broached the subject, she'd said she wanted to check with her aunt and uncle, and didn't he want to ask his family their plans?

No. He wanted to drag her down to the courthouse and get the thing done now. He hated loose ends, and their lack of wedding was a loose end that itched in all the wrong places. But he had to remind himself, just getting her to agree to move in was a big step. There was no way things would progress positively if they couldn't at least be together to figure them out.

Which reminded him. Time to start looking for houses to rent. It didn't make sense to buy at this point, when he'd likely be PCSing in another year or two. But there were always houses to lease around a military base. And he couldn't see bringing home his baby to his bachelor-style apartment.

It all came crashing down on him. A baby and—hopefully—a wife. In six months. Busy year.

"The dinner was nice," Veronica said, staring out the window. He couldn't tell if she wanted him to respond or if it was just something to fill the void. So he took a chance.

"Yeah. Skye's a sweetheart to set that all up." He thought back for a minute. "You didn't eat much though. You feeling okay?"

She stared at him with big eyes, and he realized it was the first time he'd directly asked about her pregnancy since the doctor's office.

Covering her stomach with one hand, she gave him a smile that looked a little more like a grimace. "Still sensitive, but overall, getting better. Or at least, that's what I think. Then out of nowhere, a bad day will hit me."

She could have been describing his assimilation problem word for word. It didn't take a genius to figure out that, with his relationship with Veronica up in the air and the new changes in his life all coming to a head at once, he was struggling a little to keep up with everything. And his mind was playing tricks again.

It was the exact wrong time for a freak-out. Not with a new baby on the way.

They pulled up to the apartment and she reached behind the seat for her bag. After he lifted her down from the truck, he almost grabbed her hand on instinct. But that wasn't a good idea. She was upset with him, and he was upset at… what? Her? The world? Himself? He still hadn't worked that through in his mind yet. But when he opened the door to his apartment, he couldn't deny a big urge to sweep her off her feet and play the old-fashioned knight carrying his bride over the altar.

He resisted the knightly urge. With her stomach unsettled, the gesture likely would have resulted in her getting sick, anyway. Nice way to spend the first night of cohabitating.

She walked around the living room slowly, pivoting in her little silver flats. Brushing a hand over the top of his sofa, touching the corner of a picture, eyes soaking in every inch of his apartment, as if she hadn't been there before. As if she hadn't spent night after night with him. Then her shoulders tensed up, like she took a deep breath, and she turned to look at him with a resolute face.

"I need to ask you something."

"That sounds ominous. But go ahead." He took off his suit jacket and draped it over the back of the arm-chair, then shoved his hands in his pants pocket like what she was about to ask had zero bearing on his mind. What a lie.

"Where do I sleep?"

Okay, that was definitely not what he was thinking. "In bed?"

"Is that a question?"

"I don't know, is it?"

She blew out an exasperated breath, one he could relate to. "Stop that. I just don't…"

She lifted her hands and let them fall again. "I don't know what we're doing here. There. I said it. I don't know what's going on. I don't know where you are, I don't know if you only asked me to marry you because you felt like you had to, if you're upset with me, if I've ruined everything. I just... don't... know."

The uncertainty in her eyes came close to breaking his heart. But he held firm. Blair had played the same game, and he just couldn't go through that with Veronica. Putting in the extra effort to appear nonchalant, he said, "You can sleep wherever you want, darlin'. I wouldn't mind company in bed, but if that's not what you want, then there's a guest room. Or the couch. Whatever you want."

"Oh. Okay." She grabbed her bag from the sofa and headed down the hall. A door closed, though he had no clue which one. Probably the guest bedroom, since he was basically an asshole and even he didn't want to spend time with himself.

*You've got to get over it. Veronica isn't Blair.*

*But she could be. And if Blair got the drop on you, anyone could.*

It was cynical, it was harsh. But it was true. Could he seriously risk going through that again? With Veronica, a woman he was half in love with already?

If the entire thing turned out to be a scene, it might kill him.

───※───

Veronica dropped the bag on the mattress and sat next to it, crossing her legs. What a picture she must look. In her nice dress, sitting on a twin bed in a guest room by herself while her, what, fiancé? Whoever he was, while he did who knew what all by himself.

Fiancé. She tasted the word and didn't care for it much. Though the flavor might have more to do with the situation than the person. Or maybe the person's actions…

So what did she do now? Unpack, apparently. She started taking things out of her bag, setting them down on the desk. It was a pathetic assortment of stuff she'd shoved in there last minute before heading to dinner. The rest of her things were in boxes Dwayne had unloaded in the dining alcove for the moment. Where should she unpack them? His room? Had he made space for her in the closet, in the dressers?

Questions sucked.

She slammed the shampoo down harder than necessary. No. That was just bull. Things hadn't started off in the most conventional manner, true. But they were engaged… sort of. And she loved him. And he… well. He something. He cared enough about the baby at least to want to marry her. And that said something. She wasn't going to just sit in the guest room like some child being punished. If their relationship—the family they had started—stood a chance, someone had to fight for it. And he wasn't ready to go to battle for them yet. So she would.

With more anger than conviction, she flung the door open and went to find him, prepared to give him a piece of her mind. But the anger burned out quickly when she found him passed out, facedown, on his bed. Still in his pants, shirt, and shoes from dinner. Her heart gave up the irritation and made way for compassion.

With quiet, smooth movements, she untied one shoe, then the other, placing them silently on the carpet at the end of the bed. There was nothing she could do about his pants and shirt, not the way he was lying facedown.

But she could turn off the bedside lamp and leave him to rest for a while.

But the click of the lamp was like waving a red cape in front of a bull. So fast, she didn't see him move until it was too late, as he grabbed her wrist and pulled her down to the bed next to him. Her mind flashed to that day, months earlier, when he'd pinned her to the couch in an unconscious haze of fury. The blank look in his eyes, the awareness that just wasn't there.

But this was different. Even in the dim light from the moon, she knew he was wide awake, fully aware. His eyes weren't blank, but full of something very real. Something that looked like hunger. Desire.

Something she could easily relate to. Cupping his face in her hands, she smiled in welcome. And he took it. Took her mouth in a kiss that was almost as fierce and possessive as he used to be before…

No. She couldn't do that.

"Dwayne." She breathed it, didn't mean for it to escape. But if he heard, he didn't respond, merely working his way down her neck to her collarbone, the hot trail left behind on her skin cooling in the air and making her nipples pucker under her dress. One large hand moved her until she was on her side, then unzipped her dress until it gaped in the front and he could pull it down. But he didn't pull it off.

Instead he reached under her bra and fondled one breast, lifting until it pulled out over the cup. Then repeated the process with the other. His knee dragged up, forcing her legs to widen, until he rubbed against her center.

She felt unbelievably decadent, lying there so

exposed while still in her dress. Somehow, the parts still covered made it seem even more naughty. She wanted him—God, she wanted him—but he was determined to take his time. Make her suffer. For the pleasure, or for punishment, she wasn't quite sure yet.

Slipping his hand down, he fumbled and worked until he caught the elastic of her panties with his fingers and tugged down, lifting his knee only a moment to pull them completely from her body.

"Bend your knees." He spoke into the soft skin of her breast, and she automatically shifted to do what he commanded. Anything he gave, she would grab at.

With his left hand he hooked under her right knee and brought it up as far as it would go. "Hold this."

And when she would have asked why, he answered without words. Not that he could have spoken while his mouth was *there*. It felt so wrong and so good all at once, and she almost exploded with the combined pleasure and embarrassment. But pleasure won out, slowly edging any self-consciousness to the side as he worked her with expert knowledge until she was sobbing his name. Crying out to whoever would listen that she couldn't take more.

But he knew better, and he went on. And she did, until her mind seemed to float away from her body on a haze of hedonism. Vaguely she realized he was working his way back up her body, light kisses, barely there caresses. But he was still fully dressed. For that matter, she mostly was herself. She reached with one heavy arm to undo his tie, to help him start the process, but he captured her fingers and moved them away.

Reaching in his nightstand, he pulled out a condom.

"Um, I think…" She waved at it, not sure what more to say. How did you phrase the question on your wedding night about protection?

He stared at the foil in his fingers for a moment, as if not even understanding how it got there. "Ah. Right. Yeah, that was just automatic." But he didn't set it down right away.

She waited, and waited a little longer. But it was like he was frozen, unable to move or make a choice. Put it down, or use it. She finally ended his decision-making by gently removing the packet from his fingers and placing it on the nightstand. His eyes tracked her every move.

"You sure?"

She nodded. Why wouldn't she be? The damage was done, as far as a child was concerned. It seemed a little silly not to trust him now. Maybe that was naive of her, but then so be it. She couldn't go into the marriage with anything less than her all.

But Dwayne could. She knew even as he shifted between her legs that he wasn't completely there. Mentally of course. But emotionally, the sweetness was gone. The sigh of contentment when he slid in was missing. Every move, every word he breathed, every touch felt calculated for pleasure. Not an expression of love. It was a choreographed dance, nothing more. And even as he found his own release minutes later, rolled over, and pulled her to his side, she knew a little part of him was completely detached.

It would be an uphill battle. But she'd work through it.

# Chapter 24

VERONICA WOKE TO A COMPLETELY COLD BED. NOT A hint of Dwayne's warmth. She cracked an eye open and saw it wasn't even six in the morning yet. He left for work early, but usually not this early.

She got up and found one of his sweatshirts to slip on as a makeshift nightgown, since the thing hung almost to her knees. Before opening the bedroom door, she gathered the too-long sleeves to her chest and inhaled his scent, using it like lavender might calm the senses. Then she quietly tiptoed out into the hallway.

After a quick peek at the bathroom door—open, no Dwayne—and the guest room where his desk was—also empty—she padded down the hall to the living room and found him.

With only one side lamp on, he was bathed in an eerie yellow glow, and shadows. It almost made the simple picture of getting ready for work more menacing. More serious. He sat on the couch, lacing up his boots. Unaware she was in the hallway, she had the opportunity to watch his fingers at work. As they manipulated the thin strings around each hook and expertly knotted them with efficient, fast movements, it wasn't hard to remember what those fingers felt like only hours before over her body. She shivered, and must have made some small sound because his head snapped up and he spotted her immediately.

"Did I wake you?"

"No, I... no. I just woke up and realized you were gone." She looked at the clock for emphasis. "Early morning at work?"

"Yeah." He finished the last knot, pulled tight, then stood. Six foot four inches of camouflage. And he was hers. "I don't really have the time right now to take off, sorry. Things going on at work."

"Things. Right." She thought for a moment, then decided to ask anyway. "How long have you been up?"

"Few hours." He shrugged like it was no big deal, like there wasn't a massive wall between them.

"Did I—"

"No." Short, curt, the reply left no room for arguments. "You didn't. I just needed to get up and move around."

A lightbulb went on. "Did you have a bad dream?" He didn't answer, but even in the dim light she could see a muscle twitch. "You can wake me up, you know. If you have a bad dream. If you need to talk about it."

"I'm fine."

He might be, but she wasn't. But she nodded just the same. He brushed past her to open the fridge door, grab a bottle of water, and shut it. "I'll be home later. Not sure when. I'll text you and let you know." He pressed a firm kiss to her forehead—robotic almost—and grabbed a gym bag before walking out the front door and closing it quietly behind him.

It wasn't even dawn yet on their first day of living together, and already she started to feel like a failure.

—~~~—

"Tim must be a liar. You're over here way too much for married life to be any good." Jeremy killed his beer and set the empty bottle on the table in front of him.

"Not married yet." Dwayne rolled his eyes.

"But you're engaged, and there are plans in the works, and you're living together. It's just semantics."

Time to deflect. "What's Tim got to do with this?" Dwayne rubbed a hand over his head and fought the urge to tug at his hair… what little of it he had. Why was everyone so damn concerned with his relationship? First Madison's texting him to see how things are going—as if she couldn't just ask Veronica herself—and now Jeremy. What the hell?

Jeremy shrugged and kicked back in his recliner. "It used to be the three of us, you know? Then he married Skye. Then he fell in love with her."

Dwayne snickered at the ass-backwards way he described it, though he spoke the truth.

"And now he's not around as much. I figure, if it sucked, he'd duck out more often. But this is the third time this week you've followed me home from work like a lost freaking puppy instead of racing home to your soon-to-be-wife. So really, can't be all that great, can it?"

He concentrated on loosening his grip on the beer. Crushing the glass would definitely not make him appear as sane as he would like. "I think that's just a matter of opinion. Besides, aren't you and Madison basically living together right now? Why are you always over here at your old apartment? I think that answers your questions."

"We're not officially moved in yet. Veronica still has some stuff left over, and I'm taking my time. Plus, my lease isn't up here for another three months, so we're not in a rush to get there. We know that's the end goal, and we're doing it smoothly. It works for us." Jeremy shrugged, as if it wasn't a big deal.

Dwayne said nothing.

Jeremy shook his head. "You're a dick, you know that?"

"What for this time?"

"Ha." Jeremy reached over and pulled the beer away, lifting a brow when it took more than a little effort to pry from his fingers. He set it down with his empty one on the table. "For proposing like that." Dwayne gave him a look, and Jeremy shrugged. "Madison told me. Veronica told her. Word gets around in our little group. Get used to it."

That wasn't expected. He reared back, confused. "I'm sorry—doing the right thing makes me a dick? If you missed the memo, she's pregnant."

"Yeah. So I heard."

Then what was the problem? He lifted his hands, at a loss of where to take that.

Jeremy sighed and shifted. "I just want to go on the record as saying it's not a good day when I'm the one with the most women-sense in the group. So there's that disclaimer." With obvious reluctance, he leaned forward, hands clasped between his knees. "Veronica is not some girl to hop from bed to bed with different guys."

The mere thought of Veronica moving on to someone else, with or without his kid, had the color red edging around his line of vision.

"And correct me if I'm wrong, but y'all didn't exactly jump in the sack from the word go either."

Not really comfortable with talking about his sex life,

not with Veronica, he just lifted one shoulder. Let the idiot make of that what he would.

"Thought so."

Okay, so he made of it the right thing. Maybe not such an idiot.

"She cared about you, you big dumbass. Probably even loved you."

"Never said so."

"Well, hell." Exasperated, he flung himself back in the seat, tipping the whole thing on its back two hinges before it thumped down even again. "Do you think that's a requirement? You have to say it out loud or it doesn't count?"

"It'd be nice," he grumbled.

"Yeah, well, I'd venture a guess you didn't really shout your feelings from the rooftops either."

He had a point. Dammit. "She knew how I felt."

"Felt? Or feel?"

It was a good question. One he'd been avoiding himself for the past few weeks. He'd been on the edge of love, ready to jump with abandon before she mentioned the baby. Before he knew he was right back where he started… a woman and her uterus leading him on.

"She didn't do it on purpose."

The quiet conviction of Jeremy's statement slapped at him more than any insult or curse could have. "You can't know that."

"Neither can you, until you talk to her about it. There's just no way to know. But she's not Blair. I can tell you that right now. She's not someone looking for a meal ticket, or security."

"Then why'd she say yes? She didn't have to. I would

have helped her no matter what." More than helped. He would have done everything in his power to see her and the baby taken care of.

"Did you give her a choice?"

"Yeah I gave her a… " He sat back a moment and replayed their conversation in the truck. Had he? "She's got a voice. She could have said no."

"And if she still loves you? Why would she say no?"

The thought that she could seriously still love him kicked him in the 'nads. More so than the fact that Jeremy was suddenly starting to sound like a relationship counselor.

---

Veronica smiled sadly at the computer camera. "I miss you guys so much."

Through the computer screen, her uncle grinned. "We miss you too, sweetie. Next chance you get, bring that man with you to Texas. Check with Skye and Tim when they're visiting next. You can all travel together!"

"That's a good plan."

"How did both our girls end up with military men?" Uncle Peter grumbled. And she smiled, because she knew that was what he wanted. But the thought that he considered her one of his girls made her tear up.

"Oh, honey, are you all right? He doesn't mean it." Aunt Amber watched her with wide eyes. "It's okay you fell in love with a Marine. Just because we're pacifists doesn't mean—"

"No," she choked out on a watery laugh. "No, that's not it. I just… I really miss you both."

"We're only a Skype call away, remember." Her aunt

smiled. "Now, you need to calm down. It's not good for the baby to be so upset. Maybe you should try writing your parents an email. Have you told them about the baby yet?"

"You told her *not* to get upset," Uncle Peter said under his breath, but she heard him anyway.

"Oh, or, you know… study?"

This time her laugh was stronger. "Studying is definitely not going to make me feel much better. But thanks. I do need to tell them. I love you."

After a quick good-bye, she ended the call and signed out of Skype. Her stomach felt tight, disturbed, nauseous. And it had nothing to do with the baby.

The thought of telling her parents about her pregnancy turned her into a knot of tension. Talking to her parents, under the best of circumstances, was never the easiest task in the world. And as far as her parents were concerned, *this* was definitely not the best of circumstances. Not even close. At least she had the legitimate excuse of breaking the news over email. With her parents in who knew what country that month, their transient lifestyle meant phones were not an option often. Even email was spotty, and they often went weeks, or even months without it. In their mind, there were few people outside of their fellow missionaries they even wanted to hear from regularly. That included their daughter, as it seemed.

Her fingers hovered over the keyboard, not sure how to start.

*Hey, Mom and Dad. How are things going over there? Staying safe? Great. Just wanted to let you know that I'm pregnant. But it's okay, because I am getting married. When? Oh, few weeks or so. Maybe a month. Or two. Have a good day!*

The next email she'd likely receive was that her parents died in a freak double heart attack.

Not quite the desired effect.

She waited for inspiration to strike. Nada.

Skye had given her the week off from work, partly because she was exhausted from the pregnancy and planning the move, and more importantly because she thought her cousin would want some time with her new fiancé and settling in.

Unfortunately, her fiancé didn't want time to deal with her. She might not be too well-versed in the ways of a Marine, but she figured he could have taken at least one day off to spend with her. It was his choice to leave each morning before she woke up, and his choice to come home when she was already curled up in bed.

Okay, she could practice the email first. If it was awful, she wouldn't have to send it. Opening a blank Word document, she focused her eyes only on the keyboard, positioned her fingers, and let them fly, mindless words pouring from her. When she finally looked up, it shocked her how much she'd written.

But it was the first sentence she wrote that scared her the most.

*The man I love wants nothing to do with me.*

Sitting back in the desk chair, she read it over and over until the words felt burned into her eyelids. Hesitating only a moment, she printed the page of rambling and glanced over it once more in ink form.

It was clear now she had to do something serious to fix their relationship. Even if it hurt.

# Chapter 25

DWAYNE WANDERED DOWN TO TIM'S OFFICE AND knocked once before pushing in. He was on the phone and held up a finger. Dwayne sat down in the chair across from his desk, then stood up again. The restless energy in his legs wasn't going to let him sit still. It was like ants crawled into his bloodstream and wouldn't give up their skittering around. He couldn't sit for more than a few minutes before feeling the urge to shake his limbs out.

With a click, Tim hung up and leaned back in his chair. "Hey, stranger. I know you've been in every day, but I haven't seen you. Avoiding me?"

"Nah. Just running around. Busy." *Busy avoiding you.* He didn't need another lecture. And if anyone gave a worthy lecture, it was Tim.

"I'm a little surprised you didn't take at least a three-day weekend to help get settled in. I know what it's like living with someone at the last second. A few days wouldn't have killed you."

"Shit to do." He stared at a picture of Tim hung on the wall. A shiny new lieutenant with his commission papers in hand, fellow Academy grads standing around him. Another hung next to it, of him and Skye. Just sitting on the back porch, her legs draped over his thighs, looking at each other like nothing else in the world existed.

"You know, you have a lot of nerve, making it seem easy."

"What?"

"Marriage. Your relationship with Skye. Being happy with one woman forever and ever, amen."

Tim scoffed. "I'm sorry, did you choose to just block out the entire first six months of my marriage? Including the part where I forgot I *was* married?"

"But now." He turned and stared at his friend hard. "Now it's easy."

Tim shook his head. "Sorry, bud. Not true either. Don't get me wrong, I love my wife. But easy is definitely not one of the words I would use to describe my relationship. It's work. Daily work. Some days come easier, some days harder. But anyone who told you once you find your soul mate your troubles melt away was a liar."

Dammit. If only it seriously were that easy. "I think I fucked up."

"Probably. But could you be more specific?"

He shot his friend a withering glare. "Cute. I mean with proposing to Veronica. I shouldn't have."

Tim swiveled a little in his chair, as if thinking, then shrugged one shoulder. "Maybe."

"Helpful."

"Maybe it was just the way you went about it."

"Maybe."

"Now who's being helpful?" Tim smiled, and Dwayne could feel the pity from a mile away. "I can't do this for you. I can't make up your mind on whether you want to be married or not, engaged or not, together or not. That's not how it works."

"Well, hell." He flopped back down in the chair and waited for a divine answer from God.

Nothing.

"I shouldn't have asked her to marry me if I didn't love her."

"Don't you?"

He closed his eyes a moment. "Why is it everyone thinks they know me and my feelings better than I do?"

"'Cause you're an idiot?" Tim asked helpfully. Then he chuckled. "We're all idiots when it comes to women. That's just the way the game is played. If we knew everything there was to know about the female species, then we'd get bored. The mystery is specifically designed to keep us crazy and wanting more."

Despite the situation, he laughed. "Probably."

"Let's go grab some lunch. Taco stand?"

As Dwayne followed Tim out the door, his friend asked, "Would it kill you to ask her how it happened? You seem so sure there was some evil, nefarious plot behind the entire thing. But couldn't it have just been a mistake?"

He tried to picture how that conversation could go. *Hey, dear, how's dinner coming along? Smells great. Did you lie about being on birth control?* Yeah. Great idea.

"I can see the wheels turning, and I doubt they're going anywhere good."

"Probably not," he agreed.

"You didn't have a problem confronting Blair over what she did," Tim said, opening his car door.

"I didn't feel…" He drifted off, hand frozen over the door handle, staring at his best friend over the top of the car.

His best friend, who had the nerve to look smug. "Feel what?"

Snapping out of it, he opened the door and gave his friend a sardonic glance. "Yeah. What."

As they each shut their doors and Tim started the car, he turned. "Just talk to her, ya dumb jarhead."

When the result of that simple talk mattered more than he wanted to admit, it was easier said than done.

—⁓—

Throughout the day, Veronica tried to distract herself from the white noise of disappointment filling her mind by washing dishes and folding laundry. She went so far as to get down on her hands and knees and scrub around the corners of the kitchen floor before it was too much. Tossing her rubber gloves in the sink, she gave in to temptation and stormed back to the office-slash-guest room and found her bag where she kept her schoolbooks, and conveniently stashed the page. Dragging the whole thing out to the living room, she plopped the bag down, curled up on the couch, and dug out the paper.

No. No, she wasn't going to do this again. Folding the paper in half, she grabbed her thick GED test prep book and shoved the paper in the front where she wouldn't have to look at it. About to shove the book back in her bag, she realized there were still a few hours before Dwayne was home. Best to study before he got back. Only a few more weeks to drill herself before the test.

And once she had her GED, she could tell Dwayne about it. You know, if it ever came up in conversation. But until that time, she was going to just work her butt off and get done what she could.

Curling up on the couch, she settled with a pad of

paper, a pencil, and her book, ready to copy equations over and over until they were burned in her brain.

But when she jolted awake some time later, she had no idea she'd even fallen asleep. She rubbed grainy eyes, stretched her sore neck, and stared straight ahead into cammie-clad legs. Craning her neck, she looked up to see an amused smile tilting his lips.

"Must be riveting stuff."

"Yeah. Well, you know. Numbers make me sleepy." She tried to close the book without drawing attention to it. "What are you doing home so early?"

He rubbed the back of his neck and sat down next to her. "I went in early, so I figured I could leave early."

She smiled. "I'm glad." Taking a chance, she added, "I've missed you."

"Really?" He looked a little surprised, though she had no clue why. But before it even registered what he was doing, he reached over and took the book from her hands. "Maybe I can change and help you study. Whatcha working on?"

Panicking on the inside, she tried to keep her voice calm as she reached for the book back. "Oh, I'm good. If you want to—"

"GED prep?" He gave her a funny glance. "I think you picked up the wrong study book. You probably meant the GRE, babe. They talk about pregnancy brain, but I didn't believe it until now."

She laughed weakly.

"I don't think I asked you before, but exactly which classes are you taking? I assumed online courses, since you never mentioned going on campus."

"True." Well, it was. "Okay. Look, here's the thing."

She gingerly took the book back and scooted until her back was supported by the arm of the couch, making it easier to watch his face. "This is actually the right book. I'm studying for my GED."

She could almost see each step of the process as her words filtered through his brain, what that meant. The confusion, the irritation. The anger.

"I'm working hard," she rushed on. "I'm almost done, and I should be testing in the next few weeks. So it's basically a done deal. I'm sure I'll pass but—"

"So you lied."

From the top of his head to the toes of his boots, she watched as any form of discernible emotion drained from his body until he was a blank slate.

"I'm almost done," she said weakly.

"But you lied. You're not actually in college."

"I didn't want you to think I was an idiot. It's embarrassing."

"That's bull and you know it." He exploded off the couch and paced in front of the coffee table. Why was it, in his uniform, he was exponentially more intimidating? "I know you're not an idiot. I don't even want to hear you think it. That's not the point. It never would have been the point. But you told me you were in college."

"I never actually said—"

"You let me believe it. You didn't correct me. All the time we spent together and you didn't correct me. It's the same thing, and you know it. Don't play semantics."

He was so angry. Angrier than she ever considered he might be when she told him the truth. But oddly, for a different reason than what she expected. "I'm sorry."

"Sorry? For what?" He stopped, his huge boots

inches from her bare feet, making her look tiny by comparison. "It's a pretty simple thing, you know. I don't care that you're still working on your GED. You could have told me."

"I was embarrassed. I still am. I'm twenty-six." She held up her hands, at a loss for how to explain to him exactly how hard it was for her to know people thought she was an idiot for not having finished high school. For not ever being to high school. For the way she was raised, her lack of friends, her lack of updated culture. Everything.

She wanted to say it. She was finally ready to say it. But he wasn't ready to hear. Even she knew that.

"How the hell… I mean, how do I… Dammit!" He stomped off down the hall, leaving her mouth hanging open at his curse. A moment later a door shut, and she could only assume it was the main bedroom.

That was definitely not how she saw the whole thing playing out in her head. And worse, the frustration he felt for being kept in the dark about this was only adding onto his frustration with the way their marriage came together in the first place.

*You dug yourself a nice deep hole, Veronica. Time to start clawing your way out.*

---

Lied. She lied. What the hell was she lying about?

He let his boot drop from his hand to the floor with a heavy thud, knowing it was the best he could do. What he really wanted was to work it out with a sparring partner. Or go a few rounds with a punching bag. Something. But no, he was now stuck in his room because he stomped off like a child. And like hell was he going back out there right now. No. Even he knew he needed a cooling down time-out from the rest of the world, and he wasn't leaving until he had things under control.

His lack of control over his temper, just now in front of Veronica, was going to haunt him that night. The normal Dwayne wouldn't have gone off like that. Or was this the new normal? How was he supposed to know anymore?

And why had she lied about the whole GED thing anyway? People had to drop out of high school; it happened. His own mom did, thanks to being pregnant with him. She went back eventually, finished school through night classes. Busted her ass to get it done. There was no shame in that. And she knew. Dammit, she knew. He'd told her all about his mom. And she didn't use it as a time to air out. Just sat there, nodding, saying she sounded like a good woman.

What the hell else was she hiding? Hard to tell at this point. But he needed to get a grip or else he was going to lose it. And they still hadn't even had the big talk. The one that he would rather gouge his eyes out than have.

With the news that she'd been withholding on this, he wasn't overly excited to hear what else was going on.

---

Veronica crawled into the twin bed and debated whether to suck it up and head to the main bedroom. But no, this was probably for the best. Shifting, she tried wedging a pillow against her chest and wiggled a little. She'd holed herself up in the second bedroom for the rest of the day, studying and generally feeling ill. Her stomach hurt, but that was just a part of pregnancy. So she wasn't looking forward to dealing with Dwayne, not when she felt awful. Maybe tomorrow, after some rest… if rest would ever come. She tried again with the pillow, anchoring her from behind now. No, that wasn't going to work.

She flopped on her back and stared at the ceiling. She wasn't even showing yet and she couldn't get comfortable. How in the world was she supposed to get comfortable at nine months? She shuddered at the thought.

No sooner had she turned to her side and found a comfortable position than the door swung open.

"What are you doing?"

"Sleeping." She didn't move. It took her ten minutes to find the position she was in and she wasn't about to lose it just because he—

"Dwayne!" She shrieked and her hands scrambled around his neck for a good grip. "What are you doing?"

He turned sideways to get through the doorway, and again to get through the main bedroom's door. "Going to bed—what does it look like?"

"And why am I being dragged into this?"

He set her gently on the edge of the bed and put his hands on his hips. "Because you didn't come to bed yourself. If you're going to make me do all the work, then I will. But I don't have to like it."

She wanted to argue, she really did, but she felt awful. The only thing she wanted more was to sleep. And since making a break for the guest room was out of the question, she growled and crawled under the sheets to start the process of finding a comfortable position all over again.

He turned out the lights and the bed dipped behind

her as he joined her under the covers. But when he didn't turn and gather her to him, she let everything that churned low in her belly fall out.

"I am a freak."

He shifted and rolled, though she didn't know where he was facing. She kept her back to him.

"Do you want to expand on that, darlin'?"

Well, she opened the door. Time to step through. "My parents are missionaries. I've lived in more third-world countries than I can count. Probably more than most people know exist."

He said nothing.

She blew out a breath and crunched her knees up a little more. Any week now, the first trimester stuff should pass. Any week now. "I almost never had friends. Nobody around me spoke my language. Anyone who did was too old for me to play with. Or they were a boy, and I wasn't allowed to fraternize with them after about age seven. Something about the evils of the opposite sex." She sighed. "My parents took things to extremes more often than not."

A large hand covered her shoulder, tugging gently until she willingly rolled onto her back.

"You don't have to talk about it."

"I do. I should have already. But it's just become habit to hide this." Another deep breath. "My parents' entire calling was to serve those around them. Even if it was to my detriment. I could fare for myself, but they had to save the poor souls around them. I accepted that after a while. That other people were more important than their daughter. It's why I never got my diploma. Sort of hard to attend high school while you're in the middle of nowhere. And since they didn't put an emphasis on education, it just didn't happen."

His thumb brushed over her cheek, and in delay, she realized he was brushing away a tear.

"The few times I had a chance to talk with people my own age, I was sort of... well, a freak. I came back once to stay with my grandma on my father's side. It was awful. I had no social skills, I could barely force myself to talk. And I had no idea how to interact with them. It ended badly."

"You're not a freak, baby." His voice was hoarse, like he was talking around something in his throat.

She smiled wryly. "That's sweet, but trust me. Hindsight is so clear. When I finally broke away from everything I knew—which was quite a tiny little box, really—I ended up at Skye's parents' home. Then she brought me here. And suddenly I wasn't just in some remote place where it didn't matter if I was awkward, since I couldn't talk to people anyway. I was surrounded by people who cared. And there I was, a twenty-six-year-old with nothing to her name. Not even a GED."

"You don't have to go on."

"I was embarrassed and ashamed. I still am, really. I realized people would think I was stupid, so I started hiding it. Stretching the truth, or outright lying about it until it became habit. But I'm trying to fix it." The words were so soft, even in her own ears. "I'm trying to fix it." She hiccupped and swallowed against the ball of tears welling in her throat. But they wouldn't be ignored.

"Okay. All right, baby." He pulled her over, cradled her close. "Let's let it out. Let it all go." One large hand rubbed circles over her back as she dampened his shirt with tears.

Had this all truly been building up inside her for so long? Embarrassment, yes. But it almost felt like shame she was letting go of. And a huge, thick weight dropped from her shoulders.

As her breathing calmed, as her tears slowed, then stopped, he squeezed gently and settled her more comfortably beside him. Smoothing fingers over her forehead and cheeks,

"We can talk about it tomorrow if you want."

She nodded, exhausted, and bit back a little groan when her stomach tightened again. "Yeah, that'd be good."

"Sleep. Go ahead and sleep, baby. We'll talk it through tomorrow."

His smooth drawl was like a cool balm over the worst of the hurt. Details weren't going to come easy, but the biggest hurdle had been jumped.

# Chapter 26

"Dwayne."

The sweet whisper filtered through his brain before he was ready to wake up.

"Dwayne."

A small hand gripped his shoulder, and he smiled, knowing what she wanted. He reached back and felt…

Nothing. Okay, where'd she go? How were they supposed to make love in the warm, sleepy cocoon of the night if she was gone?

"Please wake up?"

Finally—reluctantly—he cracked his eyes and found Veronica standing in front of him. Her brow was creased, her eyes were wide, and she chewed on her lip.

"What is it, darlin'?" He rolled onto his back and sat up against the headboard.

When she kept standing despite his patting the bed in invitation, something clicked in his head that this wasn't a nighttime nookie moment. Keeping an outward calm he was starting to lose inwardly, he circled her tiny wrist with his hand and guided her down, and repeated, "What is it, darlin'?"

"I just got off the phone with the on-call nurse. I think I need to head to the ER, if you wouldn't mind driving me."

Nurse. ER. Not what he'd expected to wake up to. "Wait. Back up a second. What's wrong? Are you hurt? Where does it hurt?" His hands immediately started roaming over her body, looking for injuries, broken bones, something. Anything.

She captured one of his hands with two of hers. God, she was so small. Fragile. "The nurse just said I should head in for an ultrasound. I'm bleeding a little and—"

"Jesus!" He leapt out of bed, except his feet were still tangled in the sheets and he fell shoulder-first onto the floor with a bone-jarring thump. Kicking once, he freed himself and reached around on the floor. His hand managed to snag something that felt like denim tucked under the bed and he grabbed them. Looking at her while hopping one leg in, he asked, "You're bleeding and you didn't wake me up? Why am I just now hearing this?"

"I didn't want to worry you if it was nothing." But he saw it in her eyes. She knew better. Knew it was something that they couldn't ignore. Not like they'd been doing up to now with their marriage. This was serious.

"You should have—" He stumbled a little and tried again. "You should have woken—" His elbow hit the dresser and he stood. "Why the hell can't I put my pants on?"

"Because they're mine." She gently took the jeans from him and handed him a pair of cargo shorts. How was she so calm right now? His mind was completely shut off.

"If it was nothing, we wouldn't be going in. Which we are. And why aren't you getting dressed?" He found a polo and yanked it on, cursing when he realized he'd pulled it over his head backwards. His arms finally found the holes and when his head popped through, he found Veronica still sitting, motionless as a statue, on the bed. Hands clasped in her lap, face bone-white. "Veronica?"

She didn't move. He couldn't see her eyes well, but he'd guess she didn't even blink. Foregoing finding his shoes for the moment, he crouched down in front of her and tilted her chin up with one finger until she met his eyes. Her own were watery, as if she were afraid to blink and let them spill over.

"I'm scared," she whispered. And then she blinked, and the tears tracked down each cheek.

"Baby, come here." Sitting next to her, he pulled until she sat in his lap, head on his chest. He did what came natural and slowly rocked as if she were an upset child, instead of just carrying one. "It'll be okay." *Please let it be okay.* "I'm sure they just want to be cautious. So let's get you some clothes and get a move on, all right? Faster we get there, faster we can come home and crawl back in bed." When she sniffled, he added, "Something to put in the baby book, right? First time Junior scared the crap out of his parents."

She gave a watery laugh at that, and his heart felt marginally lighter. It was lame as hell, but he didn't care. The woman he loved was scared to death and he'd do just about anything to make it better.

Anything except analyze the fact that he just mentally referred to her as the woman he loved. That, he didn't have time for. Later.

With a pat on her bottom, he got her up and moving, supervised her getting ready, and scooted her to the truck as fast—and careful—as possible.

And the whole way to the emergency room, as Veronica sat quietly in the passenger seat with her forehead pressed to the window, he prayed to whoever was on duty upstairs that his promise that it would be okay was one he could keep.

—∞—

"Where's the doctor? Honestly, where is he?" Dwayne paced back and forth, and Veronica was at a loss for what to say to calm him down.

"They'll get here when they can."

"This is the emergency room. The key word being emergency. What do you have to do to get some service in this place—cut off a thumb?" He shoved his hands in his pockets, took them out again, and did another lap around the little cubicle she'd been assigned to. Outside the curtain, life bustled and moved, but inside their own little bubble, the world was muted. Silent. Scary.

He was worried, maybe even afraid. And she could relate. But he was going to wear a hole in the tile, and he didn't need to stress out. She was doing enough of that for the two of them. Someone had to be the calm one. She sighed a little. Why was it her? Finally an idea struck.

"Dwayne, your pacing's making me a little dizzy. Do you think you could—"

Before she even finished her sentence, he was in a chair beside her, holding her hand lightly between his. "I'm sorry. Lie back."

She did, but restlessness made her leg twitch. Curling up on her side helped, but not much. The cramps felt the same, no better or worse. But being in the hospital, with doctors a step away, made her feel a little better. But why was it happening?

*God brings justice in whatever way He wants.*

But her mother's words no longer bothered her. Maybe that's how she was raised, to live in constant fear of God's wrath. But she was a big girl now, not dependent on her parents for guidance. And she knew in her heart this wasn't punishment.

She reached out and traced a line furrowed into Dwayne's brow. "Distract me?"

"Hmm?" The line receded a little, as if her touch erased it. "How? I'm not a good storyteller. And you don't wanna hear me sing."

"Tell me how your acclimation issue is." There. That should keep them both distracted.

On cue, his face soured. "I'll pass, thanks."

"Please? I just want to know if it's better." Tracing another line lightly, she sighed again. "I feel like you didn't want a relationship at all. Certainly not a fiancée. Or maybe just not me."

Wrapping fingers around her wrist, he pressed a kiss to her palm. "That's the farthest thing from the truth." He took a deep breath, and she waited for the speech about backing off, giving him his space, his privacy.

"My last girlfriend was pregnant."

This was not backing off. She shifted uncomfortably, the paper covering the exam table crinkling under her.

"Okay, that's not right. She told me she was pregnant. And I believed her. Put a ring on her finger. Wanted to do the right thing."

The right thing. It should sound noble. Instead it sounded like a little piece of her heart breaking off, both in empathy for his own situation and for hers.

His chair rolled away a little so he could peer out the slit in the ugly orange curtain surrounding them. "She wasn't. Never had a doubt. Not a scare. Just knew I was about to move to a new duty station and our relationship wouldn't go the distance. So she faked the whole damn thing. And I found out—luckily—before we got married."

"That was a horrible thing to do." And explained so much. He'd trusted her, started to plan a life with her, and she'd been lying to him the whole time. About such an important, serious issue.

No wonder her omissions were hard for him to swallow. And the pregnancy.

"I'm sorry."

He shrugged. "If I'd loved her, it would have hurt a hell of a lot worse."

Do you love me? It was on the tip of her tongue, but before she could decide whether to hold back or let loose, the curtain jerked open. A man with a white coat and hair that stuck straight out every which way, as if he'd been tugging on it in frustration, came in.

"Veronica Gibson?"

"Yes." She struggled to sit up a little, but managed with Dwayne's help. He stood up, moving close to her side as if ready to leap in front of her at any moment. "Sit down, please." When he did, she reached out and rubbed his arm. Poor man. On his last nerve, and then some. And oddly, a sense of peace she didn't think possible at that moment washed over her. She had no clue what came next, but she simply knew it would be fine, whatever it was.

"I'm Doctor Barton." He stepped forward to shake her hand, then held his out expectantly to Dwayne.

"Dwayne Robertson. Her fiancé."

Such a difference from the last appointment, when they had no clue how to refer to each other.

The doctor checked his chart and rubbed one eye

tiredly. A nurse filed in behind the doctor, pushing a machine, and closed the curtain behind her.

"A little bleeding here, looks like. Starting the second trimester. Well, we'll give it a check and see." He gestured to her top and she rolled it up while lying on her back. After a little cold gel that had her hissing in a breath, he spread the stuff around with the ultrasound wand and flipped a switch.

Instantly the sweet rhythmic whooshing sound filled her ears, and a tear broke free, rolling down her cheek into her hair.

Dwayne leaned in and wiped it away with the pad of his thumb. "What's that sound?"

"Heartbeat," the doctor said succinctly. "Sounds good. Let's just check measurements quickly here." A few clicks and the screen filled with some numbers off to the side.

Veronica couldn't tear her eyes away from the little gray object that bounced. One tiny sticklike thing popped out and wiggled.

The nurse giggled. "Oh, cute. He's waving."

"Kidney Bean can wave?" Dwayne's voice was full of awe and amazement. And, to Veronica's amusement, a little pride. "Kid's not even born yet and he's waving. He's a genius."

"Kidney Bean. That's one we haven't heard before." The nurse scribbled a few notes on the clipboard as the doctor softly read measurements off.

"So does he look okay?"

The doctor finally met her eye. "Oh, yeah, baby looks just fine. Right on schedule. Sometimes bleeding just happens without any real explanation." He clicked the ultrasound machine off and put the wand away. The nurse handed her a paper towel to wipe her stomach off.

"So… so I didn't do anything wrong?"

Dwayne squeezed her hand. "Of course not." He stared hard at the doctor. "Right?"

"Absolutely," the doctor was quick to agree. "I mean, absolutely not. I mean, it just happens sometimes, not as a result of anything the mother has or hasn't done. Though I'd like you to stay off your feet for a few weeks, pelvic rest included. And call your regular doctor tomorrow morning to follow up."

Veronica nodded, but Dwayne stopped the doc as he parted the curtain. "Pelvic rest?"

The doctor gave him a small smile. "No intercourse."

Dwayne made a face like he'd sucked on a lemon and muttered something that sounded suspiciously like a curse. But Veronica giggled. That he cared was enough of a good sign to her to be happy.

"So we're good to go?"

"You're all clear, Ms. Gibson. Have a good one. And rest for a little bit."

After the doctor left, Dwayne picked her up in his arms. She grabbed around his neck and laughed again. "What are you doing?"

He shot her a playful grin and affected a thicker-than-normal twang. "That there doc told you to keep off yer feet, missy. I aim to help ya."

She slapped his chest and pointed toward the exit. "Let's go home, Dwayne."

Home. With Dwayne. It's where she wanted to be.

Veronica slept the sleep of the dead. More than once, Dwayne had checked just to make sure she was still breathing. She didn't move, didn't reposition, didn't even make those cute, light snoring sounds she was prone to make. But she was so exhausted, both with being up so late at night and the emotional toll the trip to the ER had been, she was dead to the world. But he was wired, couldn't sleep, couldn't even sit still. Everything in him pulled him to her, to watch her sleep, protect her, make sure nothing bad ever touched her again. Illogical, but he couldn't help it.

As dawn broke through the shades, he crawled out of bed and got dressed. Knowing she would sleep in well past normal time to get up, he left her a note telling her he was running an errand and would be back soon. And to text him if she felt the slightest twinge of pain or worry.

Then Dwayne shuffled out of the apartment before Veronica would realize he was gone. He hated doing it, when everything in him screamed to stay home and take care of his woman and their kidney bean. Be there if she needed him. And if he hadn't seen with his own eyes that Kidney Bean was doing fine, he might have.

But Veronica wasn't one to be pampered over. Staying there just to wait on her would probably annoy her more than help. She was safe and sound, asleep in their bed.

Their bed. God, that felt good.

And he had someone to talk to.

He drove to the battalion and headed straight for the chaplain's office. He knocked and waited, but there was no answer. Turning on his heel, he slammed into someone, papers from the man's hand scattering.

"Sorry, I—Chaplain. Ah, damn. Darn. Sorry. Didn't see you there."

The chaplain smiled as he bent down with Dwayne to start gathering papers. "I assumed as much. Unless it's your new greeting to run a man over as you say hello. Just glad I hadn't brought my coffee with me." As he stood up, the messy stack of papers in hand, he glanced at his watch. "You're early."

Dwayne rubbed the back of his neck. "Sorry, just got an early start to the day."

Unlocking his door, he opened and beckoned Dwayne in. Dwayne waited until Major Dunham had settled his folder.

"Okay, Robertson, I've got a few minutes. Let's talk."

Suddenly, Dwayne wished he could make an invisible exit. Words weren't his thing, and he certainly didn't make a conscious plan to come in and talk things through. But the minute his mouth opened, his instinct took over. "I just wanted to say thanks."

"You're welcome." The chaplain smiled. "Mind telling me what you're thankful for?"

"Mostly listening. Being a neutral ear. Convincing me I wasn't crazy." He studied the toes of his boots. "We're getting married."

"Congratulations." He paused. "I take it this is a happy thing?"

"It is. It really is."

"No problems, questions, or concerns?"

Dwayne smiled. "All three. But we'll figure it out."

A knock sounded on the door, and Dwayne stood. "I hope I didn't make you late."

"Not at all. He's a little early. But Captain, my door

is always open if you need help weeding through any of the above." Major Dunham stood up and extended a hand. "I have a feeling our impromptu get-togethers are coming to a close, don't you? It was a pleasure meeting with you. And I hope you'll keep me updated on things."

"Yes, sir." Dwayne stood and shook the chaplain's hand. Odd to think he wouldn't be walking through the doorway again feeling as broken as he had the first time through. And relieved, on top of that.

As he walked out, he saw Captain Beckett sitting on a chair in the outer office. "Hey, man. Did you need the chaplain? I think he's got someone coming in, but—"

"That'd be me." Beckett gave him an easy smile. "I'm his appointment. You just beat me to it this morning."

"Oh, wow, sorry." He ran a hand over his hair. "So before, when I thought you were running errands, you were…"

"Coming here for counseling? Yup." Beckett shrugged, fresh-washed cammies rustling in the quiet of the office. "No big."

"Right. No big." He glanced back to the closed door and waved toward it. "I hope you get what you need out of it."

"Yeah. Me too." He nodded as Dwayne passed by, then knocked and entered.

That was awkward. But Dwayne felt marginally better knowing he wasn't alone in seeking help for shit he'd seen, experienced, been through. Of course, he knew instinctively he wasn't. But it helped to know all the same.

He headed to his office and did a quick email check, sending some info that was time sensitive and writing down notes for the administrative assistant the captains shared. Then after a quick detour to the CO's office, he headed down the hall to Tim's door. Knowing his friend would be there—who was always in first? Tim—he pushed open and waited for his friend to look up from the computer.

"How did you know?"

Tim sat back and laced his fingers behind his head. "I'm afraid to ask, but I will anyway. Know what?"

"Know that you loved Skye?"

"Ah." A satisfied look crossed Tim's face. "That's a kind of personal question, don't you think?"

"Oh, cut the bullshit, O'Shay." He walked to the window and watched as the first trickle of morning traffic worked its way down the streets behind the battalion building, on their way to their own offices around base.

Tim chuckled. "You know, it's just hard to think, physically, how a little thing so small as Veronica can take down such a big guy."

"She's small, but potent." He smiled wryly. "And she's got me tied up in knots."

"Couldn't tell," was the smartass reply. "That right there should tell you something big. That she's got the power to twist you around."

"And that's how you knew?"

Tim pointed to a chair. "Sit down, you giant. I'm not having this conversation with my head tilted up to stare at your tall ass." After he grudgingly sat, Tim kept going. "I knew I loved her because I knew I could move on through life without her."

"That doesn't make sense."

"Of course it does. Do you think I was going to trust some all-consuming sort of feeling where if I couldn't have her I couldn't go on? That sort of removal from all things controlled?"

Dwayne snorted. Feelings like that—the stuff that drove Shakespeare's best work—would be Tim's idea of hell. "You would have hated it."

Tim stabbed the air with a pen. "Exactly. That sort of stuff, the dramatic, life-or-death fairy-tale stuff, it's not real. It's some manifestation of lust and a lack of logic."

"Sort of like how you met Skye in the first place?"

Color swept over his friend's cheeks. "Okay. Bad example. But the point is, I knew I could live without Skye. But I didn't *want* to. That's the difference. Or at least it was for me. The fact that I could go on. I could move on with my life and function and be okay. I just didn't want to. Because all forms of future happiness, in my mind, were wrapped around that one stubborn, completely bizarre woman."

He couldn't hold back the laughter at the way Tim described his wife. And it was all true. "I see what you're getting at now."

"So do you love her?"

Dwayne raised a brow. "I think that's something I should be talking to her about."

"Well, have fun with that tonight."

"Today," Dwayne corrected. "Just got done with the CO. Told him I needed a few days off. Wedding stuff." He winked and stood up, stretching his back as he did. "The idea of spending a few days curled up with Veronica and sleeping in are more appealing than I want to admit. I thought I bled red and gold, but damn. Now that there's something to go home to—"

"You can't wait to drop your boots at the door, can you?"

"Not at all. So I'll be heading out now. I've got a woman to talk to."

Tim glanced at his cell phone. "Well, you might have to save that convo for a few hours. She's over at the old place with Madison and Skye."

Dwayne froze. "What?"

Unaware of what he'd stepped into, Tim shrugged. "Yeah, Skye texted me a little bit ago. She's not on 'til late tonight and Madison's off for the next few days, so the girls are over at Madison's helping Veronica pack up the last few things she didn't have time to grab before."

"She's packing?"

"I'm sure they're doing more talking than packing. You know females."

"She's *packing*?" Dwayne thundered. "What the hell?"

"It's not a big deal; she's—"

"Dammit." Dwayne stormed out the door and let it shut behind him, cutting off Tim's conversation midsentence.

Packing, for the love of Christ. She was supposed to be taking it easy! What the hell did she think she was doing? He would have packed for her. Hell, he would have done anything she asked.

He passed by Jeremy's office, not stopping when his friend called out in greeting. A lance corporal scurried out of his way in the hallway, as if the sight of him freaked the Marine out. Luckily, he thought as he started up his truck, traffic heading out the main gate would be all but nonexistent at this time of the day. Because he had a bone to pick with his wife and it was not going to wait.

# Chapter 27

Skye held up another book. "This one?"

Veronica squinted. "No, donate." She rolled over onto her back and sighed. "You guys, I hate this. Can I just do one box? The light stuff, no books."

"No," Madison and Skye said in unison.

"You're supposed to be on bed rest," Madison went on. "So stay up there on the bed and rest. Doctor ordered, nurse enforced."

"Thanks, Nurse Ratched. I'm not an invalid. I'm just pregnant," she grumbled back.

"Well, then the fetus needs to be on bed rest. And since he can't rest on a bed without your help, I think that you would want to help him," Skye pointed out in a softer, more reasonable voice.

"Oh. Right." She laid a hand on her stomach, a little confused and a lot amazed that almost overnight, her mostly flat belly had morphed, now with a barely perceptible curve to it. You couldn't even see it when she stood up, just lying flat on her back. But not like she'd eaten too many cupcakes. It was hard, firm to the touch. Definitely a new development. It still was beyond her comprehension how something so tiny would become a baby in a few months. But according to the book Madison gave her, that's just how it worked.

A pounding sound echoed through to the back bedroom. Madison glanced up at Veronica. "Did you call someone to come over?"

Veronica shook her head. "No. The guys are all at work. I don't know who that is."

Madison shrugged and kept going through another box Veronica had put directly into storage when she'd first moved in.

The pounding continued.

Skye looked up at Madison, a sweater dangling from her hands. "Shouldn't you see who that is?"

"I'm not expecting anyone. Probably a vacuum sales-guy. I saw one of their vans in the complex yesterday. I'm not getting up to answer in my pajamas."

"Hmm. Keep?"

Veronica nodded and Skye moved the sweater to the Keep for Storage pile.

"Veronica!"

She sat up quickly, then slouched down a little when Madison gave her a look that said either lie back down or I will strap you down. "Was that—"

"Veronica!"

Skye ran to the bedroom window and peered down a little. "Oh my God, it's—"

"Open up the dang door, darlin'."

"Dwayne?" all three asked simultaneously before Madison jumped up and shuffled to the hallway in her slippers. A moment later, the sound of a door opening and Dwayne's disgruntled voice filled the apartment.

"Where is she?"

"Easy there, cowboy. She's back in her old bedroom."

A moment of thundering almost shook the walls before Dwayne, in full cammies, stopped in the doorway, his head and shoulders centimeters away from actually touching the frame. The scowl on his face probably should have had her knees knocking, but she just wanted to laugh at how disgruntled and adorable he looked.

"You mind telling me what you're doing over here?"

Veronica spread her arms out across the bedspread, as if she were making snow angels. "Packing, of course."

"Uh-huh." He shot a hard glance at Skye, who was quietly giggling. "You shouldn't be encouraging this."

Madison snickered behind him.

Whirling around, he pointed a finger at her chest. "And *you* should know better. You're the medical person."

"Yes, medical person. I think that's what it says on my state certification," Madison said dryly.

"She's on bed rest, for God's sake!"

"Modified bed rest," Veronica said. "And where am I?" She held up her hands to prove a point... that she was still flat on her back in bed.

"Exactly." Madison slapped his finger away. "Don't point, Casanova. It's rude." And she waltzed around him and plopped back down on the floor as if he hadn't disrupted their morning of girl-time and work. "This book?"

"Donate. What are you doing here?" She propped herself up on her elbows.

"Took a long weekend." With a sigh of what could only be resignation—Veronica bit back a grin at that—he thudded in with heavy feet and sat next to her on the bed. With one giant hand he gripped her ankles and dragged her feet into his lap, absently massaging her ankles.

She nearly wept with gratitude. Instead she fell back to the bed and let his hands work their magic.

"I don't think you'll have much to take with you at this rate," Skye said a few minutes later. "I mean, you didn't even unpack this stuff when you originally moved in here."

"It's because I didn't want any of it," she answered, closing her eyes and letting the amazing feel of Dwayne's fingers seep in. "It's just what I had with me when I came over to the U.S. and so I kept it." Not sentimental, she knew. But something at the time hadn't let her throw away the things from what she now thought of as her previous life. It was almost as if she knew eventually she would look back and see how far she had come. Like a scrapbook.

"I think we're almost done then, unless you had anything stashed in the patio storage." Madison stood and wiped her hands on her pajama pants.

"No, I think that's—"

"What is that?"

She turned her head to look at Dwayne. "What is what?"

He pointed, then placed a hand over her stomach. "That."

She covered his hand with one of hers. "That would be a stomach. It's usually located above the hips but below the chest."

"Oooh, I can play this game. Anyone want to know the scientific name for organs in there?" Madison bounced up and down with her hand in the air like an overeager first grade teacher's pet.

He shot her a look. "Smart alecks. Both of you."

"It's why you love me," she sang as she left the room, Skye hot on her heels. Apparently, under some unspoken agreement, they'd decided to give her and Dwayne some alone time.

"Why is it all bulgy?"

"You do make my head spin with your compliments." When he raised one brow, she sighed. "It's the baby. It just sort of… popped. This morning."

His eyes grew wide and she laughed. "It's supposed to happen. Calm down. Actually…" She pointed to a bag that was in the keep pile on the floor by the closet. "Go grab that for me, if you could."

He shifted her feet off his lap gently and did as she asked. When he handed it to her, she pushed back. "No, open it. It's yours."

He did, letting the plastic bag flutter to the floor as he read the book's title.

"It's a book."

That didn't sound promising. He just kept staring at the cover, as if it was going to morph into something more exciting. "The guy at the bookstore recommended it."

He kept staring.

"It's supposed to be good for information, but funny too, sort of keeping you in the loop with humor. So you know what's going on with the baby but don't get all the emotional mushy stuff… or so said the bookstore guy."

"Yeah." He turned the book over in his hand, inspecting the back cover, the spine, flipping the pages quickly with his thumb.

"If you don't like it, I can take it back."

"No. No, don't do that." He set the book on the nightstand and leaned over her, one hand over her belly. "It's great. Thank you."

They were the right words, but what was he feeling? His face didn't give anything away.

"Can I take you home now? I assume Skye drove you, since I'm praying you weren't crazy enough to drive yourself."

She smiled. "I'm crazy, but not stupid. Yeah, take me back home."

An expectant father book. Jesus, the hits just kept on coming. He wasn't sure what to do with that information. Well, clearly he was supposed to read it. But damn, she took him by surprise with that one. In a very good way.

After tucking Veronica in for a nap, Dwayne sat in the living room, wondering exactly how long he could hold on to his feelings. Keep control of them. Could he make it until he knew how she felt?

"Damn it," he muttered, leaning over to unlace his boots. Something by the side of the couch caught his eye and he reached for it. Veronica's tote bag, full of her stuff for school. Or, well, studying for the GED. He grabbed the huge textbook and flipped through it absently, remembering his own high school days. Now *there* was a distraction.

He felt sixteen again, hoping to win over the cute girl in fourth period by doing her math homework with her.

The book dangled from his fingertips and a loose piece of paper fell out. He reached for it, not intending to read the study material until his eyes caught the words *man I love*. Then he couldn't go back.

Starting from the beginning, he read. And read again. And another time, until the sentiments were burned into his memory.

She awoke to the sounds of banging in the kitchen. After a quick side-trip to the bathroom, she weaved her tired way down the hall and squinted into the bright light.

"Morning, darlin'." Dwayne turned to smile at her from behind the refrigerator door.

She stifled a yawn. "It's like three in the afternoon. And I woke up from a nap, not from the night."

"You say tomato… Sit down and let me get you something to eat. Juice? You want juice?" He scooted her onto a stool and flew around the kitchen, grabbing a glass of juice to sit in front of her before heading back to the stove to poke at… something.

"Dwayne? What's in the skillet?"

"Eggs."

They most certainly did not look like any eggs she'd seen before. For the most part, Veronica had taken over the meals, mostly because she didn't mind working in the kitchen. Unlike what the books seemed to say, being around food all day didn't dampen her desire to make her own meals at home. "Do you like to cook?" How odd that she still had to ask that, after agreeing to marry the man.

"Nah, I'm not much of a kitchen guy. I've sort of lived off takeout and frozen pizza. But I figured eggs were a no-brainer. Who could screw up eggs?" He set the spatula down, turned to face her, and crossed his arms over his chest. "You good with an egg sandwich for a late lunch?"

She gave it a moment to sink in and see if her stomach would rebel at the mere thought of eggs. But everything seemed calm on that front. "Sure."

"Good. And after that, I'm hoping we can have a nice talk."

"Talk?" The gulp of juice she'd taken expanded in her throat like a balloon, and she fought the urge to choke. "Talk about what?"

He propped a hip against the counter and looked completely at ease. "Things in general. How everything's going. Our relationship."

Tears stung the backs of her eyes, but she blinked rapidly to stall any tears. "Of course."

He stared at her a moment, the infuriatingly blank look on his face, and then pointed to her glass. "Drink. I don't know if you ate a good breakfast or not before you went over to Madison's. Which," he added with a pointed look, "I'm not all that thrilled about."

Veronica rolled her eyes, but diligently picked up the glass and took another sip. This one went down better. "I'm capable of eating when you're not here. I've done it enough times when you're working late."

Something that looked like guilt crossed his face. "That's going to come up in our talk. But until then, just humor me and eat good meals, please?"

She smiled placidly. "I think your *good meal* is burning."

He froze, then turned around and grabbed the spatula, shoveling blackened egg around the skillet in a fruitless effort to save them from singing. "Well, hell." He flipped the burner off with a flick of his wrist and tossed the skillet—egg and all—into the sink. With a sheepish smile, he shrugged. "How about cereal?"

"How about we talk? And then you can order a pizza for an early dinner." She might have her appetite back, but her energy was still lagging a little. And fixing another meal wasn't really on her to-do list at the moment.

She walked into the living room, propping herself up on the arm of the couch. Dwayne followed, surprising her by sitting on the couch with her rather than in the armchair on the other side of the coffee table. That had to be a good sign, right?

She motioned with her juice glass. "Talk."

He blushed a little up the back of his neck, over the tops of his ears. "I have a confession first."

Suddenly, her stomach roiled and she was glad she hadn't had a chance to eat the eggs.

"I was flipping through your GED book, just thinking about stuff and wondering if you might need help, and a paper fell out. I shouldn't have read it, but I did." Leaning to one side, he reached in the back pocket of his jeans and pulled out a folded piece of paper. The lightbulb turned on when he unfolded it and held it out.

Her hand darted out to snatch it away before she even knew she was moving. Her private, intense, overly emotional, hormone-driven thoughts. And he knew every single one of them.

"I'm sorry. I really am. It fell out, I meant to just shove it back in but something caught my eye and I couldn't stop myself. It was wrong."

She clutched the paper to her chest like a shield.

"I'll ask for forgiveness in a minute, but I have to say something before that."

"What?" she croaked out, fighting a losing battle to swallow down the lump in her throat.

"You were wrong." His voice was low and husky, but carried perfectly. "I want something to do with you. I want everything to do with you."

Confusion momentarily blocked out her embarrassment and she glanced down at the first line of her hastily typed message.

*The man I love wants nothing to do with me.*

"I might have given you that impression, and I know exactly how I did it. But I wasn't staying away because of you. It was me. All me. I thought I needed distance to keep things square in my mind, but that was just bull."

She waited for more, her heartbeat pounding a tattoo in her eardrums.

"And you were wrong about something else. In there you said you'd have to love enough for the both of us. But you don't." Reaching out, he gently pried one of her hands away from her chest and held it. "Darlin', I love you. I have for a while; I just didn't trust myself, my situation, my own self to say it. I let stuff from the past get to me because I wasn't sure if I could believe. If I was ready to take that step, or if things were going to fall apart any minute. My mind was still in survival mode, even if my heart was five steps ahead of the game."

She choked out a watery laugh. "I—"

"No, wait. Let me get it all out." One corner of his mouth tilted up. "I'm not great with words, remember? I had this whole thing planned out. I'm sorry. I couldn't be more sorry for how I let things fall apart between us. I made some serious mistakes, and I can't change them. But I know what went wrong and I won't let it happen again."

With a shuddery sigh, he rolled his shoulders. "So, can you forgive me? Or have I really screwed things up for good?"

She stared at him, taking in the hesitant expression on his face, the way his body was coiled, as if ready to run at any second. Did he seriously doubt for a moment? "Of course I do. I screwed up too. I shouldn't have led you on with the whole school thing. And then not knowing better about the birth control so I—"

"No." His voice, so fierce, cut through her apology like a knife. "Don't. I know it wasn't expected, but Kidney Bean's here now. And I don't want either of us to want to take that back. I love the bean already. No way would I give that up."

One hand instinctively went to her belly. "Neither would I. And I love you. I do. Still, always."

He grabbed under her arms and tugged until she sat with her legs draped over his, her head resting on his shoulder.

"Good. Very good."

She sat for a moment, breathing in his scent, being lulled into a happy state by the feel of his arms around him.

"I'm sorry, did you call our child Kidney Bean?"

His chin rested on the crown of her head. "I think it has a certain ring to it, don't you?"

"Why not Dwayne Junior?" she teased.

He groaned. "I love him too much to do that to him. We'll figure something out."

His hand covered hers, resting protectively over their child.

"You're right. We'll figure something out."

# Acknowledgments

This series has been such an eye-opening experience, from beginning to end. It was the birth of my first paperback, my first full-length series, and my first time working with my agent. I learned how to shoot a gun while researching this series, I moved twice while writing it (one move was a five-stater!), and survived the terrible twos as a mother. Talk about a learning curve, in every way possible. On-the-job training doesn't come close to writing a series like this. But I loved (almost) every minute of it.

There are too many people to thank from throughout this entire series, and I'll forget 67 percent of them just due to excitement, so to be fair I will give everyone a shout-out combined. To those who have touched my life or these books in some way, thank you for your positive thumbprint on my life and the life of this series.

There's one group I can't help but single out... the readers. I can't thank you enough for joining these three Marines on their journeys to find love, and for joining me on this equally special journey. Stick with me, guys. I've got more in the tank!

# About the Author

Jeanette Murray is a contemporary romance author who spends her days surrounded by hunky alpha heroes... at least in her mind. In real life, she's a one-hero kind of woman, married to her own real-life Marine. When she's not chasing her daughter or their lovable-but-stupid Goldendoodle around the house, she's deep in her own fictional world, building another love story. As a military wife, she would tell you where she lives... but by the time you read this, she'll have already moved. To see what Jeanette is up to next, visit www.jeanettemurray.com.